THE SHOW GIRL

Also by Nicola Harrison

Montauk

THE
SHOW
GIRL

Nicola Harrison

ST. MARTIN'S PRESS

New York

First published in the United States by St. Martin's Press, an imprint of St. Martin's Publishing Group

THE SHOW GIRL. Copyright © 2021 by Nicola Harrison. All rights reserved. Printed in the United States of America. For information, address St. Martin's Publishing Group, 120 Broadway, New York, NY 10271.

www.stmartins.com

Design by Donna Sinisgalli Noetzel

Library of Congress Cataloging-in-Publication Data

Names: Harrison, Nicola, 1979- author.
Title: The show girl / Nicola Harrison.
Description: First edition. | New York : St. Martin's Press, 2021. | Includes bibliographical references.
Identifiers: LCCN 2021006970 | ISBN 9781250200150 (hardcover) | ISBN 9781250200167 (ebook)
Subjects: LCSH: Showgirls—Fiction. | Ziegfeld follies—Fiction. | GSAFD: Historical fiction.
Classification: LCC PS3608.A7835785 S56 2021 | DDC 813/.6—dc23
LC record available at https://lccn.loc.gov/2021006970

Our books may be purchased in bulk for promotional, educational, or business use. Please contact your local bookseller or the Macmillan Corporate and Premium Sales Department at 1-800-221-7945, extension 5442, or by email at MacmillanSpecialMarkets@macmillan.com.

First Edition: 2021

10 9 8 7 6 5 4 3 2 1

For Greg, who's always up for an adventure

THE SHOW GIRL

We'd been expecting Mr. Elvie, too—he usually knocked on the dressing room door soon after the show to give us his notes onstage while they were fresh in his head.

"He hasn't come backstage yet, I'm afraid. I can pass on a message if you'd like."

"Please do. Tell him that Florenz Ziegfeld came by to compliment him on his production and on his spectacular cast."

I nodded, trying not to appear too eager to meet him.

"And you, you were quite spectacular yourself, Miss . . . ?"

"Miss McCormick," I said. "Olive McCormick."

"Yum-Yum indeed." He took my hand and kissed it, holding a beautiful bouquet of flowers in his other hand. "You saved the show this evening."

"Oh, I don't know about that."

"Indeed, your bravery, your calmness and your presence of mind to keep singing in that beautifully sweet voice of yours averted what could have resulted in a stampede."

I hadn't thought of it that way; I'd just really wanted to sing. In fact, since the show had ended, and I'd heard the cast members in the dressing room talking about the terrifying earthquake and how we could have all been crushed to death in the rubble of the theater, I briefly thought that my continuing to sing could have actually done a lot more harm than good if there'd been another tremor.

"Truly, Miss McCormick," he continued, "hundreds of lives could have been at risk if everyone panicked and tried to flee."

"Well, I suppose you're right; I did save the day. Thank you for the lovely flowers," I said, reaching for them.

THE SHOW GIRL

CHAPTER ONE

I saw the marquee first, jutting out onto West Forty-second Street with bright white letters—ZIEGFELD FOLLIES OF 1927—all full of light bulbs and ready to illuminate the street when the sun began to fade. The building above the New Amsterdam Theatre towered over its neighbors. The names Eddie Cantor, Lora Foster and the Brox Sisters were painted in huge lettering on the side. I allowed myself to imagine for a moment that it was my name up there—big, bold lettering, shouting out for all of New York City to see.

During the walk over from Lord & Taylor to the theater, I'd felt quite proud of myself. Mr. Ziegfeld had approached me at a show in California and told me to call on him if ever I was in New York. And look at me now, I thought. Despite everything, I was about to knock on his door, ready to get on that stage. A twinge of nerves fluttered through me as I approached the theater entrance, but I shooed them away.

Inside was equally impressive—black-and-white marble floors, elaborate carved wooden friezes, illustrations of beautiful women adorning the walls. But there was no one in sight. The box office windows were closed, the glass doors to the theater were locked. Looking around, I could see no indication of where to go, so I called the elevator and heard the churning of machinery as it slowly made its way down to the lobby.

"Good morning, miss," the elevator attendant said as he opened both doors. "How can I help you?"

"I'm here to see Mr. Ziegfeld," I said.

"Of course. He's on the sixth floor. Is he expecting you?"

"Yes, I believe he is," I said, smirking slightly as I stepped inside. It had been a little over a year since we'd met, and in that time my life had been turned upside down and back again, but Mr. Ziegfeld didn't know any of that. Surely he was expecting me to show up at some point.

In his office I gave his secretary the same answer I'd given the elevator attendant because it had worked so well and it tickled me as I said it.

His secretary looked through the calendar. "I don't see a meeting scheduled, Miss McCormick."

"Really?"

"Are you sure he's expecting you?"

"Oh yes," I said, enjoying this more than I should be.

"Okay, let me see," she said, getting up and going through a heavy dark wooden door. When she reappeared she said, "You can go in now."

I quickly walked into the office before anyone had a chance to change their mind, taking a deep breath, willing the confidence to stay with me.

The rich burgundy-and-gold carpet was thick under my feet, as if I were in someone's bedroom, not their office. Mr. Ziegfeld stood up from his large mahogany desk and walked around to the front to greet me. He looked just as I remembered, slight of build but tall, a full head of silver-grey hair, thick black eyebrows and an impeccably tailored suit.

"Hello, Mr. Ziegfeld, so lovely to see you again."

He stopped and appraised me, frowning slightly. He looked confused or possibly angry at me for showing up without an appointment. I couldn't decide.

"And you are?"

"Olive McCormick," I said, laughing a little nervously. "We met in California at the Manila Theater." He looked at me blankly. "San Jose, California. I sang in the performance of *The Mikado* with a traveling opera company." I was sure this would bring that moment back to him. But nothing—just a blank look. "There was an earthquake, remember? You said that my singing stopped a moment of sudden panic." Panic? I was in a panic. This was not going at all as I'd expected. How could he not remember? He'd been so complimentary. I had imagined how this second meeting would go just about every day of the past year, envisioning it as a turning point in my career, a necessary stepping-stone in my life, yet he couldn't recall ever seeing my performance.

"I'm terribly sorry. I see a lot of beautiful women, a lot of talented singers and dancers. I cannot possibly remember them all."

"Well, let me jog your memory," I said, a little sternly now. "You told me you'd like me to come to New York and be in your show."

He raised his bushy black eyebrows, and a slight grin appeared under his thin mustache.

"Or, perhaps you said if I was ever in New York then I should pay you a visit at your theater, or something to that effect. Anyway, here I am." I curtsied sarcastically.

This time he smiled and sat on the edge of his desk. "Well, Miss McCormick, you've certainly got the spirit of one of my girls. I can see now why I must have liked you. Please take a walk to the wall, slowly, turn, and walk back towards me."

I did as he instructed, trying not to rush, trying to calm myself down. I was here now, he'd already seen me perform, he'd already complimented my voice, my figure, what more did he need? It felt strange and uncomfortable to be observed doing a simple, everyday act such as walking. His eyes on me made me feel as though I were doing it wrong.

I'd read a few magazine articles about Ziegfeld over the past year. One was called "How I Pick My Beauties," and I remembered it saying that personality is what gets a girl into the *Follies* and that she should be jolly, happy, and lighthearted. Another article, "When Is a Woman's Figure Beautiful: Florenz Ziegfeld Tells How He Judges," was more specific, saying that a beautiful, rounded, lovely figure is an attribute to the stage and that the measurements he considers right for the girl of today is height: five feet five and a half inches—I was spot-on there. Weight: 120 pounds—well, in my normal state I danced back and forth between 118 and 122, and in the past few months I'd worked harder than ever to stay right in the middle.

Shoe size: five. Mine was a whopping size seven—I curled my toes in my boots as I recalled this detail. It went on to say he tried to choose the "American type," with a perfect profile, a straight nose, a short upper lip, rose-and-cream-colored skin, large melting eyes, an expressive mouth and a mass of crinkly, bright golden hair—well, I was a brunette, but I knew he'd selected brunettes before; even his former wife was a brunette. When I'd read these articles, I'd thought I fit perfectly, but now, as he took his time looking me up and down, I started to wonder and sucked in my stomach.

"Thank you, Miss McCormick, do sit down."

"Do you recall the evening we met now?" I asked, smiling, remembering to appear jolly.

"It's coming back to me, yes."

"It would be an honor to join your show, Mr. Ziegfeld, I live in New York now and I'm . . ."

He held his hand up to stop me. "Before you go on . . ." He paused, as if to make sure that I was willing to listen, which I was, obediently yet reluctantly. "This is a wonderful time for the theater. It's a time when we as producers and performers"—he nodded to me, which gave me a little hope—"know that we are doing something good for our country. We entertain, we lift spirits, we make people laugh, we tell stories, we bring communities together, we celebrate and glorify the American girl and therefore we celebrate our country and our heritage."

He paused as if for some applause or a pat on the back. "That's wonderful, I agree," I said, not sure what else to say. "I think it's brilliant and that's why I came here to tell you . . ."

He put his hand up again. It was really starting to bother me when he did that.

"Having said all that, I'm afraid that we don't have any openings for chorus girls at the present time. With your proportions, your long legs, good features and"—he opened a drawer and pulled out a transparent screenlike mask, with various lines and measurements, and held it up to my face—"yes, and with your near perfect facial symmetry, you would make an excellent chorus girl. I believe I said you'd be perfect for the ponies, but on second thought you'd make a marvelous chorus girl."

He did remember me! He'd told me when he came to my dressing room that I could be one of his ponies, and I remembered thinking how awful that sounded until I read up on it and realized it simply meant a dancer. But now he saw me as a chorus girl—even better, I thought.

"So a chorus girl, then?"

"Yes. But I'm afraid not at this time."

What was wrong with this man, getting my hopes up and then shooting them down repeatedly? Maybe I wasn't good enough, maybe performing in small-town shows had allowed me to believe I was better than I really was. I suddenly felt foolish for barging into his office, but I refused to let those feelings get the better of me or to let him see my weakness.

"It's all very well to have the looks, Mr. Ziegfeld," I said. "But let's not forget the importance of talent supported by a lifetime of training. No one is going to light up a stage if they can't sing or dance. I can do both, very well I've been told, by newspaper reviews, audiences and very important producers such as yourself." I got up to leave.

"Do come back. We'll be holding auditions again early next year."

I was mad as hell. Really, who did this man think he was, anyway, God? Picking out what he considered to be the perfect specimen of a woman with no account for her talent and perseverance? I might not be the best dancer out there, but I sure worked at it. He had no idea what I'd been through in the past year, and in that time I'd worked on my voice constantly. It was about the only thing I could do. Before that, I'd taken any part I could get in any theater company in town just to continue my training onstage. Sure, they were small-time, amateur productions, but he didn't need to know that, and I did it all to be ready to finally show off my hard work in New York City.

"Auditions?" I turned back toward him with my hand on the door. "Yes, I'll have my—"

I held my hand up this time, stopping him midsentence. "Oh, Mr. Ziegfeld, I can't simply wait around for you. I'm sure I'll be cast in another show by then. Hopefully, we'll meet again sometime."

CHAPTER TWO

I met Florenz Ziegfeld for the first time the previous year when I was nineteen and traveling with the Pollard Opera Company, much to my father's dismay. We'd been performing *The Mikado* at the Manila Theater that night in San Jose, California.

I'd had a wild streak in me since I left Minnesota. My father and I had gotten into a rip-roaring fight where he all but forbade me to go on the road, saying this "performing hobby" of mine was turning out to be some sort of crass ploy for attention and that no daughter of his should be parading herself onstage for other people's Saturday night entertainment. He hadn't minded so much when I sang in small shows in our hometown of St. Cloud or even over an hour away in Minneapolis, but I was itching for something bigger.

"I'm going to make it big, Pa, just you wait and see, and you'll feel differently about it then, I know you will."

"Ha," my father scoffed. "That'll be the day. I've told you once already I don't want you showing yourself off like that, it's vulgar."

"For goodness' sakes, Pa, I'm singing light opera, not selling my body on the streets."

The minute it left my lips I knew I'd gone too far. My outburst sent his large, broad hand searing across my face and me and my travel bag out the front door as fast as I could move.

The whole train ride from Minneapolis to San Jose I'd been furious, still feeling the burn on my cheek, yet I was quietly thrilled at the thought of him worrying about me—wondering where I'd stay and how I'd get by—and I was determined to prove him wrong. I didn't need his money or his approval, and if my mother couldn't stick up for me, even though she'd always encouraged my talents, then I didn't need her either.

The theater was packed door-to-door with patrons, and I'd caught wind that there were some important people occupying the boxes that night, a governor-general of some sort and the famous Florenz Ziegfeld from New York City. It was unusual for our traveling company to draw that kind of crowd, but that only thrilled me more. While some of the girls in the group got wobbly when they heard about a full house or dignitaries in the boxes, I got bolder, more excited. Minutes before the curtain went up I always had a buzzing sensation surging through me, a desperation for it all to start; the sound of the applause only intensified that feeling, until I felt I was lifting off the ground, gliding inches off the stage as I heard my voice fill the space around me.

That night, in Japanese dress, my face painted white, my lips red, I entered stage left and began to sing Yum-Yum's aria "The sun whose rays are all ablaze" when my voice was overtaken by a tremendous rumble, as if a roar of thunder were right outside the theater doors. Almost instantly there was a great jolt, the whole theater shaking violently from side to side for no more than a few seconds. The red-and-gold Japanese lanterns hanging from the catwalk overhead began to swing left to right, and someone in the orchestra screamed, "Earthquake!"

Members of the audience began to jump from their seats with cries of terror, but I suddenly had the strangest thought. Rather than fear for my life or panic that the ceiling would fall in on us, I was distressed that they would all leave, I wouldn't be able to perform and then I'd be devastated. What would I do with all this pent-up, buzzing energy, this absolute need to sing?

"Sit down!" roared an official-looking man from one of the boxes. The audience looked up at him, and without a second thought I picked up where I had left off, three lines in, with more intensity than I'd started out with. The thunderous noise was gone, the shaking ground below us was still and people stood for a moment, seeming unsure whether they should stay or go. Then they began to find their seats again. The orchestra had stopped playing, but that didn't bother me. I gave one hell of a performance, and when I sang my last note everyone stood up and frantically applauded. The show went on, the orchestra resumed and it was as if nothing had happened. That is, until Mr. Florenz Ziegfeld knocked on the dressing room door at the end of the night.

"I'm looking for the director, Mr. Elvie," he said.

"Oh." I pulled my robe tighter around me. I had taken off my kimono and was about to remove the white makeup and red lipstick.

We'd been expecting Mr. Elvie, too—he usually knocked on the dressing room door soon after the show to give us his notes onstage while they were fresh in his head.

"He hasn't come backstage yet, I'm afraid. I can pass on a message if you'd like."

"Please do. Tell him that Florenz Ziegfeld came by to compliment him on his production and on his spectacular cast."

I nodded, trying not to appear too eager to meet him.

"And you, you were quite spectacular yourself, Miss . . . ?"

"Miss McCormick," I said. "Olive McCormick."

"Yum-Yum indeed." He took my hand and kissed it, holding a beautiful bouquet of flowers in his other hand. "You saved the show this evening."

"Oh, I don't know about that."

"Indeed, your bravery, your calmness and your presence of mind to keep singing in that beautifully sweet voice of yours averted what could have resulted in a stampede."

I hadn't thought of it that way; I'd just really wanted to sing. In fact, since the show had ended, and I'd heard the cast members in the dressing room talking about the terrifying earthquake and how we could have all been crushed to death in the rubble of the theater, I briefly thought that my continuing to sing could have actually done a lot more harm than good if there'd been another tremor.

"Truly, Miss McCormick," he continued, "hundreds of lives could have been at risk if everyone panicked and tried to flee."

"Well, I suppose you're right; I did save the day. Thank you for the lovely flowers," I said, reaching for them.

"Oh . . ." Mr. Ziegfeld hesitated, laughed, then handed them over. "I like your confidence."

I realized as I took them that they weren't intended for me. After all, we'd only just met. He hadn't come backstage to meet me, he'd come to meet the director. I suddenly felt foolish, but I wasn't about to let on, so I breathed in the scent and smiled one of my best.

"I have a little show in New York City," he said. "You might have heard of it."

Of course I had. This was the Broadway showman and creator of the *Ziegfeld Follies*, the man who turned young women into overnight sensations if they could sing or dance. But I'd be coy, play it as if I hadn't a clue.

"I don't believe I've heard of it."

"Oh yes, the *Ziegfeld Follies*. I have the most beautiful, most talented girls in the country. I know from one glance if they have the proportions and beauty to be a Ziegfeld girl."

"Really? One glance? And I suppose she must disrobe for you to have such insight?"

"Not at all. She can be fully robed. One look at her ankle and her neck will tell me exactly how her whole leg will look. I like a straight American girl's nose and a short upper lip." He eyed me, moving his head to the side to analyze my facial structure.

"And how do I hold up to your high standards?"

"Quite nicely. You've got the face for it." He looked down, and while I was wearing a robe he allowed his eyes to follow the length of my legs from the ankle up to my thigh as if he could see right through the fabric. "The proportions are perfection, and if you could sing on Broadway the way you sang on that stage tonight, then you'd be just fine as one of my ponies."

I gave him a cockeyed look—what the heck was a pony? I was an opera singer. I laughed and started to turn away.

"You must come and visit me next time you're in New York City," he said. "The New Amsterdam Theatre on Forty-second Street. You can't miss it, it's got my name in white lights out front."

We played in San Jose for one more night and then went to San Francisco, Sacramento, and then Hollywood for the final show. It was a matinee: apparently everyone in Hollywood was more interested in going to the movie show in the evenings than in watching a live opera. But that was all right with me, because that evening the producers took our whole troupe to the Brown Derby for dinner. It was a rounded brown dome of a restaurant made to look like a derby hat right on Wilshire Boulevard. They ordered for the table— chopped chicken livers, spaghetti and a Derby plate of crabs' legs, celery, avocado and Thousand Island dressing. Afterwards some of the girls ordered ice cream and sherbets and made their way back to the hotel, but I was dying to see a little more of the Hollywood I'd heard so much about. After we said good night and went back to our rooms, I sneaked out and walked across the street to where I'd seen a big sign that read, "Ambassador Hotel—Cocoanut Grove," and underneath, "Ray West and his Cocoanut Grove Orchestra."

I approached the heavy glass doors with as much confidence as I could muster and smiled at the doorman.

"I'm meeting my friends inside," I said, not stopping as he tipped his hat and opened the door for me. Thrilled by my subterfuge, I sailed past him. The minute I stepped inside, the music hit me, swirling around a room full of tables dressed in white linen, a frenzied dance floor and actual full-size palm trees grazing the ceiling. The atmosphere was electrifying, and I tingled with excitement. Looking around, taking it all in, I noticed an empty seat at the bar, where I might be able to linger without my being alone getting too much notice.

"A Coca-Cola, please," I said to the barkeep. "And a straw."

"How about I put it in a glass for you, so you can sip it like a lady?" He laughed.

"That would be great." I took the glass of Coca-Cola and turned around to face the orchestra. It was wildly fun, and I wished more than anything I could get up there on the dance floor.

"You're not here alone, are you?"

It was the gentleman sitting to my left. I hadn't even noticed him when I sat down. He was at least twenty-five years older than me, maybe more, but slightly handsome in a slick kind of way, hair greased back, his tie loosened a little at the neck.

"Me? Oh no, I'm not alone, I'm here with a whole group of people." I looked around as if I'd lost them in the crowd.

"What kind of people?"

"We're a traveling opera company, and we've been performing along the West Coast. Today was our last show, actually—we head home early in the morning."

"Opera, huh?"

"Singing, dancing, performing, you name it," I said with a laugh.

"Do you act?" he asked. "I only ask because I'm a studio executive and, well, you certainly look the part."

15

I looked down at my Coca-Cola, trying not to beam at him. A studio executive? What exactly did they do? It had to be good, and what were the chances that I'd meet one, in real life, my last night in Hollywood? When I had myself under control, I looked up at him coyly and smiled. "You really think I look the part?"

"Well, I don't know if you've got any talent, but you've got a famous face, that's for sure."

"Oh, I've got talent," I said, and he laughed.

"Good, I like a girl with some charisma. If you've got that you're halfway there." He looked at my drink. "How's that Coca-Cola treating you?"

"It's delicious," I said.

"Want me to spruce it up for you?" He raised an eyebrow, then took a silver flask out of his jacket pocket and poured a good amount of something into my drink and then into his. "Fill me up, will you, Joey," he said to the barkeep, who looked around, then quickly took the flask along with some bills. I watched him go to the other end of the bar, turn his back to the crowd and refill it from an unlabeled brown bottle. A few moments later he came back and returned the flask under a napkin.

The man poured some more into our glasses, then raised his glass and looked at me expectantly. "What do you think?"

"I don't even know your name," I said, trying to buy myself some time. I'd had a sip of my father's whiskey before, which tasted like fire mixed with a mouthful of dirt, and I'd sipped my mother's gin fizz, which was decidedly more palatable, but I didn't even know what this was, and I was worried I'd take one sip and spit it back out again.

"Richard," he said. "But you can call me Ricky."

It was rum, and as it turned out I liked rum with Coca-Cola more than I would have expected. After I finished the first one, Ricky bought me another soda and topped it up just the same. It was getting warm in that room, but the drink was making me feel energized, as if I couldn't wait another minute before I got on that dance floor, so when Ricky asked me to dance I just about lunged at him.

He slipped his hands around my waist and danced with me, pulling me too close, but I let him do it anyway. I was in Hollywood for only a few more hours and then it would be back to regular old St. Cloud. I was dancing at the Cocoanut Grove in Hollywood with a studio executive—life didn't get much more exciting than this.

"Hey, have you seen the view from the top of the hotel?" he said into my ear over the music.

"No," I called out.

"Oh, you should, you can see the HOLLYWOODLAND sign from the balcony. I'm staying on the top floor, it's the only way you can get a glimpse—if you're staying here. Want to take a peek?"

I was reluctant to leave the dance floor behind, but I did want to see as much of Los Angeles as I could before I had to leave, so I let him grab my hand, navigate us off the frenzied dance floor, weave me through the tables and lead us out into the lobby of the hotel. The rum had hit me, and I felt wobbly on my feet. Everything seemed amazing: I couldn't take my eyes off the long sparkling chandeliers, the artwork on the walls and the fabulously dressed women. I grabbed hold of Ricky's arm so I could take it all in without falling over, and he whisked me into a shiny golden elevator.

"Have you ever thought about being in the pictures?" he asked.

"I've always dreamed of being on the stage," I said. "I'm going to be a Ziegfeld girl, you know."

"Really?" He seemed to think it was a coincidence. "I know people who know Florenz Ziegfeld."

"You know him?" I squealed.

"Sure thing, babe," he said, cool and calm as he brushed a piece of hair out of my eyes and tucked it behind my ear. "I told you, I'm a Hollywood man. I know a lot of people."

"I just met him in San Jose; he said he might put me in his show. My father is waiting to get a seat on the New York Produce Exchange, and then we're going to move to New York, though he's been saying that for years. I have to get there."

"Oh, you'd make a real pretty Ziegfeld girl," he said, placing his hands around my waist, then sliding them down to my rear and pulling me in toward him. Even in my tipsy state, I knew he was getting way too familiar, and I didn't like it. He could have been my father's age, and the only other boy who'd got up close with me like that was Henry Dickerson at my final school dance—this was far more presumptuous.

"Hey, wait a minute," I said, pulling away, flushed and a bit dizzy. But he went on as if he hadn't heard me.

"You want me to give Ziegfeld a call, tell him I think you'd be perfect for the show?"

"You'd do that?" When I spoke, my voice didn't sound like my own.

"Of course—better than that, I'm going to tell him he's a fool to wait for you to show up, that he needs to get you a train ticket and a place to stay lined up immediately, along with a generous contract, or you're going to get snapped up by the Shuberts."

"You'd really tell him that?" I said, gasping, then reaching out to the wall to steady myself. This was the most exciting news I'd heard in my whole life.

"I'd do anything for that pretty little face of yours," he said, leaning in and kissing me on the lips. I cringed at the feel of his moist mouth on mine; it was uninvited and unwanted. I tried to pull away, but he held my face tight in his hands. I held my breath. He'd said something about being in the pictures. I imagined being in front of the camera. "I'd do anything for you," he said, pulling back, holding my face a little too firmly in his hands. "Anything at all, if you'd do something for me."

I never did see the HOLLYWOODLAND sign. I just stared up at the white, swirling ceiling in his hotel room, then squeezed my eyes tightly shut and forced myself to think about my first night onstage at the New Amsterdam Theatre.

When I got back home to St. Cloud, Pa felt guilty as hell for slapping me across the face, I could tell. He didn't mention it, but he was sugary sweet for a few days. I continued with voice lessons and my part-time job as salesgirl at the local women's clothing store, but I was repulsed with myself. I couldn't believe I'd let myself get drunk off that man's hooch and that I'd let him do what he did. It was a blur, the rest of the night; I didn't even remember how I got back to my hotel room. I vowed to never let myself think of that night again.

Over the next few weeks, I read up on Mr. Ziegfeld in magazines and looked for auditions for every play and traveling performing group that could end up as an excuse to get me to New York City, where I could pay him a visit on Broadway. But nothing came up to send me east.

And then, a little over a month after returning home, after my father had been traveling for business, my parents sat down with me and my brothers George and Junior and told us we were moving. Erwin, the oldest, was already out of the house by then. They'd bought a Victorian house in Flatbush, Brooklyn, and just as they'd hoped, Pa was going to leave his job in banking to be a grain and stock broker in Manhattan. He'd been waiting for the opportunity, and it had finally presented itself.

I couldn't believe it. My brothers complained like hell, but I could barely contain myself. I didn't have to lie, cheat or run away to make it happen. I kept quiet, shocked by my unbelievably good luck, since I didn't think any of us had ever thought it would happen.

Keeping my excitement at bay, I obediently organized my things and helped my mother pack up the house with such determination that my father held me up as an example to my brothers. If only they could be more like me, he told them for the first time in my life, helpful and cooperative instead of sitting out on the front porch sulking. As far as I was concerned, the faster we packed up our old life into boxes, the faster I could start my new life in New York City.

One morning, while my mother and I carefully wrapped the china in newspaper, our hands blackened with ink, a wave of nausea came over me.

"Ugh," I said, setting down a stack of teacups and rubbing my stomach.

"What is it, honey?" my mother asked.

"I don't know, the smell of this ink. Or maybe I'm hungry."

"Do you want me to fix you something? I just got eggs at the market today, I could fix you fried eggs with the runny yolks the way you like them."

The very thought of runny yolks made my stomach lurch toward my throat. I stood up and ran to the bathroom, making it just in time.

The same thing happened every day for a week, the same time, right around breakfast, and my mother thought the stress of moving was making me ill. I assured her it couldn't possibly be that, because I was quite looking forward to the change of scenery—a slight understatement if ever there was one—but she insisted that we see a doctor. And that's when we got the news.

"Pregnant!" my mother's voice screeched as she stared at me in disbelief.

I stared right back at her, speechless, then she marched out of the office and slammed the door behind her. The shock of what he'd told me didn't sink in until the door made me jump.

"I don't understand," I said, staring dumbfounded at the doctor, who tidied up his instruments and scribbled something onto his notepad.

"Really?" he said harshly. "I think you do." And he walked out, too, leaving me there on the cold metal examination table, seeing my hopes and dreams shatter around me.

Outside, my mother was pacing.

"How could you do this to us, Olive? How could you do this to your father? We've given you everything, everything you've ever asked for, and this is how you repay us? Good God, what have you done?"

"I'm sorry," I said, starting to sob.

"Oh, save your tears and pull yourself together, there's no time for this. Who did this to you?"

"I don't know."

"For God's sake, Olive, what does that mean? Tell me the truth."

I'd never seen my mother so angry.

"I honestly don't know. His name was Ricky, I met him in California. He said he worked at a cinema studio in Hollywood. I don't know anything else about him. He gave me a lot of rum and said he'd help me get into show business."

"You stupid, stupid, selfish girl. You could have had the world. But not anymore. And this poor child, this poor bastard child."

"I'm sorry, Mama," I said, trying to hold back the tears. "I didn't want to, I didn't mean to."

She pulled at the roots of her hair so hard, I thought a clump might come out in her hands. "You can't go to New York in this condition, you'll ruin your father's reputation before he's even gotten a start. He'll disown you if he finds out."

"I have to go to New York," I said.

"You can't."

"Well, what am I supposed to do?" I cried, tears now rolling down my cheeks. "Stay here in Minnesota?"

"Yes," she said. "That's exactly what you'll do."

"No!" I cried.

My mother looked off into the distance and rubbed her temples.

"You'll stay here and have the baby, and I don't know what will happen next for you, I really don't."

"Mama, please," I cried frantically. I couldn't have a baby, I couldn't even fathom it, and I certainly couldn't do it without my mother. I still needed her, I still felt like a child myself.

This was a curse—that man had cursed me, and I had no one to blame but myself for letting it happen.

But over the next week, my mother made the necessary arrangements. I would stay with her widowed sister, my aunt May, in Rockville, a few hours southwest of St. Cloud. There was a place she'd heard of not too far from where Aunt May lived, Birdhouse Lodge, where unwed women went to give birth and put their babies up for adoption. She told my father that Aunt May had taken ill and that someone needed to stay behind and take care of her until she was better. She told my father that she would have to do it, knowing full well that he needed her to set up the new house in Brooklyn and get the boys settled. So she let it be his idea that the only person who could stay behind and care for her sister was me.

I hadn't seen much of Aunt May after her husband, Henry, died overseas in the war eight years earlier. She'd become something of a recluse since he'd passed, and at first the thought of staying with someone like that for the next seven months made me incredibly uneasy. As a young child, I'd loved her. A few years younger than my mother, she'd been fun and caring and always made the effort to spend time with me away from my brothers, which I'd thoroughly

23

enjoyed. But after Henry died my mother said she'd changed, and it worried her and frightened me. Her lively, chatty and fun-loving demeanor had been extinguished and what was left was a quiet, dreary and inattentive woman whom no one could recognize.

"Let's get you settled, then," she said when I arrived. Her house was simple and a little cluttered with newspapers and magazines. "Yours is the little room at the top of the stairs; we'll bring your luggage up later. Now I haven't had many guests over the years so you'll have to let me know if you need anything." She looked a little uncomfortable herself, and I longed for my own mother to be there with me, even though in the past few weeks she'd barely been able to stay in the same room as me for more than five minutes.

While I didn't know anyone in Rockville, I didn't want to draw attention to myself and couldn't risk anyone seeing me in my swollen state, in case news got back to my father. So I stayed home mostly, as Aunt May did, with the exception of her early morning walks to the store and her afternoon gardening. We played cards and I read magazines that she picked up at the store for me, and when she was outside gardening I practiced my scales and all the songs I knew from my previous performances.

She was thirty-eight or so, and she had a pretty face, if only she'd tame her wild hair. In a picture she kept on the mantel of Henry and her on their wedding day, she was breathtaking. She told me they'd met at a dance at the church hall and that he'd come calling the next day and every day after for a week. At the end of the week he'd asked her to marry him, and she'd said yes. I smiled at the thought of her, young and giddy with all the possibilities of love waiting for her.

"Thank you," I said quietly one afternoon as we were having a cup of tea in the living room. "For letting me stay." I looked down at my slightly protruding belly and sighed. "I got myself into a real mess, Aunt May."

She pressed her lips together. "Yes, poppet, yes, you did. But it doesn't look like you had many options."

She walked over to me and gave my shoulder a squeeze. It was the first act of affection she'd shown toward me in the three weeks I'd been there, after all those hugs and kisses she'd bestowed upon me as a child. I wondered if it was because she'd become so used to being alone that she'd forgotten.

"I'm scared," I said, finally letting out the words that had been twisting and turning inside my head night after night. "I'm really scared."

"I know you are," she said, not offering any empty promises that everything would be all right, and for that I was strangely grateful. "When you were a child you used to get more scrapes and bruises on your legs than your brothers combined. Don't tell them that I told you this, but they used to cry and cry, and you, well, you just brushed yourself off and got on with whatever it was you were doing. You were the strongest of the four of you, always have been. You're going to come through this. You'll be all right, Olive, I know you will."

When the time finally came, I packed a suitcase as I would if I were going away on a family trip, not to some Catholic boardinghouse where disgraced women gave birth.

"Are you sure I can't have the baby here at home?" I asked. As the months went by, Aunt May's house felt like a safe haven and I was terrified of what would happen once I left its confines.

"You've got the baby to think of now, Olive," she said. "They'll find a home for your child. That is still what you want, isn't it?"

"Yes," I said quietly, though all of this just felt so wrong. I couldn't raise a child, not like this. I was young, I had no husband, and there were so many things I wanted to do with my life, but the thought of giving my baby away to strangers was excruciating.

"That's what your mother wants for you, too. She gave me strict instructions to follow, so that you can get back to your family where you belong. The sooner you get through this, the sooner you can get back to your old life. Now, come on"—she put her weight on my suitcase and zipped it closed—"we don't want you missing that train."

She placed her hand on my belly, now firm and tight, about the size of a watermelon. "It won't be long now."

When I arrived, it was nothing like I'd expected. The name Bird-house Lodge sounded quaint and peaceful, but women were four or even six to a room in bunk beds, nuns enforcing that everyone take shifts scrubbing the floors, cleaning the bathrooms, cooking in the kitchen and earning their keep right up until they gave birth.

At forty weeks I waited for my turn, terrified of the pain that was to come, that we'd all heard in the screams from the delivery room and that we'd seen in the blood that we'd washed from the sheets and towels. Up until this point it had all felt unreal. I hadn't discussed my body's transformation with anyone, not even Aunt May; I'd just watched my

stomach grow and grow in stunned silence. But now that I was surrounded by other women with the same fate, hearing their screams,
seeing their sadness, it all became frighteningly real. I lay awake at night
petrified of dying, of never having the chance to live out my dreams.
This is just temporary, I kept telling myself when I was down on my
hands and knees scrubbing the kitchen floor, this will be over soon.

And then, one afternoon when I carried the bucket of water to
the outdoor drain, I had to set it down suddenly. I'd managed with
every task asked of me up until that point, trying to just get on and
get this done, but at that moment it all felt too much. Everything felt
too heavy—the bucket, my legs, my stomach. Extra weight seemed
to be pushing down on me, even my shoulders seemed to be pulling
downward. I slumped to the ground.

When one of the nuns, Sister Margaret, came to me, I told her
I had to go to the bathroom, and when I did, a clump of something
jellylike came out of me with my urine, which she told me was a
sign that the baby would be here soon. A few hours later, after I
was allowed to rest, I tried to get out of bed. I thought I needed the
bathroom, but I didn't make it: warm liquid pooled around me. After that, everything happened so fast. The contractions started, light
tightening at first, but they soon progressed to painful clenching that
gripped me so hard I could barely breathe. I was taken to the delivery room and positioned in the delivery chair—a school desk–like
contraption with footrests to push down on and a hole where the
seat would be. Other pregnant girls came in with clean towels and
buckets of water, stealing terrified glances my way.

No one had prepared me for any of this, and I didn't really understand what was happening to my body, but I'd told myself I wasn't

going to cause a fuss or yell or scream for the whole house to hear, that I was going to get through this and move on. But I couldn't control myself. The pain became so intense it made me vomit. At times I thought I'd pass out from the agony, and I hoped I would, that I would just wake up when all this was over, but the nuns gave me smelling salts to revive me when I felt faint, and when the doctor came, he gave me a combination of morphine and scopolamine, which dulled the pain and made me woozy. I pushed and pushed and pushed, as they told me to, and the girls took away blood-soaked towels, returning with clean ones.

"There's a lot of blood," the doctor kept saying. "Bring more water."

The morphine made me hot and sweaty and then cold and delirious; I was in and out of consciousness.

"Wake her up!" I'd hear someone yell, and I'd be jolted back to consciousness with the smelling salts.

"Push!" the doctor yelled. He sounded desperate, and I knew something was wrong. "Harder, push now!" He placed his hands on my stomach and pressed down. I screamed in pain.

Finally, I felt it happening. It was excruciating, but I knew it was almost over now, so I gave it all I had until I heard the sound of catlike cries.

"It's a girl," someone said, and I felt so relieved, but I could feel myself slipping into sleep again. The baby was wrapped and cleaned and brought to me briefly. When I held her she seemed so small and fragile; she looked at me and stopped crying for a moment, her deep blue eyes searching, confused, seeing things for the very first time.

"No time for that," the doctor said. "Get her to the bed!" And I was picked up under the arms and shuffled to a bed nearby where they frantically stuffed towels between my legs.

When I awoke, I'd been moved to the recovery room, and Sister Margaret sat in a chair by my bed. She was holding the baby in her arms.

"Thank the Lord," she said, standing. "She's awake."

I looked at the tiny bundle in her arms, wrapped in a blanket and fast asleep.

"What happened?" I asked, my throat hoarse. She brought a glass of water to my lips and I gulped it down.

"You've been asleep for two full days, we couldn't wake you," she said. It felt as if it had been longer. The doctor came over and took my temperature, looked in my eyes, listened to my heart.

"You've been very lucky," he said finally. "You had childbed fever. Many women don't make it through that, but the fever seems to have broken." He looked at me seriously.

"Well, that's good, isn't it?"

"We'll have to monitor you for a few more days." He looked from me to Sister Margaret as if there were something else. "You hemorrhaged a lot of blood. There was a rupture in the uterus. We were able to stop the bleeding, but I'm afraid it's done a significant amount of damage."

"What does that mean?"

"Miss McCormick, it means you won't be able to have any more children. Your uterus is torn."

I'd thought, from his tone, that he was going to tell me I was dying.

"What about the baby?" I tried to get out of bed to get a look at her again. When I tried, the pain wouldn't let me. "The baby's okay, though, isn't she?"

"Yes, yes," the nun reassured me. I strained to sit up and see her face and felt a tremendous amount of love for the little creature, not quite like a mother, I supposed, but as if she were my baby sister. Her tiny features, her pink hands, her dark wisp of hair. I wondered if it was only relief that she was out in the world now and safe. I squeezed my eyes shut. Was she safe? She was so tiny, fragile, help-less. What would become of her?

"Is she going to live?"

"Yes," the doctor said. "She's perfectly healthy."

"Good," I said, trying to remain practical. "And me?" I asked, forcing myself to change the subject. "Will I live, too?"

"Yes," the doctor said, almost cracking a smile. "Yes, Miss McCor-mick, you're going to live. I just had to inform you of the news . . ." He paused and regained his serious expression. "The news that you won't be—"

"I understand, thank you, I understand that," I said. "It's okay."

The truth was, at the time I thought that it would be. I'd never even considered becoming a mother before, so the news that I couldn't go through all this again wasn't as devastating as they might have expected it to be. I'd been so focused on everything else that life had to offer. As the pregnancy had progressed and my stomach had grown, I'd felt a tremendous amount of responsibility to this baby, to make sure it was healthy and do my best to find her a good home, but I hadn't considered changing my mind about the adoption. If I did, I'd be alone, I'd be disowned by my family, I'd be poor, and that was no way to raise a child. Anytime my mind wandered into those murky waters, I had reminded myself of this.

It was a full week before I was strong enough to walk around unaccompanied, and once the baby was deemed to be in good health and cleared of any abnormalities or deformities, which would have made it too difficult for them to find adoptive parents, I was told by Sister Frances it was time to leave. Tall and masculine looking in her black-and-white nun's habit, Sister Frances wore thick glasses and had yellowing teeth.

"What will she drink if I just leave like this?" I asked.

"Evaporated milk, that's what your money goes to—care and feeding of the girl."

"And what do I do about these?" I looked down to my engorged breasts.

"The milk will dry up when you're away from the baby. It'll take a few days, but it'll happen. Your body knows what to do."

"Shouldn't I take her home for a little while, just until she's a bit stronger, and bring her back in a couple of weeks?" I said.

"Are you planning on keeping her?" she asked, her eyes squinting at me through her glasses.

"No," I whispered.

"Then she stays," she said. "This is a baby we're talking about, not a piece of furniture."

"I know, I didn't mean it that way." I was already feeling awful for doing this to the poor child, abandoning her, but I told myself it was for the best. I knew she deserved a family who desperately wanted a baby, whose lives and hearts had room for her.

"It just seems wrong to separate a baby from her mother so soon," I persisted, glancing up at her, then looking away. It was the first time

I'd used that word, "mother," and it felt strange on my lips. "She's so helpless."

"Yes, well . . ." She made the sign of the cross, and I wondered what she must think of me. "The Blessed Mother will take care of her now." She made the sign of the cross again. She must have thought one cross wouldn't suffice—this poor child needed as many as she could get. "We will find her a home as soon as possible. The younger they are the more likely they are to be taken in, so the new mother can feel an attachment, as if she's her own."

She swaddled her and carried her to the door. "Now strip your bed and take your sheets to the laundry room, then sign your papers on the way out." I stood frozen, though my mind was darting from one thought to the next. Should I do something, say something?

"Peace be with you," she said, walking down the hall with the baby in her arms. And I wondered if that would ever be possible again.

It took four weeks of wearing a girdle day and night at Aunt May's house and dining on nothing but broth and cucumbers before I could fit into my old clothes again—and just as long for the bleeding to stop. Though I looked almost the same from the outside, I was plagued by the notion that my father and brothers would notice a difference in me. I wondered if I'd been changed from the inside out.

When she found me sobbing into my sheets those first few weeks, Aunt May assured me that it was normal for me to feel that way, that sometimes women who gave birth cried a lot for no reason, even if the baby was wanted.

"What if nobody wants her?" I said one night. "What will become of her then?"

"Someone will want her," she said, smoothing the hair back from my face. "She's going to grow up and have a good life with someone who loves her very much. I promise you."

CHAPTER THREE

The house on Marlborough Road in Flatbush, Brooklyn, was painted a cool mint with pink and dark green trim around the eaves and windows. All the houses on Marlborough Road were new, lined up in different hues with wraparound porches and picket fences. My parents had been sold on the location because it was desirable for families who wanted to be close to Manhattan but had an appetite for a more suburban life.

It made sense for my mother, who wouldn't have lasted five minutes cooped up in a city apartment, and for my father, who planned to commute into Manhattan each day but would want to return home to dinner in a proper dining room and retire to the backyard for a beer after. My brothers settled in fairly well. George had started Brooklyn College in the fall and had already joined the men's basketball team, and Junior, though he missed his buddies back home at first, soon made plenty of friends at his new school. My oldest brother, Erwin, had been out of the house for four years already. He'd joined the navy the minute he turned seventeen—after watching so many young men go off to war when he was in his early teens, he'd vowed to do his part as soon as they'd take him, so he hadn't even seen the new house.

The first few days after arriving in Brooklyn, I tried to quell my eagerness to bolt out the door and head into the city. I knew if I was too eager, it would backfire.

I helped my mother around the house; she'd made new curtains and wanted me to help her replace the ones she'd hung in the living room. She didn't speak of the baby, the birth, or my time with Aunt May, so I didn't speak of it either. It was as if the whole thing had never happened.

"What do you think?" my mother asked. "Will you look for a job in a little clothing store, like before? Maybe you'd meet some nice girls, make some friends in the neighborhood?"

"I don't think so, Mother, being a shopgirl is very dull."

"I don't think it would be dull if you worked somewhere like Lord and Taylor, that gorgeous department store on Fifth Avenue."

I rolled my eyes. The thought of selling perfume just about sent me to sleep.

"Your father's heading into the city tomorrow morning, why don't you see if you can ride in with him."

"I could do that," I said, perking up. "I mean, I suppose I could keep him company, take a look around while he's at work."

"Wonderful. I'd come along with you, but I've got some neighborhood ladies coming for tea tomorrow, and I need to bake a sponge cake in the morning."

The next day, while my brothers were still sleeping and my mother was cooking breakfast for my father, I slipped on a yellow georgette crepe blouse and my shepherd check skirt with the big pockets. I'd been eating like a bird for the past month, anticipating meeting Mr. Ziegfeld at some point in the near future, and the skirt even felt a little loose around my waist, thank God! I buttoned up my boots, quickly removed the pins from my hair, arranged my curls and slipped into the kitchen holding my father's briefcase.

"Good morning, Papa," I said, sitting with him at the kitchen table. "I was thinking I might accompany you into the city today. I'm going to inquire about finding work, too."

"You don't have to do that. Your mother probably needs you here." He shoveled a forkful of eggs into his mouth and washed it down with coffee. "I don't know if you should wander around Manhattan unescorted."

"Actually, it was Mother's idea, and now that I'm finally here in New York City I'd better catch up and learn how to get around, don't you think?"

The truth was I hadn't a clue how to get around Manhattan, but there were streetcars and taxicabs and I had a feeling I would know exactly where I needed to go.

It was a cool March day and the energy of the city was pulsating. My father's office was on Wall Street, so I asked the driver to drop me near Lord & Taylor.

Men in blue serge suits and charcoal pinstripes walked past me in a hurry, everyone tipping their hats against the chilled spring air. The men in this town were well dressed and handsome. Fifth Avenue was dominated by streetcars, which shared the road with the occasional horse-drawn carriage. I looked up at the enormous ten-story building, which took up an entire city block from West Thirty-eighth Street to West Thirty-ninth. I'd never seen a store so large. When the wind calmed for a moment, I felt the rays of the sun shining between the buildings that sprouted up from the concrete sidewalks. A warm summer wasn't too far off; I could feel it.

Walking through the glass doors, I was amazed to see that people were already browsing and shopping. A dazzling selection of beaded evening purses, sequined headbands, tiaras and hair clips sparkled up at me, and I felt a thrill as I pictured the costumes and headpieces of the stage. I could feel it, the pressure of the headpiece, the contracted abdomen, the pinch of the dance shoes, as I walked toward the audience, arms outstretched, receiving the applause.

"Welcome to Lord and Taylor." A lithe young woman startled me. "Can I assist you with the accessories, miss?"

"Oh no," I said, "I was just passing through, I'm not here to shop."

"Of course. Luncheon will be served on the tenth floor at eleven A.M. in the Wedgewood Room, and afternoon tea will be served at two P.M. in the Mandarin Room."

"I'm not here for that either, actually. I'm heading to Times Square," I said, suddenly feeling the urgent need to get out of the store. She pointed me in the right direction, and I walked, faster now that I knew I was close to the New Amsterdam Theatre.

CHAPTER FOUR

fter my disappointing meeting with Mr. Ziegfeld, I left the
theater, dashing out of the grand lobby, past the two enormous gold
peacock sculptures, letting the doors slam behind me. The bright
sunlight blinded me after having been inside, but I just started walking. After turning on Broadway, cars whizzing by, people dashing
past with somewhere to go, I realized I had no idea where I was going. Advertisements for "Squibb's Dental Cream" and "Coca-Cola—
Delicious and Refreshing" and "Arrow Collars" all loomed above me.
An immense image of a man smoking a cigarette looked down on
me with the words "I'd Walk a Mile for a Camel," but I couldn't walk
another block. I just needed to sit down for a minute—I felt deflated.
Mr. Ziegfeld hadn't picked me on purpose, just to knock me down a
peg or two; I was sure of it.

I moved away from the busy street, leaned back against the wall
and closed my eyes. I had to plan out my next move. I'd promised to

meet my father and his driver at three o'clock and it was only eleven A.M. There were theaters and vaudeville houses all along Broadway and West Forty-second Street—some big-time charging $2 a show, some small-time charging ten cents and showing six times a day. The *Ziegfeld Follies* was $10 a ticket, making it a real special occasion to see.

I didn't know what to do. I hadn't considered the idea that I might not get cast; it hadn't even been a possibility. I'd gotten through the previous eleven months by picturing the moment when I'd walk into Ziegfeld's office and claim my spot on the stage. This was simply not how I'd imagined things. I walked back to Lord & Taylor glumly and spent the afternoon alone in the Mandarin Room.

The next day, I went back to the city and found myself in the dingy little office of theatrical agent Moses Sherman. I'd seen a tiny ad for him in a free paper I picked up outside the vaudeville houses. There wasn't an open seat in the cramped waiting room packed with other young men and women, so I stood by the window surveying the crowd, waiting for someone to call my name. In the far corner was a tall, slim woman draped in an armchair, her limbs all right angles, her facial features masculine and sharp, yet she was striking in the most unusual way. She caught me staring, and an enormous smile grew across her cheeks. She looked amused, as if she could tell immediately that I was new in town. Oh, I might be new, I thought, but I'm as determined as they come, just you wait and see.

A couple of men were seated by the door, dressed in identical pin-striped three-piece suits, bow ties and straw fedoras. There were dancer figures, and opera figures, and a few who looked as if they'd come in off a night on the street.

Eventually Mr. Sherman called my name. He was short in stature and round everywhere: his head and chin formed one blob, his chest and belly formed another.

"All right, Miss McCormick . . ." He looked up at me and wrinkled his nose. "You're going to have to change that name if you want to be in showbiz." He glanced at the paper I'd handed him that listed my performances and training. "So you can sing and dance?"

"That's right, Mr. Sherman."

He seemed in a hurry to be done with me.

"Okay, head over to the Olympia Theatre this afternoon. It's a thrice weekly variety show. One of the girls dropped out of a three-person act, got herself knocked up, or a sinus infection, or something." I held my breath as he said it. "Anyway," he continued, "she's out, and they need someone who can learn fast, two days fast. Can you do that?"

"Of course," I said. "Just tell me where to go."

He scribbled down the address on the back of the paper. "Come back here after you're done, and I'll let you know if you're in. We'll sign contracts, and if it all works out you start in a couple of days."

"That sounds perfect," I said. "Thank you so much."

He was already walking past me to his door. "Miss Leggington?" he called out.

I quickly picked up my handbag, my coat and the paper with the address and hurried toward the door.

"Oh, and Miss McCormick," he called out. "Change the name— you need something with some pizzazz, something that sounds like a star, not some woman who should be at home cooking her husband a lamb chop."

I nodded, a little taken aback, and he shut the door.

I auditioned for the part while their rehearsal was in session. I met the two girls I'd be performing with, Eileen Ray and Doreen Williams, and watched them dance their number. They taught me a short part of the sequence, then I danced it with them right there and then.

"You're going to have to learn the rest of this choreography in a jiffy," the director said.

"Yes, sir," I said. It was a soft-shoe ballet number—thank God, because I wasn't as confident on pointe—where three butterflies emerged from their cocoon to flit from one flower to another, a moment that, he explained, also signified their blossoming into women, until they fell asleep again on flower petals. The act was a bit ridiculous, really, but I just wanted to be onstage, to prove to myself that I could get cast right away, so I was willing to take anything I could get. "I could learn it today," I said.

"This is where the two other butterflies leave the stage and you'd sing your solo." He handed me the sheet music. I listened to the orchestra play the first half, then I walked onstage and sang the second half. When I finished, the director and stage manager clapped their hands in approval.

"Well, I think we've found our girl," the director said. "The show goes on three times a week at seven P.M., with practice on Tuesdays and Thursdays. Be here tomorrow for your first rehearsal."

"Okay," I said.

"We'll just be running through the acts to get the orchestra familiar with the music and determine the order for the program."

"Great!"

"What did you say your name was again?" He stood poised to scribble it down on his clipboard.

"Olive," I said. I wished I'd given it some thought before I charged in there an hour earlier. He glared impatiently. "It's Olive," I said. "Olive Shine."

The first few rehearsals and performances were quite exciting, just like any new show. It started with a newsreel so that anyone arriving late wouldn't miss out on the live acts, followed by a singing baseball pitcher, a short drama and a return engagement by Sally Holland, an older performer I'd never heard of, whom everyone seemed to love. The headliners were a tap dancer named Lou and a singer named Cliff. And then there was our dance, my solo, and then it was on to the next act, each one lasting about twelve minutes.

I liked the girls in my act, but the show itself was disorganized and at times amateurish—a fact that we all seemed to know but no one acknowledged. It felt good, of course, to have somewhere to go, a purpose, a job, even though it paid next to nothing. But I certainly didn't want my parents or my brothers to see it. The theater itself was shabby and the orchestra was often a few beats behind. It was on Broadway, just barely, but my father still wouldn't approve. He'd made it clear that he didn't want me performing for much longer, but even if I could persuade him, he'd see this mediocre performance as a reflection of his reputation. If only I could explain to him that this was just one step toward something better, if only I could convince him that it was worthy, though at times with this show, I wondered that myself.

"Olive," my mother said at dinner one evening, "your father and I want to have a word with you."

I knew what was coming. "We're happy that you're settling in here, but you agreed that your last show in Minnesota would be your last. And now you're telling us that you have a part in a new show."

"Yes, but it's on Broadway, it's not some little show from back home."

"Humph," my father grumbled as he ate his meal.

"Well, then we at least want to see it, don't we, Ted?"

"Ma, not yet. Honestly, the show will be fantastic—it really will—but we need a lot more practice. Give it another month or so and then come see me, all of you." I looked to my brothers and then to my father to gauge his response to this, but he was intently cutting his pork chop, head down.

"But Olive," my mother pushed on, "why would the show go on already if it isn't rehearsed enough?" I knew she was speaking on behalf of my father, that they'd probably had an argument about it and she'd promised to set it straight. Now she was trying to smooth everything over by asking the questions sweetly, while letting him know he'd been heard and that something would be done about it. "Are you sure it's reputable? We are concerned that it's beneath you."

"It's not beneath me, Ma, it's a wonderful theater and a stellar production. It's the Olympia," I said emphatically, knowing she had no idea if that was a top-notch theater or a hole-in-the-wall. "And the director is very well-known in the theater world, oh, he's introducing me to all kinds of people."

My father scoffed.

"What is it, Pa? Why are you so disgruntled by this?"

"I don't like it, Olive. Where's it going to take you, huh? Sure, we let you do those dance classes and singing lessons because you were a little girl, but you're twenty years old, Olive. It's time to find yourself a nice man and settle down, have a family—what do you think, you're going to do all that and be on that stage?"

"I don't see why not."

"You're nuts." He took a swig of his beer and set it down a little too hard. My mother and I both flinched. "We raised you well, you don't need to be doing this, you don't need the money. It's crass—you off dancing at some place we've never even heard of."

"For goodness' sakes, Pa, this is my first show on Broadway, no one knows me here yet. Give me a chance to prove myself, prove that I can do this and do it well." I tried not to let things get too heated, recalling the sting of his hand across my face the last time I tried to defend my performances. I considered telling him about the meeting with Mr. Ziegfeld and that my goal was to work my way up to one of his shows, or the Shuberts, but I didn't know if that would make him see things any differently. "Just give me a few months, please."

He shook his head, but I sensed he was easing up a little. "I promise," I said, placing my hand on his arm. "I promise I'll make you proud."

What I realized, soon after I started at the Olympia, was that there were thousands of girls like me in Manhattan. I saw them everywhere.

Clean faced and perky, walking in groups of three or four to early morning rehearsals. I saw others a little puffy, eye pencil residue left from the night before, as they ran up the stairs of the subway station late, a hint of hooch in their wake. I had my own nine A.M. call time, but I couldn't help wondering about their shows, imagining that they were bigger, more polished, their audiences more important.

As the show went on, it became very apparent that ours was a third-rate affair. On more than one occasion, Sally Holland showed up drunk but went on to perform anyway. Twice in one week we performed to a crowd of about five people and the director flew into a rage about it after the show, blaming the cast and their uninspired performances. My parents had been right to voice their concerns. I would definitely be tarnishing their reputations if anyone my father knew heard about his daughter performing in this dingy show. I knew I should walk away, but I didn't know how. I could hardly go back to Moses Sherman and tell him I wanted to quit the first gig he'd helped me land, so I kept showing up.

Then one night, after a month of performing, a tall, slim man approached as I was going out the stage door. "Miss McCormick?" he asked. "Or is it Miss Shine?"

"It's Shine now," I said, looking around. There were crowds of people leaving the theaters half a block away on Broadway, but West Forty-fourth Street was relatively quiet.

"I'm sorry to startle you." He put his hand out to shake mine. "Mr. Brock. Nice to meet you in person. I meant to arrive earlier and deliver a message to your dressing room, but I was needed at the theater."

I perked up. "The theater?"

"The New Amsterdam." He held out a small envelope and paused. "A message from Mr. Ziegfeld." It took everything in my power not to snatch it out of his hands and rip it open right there and then. "He'd like you there early tomorrow morning, so I've taken the liberty of having our driver take you home if that's acceptable to you." He nodded to a parked car at the sidewalk, and the driver tipped his hat.

"Thank you," I said, taking the note from his hands a little too eagerly. "Does this mean he wants me in the show after all?"

"I believe so. There's a note inside," he said, tapping the envelope in my hand and opening the car door for me. "He's spoken with your agent and relieved you of your contract. Best of luck to you."

I kept my composure until the car pulled away and Mr. Brock waved and walked toward Broadway, then I ripped the envelope open.

Dear Miss Shine,

I simply can't allow you to waste your talent in that terrible show. If you're still interested, a space has opened up in the Follies. *Please arrive promptly at 9 A.M. tomorrow morning for rehearsal. Allow me to make you a star.*

Very best,
Florenz Ziegfeld

CHAPTER FIVE

I t was the finale of act one, the theater was dark, and an edgy, serious air pervaded the empty orchestra pit where only the lighted glow of a cigar betrayed Mr. Ziegfeld's presence. We'd been going for almost fifteen hours, repeating the numbers again and again, and we were finally nearing the end.

The lights went up and the curtains parted to reveal "the Ingénues," a nineteen-member all-female orchestra. They played center stage while two men and twelve women played pianos perched on the steps of a dramatic double staircase. You'd think I would be used to it by now, after eight weeks of rehearsals every single morning, followed by more dance lessons in the afternoon at Stage Dance Studios—apparently Ziegfeld thought my pirouettes and piqués needed some fine-tuning—but this was the first time we'd done the full dress rehearsal, onstage, all the way through.

The costume and set designers hadn't let us get a glimpse of the full feathered costumes until that day, saying the plumes could get ruined with too much use. But here we were, the chorus, wearing nothing but cream silk leotards the color of our skin and enormous white ostrich feather fans strapped to our arms.

When the principal dancers came onstage in white costumes, with gold fringe and gold feather hats and headdresses, for the final few moments there were more than eighty people onstage. I couldn't believe I was one of them.

Ziegfeld came into the light and removed his coat.

"When he takes off his coat, he means serious show business," one of the girls whispered next to me.

"Blue foots up on a dimmer at the start of the overture," he called out to the electricians in the wings as he walked up the stairs to the stage. "White and amber foots up on dimmer at the end." We all froze in our final position, still smiling, hoping we wouldn't have to run through the whole thing again. "Next scene, all lamps floor until finish, then dim down to blue and white one-quarter up and palm curtains open."

It was all Greek to me. He walked across the front of the stage and surveyed us. "The final act dragged," he said to no one in partic-ular. "It has to be perfect. Howie?"

Howie, the choreographer, appeared by his side. "Bring the prin-cipals on earlier, I want a full ensemble, everyone onstage for longer than just the last few moments."

He walked over to my row of girls in feathers and stared at us as if we were dolls he was surveying in a toy store window. My pulse raced. What was he going to say about us, what was he going to do with us?

"I want this row up front," he said. I nodded to show I was willing. "Now," he barked.

We shuffled forward as best we could without rubbing our ostrich feathers against one another. Eighty people on a stage felt hot and crowded.

"Final moments before the lights go dark, you open your arms to reveal your figures." He demonstrated, and we copied him. He didn't look satisfied. "Wallace?" he called out. "Where's Wallace?"

Within seconds the costume designer was onstage. "I want these outfits remade into two pieces, top"—he gestured to the bosom of one of the girls—"and bottom. I'd like to see more of their figures." One of the girls gasped, but Ziegfeld, if he heard, chose to ignore it. I thought the costume change was a wise choice, a more dramatic reveal.

"Yes, Mr. Ziegfeld." Wallace nodded, his slim fingers scribbling down notes in a well-used, scruffy notepad.

"But not vulgar, you know how our competitors offend my artistic sensibility with their vulgarity and nudity. I want elegance, class and artistic integrity when we undrape our women."

Draped or undraped, I didn't care. The splendor of it all—the lavish costumes, the scenery and props, the sheer intensity and passion he had for his show and the determination of every one of the girls around me to make it big—was electrifying. But looking out into the empty house gave me the biggest thrill. I'd been told tickets for opening night were selling for $200 a pop and all seats would be filled. I couldn't wait for it all to begin.

Opening night was magical, but it was not without its blunders. In the second act, Marylin rode an ostrich with a rhinestone collar across the stage. In every rehearsal it had gone off without a hitch, but on that night the roar of applause that filled the theater must have spooked the poor thing. It looked around frantically, then fixed its eyes and aimed straight for me. I leapt out of the way, breaking formation from the other girls, but it seemed determined and raced toward me. In hindsight it was likely the ostrich feathers I had strapped to my arms, which I'd been pulsating like some kind of mating dance, that sent the bird into a whirl of confusion. Once I stopped moving and stood still for a few moments, it turned and ran in the opposite direction, and then into the wings, looking for its trainer, or an exit, sending Marylin to the floor in its frenzy. She handled it like a champ, of course—stood up, brushed herself off and took an exaggerated bow as if it were all part of the act, and then she went on with her next number. But offstage she was livid and said she refused to share the stage with that animal again.

We all planned to meet at Casa Blanca after the show to celebrate a successful opening night, despite the ostrich incident. Ruthie, who'd been in the *Follies* for a few years already, had been showing me the ropes. She had shocking red hair, huge blue eyes and a face that was more interesting than traditionally beautiful.

"Now when the two of us walk out the back of the theater, there'll be a big crowd waiting—men and women, but mostly stage-door johnnies."

"Stage-door johnnies?"

"You'll get used to it," she said. "We just smile, thank them and walk on. You ready, Olive?"

"You bet I'm ready," I said.

We pushed open the back door and there they were, just as she'd promised.

"Miss, miss, you were stunning tonight, can I take you out to celebrate?" one called.

"I heard you're new in town," another said. "My friend told me to look you up, show you around."

"Ignore them," Ruthie warned. "They say that to everyone."

Some johnnies were looking for specific girls, bouquets in one hand, jewelry boxes in another, while other gents were there to take out whoever would say yes. But it didn't matter, it was all such fun.

"Let me treat you, miss . . . miss . . ."

"Hey, Miss Spicy," said one johnny as he pushed through the others toward Ruthie and me. "Come on," he said, leaning right into me, smooth as pomade. "Let me take you away from all these boys." He reached into his inside jacket pocket and pulled out a slim navy box and gave me just a peek. I couldn't help staring at the string of pearls inside.

"Stick with me, doll," Ruthie said as she took my arm in hers. "We won't have any shortage of champagne and lobster once we get there, and there'll be plenty of fellas showing you lots of ice as the days go by, just wait. Why don't you take it all in before you say yes, see how it all works?"

The guy wasn't my type anyway, not that I really knew what my type would be. I hadn't had an appetite for romance in the last year, but he was a sharp dresser, and my, those pearls, were they for me or anyone who'd take him up on his offer? I wondered. I glanced back at him and smiled. "We're going to Casa Blanca on Fifty-sixth Street," I said excitedly. "Maybe I'll let you buy me a drink."

"Oh, boy," Ruthie said, tugging me along to Broadway. "You have a lot to learn. Come on, or we'll never get out of here."

Just five months earlier when I first set foot in New York City, I'd looked up at the bright lights on Broadway with the celebrated names of headliners and the towering billboards advertising all the things they assumed I needed to be prettier, thinner, more elegant, more capable. But now, walking up Broadway, made up like a doll, with a buzzing high from the first performance, I felt as though the lights were just for me, that the man smoking his cigarette above the Great White Way was tipping his hat in my direction. Well done, Olive, he was saying, you do know how to shine.

I felt like skipping. I didn't even feel the blisters on my toes or the tightness in my neck from the twenty-pound, foot-and-a-half-high headdress I'd worn along with the rest of the girls in the last act. All I could feel was the giddy sensation rising up in me, a mix of pride and excitement at what would come next.

When we arrived at the club, there was a line out the door, but Ruthie walked us right up to the front, introduced me to the doorman and led us through the revolving door into a grand and ornate gilt lobby.

Ruthie pointed across the expanse to a commanding staircase. "Loraine, Marylin and the other principals will wait until we've all arrived before they make their grand entrance down those stairs," she said. "But don't worry, we'll have our chance one day."

The dining room must have seated at least five hundred, and the walls were covered in green velvet with gold trim everywhere. Trumpets and saxophones and the roar of chatter and laughter filled my head. I couldn't hear a thing Ruthie was saying, but she was already laughing, as if some laughing gas were filling the atmosphere and we were all drinking it in. The dance floor up front was small in comparison with the room and crowded to no end, but the people— they were the most beautiful people I'd ever seen, all under one roof. And everyone had a drink in hand, clearly not giving two hoots for the Volstead Act. It was festive and gay and here I was, right in the middle of it.

Ruthie caught sight of some girls from the show and waved them over. They swarmed toward us, enveloping me into their circle. Someone grabbed my hand, another put her arm around my waist. Ruthie handed me a glass of champagne out of nowhere, and I felt that I was being carried en masse by these beautiful girls. We approached the teeming dance floor and it welcomed us into its heaving, spirited arms, opening up for us, then closing in around us. I had arrived exactly where I wanted to be.

I was one of the Ziegfeld girls.

CHAPTER SIX

Edward, the Prince of Wales, had been to see our show on opening night. The stage manager came to the dressing room right before
the curtain went up and told us of Prince Charming's attendance. It
sent some of the girls to pieces, but it didn't rattle me. In the paper
the next day he said he'd never laughed harder in all his life than
when he heard Eddie Cantor, with all of his peculiar inflections
and slurs, sing "The Star's Double," about an actor who called for
his double when he was about to be slugged by an irate husband
who'd caught him with his wife. A handful of girls were in a huff
that the prince hadn't mentioned their performance. Rumor had
it that one of the principals, Irene, had allowed him to take her to
dinner, but she wouldn't admit or deny it, which led me to believe
it was all horsefeathers.

The Prince of Wales could sit in the box and watch me perform
any day of the week, and it would just make me sing sweeter and
dance lighter on my toes, but it was my father's attendance a few

nights after opening that had me sweating in the dressing room ten minutes to call time.

Though they didn't say it outright, my parents had been mildly impressed that I'd been cast in a Ziegfeld show, or it could have just been relief that it was more reputable than the show at Olympia Theatre. My mother had insisted that they come and see it right away, I think as a way to assuage my father's concerns, but it didn't help; in fact, it made everything worse.

The performance opened with "The Follies Salad," a number featuring several girls from the chorus and me dressed as ingredients for the dish, while Eddie played chef and sang about his culinary creation. We all knew, of course, that it was a metaphor for the show: Eddie was Ziegfeld, the creator, and we chorus girls were the essential ingredients for the revue. At first I'd been over the moon when I was cast as "Spicy" while some of the others got stuck with "Chicken" or "Lettuce," but then, when I knew my father was in the audience, the thought of walking onstage in a skimpy red lace costume while Eddie sang that the spice adds "just a little tingle" and that it's "not *too* naughty," well, it had me biting my nails off with worry. It was obvious that I had seduction written all over me. I cursed myself in the minutes before the music started. Why couldn't I have been cast as "Oil" for the orchestra with a melody that makes the show run smoothly, or "Salt" for the proper seasoning, or "Paprika" to add a dash of "class and smartness." Hell, I'd even be "Chicken"—"young and tender," he sang—anything was better than "Spicy" with my father sitting up front.

Up until that evening, the audience had just been a mass of people that formed one body; I didn't think of them as individuals.

They applauded, they stood, they applauded some more. I'd never caught the eye of any one person, and I told myself this had to be the same as any other night. But as soon as I set foot on that stage, I saw the sheen of my father's parted hair. Lower right, orchestra. The grey plaid suit and burgundy tie he'd worn to work that day. Arms crossed tightly across his chest. My mother to his left, my brothers to his right. I repeatedly looked away, out to the blur of the audience, but my eyes kept going back to him, that shine of his hair transfixing me. It made me nervous as hell.

As the number was coming to an end and all of us girls, the ingredients, sashayed across the stage and gathered around Eddie, some drunken fool in the audience began calling out obscenities and was quickly escorted out of the theater to the street. We did exactly as we'd been told to do in rehearsals in a situation like this: we carried on with grace. But I could feel the weight of disapproval from my father's seat and it stirred in me a heavy mix of emotions. Worried that he'd think the whole thing was too provocative, I felt my stomach twist at the thought of how he'd react. But I clung to a faith that he'd see this performance was more than that, hopeful he'd see that most people in the audience were wealthy, respectable gentlemen taking their wives out for an elegant show of beauty and charm. In the next instant, I felt angry, knowing all too well that it was too much to ask of my father to think that way, my defenses up already at the thought of his bristly response at the end of the night.

Later, as part of the chorus, I sang "Shaking the Blues Away," in front of a beautifully designed backdrop of a cotton field and a white wooden house with real Spanish moss hanging from a cut drop, and I had a short solo in the sweet "Maybe It's You" number wearing a rose-trimmed hoop skirt and a floppy hat. I thought I'd given the previous night's performance my very best, but this night I sang with everything I had. When I walked slowly down the enormous staircase in a gorgeous full-length gown with fifty other women while Franklyn Bauer sang "The Rainbow of Girls," I walked with all the grace and elegance I could muster; I was going to impress my father if my life depended on it. But despite all of that, I knew that damned salad number was the act he would latch on to.

After the show, I took off as much of my stage makeup as I could and met my parents and brothers in the front of the theater—I didn't want them to see the shenanigans going on at the stage door with the johnnies begging for our company.

My mother hugged me. "Darling, you were wonderful, just wonderful," she said more enthusiastically than I would have expected from her. "You were a star, I'm so proud of you," she whispered into my ear. She had forgiven me for all that had happened, I thought with relief. My time in Rockville with Aunt May was all in the past now. Maybe we could move beyond it after all.

I glanced at my father standing with his arms crossed, staring straight to the street, his lips pursed tightly into a downward frown. I walked over to him slowly.

"Olive, you were the best!" my brother Junior said, jumping in, hugging me. "The berries, I'm telling you, blew the rest of those girls right out of the water." He was always my biggest fan.

"Aw, thanks, JJ, you're sweet to say so," I said, kissing his cheek. "I messed up a few steps in the final act, coming down that staircase."

"I didn't notice. Really," he said.

"Wow, what a show, though," George said. "I've never seen anything like it." I knew he'd be asking me about the ladies later.

"What did you think, Pa? I know it's not exactly your cup of tea, but did you find something you liked in the acts?" I stepped in front of his gaze, trying to get his attention. "How about the pet act, Pa? We always laugh backstage when the dog asks his owner for a whiskey."

He stood firm. "That's enough now, Olive," he said, straightening up even more. "We'll talk about it when we get home."

"But Ted, we're going to dinner, remember?" my mother said, putting her arm through his.

"Not tonight, Doris, I said we'll talk when we get home. Now all of you get in the car." He walked to the car waiting at the sidewalk, got in the front seat and slammed the door shut.

I looked pleadingly at my mother, but she was defeated. "I'm sorry," she said. "Maybe he'll come around at home. Come on, Junior." She put her hand on my little brother's back and ushered him into the waiting car. "I've got some bread and cheese, I'll make us some sandwiches."

When we got out of the car in Flatbush and closed the door behind us, my brothers made themselves scarce. My father took a beer from the icebox and my mother fixed herself a gin rickey and began assembling sandwiches at the kitchen counter.

"I don't want you in that show, Olive," he said, finally looking me in the eye.

"But, Pa—"

"No, Olive. You looked like a chippie up there, and no daughter of mine is going to parade herself around the stage like that for every man in Manhattan to drool at."

"You're talking about that one act, the stupid salad, but what about the others? They're just good old fun, nothing harmful there."

"I said I don't want you in that show." He grabbed the kitchen chair he was leaning on, lifted it a few inches, then slammed it down again. I stepped back. I hated it when he got like this, all blustery. I knew that any small thing now could push him over the edge and I didn't want that.

"Teddy, relax, will you?" my mother said quietly. "Let me pour you a whiskey."

"I don't want a goddamn whiskey, I want my daughter to wipe that makeup, and that smug look, off her face and give me her word that she won't set foot on that stage again."

I rubbed the back of my hand across my lips. "I did wipe it off. . . ."

"Don't you talk back to me," he snapped, leaning into me, and I flinched just a little and wished I hadn't. It showed weakness, it showed fear. "You heard that blotto in the audience calling out to you."

"It wasn't to me, he was just some drunkard, he was out on the roof, so far gone."

"Oh, he was calling out to you all right, dressed up like a good-for-nothin' harlot."

"Teddy!" my mother said.

"Shut it, Doris." He took a deep breath, and I could see he was trying real hard to keep a lid on it. He took another swig of his beer and shoved his hands down into his pockets as if to will them to stay there.

I was boiling mad. I was working so damned hard. When I was on that stage, I was bursting with life. How could a father not want that for his own daughter? Sure, Ziegfeld was glorifying us, he was dressing us up in the most elaborate and expensive costumes that had ever seen the lights of Broadway, and he made us feel like the most beautiful women in all of America, but he wasn't exploiting us. I knew the difference. I didn't care if a guy in the audience had the hots for me or not. I didn't care if I was dancing for Prince Charming, someone's grandmother or someone's daughter. It was still the performing that made me soar. How could he not see that, how could he not be happy for me? I'd paid a price for being too naïve, too gullible, and I thought about that fact all the time, but that was my business. Now I'd earned some recognition, some appreciation, because of hard work. I hated that I couldn't tell him this.

"Pa, I'm a trained singer and a dancer too now. You know this is what I've always wanted to do. Mr. Ziegfeld even said he was considering giving me a comedy song—he thinks I'm funny."

"He thinks you're funny?" he scoffed. "Well, I'm not laughing."

I was keeping my voice down, I was choosing my words carefully, I was really trying not to send his hands flying, but inside I was reeling.

"You let Erwin follow his dreams," I said quietly. My parents certainly hadn't been happy when Erwin joined the navy, getting shipped off to Illinois just days after enlisting, but within weeks the talk in our house went from concern and disapproval to tremendous pride, and now that he'd been one of a few selected to transfer to a brand-new training facility in San Pedro, California, he was the one in the family who could do no wrong.

"Your brother is serving our country. Are you really comparing your song and dance to his patriotic duty?"

"No, just noting your response to it. But I'm making pretty good money, Pa, I'm contributing to the house, seventy-five dollars a week." I tried to appeal to his financial mind. He knew there were very few places where I could work and bring in that kind of money, but he didn't think it was right for a woman to work anyway. He thought a woman's job was at home, making some man happy. He already had my life planned out for me, indentured to a man none of us had even met yet. But what about me? What about my happiness?

"Olive," he said more quietly now, giving me hope that my reasoning had reassured him, "if you quit that show first thing tomorrow morning, then I will pay you one thousand dollars."

My mother gasped, but my father kept his eyes fixed on me, wanting an immediate response.

"Papa," I said, almost in a whisper—this was pointless, he wasn't listening to a word I said.

"Hell, I'll give you two thousand. Three thousand."

"Pa, stop this," I said, hot and angry now. How could he think this was about the money? This was about life, this was about living. "I'm not going to quit the show."

The intensity in his eyes turned to fury, and his lips pinched into a snarl. "Then you'd better damn well start packing your bags and looking for a place to live, because as long as you keep doing what you're doing, prancing around like a good-for-nothing quiff, you will not live under my roof."

"Teddy, don't say that," my mother cried out, but he had stormed out the kitchen to the backyard and let the door slam behind him.

———

That night I lay in bed staring at the darkness. We'd been leading up to this for some time now. My father had never liked me being on the stage. He hadn't liked the way people looked at me; it made him angry. But what if he knew everything about me? What would he think of me then? It cut me deep inside, knowing that the possibilities for disappointment were endless. I knew he'd think I'd quit, that I'd be too scared to disappoint him. And he'd be right, I was scared. I was scared that I wouldn't be his little girl anymore, that he'd never forgive me, that our relationship would be forever changed. But I also knew I didn't want to be like them, married at seventeen, a kid at nineteen, a second at twenty-one, a third at twenty-three, a fourth at twenty-six. To me that sounded like living a prison sentence. I'd known since I was a little girl that this domesticated life didn't appeal to me. Maybe one day I'd change, but not yet. I still had some living to do.

The next morning, I got up and went to early morning rehearsal as usual. We had a two-hour session on nothing but the walk. Mr. Ziegfeld had watched from his box the night prior and said that many of the new girls—me included—didn't have it quite right. The walk was what most of us did ninety percent of the time we were onstage, either while another girl or guy was singing, to walk the staircase (often with a long line of other chorus girls following along behind), or simply to cross the stage. It was an essential part of the show and it had to be perfect. Arms elegantly outstretched to both sides with a slight dip of the elbow and a slow and steady saunter—no hip swaying—in heels and, more often than not, with a very heavy headpiece.

My arms felt as if they were going to drop off my body by the end of rehearsal, and my neck was as stiff as a board. I laid my head down on my dressing room table and closed my eyes.

"Hey there, Olive, what's the matter with you?" It was Ruthie coming in from her voice lesson. She looked in my mirror and checked her rich red hair, giving herself the lips and turning her head from side to side, admiring her high cheekbones. "You have a rough one last night? I didn't see you at the club."

"I just need to soak in a bathtub for a few hours," I said, thinking of the tub at home. "Say, do you know if there's any space available at the rooming house where you and Lillian stay?"

"There's a wait list, but after next week some space will open up. Lillian and I are getting our own apartment uptown. You should come with us. That rooming house is no place for us Ziegfeld girls. There's going to be a third roommate—someone Lillian knows from the *Scandals,* but you could sleep in the living room, and then it would be a better price for all of us."

"Really?"

"Sure, honey, it'd be swell, wouldn't it? And you should see this place—it's a stunner, views of the water, a straight line down to Times Square. You want in?"

"Sure, I want in, but I might need someplace to go this week. Do you think I could bunk with you at the boardinghouse for a few nights?"

She raised an eyebrow. "What's wrong, you too good for Flatbush all of a sudden?"

"My pop is all sore about the show, wants me to up and quit."

"Oh, Olive. You shouldn't have let him see it—what did you think he was going to say?"

"I don't know, I guess I thought he'd be proud of me or something."

"Honey, no one brings their fathers. They want to take care of us—all men, fathers, husbands, lovers—if they feel you slipping away, like they can't take care of you no more, they act up. I've seen it here a thousand times. But you can't quit, honey, you just got here."

"Oh, I'm not quitting," I said. "Not now, not ever."

I crept around my parents' house for the next few days, coming home when they were already in bed and trying to be up and out the door before they were awake in the morning. The first few days I left a note on the kitchen table for my mother, letting her know I had an early rehearsal and that I'd be back after the show—no need to wait up. It was exhausting and the girls often found me napping in the dressing room at the Amsterdam when they came in for morning rehearsals.

On Saturday, I tiptoed into the kitchen well past one A.M. and my mother was sitting at the table with a magazine in front of her. She closed it when I walked in.

"It's late, Olive," she said.

"I know, we had to stay after, to go over some steps . . ." I trailed off, then walked to the kitchen cabinet, took a glass down and poured myself some water. I'd had two glasses of champagne at the speak and I hoped she wouldn't smell it on me.

"Why don't you sit with me for a minute."

"All right." I stood at a distance and gulped down my water, then took the seat opposite her, my hands folded on the table between us. She reached out and took my hands in hers as if she'd been waiting all night to do this. We hadn't spoken since the blowup with my father, and now there was a softness about her, a kindness.

"I think you're wrong, Olive," she said gently. "You're wrong to be doing all this."

"What do you mean?"

"Disobeying your father's wishes. Singing, dancing, going out like this until"—she looked up at the clock on the wall—"all hours of the night."

I shook my head. She'd been on my side, at least I thought she had been, and now she sounded just like him.

"You said you loved my performance, that you were proud of me," I said. "You said that less than a week ago." I'd been holding on to that one small moment from the night they had come to the show. *You were a star,* she'd said. I'd been keeping that in my mind.

"Well, I've come around to his way of thinking. Your father is right, Olive, you can't be doing this, it's disreputable for you and for your family. It casts a bad light on all of us. And I'm worried about what will become of you. Look what happened to you last time you were in a show—you got yourself into a disastrous situation," she said in a low whisper. "What if that happens again? There'd be no fooling anyone a second time."

68

I stared at her in shock. How could she not mention my pregnancy or the baby at all since I'd arrived in Brooklyn, not even to ask how I'd fared or if the baby was healthy, and yet choose to bring it up now, to shame me?

"That would never happen again, never, ever."

"How can you say that? You did it once already. One night out on the town and you ended up getting yourself pregnant," she said in an angry whisper.

"Mother! He took advantage of me, I didn't know what was going on, he was older and he was pouring hooch into my drinks."

"But you drank them down, didn't you?"

"I didn't know that would happen, I was, he was . . ." What was the point? I could blame him all I wanted, but it wasn't going to make a difference. "I would never get myself in that situation again. You have to believe me, Mother, it was awful. I could never go through that again."

She shook her head. She didn't want to talk about that.

"Well, I'm sorry, Olive, but I have to agree with your father on this," she said, her face cold. She'd made her mind up on this one.

"Why? You were the one who encouraged me when I was younger, all those singing lessons you took me to."

"We wanted you to have a hobby. Something you could talk about at social engagements. We never imagined you'd do this with it." She sighed, exasperated with me. "Don't you think I've looked at my life before and thought, What the heck happened? Don't you think I might've had days where I would have liked to run off with the circus instead of making dinner each night, making sure you kids are clean and fed and have shoes that fit? Making sure your father's beer is cold for when he gets home from work? Life isn't always one big party. Life comes with responsibilities, Olive, whether you want them or not."

I was taken aback. I'd never considered for a moment that the life she had might not be the one she wanted for herself or that she fantasized about something more reckless and freeing.

"But you don't have to agree with him all the time," I said, more cautiously this time. "Why would you take his side when you know I have some talent and a chance at a different kind of life?"

She looked at me, miffed. "Because he is my husband. He's my husband, and that's what I'm supposed to do, that's my role as his wife. Honestly," she said, baffled that I couldn't grasp this simple fact. "He provides for us, he is the head of this household and we are to respect him and his wishes. Just like you will when you get your head out of the clouds and find yourself a husband of your own."

"So you're kicking me out, too?"

"I'm not kicking you out. I'm asking you to stay. I'm asking you to give up the theater and do something more respectable. You're my daughter, of course I want you to stay, I want what is best for you."

I glared at her.

"But if you are going to disrespect your father and defy him, go against his will, then yes, I have to support him and stand by his decision."

I stood up, shocked. Over the past few days, I'd thought somehow that she would help me fix this rift with my father. In the back of my mind I thought that it would blow over.

"I'll be out by the morning, then," I said.

She rolled her eyes. "You're not leaving. You're being ridiculous. Where would you even go?"

"I'll stay with a friend. What does it matter to you where I go?"

"Olive," she said, grabbing my wrist. "Think clearly, for goodness' sake, this is your future we're talking of, your prospects."

I pulled my arm away and ran upstairs, tears pushing at the backs of my eyes. I dragged out the old suitcase I had stored under my bed, laid it open on the floor and began stuffing the case with clothes.

It wasn't that I desperately wanted to stay; in fact, the thought of getting an apartment with the girls sounded like a whole heck of a lot of fun and far less tiptoeing around. It was the fact that my parents hated the life that I'd created for myself, the life I'd worked so hard for, the life I loved. Not having their approval felt as though I didn't have their love, and if I didn't have their love, then who was I? What did it say about me if they couldn't even love their own daughter? I sat down on the edge of the bed and put my head in my hands. I'd given a baby girl away to strangers. One day she'd grow up and learn this. She'd feel unloved, too. It felt awful, it would haunt me always. I suppose this was exactly what I deserved.

There was a knock on my door. I quickly wiped my face. Junior walked in and his eyes went straight to the half-packed case.

"Hey there, JJ."

"Are you moving out?" he asked.

"It's for the best," I said. "You know Pops doesn't like me performing and it's not worth fighting about it anymore."

I tried to sound light, breezy, as if this were no big deal, but inside I was seething, angry as hell at the two of them, my mother and my father. And my head was spinning from what my mother had just said. Was there a hint of envy at the life I was living now? A glimpse at a life she'd never had the chance to explore? But she knew what I'd just been through, she knew it was a miracle that I'd managed to get myself cast in the *Ziegfeld Follies* so soon after everything that happened in Rockville. It was sheer determination and sass that had gotten me that job, and yet here they were booing me from the sidelines. Well, to heck with them. I didn't need them or their approval. I'd be just fine on my own.

"Where will you go?"

"I've got a place lined up with the girls from the show."

He looked shocked. Where we came from, it was unheard of for a girl to move out of her parents' house until she was well and truly married off.

"It's okay, I promise you," I said, walking over and putting my arm around him. "I know it's not what we're all used to, but it's different here—actresses, singers, dancers, so many of the show girls—they all live together in apartments near the theater, it's easier to get to and from rehearsals."

"But Papa will be so angry," he said, his forehead creasing with concern.

"He's already angry," I said. "At least I won't be under his nose all the time, taunting him by going back and forth to the theater." I said it as if it were my choice to leave, as if he hadn't given me an ultimatum to quit or move out of his house.

"But if you go he'll never forgive you."

He was right, he probably wouldn't, but what choice did I have? I wasn't going to be ruled by him, stifled by his old-fashioned ideas.

"Of course he will, he just needs some time, that's all. Come on, help me get these down, would you?" I pointed to three hatboxes I had all the way at the top of my closet. Junior may have been the baby of the family, but he was still taller than me by a long shot.

"You'll come back, though, won't you, Olive?"

"Of course I'll come back, Junior. I'll always be here for you."

The apartment was at the far end of Manhattan on West 213th Street in an area called Inwood. And I didn't know what Ruthie was thinking, because it was no stunner. One window in the living room and one in the kitchen—that was it. The carpet smelled damp and it was on the tenth floor, the elevator was broken, so not only was I sweating like a man by the time I climbed the stairs on those sticky summer days, the apartment heated up hotter than a two-dollar pistol. There were Jewish families living there mostly, and Irish immigrants, and when we walked to and from the train station before or after a show, we were often stared down with looks of disdain. Ruthie said they must've thought we were cheap flappers making some money on the side.

"We're show girls, not prostitutes," she called out one evening after a few too many drinks and with a face full of makeup, to a couple pushing a baby carriage who were glaring in our direction. "There's a difference."

Our building was surrounded by trees and open fields, and during the day there were always children running around the neighborhood, but inside, the apartment was dark and dingy, so I spent as much time at the theater as possible, and in the afternoons, rather than ride the hot, sticky train forty-five minutes from the theater district back up to Inwood, I'd practice my numbers at the rehearsal halls.

Luckily, we didn't have to stay in Inwood too long. Within a few months Ruthie was given the extra responsibility of auditioning new dancers for the *Follies*, because, though he seemed to love every minute of it, Ziegfeld told her he didn't have time to hand select the girls anymore. There was a constant flow of dancers and singers coming and going, getting married, getting lured to other shows, getting promoted to the chorus or taking the show on the road, so the company had to be replenished often, staying at around one hundred girls altogether, more than any other show on Broadway. Ruthie had her work cut out for her, but her paycheck doubled.

A month later, Ziegfeld called me into his office.

"Do you know why I started the *Midnight Frolic*, Olive?"

"Sure I do, Mr. Ziegfeld, you wanted to keep the party going."

"That's right, and quite a party it has been."

When I first started he wasn't shy in telling us that he created the *Follies'* sister show, the *Midnight Frolic*, because he had always hated seeing his audience members walk out of the New Amsterdam Theatre at the end of a *Follies* show and go spend their money to eat, drink and dance at Rector's or Delmonico's, and more recently at the Backstage Club or Casa Blanca. So he built a 680-seat rooftop supper club, serving the highest-quality food you could find at any of the nightclubs in town, and he gave everyone a reason to stay. He built a revolving stage, tables surrounding the dance floor where guests could eat and drink, and a transparent glass walkway above the audience, with blowers and spotlights shining upwards, where some of the chorus girls gave patrons a new perspective. The performances were far more risqué than the original *Follies* shows that went on earlier in the evening, and for the extra skin and racy jokes, he charged a higher price for tickets and tables.

"Things are changing, Olive, and we need to change, too," he said. "We need to give them a new reason to stick around after the show."

"I've heard the food and the hooch you serve is pretty outstanding."

"I still want to give my patrons a buzz. But that buzz doesn't always have to be in liquid form—that reason to stay, that could be you."

I felt a rush of excitement at being chosen for this special distinction. It was certainly more provocative than the *Follies* and my father would cringe at the thought of me now, but he'd already kicked me out of his house and accused me of being a harlot, so there was no sense in trying to please him anymore.

On my first night in the *Frolic*, after dancing all night in the *Follies*, I came out on the platform in a skin-colored, lace, barely there costume that looked more like an undergarment, covered in balloons. I sauntered down the wide glass stairs and paraded through the audience, encouraging the gentlemen to pop my balloons with their ten-cent cigars. From the stage, Will Rogers sang "Girls of My Dreams," and as the balloons popped and popped and popped, I was left with nothing but my lacy negligee. Ziegfeld put small wooden mallets on the tables, and when the audience liked an act they didn't just applaud and hoot and holler—they'd bang their mallets on the table, sending a vibration of approval through our bones.

I was in heaven on that stage. It was everything from the *Follies*, but more fun, more singing, more flirting, more dancing, and Ziegfeld paid me $75 a week in addition to my *Follies* pay. I was on top of the world.

The stage-door johnnies started calling my name louder as we walked out the theater doors to set off for our evening's adventures, and I reveled in it.

"Olive, Olive," they'd say. "Miss Shine, Miss Olive Shine . . . let me take you out, let me take you dancing. Olive Shine, let me show you what a gentleman I am." Of course they were calling for the other girls, too, but all I could hear was my name.

There was usually a group of us heading out for a night on the town—Gladys, Lara, Ruthie, Pauline, Lillian and me—sometimes more, sometimes fewer, depending on who had a date that night. I'd be lying if I said I didn't love every minute of it, the attention, the desperation in those boys' voices, the applause as we walked out into the New York City night. If I didn't have a date already, I might look around the crowd of gents and survey my options, then pick the handsomest fella of the group.

"Come on then," I'd say, pointing to one of them. "But if you want to show me a good time, you've got to show us all a good time." And all of us girls would link arms, with the one lucky fella in the middle, and we'd walk down the street that way, or walk to his car, and sometimes I thought I noticed a look on his face that I'd just made his week.

Now that I was in the *Frolic*, the gifts and bouquets of flowers that showed up in the dressing room doubled, tripled, quadrupled. At times it was absurd how many vases of roses stood on my dressing table. They'd always be accompanied by a note and an invitation to dinner; sometimes they came with a bracelet or earrings. I usually took these fellas up on their offers for dinner or dancing—not all of them, there weren't enough days in the week, but I'd pick one and send a note back to him in the audience telling him I'd be bringing a friend and that he should, too.

There were more formal introductions, too. One evening Ziegfeld introduced me to politician Fiorello La Guardia; he was shorter than me by a good three or four inches, but he didn't seem bothered by it. He invited me and Lara and Evelyn to sit at his table at the *Frolic* with a few of his friends once our show was over. They were big shots, no doubt about it; Fiorello had been elected to Congress and one gent was the mayor of Boston. But after a while I excused myself and told them I was needed backstage. Another time, while out at a club all the way up in Harlem, our group of five or six girls were approached on the dance floor and invited upstairs to a private room of what Ruthie told me were mobsters. I've never seen so much fur and so many diamonds in my life, on both the men and women.

While we certainly got to meet a lot of gents this way, and we did plenty of flirting and a little smooching here and there, I was never really, truly drawn to any of them. Some started to bore me once the initial fun of meeting them wore off. They'd start telling me about what they did for work, where they were from, and every time we got to that point I'd start thinking about what the rest of the girls were doing, how I'd rather be out with them, listening to a live jazz band and dancing and laughing with my girls. But more often, after the formalities wore off and we'd had a few drinks, they'd start to get that look in their eye, or they'd put their hand where it wasn't wanted, and I'd be up and out of there and on my way home. I don't know if it was that awful, regretful night in Los Angeles that made me feel this way, so prickly and prude-like all of a sudden, when I was as provocative as could be onstage and when most of the girls were living up their freedoms any way they chose to, but I never went home with any of them.

With our new earnings, Ruthie and I made our move to Fifth Avenue. We got the apartment of our dreams, with a window in every room. That, to me, felt like success—to pay my own way, not needing anyone to take care of me. We had our own apartment and we made our own rules and we liked to remind ourselves of that at all hours.

"No one can tell us now that we haven't made it in New York," I'd proclaim while brushing my teeth, parading around the living room in nothing but my undergarments while Ruthie wrapped her red hair in a silk scarf and put on her pajamas.

"That's right, honey!" she'd say.

And I'd kick off my shoes and climb into bed and feel so content that it was just me, no one grabbing or pawing or sweet-talking. I'd lay my head on the pillow, often still swirling from the dancing or the hooch, and many nights, in those few private moments after I closed my eyes, my mind would drift back to the baby. I'd feel the weight of her in my arms, her sweet little face, her cheeks, her eyes looking up at me. And I'd picture those dewy eyelids getting heavy, then closing as she drifted off to sleep—peaceful and trusting. She trusted me to hold her and keep her safe. And then I'd lie there, staring at the ceiling, aching.

CHAPTER SEVEN

Ruthie had started spending time with a theater director named Lawrence, who was also a patent attorney. I didn't find him to be an attractive man—he had a big forehead, with hair that swept over his crown from one ear to the other—but he was fun and Ruthie seemed to like him. She kept on pushing me to join him and one of his colleagues for a night out and promised we'd have a grand time, but I wasn't so keen on getting set up. I knew I'd be stuck with his friend the whole night, since I was too much of a softy to hurt someone's feelings if he didn't rev my engine, and I'd end up dancing with the poor fellow all night anyway, talking his ear off so he wouldn't have a chance to swoop in for a kiss—it would be too exhausting for words.

"We're going to a new spot Thursday after the show," Ruthie said. "Come along with us, we'll have the lobster."

"We've had lobster a thousand times," I said. "I'm sick of lobster."

"Come on, Olive, his friend is dying to meet you. What does he have to do? Beg?"

"Why don't you have Lawrence take you to the Village?" I kept hearing about the downtown bohemians—a quirky mix of musicians and writers and sculptors and revolutionaries—and I was intrigued to see the scene for myself.

Ruthie scrunched up her face. "I don't know, Olive. They know us up here, we walk right in anywhere we go, the martinis are the real thing. We don't want to drink some bathtub gin."

"I think too much of the same thing can make a girl dreary," I said. "We are in New York City, we should explore every dark and dirty corner." I grinned. "If Lawrence wants to do his friend a favor so bad, tell them we want a night out in the Village, that's the only way you're going to get me to take pity on this poor fella."

On Thursday night after the show, I walked out front with Ruthie and found not just one gentleman but two, waiting by the car.

"Olive, this is Ernest Patterson," Ruthie said, smiling excessively as if to make up for his slight frame, thick glasses and sweating palms as he nervously took my hand.

"The pleasure is all mine," he said.

"He works with Lawrence at the law office."

"Hi there, Ernest," I said, trying to put him at ease.

"You were a knockout in the show tonight, both of you," he said. "The real McCoy."

"Thanks, honey," I said. As we drove down Broadway, I looked out the window and didn't feel like making small talk. Maybe she was right, maybe we should have just stayed uptown.

"So what was your favorite part?" I said finally, filling in the awkward silence.

"Pretty much any part you were in, really," he said. "The pony—

where you rode the horse on the stage singing that funny song, oh, that was a hoot, a real hoot."

"That's one of my favorite parts, too," I said, warming up to him a little. "I used to worry that horse was going to bolt when the applause came, and the heat from those lights gets pretty uncomfortable, but he's such a good boy. I think they might give him a powder or two. I've never seen such a calm pony in all my life."

On MacDougal Street, Monte's felt more like someone's living quarters than a restaurant. My stomach growled—I hadn't eaten since lunch and I'd performed the *Follies* and my act in the *Frolic*.

"I'll have the lasagna," I said to the waiter when he came by. "And a peach Melba." I smiled. "For after."

Ruthie glared.

"What?" I said. "I'm hungry." I'd been dancing so much I could eat anything I wanted—in fact, if I didn't, I'd start to see my ribs, and Ziegfeld didn't like his girls too skinny.

"The shrimp cocktail for me," Ruthie said.

"And a gin cocktail for me," I added.

"Sorry, madam, you'll have to go elsewhere for that," the waiter said.

"Don't worry, Olive." Lawrence leaned across the table and spoke in a mock whisper. "As soon as you've had something to eat, Ernest and I will take you to one of downtown's finest tearooms. You won't go thirsty."

Ernest grinned. He wasn't much of a conversationalist.

"Have you been out in these parts before?" I asked him.

"Not really. Lawrence is such a man about town, he's been promising to take me out with him for a while. I usually have dinner at home," he added. "With my mother." I smiled and patted his hand, then devoured the lasagna and the peach Melba, bless him.

It was hardly worth getting back in the car to drive just a few blocks to our next destination, but we did it anyway, pulling up to the Pirate's Den, a teahouse on Gay Street. There was barely anyone inside; it was late and dark. One man sat writing feverishly in a corner booth, while on the other side of the room a couple smooched over tea and candles. Lawrence led us through the tearoom to a back door, up a flight of stairs and through another door, where we knocked and waited. I could hear music coming from the other side. A peephole slid open. "Lawrence Long and three guests," he said. The door slipped open and we were in.

Inside was a lively, raucous scene, darker, much grittier and less dazzling than the uptown clubs, but buoyant and magnetic somehow. Ruthie and I lingered at the entrance and took it all in while the gents headed straight to the bar. There were groups of people lounging around freely, some in deep conversation, others in deep intimacy. There was a freedom about the place that I sensed immediately, though I couldn't quite grasp what was going on.

Uptown it was dancing and drinking, dancing and drinking. You just kept going until you could no longer stand on your own two feet. Here there was a jazz band playing, but I could hear people talking, too. Some were dancing, others were lying horizontal on Moroccan beds and smoking from a tall metal instrument with pipes coming out of the side.

"Cheers," Ruthie said, handing me a china cup and saucer.

"Where'd you get that from and what is it?"

"Who cares? Come on, let's have some fun."

Ruthie led the way, weaving us through the crowd toward the bar, where Ernest and Lawrence were already watching the band, but a stranger with big paws reached up and grabbed my hand, pulling me down into the banquette where he was sitting with a group of people.

"I am for those who believe in loose delights—I share the midnight orgies of young men," the man whispered into my ear, the smell of liquor thick on his breath.

"Excuse me?" I said, pulling away. He pulled me back.

"Give me the drench of my passions, give me life coarse and rank."

I looked at him as if he were crazy. He might've been—his hair was wild, and he had a sheen of perspiration across his face.

"You must be a poet," I said. "Or a madman."

"I am, indeed," he said. "I'm Frank. I dance with the dancers, I drink with the drinkers."

"Like I said, a poet, a drunken one."

"And you must be a dancer."

I raised my eyebrows. "I'm a performer, I sing and dance, yes. How did you know?"

"I can tell a dancer's body when I see one."

I rolled my eyes and a gentleman across the table poured a glass of water from a pitcher and placed it in front of his friend. "Drink this." Then he turned to me. "Please ignore him, he's out of his mind."

This gentleman was far more respectable looking than the first and devilishly handsome. His eyes were so dark they looked almost black in the dim light, with hair to match, dark brown and wavy, brushed back from his face but a little wild and unruly.

"He's quite the poet," I said, looking back to the first guy, Frank, who now had his head leaning back and appeared to have fallen asleep.

"Those are Walt Whitman's words—he tries them every time."

"Words to live by, perhaps," I said.

He laughed. "I'm Archie," he said. "I apologize for my friend's behavior, but I can't say I blame him for wanting to talk to you."

"I'm Olive," I said, giving him my hand.

"Lovely to make your acquaintance." He kissed the back of my hand and a surge of excitement ran through me.

"Please, join us and meet some of my more respectable friends." He moved in and made space for me to sit down. "Emily, I'd like to introduce you to a new friend of mine." He looked at me and grinned. "This is Olive."

"Lovely to meet you," she said.

"Emily's a writer. You've already had the pleasure of meeting Frank." He gestured toward him. "He has a charming bookshop around the corner."

"And I publish chapbooks." Frank suddenly came to life again, slurring like a sailor. "When this crowd wakes up tomorrow morning around noon, you'll find them stumbling into my shop and taking shelter amongst words."

"Oh." I looked around. I couldn't imagine anyone in that room functioning in the daylight.

"I take it you're more of an uptown girl," Archie said. "You're used to a swankier establishment."

"I don't like to get used to anything. I like a little variety in my days."

Someone came over and placed a tray full of teacups on the table. Archie handed one to me.

"This is Emily's husband, Lou." Archie reached over and tapped the shoulder of the gentleman sitting on the other side of Frank. "Olive here sings."

"Wonderful, I'm a lyricist. Emily and I both write songs."

"You sing?" Emily asked. "You should come to our salon. It's on Saturday nights at our place, you'd love it."

"Thank you," I said. Everyone was so friendly. I was surprised at how intimate it all seemed, skin against skin as we pressed into the small booth together, our drinks pouring over into one another's teacups as we said cheers. "I'd like that," I said.

She scribbled her address down on a scrap of paper and slid it across the table. I reached out to take it and Archie put his hand over it first.

"You have to promise you'll come, otherwise I might never see you again," he said.

"I'll do my best," I said, sliding the paper out from under his hand and feeling a slight thrill again when his hand touched mine.

"It was nice to meet you," I said, standing up.

"The pleasure was all mine," Archie said. "But do you really have to leave so soon? The night is young." He took my hand and I desperately wanted to stay. I glanced to the front of the room where Ruthie was dancing with Lawrence, and my date for the evening was standing alone at the bar.

"It would be impolite of me to leave my friends," I said, and I reluctantly walked away.

———

On Saturday I performed in the *Follies* and then the *Midnight Frolic*. It was two in the morning when I was done and I should have been exhausted, but I wasn't ready to go home. All of us girls were in the habit of staying out all night and sleeping until noon or two in the afternoon if we didn't have rehearsal the next day. Ruthie had already left to meet a new chap after the show, a banker who'd sent a bouquet of flowers and a diamond bracelet backstage to her dressing room the night before and asked her to dinner. I'd surprised myself that week—I'd been thinking about that Archie fella ever since I met him. Ruthie and the girls would say I was crazy lusting over a bohemian from the Village when I could have my pick of the wealthy businessmen who frequented the *Frolic*, but there was something about him that appealed to me. He was dashing in a slightly disheveled way, and the way he spoke, his confidence, was magnetic. But there was something else that I couldn't let go of: he had a kindness in his eyes. I was itching to get downtown again.

Mary, one of the principals in the show, had been given a car by an admirer, but she didn't know how to drive, none of us did, so a few of us pitched in and hired a chauffeur named James to drive us around town. That night James was still parked out front when I left the theater, which meant all the other girls had dates. I handed him the slip of paper Emily had given me, which I had folded and refolded many times throughout the week. He dropped me off at 13 East Eighth Street, a block north of Washington Square Park.

Piano music poured from the top-floor apartment. When I looked up, windows were open and people were leaning out, smoking,

"Hardly," he said, taking a swig of his drink.

"Oh, come on, you love to cause a big fuss, both of you. Olive here is a performer, she might sing for us later if we're lucky. Will you?" she asked excitedly. "I have some new lyrics."

"Perhaps," I said. I always loved a chance to perform, but I was distracted. "Say, I don't suppose you've seen Archie around? I promised him I'd make an appearance."

"I haven't seen him yet," she said with a shrug. "He travels a lot. But it looks like Frankie's got his eye on you." She laughed. "He's an absolute degenerate, but he's a lot of fun."

I was disappointed. I'd really hoped to see Archie again. I didn't even know his last name.

The older dancer approached the bar.

"I was transfixed by your dancing earlier," I said. "I've never seen anything quite like it." As I spoke, I still didn't think I liked her style much, it was just different and so was she.

"How so?" she said.

"Your style is so . . ." I couldn't quite bring myself to say *beautiful.* "Quite unusual and breathtaking."

"My art is just an effort to express the truth of my being in gesture and movement. It has taken me long years to find even one absolute true movement." She stared at me for a moment as if asking me to question my own moves.

I smiled. "I could just imagine my boss, Mr. Ziegfeld, hearing this. He insists our bodies must be still as we descend the staircase onstage with fifteen-or twenty-pound headdresses on our heads." I laughed. "We have to smile and look alluring, as if it's the easiest thing we've ever done, as if the four-foot-high crystal crown is nothing but whipped air." Even after performing in two back-to-back shows that night, I was giddy when I described to her my typical night on the stage. But she wasn't taken with it the way I was.

"You're a Ziegfeld girl?" she asked, looking repulsed. "It sounds ghastly."

"Not at all, I love every minute."

Later that evening, Emily persuaded me to sing a number from the show.

The pianist accompanied me while I sang one of Eddie Cantor's songs, "You Don't Need the Wine to Have a Wonderful Time (While They Still Make Those Wonderful Girls)." This one was always a big hit when people were boozing, and partygoing crowds really loved it. I was having fun, but my eyes kept darting to the door, wondering if Archie might make an appearance. He never did.

Determined to get home before the sun came up, I looked around for Emily to ask her to pass a message on to Archie, but she was nowhere to be found, so I slipped out the door, and James drove me back to the apartment.

CHAPTER EIGHT

I received a bouquet of white roses in my dressing room one April evening after the show with a card from Ziegfeld inviting me to join him and his wife for dinner that Sunday evening.

I'd been performing in both shows every night for two months now. I knew Ziegfeld's wife, Billie, well enough from the *Follies*, but I'd never received the honor of an invite with the two of them. It seemed promising.

He picked me up at my apartment and then circled back to collect Billie, who he said needed more time to get dolled up, then we ended up at the Grand Central Oyster Bar. A big fuss was made as we arrived, and we were seated at what seemed to be the best table in the house.

For most of the evening it was all chatter and laughs, and I had absolutely no idea why I'd been invited. I began to wonder if perhaps there was no motive, that they simply liked me. But as dessert was served, and I knew well enough to decline, Ziegfeld got quickly to the matter at hand.

"As you may know, Miss Shine, it is very expensive to put on our shows. I insist on only the best for my girls. I simply will not accept cheap fabrics, or costumes," he said with disgust. "Costumes with faux glamour are for other shows. We offer real beauty. If it glitters, it's because it's made with Swarovski crystals. If it shines, it's because it has gold-leaf embellishment. I simply will not compromise."

He looked lovingly at his wife and kissed her. "But the price I pay is high, the price I pay is such that at times, rare times, I must cut back on my performers to pay for the extravagance that I insist on showering on my girls."

Was he cutting me out of the show? My heart sank, I couldn't believe what I was hearing. Was this it for me? I was only twenty-one. I had dreaded the very thought of getting older, my sagging breasts, my wrinkled skin, all the terrible things I'd been warned about leading up to the curse of one's thirtieth birthday; but this was all happening too soon. I wasn't ready, I wasn't prepared. I hadn't found a nice man to settle down with. I'd been too picky or hadn't stuck around long enough. It was over. My life was over. I might as well shrivel up and die right there. I was so preoccupied with my disastrous thoughts that I barely heard what he was saying.

"My darling, you've gone white as a sheet." Billie reached over and took my hand. Hers felt soft, like a baby's hand, and it was dripping with diamonds. "He's not telling you it's over, listen to what he has to say."

She could read my mind. Of course she could—she too was a performer and knew just as well as the rest of us what would happen when her time in the spotlight was up, except she'd played her cards right with Mr. Z.

"I'm saying," he continued, "it's just for a short spell, the rest of the season. You'll still be in the *Midnight Frolic*."

"I will?"

"Of course. That's what I've been trying to tell you. You are one of our star performers in the *Frolic*. In fact, with your spontaneity and feisty personality, it's actually where I think you excel. But I assure you, you'll be back in the *Follies* in no time. I just have to pay off my debts to keep things running smoothly, and without any changes to our prime reputation as the most luxurious, most sophisticated show on Broadway, with the most luxurious, most sophisticated women."

I sighed with relief. I hadn't intended to show how much I needed him, but as the blood finally began to flow again, I jabbered on about how grateful I was and how indebted I was to him and to Billie and to all the girls in the show.

He paid the tab and escorted us to his awaiting car.

"I'll drop Billie off first since we're closest, then I'll escort you home," he said as we climbed in.

"Oh, you're too kind, Mr. Ziegfeld, but really there's no need."

"I insist," he said firmly, and the matter was closed.

I said good night to Billie, and she patted my hand. "Please don't worry yourself with this, I'll make sure he takes care of you," she said.

As we drove across town to my apartment, we rode in silence for a while, and I wasn't quite sure what to say. The evening of laughs and stories over shucked oysters seemed a million miles away now. I'd been put in my place somewhat—it was as if I were back to being the new girl, desperate for approval, willing to do anything to prove myself.

"You're a beautiful girl," Mr. Ziegfeld said, placing his hand on my thigh and rubbing it slowly. "I don't want you to worry about a thing, do you understand? You're a star, but I could make you *the* star." His hand moved farther up my thigh and he began to squeeze gently. "I want you to know I take care of my girls, in the best possible way." He moved closer and my heart began to race. I put my hand on his and was about to move it off my leg, but I had a moment of panic—I didn't want to insult him, I just didn't want this. Instead my hand rested on his for a moment, almost as if I were encouraging it. He slipped his hand between my thighs and leaned in for a kiss, his lips already wet with anticipation, his mustache softer than the wiry feel I might have expected but foreign and unwanted all the same. He took my hand and moved it to his groin, hot, and hard, and repulsive. This man was at least thirty years my senior. I pulled myself away from him, and without even thinking, I raised my right hand and slapped him across the face.

"Mr. Ziegfeld!" I said, stunned at myself more than anything.

He looked at me, shocked, his thick eyebrows raised, as he brought his hand slowly to his face. "Why, Miss Shine, that is most unkind." He moved away from me toward the window and looked straight ahead. "Most unkind after how generous I have been to you." We were parked outside my apartment now. The chauffeur silently idled the engine and sat upright as if he weren't there at all.

I stared at Ziegfeld, astonished at his behavior but more so at mine. What had I done? But what could I have done? I would never be so deceitful to Billie, even if some of the other girls were, and I would never compromise myself in such a way. And yet I couldn't fathom what to say or do next. What would become of me now?

"I, I . . . ," I stammered, at a total loss.

"That's enough now," he said, still staring at the street ahead. "Go on, off you go."

I got out of the car as fast as I could and heard them drive away before I'd even reached my front door. I walked quickly past the doorman and rode the elevator up to my floor, and as soon as the door closed behind me, I burst into tears.

I showed up for rehearsal the next day as usual. I saw Howie, the choreographer, in the corner talking to the percussionist, and I went to the opposite side of the room. The sun was shining in between the gaps of the ragged sheets that'd been draped as makeshift curtains. Even though I knew I'd been cut from my biggest scene in the *Follies,* I still held out a glimmer of hope that I'd be part of the chorus. We were working on a new dance, the Brazilian samba that had taken off in Paris, so I sat down on the floor and put on my T-straps with the short Cuban heel and rubbed the leather soles into the resin dust left over from the day before. Ruthie had gone in for an early rehearsal, so I hadn't had a chance to tell her about getting cut, and I sheepishly kept my eyes down, taking my time to get ready so that no one would single me out. But it didn't work.

"All right, line up, girls," Howie said. Some girls were still adjusting and primping in front of the small mirror on the back wall, a few others were hurrying through the door, late. Ruthie winked at me. I stood up and got into formation.

"Uh, Olive," Howie said through his teeth, as if that would decrease the odds of the other girls noticing. He nodded for me to follow him away from the others. "Mr. Ziegfeld said he spoke to you about this and that you understood you'd be taking a break. The horse scene was cut, no point in you sticking around for these small bit parts in the chorus, just come back at three for the *Frolic*."

"Oh, okay. I thought, I wondered if I should still learn the samba for when—"

"He said no, not at the moment." Howie felt bad for me, I could tell, pity in his eyes. "Don't worry, it'll work out, you know how Ziegfeld gets sometimes. He's very loyal."

"Loyal? I thought this was about money," I said.

"Yeah, that too."

There was nothing I could do. I should have known not to show up in the first place. I tried to exit the room without anyone noticing, but I felt the girls' eyes on me, probably wondering if they'd be next or relieved that it was me and not them.

Out on West Forty-second Street, the stench of last night's debauchery clinging to the sidewalk and coming up from the drains stung my nostrils and caught in the back of my throat. It was only nine thirty in the morning. I brought in good money being in the *Frolic*, but Ruthie and I had banked on the money from both the *Follies* and the *Frolic* to afford our apartment on Fifth Avenue, and we had barely accounted for food or clothes in our budget because that was always taken care of. I started to panic. What was I going to do now that my pay had been cut in half? Ziegfeld said I still had the *Frolic*, but after that ride home the night before, I didn't even know if that was still on the table. I felt desperate. It could all be gone just like that, and for what? For refusing his advances? It was confusing. Technically he'd cut me from the *Follies* at dinner, before he tried to put his tongue down my throat, but he'd also made it seem that I could be back on top, *the* star, if I went along with what he wanted.

Maybe my father was right, maybe I'd been a fool to think I could do this, that I'd amount to any more than a biscuit in a frilly dress. I had a sudden urge to go home, to curl up on the couch and let my mother bring me hot milk. I wouldn't, though; that would mean admitting defeat, and worse than that, it would mean sitting around waiting to be paired off with someone my father thought was suitable. And even those prospects, my father had told me, would be slim after working as a show girl and living away from my own family as a single woman. He didn't know the half of it.

I found myself on the ladies floor of Lord & Taylor, staring at a heavily beaded Chanel dress in lipstick red.

"It's a beauty, isn't it?" a salesgirl said, appearing at my side. "Would you like to see it on one of our girls, madam?"

"No," I said. "I'll try it myself along with some shoes, evening, none of those daytime heels."

"Of course." She seemed excited.

"I need a new coat, too, white fur collar and cuffs, doeskin gloves and stockings, rose beige."

She scurried off, and while I waited, I perused the evening bags, settling on a lizard skin, black with white trim. I might as well spend my money while I had it.

I asked for everything to be wrapped and boxed. It came to

$436.50—a little over what it cost Ruthie and me to furnish our three-bedroom apartment.

"How would you like to pay?" the salesgirl asked.

"Put it on my account," I said. Ruthie and I had splurged a few times since I'd been in the show, though nothing as extravagant as this. She'd bought a pair of brocade T-strap sally pumps that we took turns wearing when we knew we'd be out dancing all night. I'd bought a gold chiffon dress with real metal sequins and a bejeweled cigarette case.

"Of course," she said.

Afterwards I went to the tenth floor and had lunch in the Wedgewood Room. It wasn't so bad, I thought, looking at the various groups of women gathered around me, but then two elderly women at the adjacent table eyed me suspiciously and mumbled about my eating alone. I stared into my salad, and when I looked up again, I noticed a mother and daughter sitting a few tables over. The girl was four or five, so well behaved in such a grown-up setting. I watched them for a while, the little girl picking up her teacup and taking a sip each time her mother did. The mother reached over and touched the girl's cheek. I couldn't take my eyes off them, I couldn't help imagining what my life would have been like if I'd insisted on taking the baby with me. I must have been staring longingly because the mother looked up at me and glared. I didn't belong here. I didn't seem to belong anywhere. I paid the check and left as fast as I could.

As I walked back toward the theater district, the momentary thrill of the pretty bags and boxes that filled my arms had dissipated. The thought of rehearsal going on without me, the girls' skin pink and beaded with sweat, made me sink again.

I strode all the way west to the Landmark on West Forty-sixth and went straight up to the unmarked third floor. There was one lonely blotto sitting at the bar. Alberto Ricci was playing on the gramophone, and I breathed in the vibrations of his voice, so alive, so powerful. I'd seen posters and billboards all over town announcing his return to the Metropolitan Opera House that summer. I'd loved listening to his voice for as long as I could remember, ever since my parents took me to see him perform in Minnesota. What I'd do to see him sing again, in person, in New York City. I should have bought myself a ticket two days ago. I'd never be able to afford it now.

"We're not open," the barkeep said, looking me up and down, his eyes resting on my shopping bags.

"It looks like you have a couple of customers," I said, nodding toward the gentleman with his chin on the bar, then I pulled up a seat next to him. "I'll take a bourbon, make it a double."

When I walked into the dressing room later that afternoon with my shopping bags and a jolt of confidence from the bourbon, the girls stared, then looked away—that was until Ruthie caught sight of me.

"What the hell are you doing?" she said, barging through the others to get to my mirror.

"What do you mean? A little shopping, that's all."

"You're going to get yourself cut if you act up like that! And you smell like hooch."

"I already got cut, so I can do what I damn well please in my free time. But I need to get ready for my *Frolic* rehearsal because that's the one thing I've got left right now, so if you'll excuse me ..." I felt defensive. Ruthie, though she was my closest friend, seemed like someone on the other side now. She was with the girls who had everything, I was hanging on to what I had for dear life.

Sure, I'd put down a few bourbons, I had to take the edge off, but I'd knocked back a few black coffees, too. After I finally got Ruthie to leave me alone, and the morning girls cleared out of the dressing room, I lay down on the couch and closed my eyes. By rehearsal time, I felt terrible.

Howie peeked his head in the door. "I heard you went out and drowned your sorrows."

"I didn't have many options," I said.

"We're not going to rehearse like this," he said, his face stern. "Come back tomorrow, same time, in better shape. I won't mention it to Ziegfeld if you promise this will never happen again."

I nodded solemnly.

CHAPTER NINE

I was already warming up when Howie walked in the next morning, and he looked a little surprised. I had a one-hour rehearsal for my solo in the *Frolic* and then the chorus girls would arrive for us to go through the numbers together.

Ziegfeld liked to keep the routines fresh, adding new elements every few days to surprise the repeat patrons. And there were many repeats—gents who came in night after night despite the hefty five-dollar door fee on top of the ticket price. For most, the idea of riding the elevator from the theater lobby up to the rooftop garden, where the doors would open to a party of dancing and the sound of champagne being uncorked, was far more appealing than venturing out into the busy streets of Times Square and making their way to another nightclub across town. So once they were on the guest list and they proved they could afford the front-row seats, steak dinners, Beluga caviar and the absurdity of $2.75 for a miniature bottle of champagne (about the cost of eight one-pound steaks at the butcher's shop), they were welcomed back night after night.

"I was thinking about the ribbon number," I said to Howie as I sat on the floor and stretched forward to touch my toes. "How about we jazz it up this time?"

"Sure," he said. "Everyone loves it, I don't know what else you could do. What did you have in mind?"

The ribbon number was the final act before the first twenty-minute intermission and already something of a crescendo. As I sang my solo, five other girls, each holding the end of a ribbon, crisscrossed the stage, wrapping me up like a beautifully decorated maypole. Since I was already wearing nothing but silk and a thin chiffon negligee, the ribbons wrapped around me like a full-length corset. I sang about being tied down to some old, good-for-nothing dewdropper and yearning to be free from him. At the end, after the girls left the stage, I began to spin on a small circular disk that rose a foot or so from the stage. Slowly at first, the ribbons unraveled as I turned. In the original act, a fan blew from backstage, so that as my solo came to an end the long ribbons flew off my body in long, beautiful, colorful strands out into the audience, where everyone jumped up to grab one. When the curtain dropped, the stage rolled back to reveal a dance floor, and the patrons, already on their feet, began to dance.

"What if one of the ribbons is attached to me?" I said. "And when they all catch a ribbon, one patron will realize he's got the one with me on the end of it. Kind of like fishing, then he can pull me to the dance floor, where I'll dance with him until the next act. Wouldn't that be fun? And it gives every gent a shot, no matter who they are or if they were just here the night before."

I had decided, after emerging from my afternoon bourbon haze the previous day, that I wasn't going to be defeated by Ziegfeld or by getting kicked out of the *Follies*. Instead, I was going to excel in the *Midnight Frolic* more than anyone could imagine, and I was going to steal the show. Each night, audience members were asked to vote for the girl they considered most beautiful and state why on cards handed out by the usher, and the girl with the most votes during that run of the *Frolic* had her salary doubled. I wanted that girl to be me, but it wasn't just about the money. I felt more determined than ever to win at this. I'd prove to Ziegfeld that he needed me in his show, but I'd also prove to my father that I wasn't going to make a wreck of my life just as he expected me to. I'd show my mother, too, that I could do anything I put my mind to, that there was more to life than just bowing down to your husband's wishes. But most of all, I needed to prove to myself that the things I'd done in my not-too-distant past were done for a reason. I would succeed, I told myself, I had to.

Howie loved the idea of ribbon fishing. He rubbed his hands together. "What if we put you in the flying harness?"

"What, that contraption that Terry K straps into for her act—is that thing safe?"

"Perfectly, very secure. We'd put it under your attire, of course, so when the lucky fella pulls you toward him we'd lift you off the stage, and he can fly you to him over the audience, and we'll deliver you right to him on the dance floor."

"It's darb! I love it!" I said, jumping up. "And then I'll unclip myself from the harness and we'll have a good fifteen to twenty minutes to dance while the stage set changes."

"But wait a second," he said. "You're in the next act, too, you'll need a few minutes to change and rest and have something to drink."

"It will take me two minutes to slip into my next outfit. Don't worry about me. I can go straight through."

Howie looked as if he'd known I was going to say that. "It will be marvelous and Ziegfeld will think so, too." He rubbed his chin in thought. "Hey, I'm going to call around and see if we can get some press in here tonight. All the opening nights are history now, maybe they need something fresh to cover."

The idea thrilled me. We began practice right away.

That night the ribbon act went off without a hitch. The adrenaline that ran through me leading up to that final moment of being lifted off the stage made me sing even better than I had before, with more passion and seduction and determination. When the fans turned on behind me, the ribbons flew forward and I was dazzled by the floating colors. I don't know how it must've looked from the audience's perspective, but from where I stood, it was as if I were in a storm of rainbow confetti. I stood, arms in the air, smiling, catching my breath, not even able to see the audience out front for the mass of dancing ribbons blurring my view. I felt a slight tug on my waist from the harness, and I began to lift off the stage. It wasn't until that moment that I began to feel a pang of trepidation. Had I thought this through? It was one thing to sing and dance in front of all these audience members, couples cheering, gentlemen leering, some perfectly delightful, I'm sure, but I had no idea who would be at the end of this ribbon. What if he was a drunk, hideous? What if he groped me? I tried to push my sudden reluctance out of my mind and positioned myself in an elegant midair drape as if it were the most comfortable thing in the world. The harness cut into my flesh, and my muscles ached as I maintained the seemingly easeful pose, but I could suffer it a few moments longer. I flew above the ribbons, which had mostly landed now, over the end of the stage and toward the middle of the packed dance floor. The audience roared and the room vibrated with the sound of wooden mallets pounding against tables—Ziegfeld's gimmick for aiding applause-weary guests was put to good use that night.

I saw a well-dressed gentleman smiling broadly as he pulled me toward him with the ribbon in hand. In the glare of lights from above, I was relieved that he looked respectable and had a good silhouette, tall with broad shoulders. For there was no turning back—I was making my descent, and patrons on the dance floor formed a circle around us, clapping frantically. My toes touched down and I unclipped myself from the harness.

And when I stood there in front of him, I realized it was Archie, Archie from the Village! But impeccably dressed and far more polished than I remembered.

"It's you!" I said, delighted at the sight of him.

"How lovely to see you again," he said, smiling.

I suddenly realized I hadn't given enough thought to my attire. Onstage it was appropriate, a barely there negligee at an untouchable distance, yet here I was, wearing next to nothing, in the arms of an almost stranger. As if he had read my mind, he slipped off his jacket and put it around my shoulders. I knew it would fall off the second we started dancing, so I put my arms through the sleeves and rolled them up.

"What a gentleman," I said, and we immediately began to dance. Men and women filled in the floor around us.

When the music slowed down enough for us to talk, he pulled me in a little closer, but not too close, and I didn't mind one bit.

"What are you doing here?" I asked.

"Looking for a beautiful young lady I met a few weeks back at the Pirate's Den."

"Any luck?"

"Oh, I got lucky all right."

He'd just had a shave that day, I could smell the clean scent of shaving foam when his cheek touched mine.

The music picked up again and we danced a fast one-step, and boy, this man really knew how to dance. He held me in a close embrace and took the lead around the dance floor. I laughed—he was as much a performer as I was. As we picked up the pace, the dance floor cleared out again, making room for us. The trumpet blared, the percussion sped up, and he spun me around the circumference of the floor. By the time he was done, I had to catch my breath. The audience applauded again, and we both took a bow. That was my cue—I had to be onstage for the next act—but I was reluctant to leave.

"Thank you for this wonderful moment," he said. "May I see you again?"

"I hope so," I said, surprising myself, then I dashed backstage.

The next morning, Ruthie ran into my room and leapt onto my bed.

"Wake up, Olive, wake up!"

"What is it?" I peeled the silk sleep mask from my eyes and had to shield them from the sunlight streaming in the windows as Ruthie swept back the curtain. "What are you doing, you crazy girl, I need to sleep."

"Sleep later! You're in *The New York Times*. They adored you!"

"*The New York Times*?" I grabbed the paper from her hands and stared at it in amazement. There I was in black and white, gliding through the air, the stage lit up behind me, reaching one arm out to a silhouetted man on the dance floor with a ribbon in his hand. The title read, "Olive Shines! Ziegfeld's Beauty Reaches New Heights."

"The latest edition of Florenz Ziegfeld's 'Midnight Frolic,' which had its twenty-fourth presentation of the season on Tuesday at midnight, before an audience that embraced all who live and move and have their being in Broadway, out-Ziegfelds all its predecessors. Like the others only more so, it is a show of beautiful women, frocks and tableaux designed for the businessman who is too tired to go home after the play. . . . Miss Olive Shine shone indeed last night with a dazzling solo followed by a flight to the dance floor as she surprised one lucky audience member with a dance, Mr. Archibald Carmichael, a businessman with interests in New York and Cincinnati. . . . One might search the world and not find anything quite as unique or lavish as this midnight revue."

Ruthie and I threw our arms around each other and jumped on the bed. "I'm in *The New York Times*!" I screamed with excitement.

"You really showed Ziegfeld," Ruthie said.

"Ziegfeld? I showed everyone in New York!"

"You're a true star now, Olive."

I squealed with delight.

The following evening, as the ribbons flew out to the audience, I wished I'd remembered to ask a stagehand to bring me something to wear over my outfit. I'd been lucky the night before with Archie, but there was no telling if tonight's "fisherman" would have the same manners or charm. I closed my eyes, waiting to be lifted offstage, and hoped for an instant that it would be him again, but then I felt the tug on the harness, a rough jerk, eager and greedy. It propelled me forward, waist first, and I almost fell off my elevated platform before the stagehand above quickly hoisted me upwards. For a few seconds I was awkwardly suspended in midair until the audience member began to pull me out toward him. I tried to rearrange myself more gracefully, but it was much more challenging, having gotten off to a wobbly start. When I landed, it was into the arms of a lanky gentleman grinning hungrily, with oily hair slicked back from his face in a harsh middle part. Grand, I thought sardonically, but then his date appeared by his side, clapping with excitement, and relief washed over me.

"A ménage à trois! How daring!" I said as I backed away from the man and into a more collegial formation. The girl was a charm, sweet and excited to dance. She looked lovely, too, in a long pale pink chemise with an ornate silver-beaded V in the front. We held hands and began to dance, and when the music got going, she called some friends over. They were far more fun than her date, but I encouraged her to bring him back into the circle and make a fuss. I was their dancing coach, positioning the two of them just so, then sandwiching him in the middle and nudging his feet to the right beat. Then I switched to her side, my hands on her hips, swaying them not too much, just the right amount. When I was sure they were all having a good time, I slipped away, scanning the room for Archie with no success.

I went backstage and dressed for the next act.

My feet were up for less than thirty seconds when there was a knock on my dressing room door.

"Flowers, Olive," the stage manager called. I opened the door to a huge bouquet of long-stemmed red roses along with a flat rectangular box. "Two minutes to call time."

On top of the box there was a note:

Dear Miss Shine,
Your performance and your company last night have rendered me an unproductive man. I've been thinking of you all day. Please accept this gift as a thank-you for spending your precious time dancing with me. I hope it will make your flying escapades more comfortable.

In awe and gratitude,
Archibald Carmichael

The box contained a gorgeous champagne-colored beaded and sequined evening cape. I placed it around my shoulders and looked in the mirror. It was absolutely stunning, the perfect fit on my narrow

shoulders, falling just to my elbows. What a beautiful and extravagant gesture. Who was this man? I wondered. He'd seemed so down-
to-earth when I met him at the speak in the Village, but *The New
York Times* referred to him as a businessman, and this cape definitely
had the touch of uptown luxury.

Another knock on my door. "One minute."

I spun around, looking at the beautiful craftsmanship from all
angles in the mirror, excited now to think that he must be in the
audience. Then I placed it carefully back in the box, next to my new
red dress and heels that I'd brought for that evening in hopes of
receiving an invitation.

But I didn't receive an invitation from him that night, or the next
night, or any night that week.

Within a week I was getting sick of the ribbon routine. Maybe
because the first time had been such a thrill and the ensuing
moments so dull in comparison. I'd worn my new red dress twice
after the shows that week in anticipation of an invite to dinner, and
both times it had gone to waste. The whole thing had put me in a
sour mood. Archie had beamed when we danced together, he'd sent
me a beautiful gift, and yet he apparently had no desire to spend
any actual time with me. Does he think all I value in life is a pretty
beaded cape? I found myself questioning. Doesn't he want to know
anything about me, who I am?

"What's going on with you, Olive?" Ruthie said as I slowly put
away my costumes for the evening. She was already changed and ready
for a night out. "Are you still on the lookout for Mr. Handsome?"

"No."

"Maybe he's an out-of-towner or something."

I rolled my eyes. He knew too many people to be an out-of-towner, though Emily had warned me that he traveled a lot.

"He's probably married," she said. "Come on, let's find you someone else to have fun with."

I'd been fooled before and thought I was better at sizing up men now, but maybe I was wrong. I just couldn't understand his silence.

"I'm not looking for him, I'm just exhausted, Ruthie, and my feet are pounding."

The truth was I did feel disappointed. We'd danced only a few numbers and talked briefly, but there was something about him that excited me. There was an element of mystery about him, and the thought of him had kept me awake at night. I knew nothing about this man, and yet I was compelled to find some snippet of information, to spend another evening with him in the booth at the Pirate's Den, except this time I wouldn't have to leave.

"You do look tired. I hope you're not coming down with something." She put her hand to my forehead. My sweet Ruthie.

"You go on and have fun," I said. "I'll meet you back at the apartment, I just need to get some rest."

We moved the ribbon act to the first half of the show because we added a new number in the second half—a celebration of the new Ford Model A. Rumors swirled about how Ziegfeld got the car up on the roof (some say it was a crane in the middle of the night), but he had managed to park that vehicle right in the middle of the rooftop stage. Rehearsals that week were an absolute blast and quickly got me out of my mood.

At intermission I walked into my dressing room, flung off my costume and lay on the couch naked except for my knickers. The ribbon act was over, but I was sweating and had to let my skin cool off before I'd be able to dress for the Model A.

A knock at the door. "Flowers, Olive." The stage manager brought them in, white roses, and set them on the table next to me. I covered my breasts with one arm; it was all the effort I was capable of.

"Olive, put some clothes on."

"Sorry," I said. "I'm so damn hot." I reached over and picked up the card.

Dear Miss Shine,
May I request the honor of your presence at dinner this evening? I will be waiting in front of the theater after the show in the hopes of a positive response.

With eager anticipation,
Archibald Carmichael

I smiled. What had I been so worried about? He just needed some time to come around.

In the second half, I put on one hell of a show. Knowing for definite that he was in the audience, I gave it my all. Everyone was going crazy—as much for the fact that Ziegfeld had achieved such a feat as for the shining car itself. We danced all over that thing, encircling it with our biggest feathers, then opening them up to reveal it, backbends out the window, sliding down the hood, singing "Happy Birthday" in the most seductive way we knew how. The crowd loved it—it was amazing how we could control the audience, the power we had as performers to make them laugh, cry, cheer. The mallets pounding the tables were the only percussion I needed.

"For the final act I want the flying device," I told Howie. "Instead of doing all those pirouettes on the stage, right before my very last verse, raise me up on the platform, I'll start the pirouettes there, and then I'll continue them in the air and I'll sing the last few lines from midair, then lights out."

"Olive, we haven't even practiced that. This is the final act, we don't want to mess it up."

"We won't, I promise, I know it will work."

Reluctantly, he agreed.

I wasn't that good at pirouettes to begin with, I'd always been a better singer than dancer, but it must have been the adrenaline pulsing through my veins, my absolute will to wow them. Through sheer determination I spun up onto my toe, kept my body and legs firm and tight, whipped my head around and managed six full and almost perfect pirouettes before the platform lowered and I remained airborne. It worked just as I'd imagined it. After my final note, I threw my head and arms back and draped in the air as the lights went dark, then they slowly brought me back to the stage. The audience kept on cheering, clapping and calling out praise. After I'd detached myself from the harness, the lights came up again and I bowed and curtsied. I waved for all the other girls to come out from the wings, and we held hands and bowed together. It was a magical feeling to know we'd managed to impress them once again and even more to know Archie had witnessed another roaring success.

I kept him waiting while I freshened up and dressed for dinner. Of course it was the one night that I hadn't brought my new red dress, so I put on the old gold number that was always a hit, the one with the handkerchief hemline, dropped waist and beaded bust. He was waiting for me out front, holding his car door open. When I approached, he took off his hat, revealing his tousled brown hair, tamed, but not slicked the way most gents wore it.

"Miss Olive Shine," he said, taking my hand and kissing it. "What a vision."

"Thank you for the beautiful flowers, and for the stunning evening cape you sent, Mr. Carmichael." It sounded strangely formal when I said it. I'd already been introduced to him as Archie, but he seemed so much more debonair this time around.

"Please call me Archie."

"Archie," I said as I climbed into the car. "It was a lovely surprise."

There was something reserved about the way we were treating each other, not like our meeting in the Village. He wore a pristinely tailored navy-blue suit and his car was that of the wealthy, but his friends were bohemians from the Village. I couldn't quite figure out who this fella was and where he belonged.

"I have to apologize for my delay in calling on you."

"Oh, please," I said, brushing away his comment. "I wouldn't have been available on any other night."

"Now, I'll take you anywhere you want to go, and I'd love to take you dancing after, but I was wondering if you might like to go somewhere a little quieter first, so we can talk and eat a good meal before I have to share you with the rest of the dance floor."

"That sounds perfect," I said. My stomach was growling after my performance.

We settled into a corner booth at Sardi's at 234 West Forty-fourth Street, where I ordered Duchess Soup and a pork chop with potatoes and French fried onions. Archie ordered the sirloin steak and a Waldorf salad. He'd picked one of the few places that stayed open this late to serve dinner.

"So, Miss Shine," he said, smiling. He had a wide smile, a little crooked, giving him a playful, boyish look, despite having about ten years on me. "Tell me everything about yourself," he said. "I'm dying to know."

"Everything?"

"Everything."

"Well, first, I must insist that you call me Olive if I'm to call you Archie, and secondly, you already know a little about me—where I work, that I sing, that I possess a gorgeous evening cape. Why don't you tell me about you?"

"Well," he said, sitting up a little taller, "I'm from Cincinnati, but lately I spend many of my days in New York City. I have a suite at the Plaza."

"The Plaza?" This was no bohemian.

"My business interests are both here and back home, and I find myself traveling quite extensively."

"Oh." I nodded. "Perhaps you're not who I thought you were."

"How so?"

"When I met you at the Pirate's Den you were with poets and

artists. I just assumed you were one of them . . . but it sounds like you're a businessman after all."

"Does that disappoint you?"

I shrugged. "I suppose I'll have to find out. The businessmen I've met thus far are a bit of a bore."

"Ha, couldn't agree more. I collect art, it's a hobby of mine, so I've become quite friendly with many of the artists along the way." He leaned in as if to let me in on a secret. "They're a terrible influence on me, but we do have an awful lot of fun."

I looked at him curiously. He was not what I'd expected.

"Oh dear, I'm boring you already."

"You're not. Go on, tell me everything, start at the beginning."

He laughed and shifted a little in his seat. "My first time traveling anywhere outside of Ohio was to New York. My parents didn't have much, and I knew that if I wanted to make something of myself I'd have to head to the big city. So, at sixteen I got on a train and headed east in true Horatio Alger style."

"My brothers loved his books! I read a few of them too—boy from humble upbringing rises up through the ranks through hard work, determination and some heroic act of honesty or courage. Same story over and over in every book, but so good!"

"I devoured those books as a boy. I basically mapped out my life based on them."

The waiter delivered my soup, creamy with vegetables peeking through. If Archie weren't sitting with me I would have inhaled it, I was so hungry, but I forced myself to eat like a lady.

"So, I worked as a clerk during the day and took night classes at Cooper Institute, and as things progressed, by the time I was twenty-six I was the proud vice president of a salt company. It was only a fledgling business at the time, but I got some partners, bought more interests and combined them into the National Salt Company. At the time, the United States was consuming thirteen million barrels of salt a year, and we were lucky enough to supply nine million of them."

"Wow, that's quite impressive."

"We had big plans to supply the whole world with salt, we were going to be the first international trust ever formed, but then the deal fell through."

"What happened?"

"Now, that would definitely bore you—it just didn't come together, but that was all right. I was thirty by then, and I'd made it in New York just as I'd hoped I might. I did well, but I wanted to see more, learn more, so I took two years off and went to Europe."

I carefully spooned some of the soup, scooping away from myself toward the back of the bowl the way my mother had taught me.

"I knew that if I didn't see the world, educate myself and do the things that fed and inspired me, then I would never do them, so I went to as many museums and art galleries as I could and met some wonderfully gifted artists. After two years away, I came back from Europe and got back to work. I formed Columbia Gas and Electric with a businessman I met on my travels, supplying natural gas and electricity to Cincinnati and its neighboring towns, and that's what I do now."

"Here or there?"

"Both. I was just in Cincinnati this past week, actually, or I would have called on you sooner."

I nodded, pretending not to care. I instinctively looked to his left hand. There was no ring and no telltale indent of a ring, but you could never be sure. There were a lot of things I'd do, wild things, reckless things—heck, I danced around on a stage almost naked most nights—but one thing I'd never do was get between a man and his wife. It was the utmost form of disrespect.

"And your family?" He was older than me, distinguished, and I wondered if he'd been married or had close family ties.

"You want to know everything, don't you?"

"Just curious."

"I'm not the most interesting subject at the table, you know. May I just say, I feel as if I've just won big at the races—all the money in the world. First I'm sitting in a dingy speakeasy downtown, marveling at how I managed to convince a stunning, poised and talented woman such as yourself to sit next to me at the booth. Next I'm pulling you toward me through the air, holding you in my arms, dancing with you, and now here I am, a week later, sitting across the table from you, enjoying a lovely evening."

"Don't think you can get out of telling me your life story that easily," I said. "I'm not immune to flattery, but you have to hold up your end of the bargain."

"Oh, I'll tell you everything you want to know, but I fear it's not nearly as entertaining as the story of your life thus far. Tell me a little something about you, so I don't put us both to sleep."

I gave him the truncated version of my journey to Broadway, not mentioning the parts I didn't like to dwell on myself. I told him of my family's move to Brooklyn, about my brothers and where I lived now.

I could tell from the way he spoke that he was worldly and well educated, and I had a sudden pang of concern that while he liked all that he'd seen of me so far, onstage and on the dance floor, if he really got to know me, I might be a big disappointment. I might not be fascinating enough for him, intellectual enough or cultured. While I'd always done well with vocal and dance training, I hadn't excelled in school. I was smart enough, or at least I thought so, but I'd been an impatient, restless student.

"I hope to visit Paris someday," I said. "Perhaps at the end of the season when I have a few weeks' break between the shows."

"I think you'd fit right in, it's a beautiful city. Maybe I could take you?"

I smiled. "We'll see."

We didn't go dancing that night. Instead we stayed at the restaurant talking until the wee hours, when we realized the only ones left were us and the barkeep, the poor guy struggling to keep his eyes open. Archie drove me back to my apartment and walked me all the way to my door. I felt like a teenager, my heart racing, the energy of our evening buzzing through me. He brought his face to mine, and our foreheads touched ever so slightly.

"Thank you for a lovely evening," he said quietly. I thought our lips would meet, I hoped they would, but instead he kissed me on the cheek and squeezed my hand. "I hope I can see you again soon," he said, and then he turned and walked away.

CHAPTER TEN

I'd never felt giddy excitement over a man before. You wouldn't know it from meeting me—my reputation for being loud and chatty and flirtatious seemed to precede me—but that was all just for fun. I liked to make people feel good about themselves, I always thought it darb that you could make someone's whole night just by giving them a little attention, and it gave me a sense of power to know that I had that ability. But as far as actually wanting to take anything further than a little harmless flirtation, no thank you. I didn't have the time or inclination. Ever since I let that studio executive put his hands all over me, and the rest, I'd been completely turned off by the idea of intimacy altogether. And yet here I was brushing my teeth, trying to select my clothes for rehearsal that morning, and my head was in the clouds thinking about Archie.

It had been three months since I'd written to my mother, an obligatory note letting her know we'd left Inwood and had moved to an apartment on Fifth Avenue. But I had the sudden urge to speak to her, or at least feel as though we were speaking. I grabbed a piece of paper and my fountain pen.

Dear Mother,

I hope you, Papa, George and Junior are all well, and that you've heard from Erwin in California.

I wanted to write and tell you how wonderfully things are going here at the theater.

I briefly considered telling her about getting cut from the *Follies* but reassuring her that I was receiving great reviews in the *Frolic*, but I didn't want to have to explain what the *Midnight Frolic* was yet. Besides, with a bit of luck they'd all seen the article in *The New York Times*.

Mr. Ziegfeld is treating us all very well—

That wasn't entirely true. I closed my eyes and shook my head free of his advances in the car—this was not where I wanted my mind to wander, and it certainly wasn't something I was going to share with my mother.

He insists on the very best costumes made of the finest materials.

My roommate, Ruthie—I know you think that the idea of a roommate is shocking but it's really not all that unusual among theater performers—anyway, Ruthie is just lovely and has become a true friend. She's shown me the ropes and has kept me out of mischief for the most part.

I wanted to cross out that last part—I didn't want her getting any ideas, not after the last time. I let my pen hover above the page for a moment. Nothing seemed to be coming out right. I wanted to tell her about Archie, that was the real reason I'd wanted to write in the first place, but something in me resisted. I wanted to share my excitement, my feelings, but I couldn't quite bring myself to do so. I missed her, and I missed the way we used to talk. It was as if by making the choices I'd made, I'd become unlovable.

I folded the letter and left it on the bed.

The girls in the dressing room were all chatting when I arrived. They'd seen the roses and the note and they'd all seen me get dolled up and leave with a handsome stranger the night before.

Someone whistled when I walked in, and Lillian, Gladys and Lara rushed over to me. Ruthie, who hadn't come home that night, looked over at me from her chair at the mirror and grinned.

"Tell us everything, Olive," Gladys said first. "Did you go all the way?"

"What?" I said, shocked. "No, I didn't go all the way."

"Well, did you go halfway?" she insisted.

"Give her a break, Gladys," Ruthie called out, turning back to the mirror to fix her face.

"Was he sweet?" Lillian asked. "Was he kind? He looked very handsome when he was waiting out front for you. We all went and had a peek."

"Yes, he was very sweet and very kind and very interesting, not a bore at all. I didn't get home until the sun was almost up and we didn't even go dancing."

"Did you see his bedroom at least?" Gladys asked.

"No, Gladys, I didn't, what is the matter with you? We went to dinner and stayed out talking until the restaurant kicked us out. He's a very respectable man."

"I know plenty of respectable men who'll have their way with you on a first dinner date, and send you home with a diamond bracelet."

"He's not like that," I said, wanting to be done with all their questioning, wanting to get back to my daydreaming of how it had been, just the two of us, closing down the restaurant, intent on learning as much as we could about each other.

"Come on, girls," Ruthie said, saving me, "we're all going to be late if we don't get going."

Every night that week I waited to hear from Archie again, but just like before he kept me waiting. The girls kept asking, but by the end of the week their questioning slowed. It didn't make any sense to me that he would act this way again. Why would a man express so much interest and then disappear? The whole thing made me uneasy.

And then Lillian, our former roommate, who had kept the apartment in Inwood and enlisted two other girls from the show as roommates, showed up on my doorstep before morning rehearsal unannounced. I wasn't particularly surprised—Lillian often preferred to stay in the living room at our place rather than trek all the way up to Inwood; it was closer to the theater, cleaner, and had an elevator that worked—but she usually made her decision late at night after a heavy evening of dancing.

"Do you need to drop off some things before we head to the

theater?" I asked as she walked in. She was petite, five feet two at most, and was a fantastic ballerina, her posture enviable, but today she looked hunched and stricken.

"Everything okay, Lils?" I asked. "Big night out?"

"I have to talk to you about something," she said. "Before we go to the theater."

"What is it?"

She walked past me to the living room, set down her things and went to the kitchen to pour herself a glass of water. "It's about the fella you've been going with."

"Archie? What about him?" It had been more than a week since I'd seen or heard from him, but I didn't want to let on.

"Well, you know Evelyn, the young girl who just joined this season as a pony, you know the one, blond, voluptuous." She held her hands in front of her bosoms and pretended to squeeze.

"Yes," I said. Oh God, don't tell me he'd been wooing her, too, how humiliating, poaching from under my very nose. What a fool to think he was interested in me and me alone.

"She's from Cincinnati, she just moved here recently, and she said he's very well-known in that town, very well-known," she emphasized. "In the papers weekly, apparently, comes from a wealthy family."

"Well, he built his own fortune, actually, but never mind . . . go on."

"You're not going to like this, and I'm only telling what I heard because the other girls have been talking about it in the dressing room and I don't want you to have them whispering behind your back, it's not right—"

"Just spit it out, Lillian," I snapped, furious already at whatever it was she was about to tell me.

"He's engaged."

"What?"

"To be married."

"To Evelyn?"

"No." She almost laughed and I shot her a look that made her straighten up. "No, not Evelyn, but she knows about him, and it's been all over the papers back in Cincinnati, some woman from his hometown."

"That can't be right," I said, confused, caught completely off guard. How could this be? Why would a man go to great lengths to find out where I perform, send me gifts, flowers, take me to dinner and want to know so much about me if he's already engaged to another woman? It made no sense.

"That's what I said, it seemed false, but she was adamant about it, she even brought in a newspaper clipping." Lillian reached into her pocket and unfolded a cutout. She looked at it as if she weren't sure she should show me.

"Just give it to me already," I said, standing up and taking it from her hands.

MISS MOYER AND MR. CARMICHAEL, PROMINENT
COMMUNITY PLAYERS, ANNOUNCE ENGAGEMENT

I looked at Lillian, who stood nervously watching me, then I read some more.

Miss Lutz of 62 McKnight St. last night proved a delightful hostess to the members of her bridge club in honor of Miss

Moyer, who announced her betrothal to Archibald Carmichael of this city.

A huge cake, topped with a miniature bride and bridegroom, formed the centerpiece of the attractive table. A dainty luncheon was served with an elaborate display of daffodils and snapdragons, which complemented the decorations . . .

"Repulsive." I crumpled the clipping in my hand and threw it across the room. "Who knows about this?"

Lillian looked worried and shrugged. "I'm not sure, there's been quite a bit of talk."

"To think that I wasted a perfectly good evening on him." I tried to smile, act as though I didn't care. "Thanks for telling me. Come on, let's not be late." I picked up my shoes, threw them in my bag and ushered her out the door.

I suffered through a week of silent humiliation. None of the girls at the theater said a word to me about it, though it was clear from the way they stopped talking about Archie completely that they'd all heard. When Ruthie brought it up back at the apartment, I told her it was old news and that it wasn't worth our precious time. But it felt awful to have things end so abruptly before they'd even really begun, without any proper explanation or apology.

I didn't go out after the shows at all that week; it was even hard to put on a big smile onstage. All I wanted to do was finish up my acts, go home and go to sleep. And I was furious at myself for feeling this way. I barely knew the guy, for God's sake. Three times, we'd met only three times, but each time had left an imprint on me, a swell of excitement and longing that was all new. And more than that,

I felt so ridiculous, embarrassed that I had put so much faith in this stranger, that I'd believed every word he said. How could he say those things and make me feel how I felt, and be carrying on with, not just carrying on, actually planning a life, with another woman. The whole thing made me sick.

During the intermission on Friday night's *Frolic* there was a knock at the dressing room door.

"Olive, you have a visitor." The stage manager popped his head in. "It's a Mr. Archibald Carmichael to see you."

There was a gasp. The girls in the room spun around, watching to see what I'd do. In some way I wanted to see him, to let him explain himself, at least give me some pathetic excuse to make him look ridiculous and make me feel better about it all. But I felt all eyes on me and I was no pushover.

"I'm not interested in seeing him," I said firmly. "Send him away."

A moment later there was another knock. "Flowers, Olive, and a note."

"I don't want those either, tell him to take them with him." I looked in the mirror and puckered my lips, checked my makeup and my hair. "The nerve of some men," I said loudly enough for everyone to hear.

CHAPTER ELEVEN

⬩◈⬩

After all the good press following the new *Midnight Frolic*, I'd been approached by Albolene cold cream to sit for one of their advertisements. The money was good, but more than anything, I was excited about appearing in magazines and maybe even a well-placed billboard.

After rehearsal, I freshened up and reapplied my makeup—even though I knew I'd be having it all redone when I arrived at the studio.

I was about to leave for my sitting when Howie popped his head into the dressing room. "Ziegfeld wants to see you."

"Now?" I checked the time. "Any idea what it's about?"

"He didn't say."

I hadn't been alone with Ziegfeld since the incident in his car. He'd commended the uptick in ticket sales at the late night performance in front of Howie and some of the other girls, and though he hadn't singled me out as the reason, I'd felt he was pleased with the new act. It was almost as if I hadn't slapped him across the face. I even started to wonder whether he'd really tried to kiss me, or had it simply been a friendly kiss good night; but no, as I recalled the details, it was far more than that. I took the elevator up to the sixth floor to meet him, and I wondered briefly if he might even be calling me up to apologize, though I quickly dismissed that idea, imagining instead a request to rejoin the *Follies*. Or maybe he wanted to discuss a new number in the *Frolic*—though surely Howie would have been part of that conversation.

"Mr. Ziegfeld," I said, standing the moment he opened his office door. "Nice to see you," I added slightly awkwardly.

"Miss Shine, lovely as always." Maybe it was all water under the bridge. "Thank you for seeing me. Please—" He motioned for me to enter his office, then he closed the door behind me and took a seat at his large dark wooden desk.

"How's the *Frolic* going?" he asked.

"I'd say it's going very well, Mr. Ziegfeld, don't you think? The audience seems very responsive."

"Yes, you're doing good work, and Howie tells me the flying act was your idea?"

"I just thought it would be a whole lot of fun. We should all be having fun at all times, don't you think, Mr. Ziegfeld, otherwise what's the point in it all?" I was trying to be upbeat and cheery. No need for bad feelings or hostility. It hadn't even happened.

He clasped his hands together. "I live to entertain," he said. "Actually, that's why I wanted to see you today. I have a proposition." He smiled.

I considered it a poor choice of words given our last encounter, but I didn't let on. "I'm intrigued."

"I'd like you to take the show on the road this August," he said. "I'm putting together a traveling *Follies* troupe this summer, and I'd like you to join them."

My stomach dropped. He was kicking me off the stage altogether. How could he? After I'd made the *Frolic* a big success in just a few weeks. Was he punishing me again for declining his advances?

"Well, what do you say, Miss Shine?"

"But I'm the lead in the *Frolic*," I said. Everyone knew it was the second-rate girls who made up the traveling troupes—he saved the very best for Manhattan. "You said yourself it was my act that had improved the sales."

"I don't believe I said that, Miss Shine. Besides, you'd be one of the principals on the road."

"But what about the—"

"We can find another girl to fill your shoes here, it's just for a few weeks."

He was making light of this all, acting blasé, but I could feel the weight of it. Once some other girl took over my role, I would be replaceable. But what could I do? Everything came down to Ziegfeld. He could kick me out at any time for any reason at all. I had to please him. I knew that if I didn't agree, he could simply remove me from the whole show—this would be a reason to get rid of me.

"Well, as long as I have a place in the *Frolic* when I get back...."

"Of course," he said, smiling broadly, and I had no idea if I could believe him.

"Then this sounds like a great adventure." I slapped on a smile. "Where will we go? Chicago, Los Angeles, Miami?"

"No need to cross the country. In fact, you'll be staying in New York—this show is going to the Adirondacks."

"The Daddy-what?"

"The Adirondacks. My dear, haven't you heard of the Great Camps?"

I shook my head.

"Ah, what a treat you're in for. It's about three hundred miles directly north of here. The wealthiest industrialists of our time escape to the North Woods by their private railcars, where they have built sprawling, timbered getaways along secluded lakeshores. It's quite elegant."

"But camping?" I was bewildered by this proposition and that Ziegfeld would even toy with the idea of sending us there.

"That's what they like to call it. When I first accompanied Mr. J. P. Morgan to his beloved Camp Uncas, he described it as a rustic compound and made it sound as if we were going to be roughing it in the wild. But I assure you that's not the case, they're elaborate estates, rustic luxury. Anyway you'll see for yourself. You'll stay three or four nights at each of the camps, starting with the Belmonts at the Pines Camp, then the Morgan family's Camp Uncas, Camp Sagamore, and Camp Santanoni. It will take a few days to get there and a few to get back."

I must have still had a look of shock and bewilderment on my face because he continued to reassure me that whatever I was thinking was wrong.

"Miss Shine, you will be well taken care of. There will be valets, chambermaids, chefs, butlers, a governess, a laundress and guides to take you on chaperoned walks. There'll even be staff taxidermists on hand should you care to hunt and take home your prized hunting trophies."

I wrinkled my face at the idea, then remembered not to in his presence.

"They escape to the wilderness for nature and relaxation and they invite guests to indulge in the same luxury, but what they need, what they desperately need once everyone has made the trek into the woods and they've been out on the lake and they've explored the great outdoors, what they need at the end of a long day, my dear, is to be entertained. There's nothing else out there to do. You will be everything to them. They need you."

Later, when sitting for my portrait, I was distracted and uneasy, but I tried not to let it show. The slogan was going to be "Up All Night? Do What the Ziegfeld Girls Do and Use Albolene Cold Cream for Beautiful Skin in the Morning."

I felt like a fraud: by the time this advertisement came out I wouldn't even be performing on a proper stage. I'd be relegated to some campground in the middle of nowhere. My hope of having my father see my face in Times Square was quickly replaced by a feeling of defeat. First Archie, engaged! And now this. Every setback made me feel that my parents could be right about failing, that soon I'd be used up, and then what?

The photographer had me change into a decadent beaded silver dress, silver gloves and a jeweled headband. They curled and pinned up my hair similar to how I liked to style it, mimicking the bob that I wanted so badly but had resisted since Ziegfeld preferred his girls to keep their hair long and feminine. I looked quite fabulous when they were done with me, and in front of the camera I was able to put away some of that disappointment. I had to. I'd make the most of this adventure just as I said I would. I was tired of being told what to do and how to do it—I could have stayed home for that. Each time the camera popped and smoked, with each momentary blinding flash, I became more determined to turn this into something better, just as I'd always tried to do in the past. With each shot I told myself I was taking a step up that giant Ziegfeld staircase, a step in the right direction, wherever that might be. One thing I'd always been good at was having fun and making sure those around me were having a good time, too. If that meant shipping off to the woods for the summer, then so be it.

After the sitting, I popped into a hair salon on West Thirty-fourth Street. I took out the pins and let my long dark hair hang around my shoulders one last time. I rarely ever wore it down like this, and seeing it made me feel weighed down, old-fashioned and owned. I suddenly couldn't wait to be rid of it.

"Chop it all off, please. I'd like a bob."

"Are you sure, madam?" the hairdresser asked with a look of concern, as if I were his own daughter about to sever ties with her girlish ways.

"Never been more sure," I said.

He shrugged. "As you wish." He placed a book in front of me and opened it to a page that showed three different styles of the modern bob. "Which one?"

"None of these." I closed the book and handed it back to him. "I want my own style, something that suits just me. I'm thinking short and sleek and with a fringe straight across my forehead. How does that sound?"

"Whatever you like, madam." And he started to snip, long thick clumps of hair falling to my feet like ropes being untied and releasing me. I'd give up my place on Broadway if I had to, I'd go to those Great Camps that Ziegfeld spoke of, I'd do it all, but he should know I'd be doing it my way.

CHAPTER TWELVE

As soon as Ruthie heard about the traveling troupe to the Adirondacks, she marched right up to Mr. Ziegfeld's office and asked to be cast.

"You're mad," I told her. "Off your rocker. Why would you want to leave Manhattan to be stuck out in the sticks all summer long? Think of everything you're going to miss, all those performances, all those parties, and dancing, and long summer nights."

"Ha!" she laughed. She was lying in the middle of our living room on a thick white sheepskin rug that one of her admirers had sent her. It was her favorite place for helping her back pain. She used to prefer the cold hard floor, but now she could relieve her pain in luxury. I was draped on the white sofa we'd bought on credit when we first moved in, just like the rest of the furniture. We'd planned on paying it all back as soon as we got our next few paychecks, but now with my performances cut, we decided it could wait.

"Why do you laugh?" I said.

"Because you obviously weren't paying attention last summer. It's hot as hell, and it stinks, especially in August. Everyone's off at their summer escape, and all you can think about is getting invited to Maine or Long Island, Westport, or, if you're really lucky, the Adirondacks."

"I don't think that sounds lucky at all. In fact, I'd choose any one of those places over the Daddy Long Backs any day of the week. At least those other places have beaches. Isn't that what summer is for? Sun and sand and swimming costumes?"

"Oh, Olive," she said, stretching her arms above her head and pointing her toes, "just wait until you get there, you'll feel very different about it all, I promise you."

I sighed, trying to get comfortable with the idea. "What would I even pack? What do people wear?"

"Well, your costumes for performances."

"Of course."

"Evening gowns for dinners," she said. "These camps may be in the middle of the forest, but from what I hear the evenings are still a formal affair. And then swimsuits and leisure wear for lakeshore activities—oh, and some sort of boots for hiking."

"Hiking?" I scoffed. "Do you really envision us hiking?"

"When in Rome . . ." She smiled. "And I imagine it gets cold there at night."

"I'll bring my mink, then."

She laughed. "Not that cold. A raincoat would suffice."

I nodded, thinking it through. I was definitely bringing my mink.

———

The luggage porters took our brand-new Crouch & Fitzgerald luggage from the taxi and loaded it onto a cart at Grand Central Terminal. Thank God, because as beautiful as those cases looked with their wooden framing, cloth exterior and shiny brass buckles, they were as heavy as a horse. Ruthie had taken one look at my dented metal case and insisted that we upgrade immediately. She was coming along; her wish to join the troupe had been granted.

"You never know who you might meet, and these tatty old things are sending all the wrong messages about who you are and how you live your life. Come on," she'd insisted, "we'll put it on credit."

It did feel awfully nice to know that those beautiful cases were ours, and I looked at them lovingly as the porter pulled the cart toward the station.

"This way," Ruthie said, grabbing my hand and weaving us through the early morning hustle of men striding away from the tracks and out into the city. I watched them all heading in the same direction and felt a pull to go with them.

"It's all going to be here when you get back," Ruthie said, giving me a little tug. "Manhattan is not going anywhere."

Out on the platform, we stood trying to catch our bearings. One black train car after another.

"What car does it say on our tickets?" I asked Ruthie, assuming she knew her way around.

"This way, ma'am." The luggage porter ushered us to a car toward the end of the train.

As we drew closer, we saw Howie and the girls waiting for us. They whooped and hollered as we got close. We were all dressed to the nines for our ride to the Adirondacks. We'd been given strict instructions that we were representing the *Ziegfeld Follies* from the minute we stepped out of our homes to the minute we got back. We were "the entertainment" at all times, not only when we were onstage. We should expect the press to take our pictures, and sure enough, we were approached by a photographer before we even climbed aboard.

"Miss Shine, you're leaving the *Frolic*?" a newspaperman asked.

"Just for a short time," I said. "My talents are needed elsewhere."

"Where are you going?"

I looked at Ruthie. I could never remember the name of the damned place.

"The mountains," I said.

"The Adirondacks?" he called out.

"That's right—the Great Camps await." We climbed into the car, and I didn't know what the other passengers must have thought, but we were certainly a loud and cheery bunch to put up with.

"Not bad," Ruthie said once we took our seats. "It's only a few cars away from first class."

As the train pulled away from the station, my stomach clenched—I was anxious about leaving the *Midnight Frolic* behind yet slightly intrigued about the adventure ahead. And then there was Archie. It felt strange to leave town without seeing him again. I suppose I thought I'd bump into him somewhere or that he'd make another attempt to see me, to explain himself. But nothing. It was as regretful as it was infuriating. I felt so foolish. I tried to push the thought of him out of my head, but it was hard to let those feelings go. Maybe this trip to the mountains was a blessing, a welcome and necessary distraction from the humiliation I felt at letting myself get carried away.

As we settled into our seats on the train, everyone in our group seemed to have a nervous energy about them. It was only seven fifteen in the morning but by eight thirty, we were already getting rowdy and one of the girls started singing "The Best Things in Life Are Free," quietly at first. Some of the other passengers shushed her, but that just motivated the rest of us to join in. By ten A.M. we were all getting into it, and Ruthie pulled me with her into the aisle, serenading me with "Ain't She Sweet" in a deep, manly voice. I played along, dancing between the seats and down the aisle. In no time almost everyone was up, dancing, singing and being rambunctious. The conductor came through and told us to quiet down, which we did for a few moments, but then we started singing to him, and we just got louder as soon as he left.

Word must have traveled because riders from other cars came down to ours to see the spectacle for themselves, and that just seemed to spur us on—the growing audience feeding our desire.

Just before noon Howie passed Ruthie a flask, and she took a swig, then passed it to me. "Hey, looks like we have some admirers," she whispered, nodding to a couple of gents smiling in our direction who looked as if they'd come from the first-class car.

Ruthie gave them the eyes and one of them held up a martini glass as if to say, "Bravo!" I was surprised to see them serving that kind of hospitality even in first class—this was a public place, after all, and the rail service could be shut down for serving hooch on board.

"I'm intrigued," Ruthie said. "Let's go and say hello." She took my hand and sauntered up the aisle to meet them.

"Good afternoon," one of the gentlemen said, kissing Ruthie's hand and then mine. "We heard there were some beautiful ladies making this train ride a heck of a lot more enjoyable in car number seven."

"We're just practicing our numbers," I said.

"We're Ziegfeld girls," Ruthie added.

"Yes, you are!" the other gent said, raising his eyebrows. "Say, why don't you pay us a visit in our car? It's not too shabby and there's more where this came from." He took a sip of his martini.

"Okay," Ruthie said. "We'd love to, wouldn't we, Olive?"

"Sounds like the berries."

The gents went first, one opening the door to the next car and the other holding open the door to ours. I felt the rush of fresh, cool air as we crossed over into first class. We'd been so preoccupied with all the singing and dancing that I'd barely noticed the lush green trees lining the Hudson River outside the windows. Steamboats were chugging along in both directions, and it was surprising to see such beauty just a few hours outside of Manhattan. I'd grown so accustomed to the buildings and the concrete and the bright lights of the city.

"Don't jump," the gent said as I stood between cars for a while, taking it all in.

"It's just so beautiful." I stepped in through the next doorway.

First class was quite an improvement over our standard train car. There were dining tables and booths, and people were playing cards and sipping tea. It looked ever so elegant and civilized, though not nearly as fun as ours. We walked through two more cars, one dining and lounge car, and then we reached what seemed to be the end. I looked around, confused. They held open the next door.

"There's more?" Ruthie asked.

"Isn't this where the conductor sits?" I asked.

"We're riding in our colleague's private car," the first chap said, a little too proudly. "He owns it." Geez, these guys really seemed to want to impress us, and that type of thing always left me cold. "You won't want to travel any other way after you experience this."

It was like stepping into a Moroccan jewelry box. Mahogany wood lined the walls, with a plush floral carpet underfoot. A set of deep red velvet chairs embroidered with bursts of petals, and fuchsia cushions with silk tassels, formed a cozy reading nook. Above it was an intricately carved wooden panel creating a canopy. Music played gently, and when I peered farther into the car I realized it came from a small live band set up in the corner. What kind of place was this? I marveled. I'd been transported to some exotic location in the Far East.

"Come on," the men said, eagerly checking our faces for approval, "we'll introduce you to the host."

I could barely take a step without fixating on yet another detail—the ceiling was painted in red and green paisley—I never would have imagined a train car could look like this.

We were ushered to a green velvet two-seater positioned against another wood-carved backdrop—this time lattice and Buddhas and suns and moons, and I don't know what else, were all carved into the mahogany sculpture. I tried to compose myself and not appear so struck by the opulent decor.

"Ah, here he comes, our generous host." I unglued my eyes from my surroundings and turned to see the man walking toward us from the other side of the train car. "Miss Olive, and Miss Ruthie," they continued, "please meet Mr. Archibald Carmichael."

"Archie?" I said, shocked, though my face mustn't have revealed it because he smiled broadly, as if he couldn't be happier to see me.

"I was wondering when you'd look up and recognize me. It's so lovely to see you again."

"What are *you* doing here?" I said abruptly, then took a deep breath. I refused to let him see that he'd hurt me. "This is so unexpected!" I gestured to the luxurious car.

"It's quite a place, isn't it?"

Ruthie was looking at me nervously, her eyes pleading with me to keep my calm, and the gents who'd invited us seemed even more perplexed.

"So, you two know each other, it appears," one said, trying to look cheerful, though more likely regretful that he hadn't set his eyes on another dancer back in car number seven.

"Yes," I said. "We've met. Back in the city."

"I'm so glad you're here, Olive," he said, taking my hands in his. "Traveling to the mountains, I presume?"

I pulled my hands away, momentarily stunned; I couldn't think where I was going. It was rare for me to lose my tongue or be flustered like this, but seeing him again had thrown me completely off balance.

"We're going to the Adirondacks," Ruthie jumped in. "We've been invited to perform at a few of the Great Camps—Camp

Sagamore, Camp Uncas, Camp Santanoni," Ruthie said with a flourish. "We're starting off at the Pines."

"Yes, the Pines Camp," Archie said, looking pleased with himself. "That's where I'm staying, with Anne."

Anne? The audacity!

"What a treat for you," I said. "Well, I suppose we'll see you there." I turned to head back to our car. "Thanks for showing us around, fellas. We should get back to our friends, they'll be needing us for the finale." I tried to laugh.

"Won't you stay?" Archie reached for my hand again, but I pulled it away, more abruptly this time.

"Why, yes." Ruthie stared at me. "We'd be honored to keep you company for a while."

I glared at her, furious that she wasn't catching on to my desire to leave. Reluctantly, for Ruthie's sake only, I took a seat.

"Say, do you gents have any more of those martinis lying around?" Ruthie asked.

"Sure thing, there's a stocked bar back this way," one of them said, pointing, and Ruthie walked off arm in arm with both of them toward the other end of the car, leaving me sitting on the green velvet, where Archie joined me.

A tall, slim man in a black suit appeared immediately at our side and brought a small table to us, placed a white napkin on top and asked what we'd like to drink.

"A coffee, please," I said, wanting to keep my wits about me.

"I'll have the same," Archie said, "with a shot of brandy."

When the man left, Archie turned to me and smiled, but I looked out the window. I didn't know what to do. The way he was behaving, his gentle demeanor—relaxed and seemingly happy to see me again—suggested that he didn't know that I knew about his engagement. Should I even give him the satisfaction of knowing the reason for my coldness? He thought he'd got away with having a fiancée in one state and a show girl in another. But now that we were going to be at the same camp, all would be revealed, and he didn't even seem to care.

"So, you own all this?" I asked.

"Yes, for almost a year. It required a bit of work, but I think it's looking pretty smart now, and it's running smoothly too."

"How do you end up owning a train?" I said with disdain. He didn't seem to notice.

"Not the whole train, just the train car—they hook it up to the back of the commercial trains and take us wherever they're going. We can switch tracks and hook onto other trains at various points along the way, so we can get places faster. It's more direct and it's a much more comfortable ride. I use it to go back and forth to Cincinnati quite a bit, but this is only my second time taking it to the Adirondacks."

"Oh." I attempted to sound disinterested.

"Olive, I'm sure you've been busy, but I haven't been able to stop thinking about you," he said. "Ever since our dinner."

"Is that so?" I said sarcastically.

"You're upset."

"Well, usually, my suitors don't simply disappear after a first date."

"I'm so sorry. I tried to send flowers to the theater, during my last visit, I tried to see you, but I received no response. I thought it was you who'd disappeared on me."

"Ha!" I said.

"I apologize, I was only in town for two days. I've been traveling back and forth to Cincinnati and I was hoping that I would see you this time in New York, but this trip came up, and I promised to bring some of my employees and some of Anne's guests in my train car."

I couldn't believe he was throwing this Anne woman's name around like this. Was he trying to make me jealous? He could at least attempt to be discreet. I tried not to take the bait, I wouldn't let him see that I cared, but I could feel my blood boiling.

He reached over to take my hand again, but I swatted it away and picked up the coffee the waiter had carefully placed on the table, along with some biscotti.

"Oh, Olive," he said, laughing a little. He probably thought I was being ridiculous, and maybe I was, but all this rejection was really starting to hurt, first my family all but disowning me, then Ziegfeld kicking me out of the *Follies,* and now this. I stood up abruptly.

"I don't believe you for a second," I said, louder than I'd planned, but the mention of this Anne woman infuriated me, so I kept on. "Secondly, I don't know who you think you're dealing with—maybe you think I'm just some frilly show girl who doesn't know better. Maybe you think you can woo me with talk of Paris. Well, I assure you I am more than that, and I do not appreciate an engaged man trying to seduce me."

Suddenly the train car was silent. Everyone had stopped what they were doing to observe the row. If I showed him up in front of his friends, his colleagues, even his damned fiancée, then that was his concern, not mine.

"I have far more respect for myself, and for womankind, than to go around stealing another woman's future husband. It's gauche, and it's not my style. There are plenty of true gentlemen in New York City and I don't need to waste my time on you." I turned to leave. "Ruthie," I called out, "I'm done here," and I strode down the train car back the way I came. I pulled on the door but was astounded by how heavy it was. Those men had made it seem so easy earlier. I pushed down on the handle and pulled, but the weight of it or the wind outside made it impossible to open.

Archie came up behind me. "May I?" he asked.

"You may not." I continued to tug on the door, putting all my weight into it.

"Well, then please let me explain. Surely you'll give a man that courtesy."

"There's nothing to explain," I said, fuming, not just at him but at myself, too. I hadn't anticipated caring this much. And I certainly hadn't expected to let it show. My cool and collected manner had utterly deserted me.

"Okay," he said, "I'll leave you to it."

I kept pulling on the door, a little shocked that he let me give up on him so easily. After a few moments, his butler or waiter or whoever he was came over and assisted me and I marched back to car number seven, where our crew was drunker and louder than before I left.

———

I was rattled. I felt as though I'd been dancing with a bouquet of balloons all around me in one of my *Frolic* numbers and all of them had exploded at once, leaving me half-naked and vulnerable with no prop for my act, stunned, with an audience staring back at me, expecting me to go on and perform.

The whole thing stung. How disappointing and, worst of all, how stupid I felt. He'd lured me in with his good looks, his dark, seductive eyes, his confidence and sense of adventure. The thrill I'd felt when he'd pulled me toward him on the dance floor, the anticipation of performing those next few nights with a hint of a chance that he might be in the audience, watching me. I'd allowed myself to imagine what it could be. I'd startled myself imagining a second invitation to dinner and dancing, a third; he'd hinted at travel and I'd pictured it, the two of us setting sail for London, visiting Paris. This was something the other girls did, swooning over men they barely knew, sounding foolish as they spoke of marriage—but not me, I never had such ridiculous thoughts. I'd never met a man who could hold my interest, let alone one I could picture falling asleep next to night after night.

I must have dozed off for a few moments, because when I opened my eyes Ruthie was back in our train car, sitting next to me. I took one look at her and then pretended to go back to sleep, shoving my face into the pillow I'd brought and leaning against the window.

"Olive, don't be sore with me. That Archie fella may not have been a match for you, but my two guys were a heck of a lot of fun. You should have stayed, I would have shared." She was trying to make me laugh, but I was too tired and still upset about the whole encounter with Archie. She should have left with me, showed support. But then again, why should my disgruntlement with a man spoil her fun?

"I was trying to get you to stay so you could hear what he had to say. I think you needed to hear it from him," Ruthie went on. "Did he at least say sorry?"

"No." I knew I shouldn't be angry with her, but I couldn't shake it. "No, he didn't, he acted as if he'd done nothing wrong. And now I'm going to have to see him again at the camp. Good Lord, could things get any worse?"

"It'll be okay." She wrapped her arms around me and snuggled in, using me as a pillow. "We're only at the Pines for a few days, and you, more than anyone, know how to have a good time no matter what the circumstances."

"That's true," I said, looking out the window. "I am pretty good at that."

That night we stayed at a lodge in the middle of nowhere and the next morning a stagecoach collected us and took us to a steamboat that would cruise through the Eckford lakes for the rest of the day. I had glanced around for Archie as we left the train and again on the steamer, but his group must have taken an alternate route.

The party started up again on the *Horicon II*—a handsome side-wall steamer with a huge paddle wheel on one side that slapped the water and propelled us north. Others from the train were also heading to parts of the Adirondacks, and as we all piled onto the boat people seemed to settle into either the covered furnished salon with open sides or the top deck. The sky was a beautiful clear blue, and it felt surprisingly freeing to be out on the water, in the fresh air.

Our group settled on the lounge chairs outside on the deck, and

I realized that when we traveled together—twenty women who weren't afraid to break into song or dance at a moment's notice—we could draw quite a crowd. And we did.

One fella, Andrew Stark, made himself comfortable in an adjacent lounge chair and paid me particular interest. I was indifferent at first, still brooding over my encounter with Archie, but after a few glasses of champagne mimosas I began to let loose like the rest of the girls, allowing myself to flirt with him a little, letting him boost my dented ego. I introduced him to our crew of Ziegfeld girls, and he mentioned he'd seen our show many times.

"I'll be staying at Camp Santorini most of the time, my brother-in-law's camp, you should come on over and let me take you for a spin on his boat."

"I just might," I said. "We'll be there performing at some point, so perhaps our days will overlap."

"But I'm at the Pines Camp for the first few days," he said. "I'll be visiting friends there."

"Me too," I said, excited that I'd remembered the name. "At least I think that's our first stop. There are so many Pines and Camps and strange-sounding names, it's hard to keep track." Howie was getting the girls riled up again, planning a singing competition on the main deck, and between the champagne mimosas and this gentleman's attention, I was starting to feel a whole lot better.

"Come on, darlin'," he said, "let's head downstairs to the lower deck where we can get a little privacy."

"Oh, I don't know," I said. "I'm comfortable here."

"But it's so loud, I can barely hear your sweet voice."

At his suggestion, I linked my arm through his and took the

staircase down to the lower deck, closer to the water, where the steam engine made a loud shushing sound and the rhythm of the paddle wheel drowned out the noisy patrons on the upper deck. I was feeling warm and friendly, but I could tell he was a fair bit more lit up than I was.

"You are a hot little number," he said as soon as we were at the back of the boat. There was no one else down there, and he leaned me against the railing. I let him kiss me. I needed to feel someone's warmth and wished his urgency would soothe me. He tasted like gin. He held my head in one hand and slipped the other around my rear, pressing me into the railing. It reminded me of that night on the West Coast, the recklessness in me coming to the surface. I could tell what his intentions were, and for a split second I wanted that power, to give him whatever he needed. I wanted this stranger to need me, to desire me so badly. But the railing was digging into my back and his body was pushing hard against mine, and just as fast as it crossed my mind to give in, I pushed him away.

"Steady on there," I said, twisting my way out of his overly eager embrace. "We just met."

"I'm sorry, doll, you got me all worked up all of a sudden, you talking about your dancing like you did, and you being so damn pretty."

"That's no way to treat a lady you barely know."

"I'm sorry, here, why don't you sit down, take a load off." He motioned to the wooden benches flanked alongside both sides of the boat. It was far less plush down on the lower deck, and I had a sudden concern that no one from my group had noticed I'd left or knew where I was. He had his back turned to me and was fidgeting with his trousers.

"I'm going to head back up," I said, walking toward the staircase. "And you should probably lay off that gin."

"Hey, wait. Please—we were just starting to have some fun," he called out behind me. "I'm sorry. Come on back, please. . . ."

What the hell was it with these men? What did they all take me for? I reeled at the thought of what had transpired in just a few minutes, going from flirting and light kissing to him pushing for something more. I wanted to curse him, but as I walked back upstairs, I had to admit to myself that I'd wanted him, too, even if just for a second, I'd wanted to feel something, anything.

The last few hours on the boat seemed long and arduous after that initial encounter, but fortunately that Andrew fella stayed out of my way.

That night we stayed at the Blue Mountain House—a log cabin set up for travelers just passing through. It was a quaint and simple place, but it gave us a chance to get some much-needed sleep after two full days of travel. Sharing a bed with Ruthie, just after we turned out the lights, I finally gave in and asked her what I'd wanted to ask all day. "Did he say anything after I left yesterday?"

"Who?"

"Archie. Who do you think?"

"Well, geez, Olive, you left his train car in such a huff that I wouldn't expect you to care what he thought of you."

"I don't care. But did he say anything or not?"

"No. Not a word. No one spoke of it. I don't think they dared after that scene you caused."

"He tried to woo me under false pretenses," I said adamantly.

"And you think that's unusual?"

"I thought it would be for this particular man."

"You hardly know him."

"I thought I did."

"Oh, honey . . ." She took my hand under the covers and squeezed it. "I'm sorry. We'll find you a good guy, okay? I promise you."

"I don't want a good guy," I said. "They bore the pants off me."

"Okay, we'll find you a bad boy, one of those you like from the Village. That'll get your mind off him for a while."

"I don't want one of those either."

"Well, what is it that you do want, huh?"

I thought about it for a while, and the question perplexed me. "I really don't know."

Ruthie gave me a hushed murmur; she was already almost dreaming.

---◇---

CHAPTER THIRTEEN

---◇---

Altogether it took two days and two nights to arrive at the Pines Camp. The final stretch of road was too rough for a car ride, so we were transferred to a couple of horse-drawn carriages for the last hour. As we bounced around on the hard wooden benches, I was kicking myself for agreeing to such a ridiculous journey. But then, as we got closer, it began to smooth out into a more groomed path.

At around five o'clock we knew we were close because lanterns were being set up as we crossed the guest bridge. Everything was so still and quiet except for the sound of the coach wheels, the harnesses and the horses' hooves striking gravel. Trail guides waved to us from the side of the road, and I waved back.

"What are they doing?" I asked Eugene, a guide who'd been sent to collect us from the cars.

"They've been waiting for us, so they can let the hosts know we're arriving," he said. "They run back to the camp now to alert them."

As the horses pulled us up over the hill, the clusters of pine trees opened up a little, letting the late afternoon sun stream in, and the camp appeared: quaint log cabins set on the shore of glittering Osgood Pond with a croquet lawn as its centerpiece. When we stepped out of the carriage, the smell of wood fires wafted up from the lodge and I felt a deep, healing peace from our surroundings.

"Oh my," I whispered, almost speechless. "I wasn't expecting this."

A woman in her early fifties approached our carriages wearing trousers, a collared shirt and a cardigan, looking completely relaxed.

"Welcome to the Pines," she said. "We're all so excited that you're here."

"Thank you for having us," Ruthie said. The rest of the girls were the quietest I'd ever heard them—looking around in awe at the towering trees, the cottages dotted throughout the property, separated by bushes and pathways, each cottage glowing like something out of a fairy-tale book. All thoughts of mud and bugs and sleeping in tents immediately dissipated.

"I know the journey up is treacherous, but I hope you're feeling all right now that you're here."

"We're thrilled to be here—it's been a real adventure," I said.

"Well, that's what it's all about, isn't it?" She linked her arm through mine and led us toward the cabins.

"I'm Olive Shine," I said. "Really, this is magical."

"Oh, you're Olive!" she said. "I haven't had the pleasure of seeing you perform, but I've heard so much about you." I smiled, wondering what she'd heard. "I'm going to send someone up to each of your cabins to show you where things are and make sure you're comfortable," she said, turning back so everyone could hear her. "I want you all to have a chance to rest after your long journey, then at eight o'clock we'll be serving dinner in the main dining room. Will that give you enough time to dress? Does anyone need me to send one of my maids early to help you get ready?"

We all shook our heads. "Gentlemen, do you need someone to come and brush your hair?" Ruthie asked Howie and Wallace, laughing.

"I think we'll be all right," Howie said, shaking his head.

"There's a seamstress on the property, should you need anything mended while you're here. A lost button, a dropped hem, ironing, anything you need, you just let us know and it'll be attended to. Tomorrow when you've had a chance to settle in and take in some of the scenery and activities, I'll show you the rehearsal space and the stage, and our butler, Mr. Ward, will go over the performance schedule."

"Thank you," I said, grateful for the fresh air, the smell of pines, and her hospitality. "I'm so sorry," I said as she delivered Ruthie and me to our cabin, "I didn't catch your name."

"Oh, my goodness, I was so excited to meet you, I completely forgot to properly introduce myself. Where are my manners? I'm Anne."

"You're Anne?" I said, admittedly not careful at all in hiding my surprise. She was so much older than I'd expected her to be, beautiful and generous, but I suppose I'd expected Archie's fiancée to be more youthful, more like, well, me.

"I am," she said softly—if she'd noticed my shock, she didn't let it show. "My husband, Raymond, is inside with the other gentlemen, they're all telling stories about their day out on the trails. It's probably best you meet them when they've had a chance to freshen up and dress for dinner."

"Of course," I said, stunned. Our hostess was the Anne whom Archie had mentioned on the train, but Anne was already married. I suddenly felt very foolish.

"Remember, anything you need, just ring this"—she reached inside the cabin door and pulled on a string that rang a small bell— "and you'll be attended to." She'd barely even finished her sentence before a young man in brown trousers and a white button-down shirt stood at our side.

"Yes, Madam Belmont?" He stood head down, waiting for her request.

"Oh, nothing at the moment, thank you, I'm just showing the girls around."

"Yes, madam," he said, and in an instant he was gone.

From the outside the cabins looked rustic and modest, and the interior was designed in the same spirit: wood-planked walls, bed frames made from knotted tree limbs, a stone fireplace. But upon closer inspection, I realized that nothing had been left to chance. When I lay back on the bed, it felt as though I were sinking into a pillow of the finest duck feathers wrapped in the softest, most luxurious cotton sheets you might find in a fancy hotel.

"Look at this," Ruthie called out excitedly from another room.

I jumped up and found her standing on the screened-in porch. A huge tree trunk erupted from the ground and went straight out the roof, the rest of the porch and its furnishings having been designed artfully around it. A curved two-seater with a matching curved footstool wrapped around the tree's base. I sat in it and admired a clear view straight out onto the lake, the boathouse just to the left and down a short pathway from where I sat.

"Do you think they just didn't want to cut down the tree?" Ruthie asked. "So they built around it?"

"Looks like it," I said. "It's grand to be staying here. I thought we'd be in the workers' cabins or something."

"Maybe these *are* the workers' cabins." Ruthie grinned. "What's this?" On a table at the far side of the porch there was a welcome basket with a bottle of wine, chocolates and a book about the area. Behind that, there was an enormous bouquet of red roses with a card. Ruthie picked it up. "It's for you."

I jumped up and took it from her.

Dear Olive,

I feel terrible about our encounter on the train, and it seems we've had a misunderstanding. Please can we find some time this evening to talk? I do hope you'll forgive me for upsetting you.

Please accept my apologies.

Je ne peux pas arrêter de penser à toi.

Amour de ton plus grand admirateur,

Archie

"Well, what does it say?" Ruthie was grabbing at the card, bouncing around me like a madwoman.

"I have no idea," I said, holding it above my head out of her reach.

"What do you mean you have no idea?" she said, still jumping.

"I don't know—it's in French."

"French?" She looked confused, and I handed it to her, resuming my place at the tree.

"Je ne pew paz arr-et-air dey pen-ser a toy," she read aloud. "I don't know what it says either, but he sure sounds stuck on you."

"Well, maybe he is, but unfortunately for him he's got himself stuck in another engagement."

She plucked one of the roses from the bouquet and inhaled deeply. "How on earth does anyone get their hands on a bouquet of roses like this in the mountains, anyway?"

"I suppose if you have enough money you can get your hands on anything you want."

Getting dressed in evening attire for dinner felt strange and unnecessary in the middle of the forest, but when we left our cabin the lanterns had been lit, creating a magical glow, and our guide, Eugene, was waiting to escort us to the main lodge. We met with the rest of our group on the way over, and as soon we entered the main room, Anne applauded and drew everyone's attention to us.

"Oh, how wonderful you're all here," she said. "Ladies and gentlemen, please welcome our latest guests, the wonderful and talented Ziegfeld girls." About twenty other guests turned and joined her in a round of applause. "We have the pleasure of their company at dinner this evening—please get to know one another."

I surveyed the room—magnificent tall ceilings with dark wood beams, an enormous wood fireplace set with grey stone that took up the entire back wall. The room was heavily decorated with taxidermy, including an owl, wings spread as if it were about to take flight and pick its prey from among us, and a giant grizzly bear keeping watch over the room.

"Menacing, isn't it?" Anne said as she walked over. "I shot him myself while traveling through the West." She had a gleam in her eye and I couldn't quite tell if she was serious. I tried to picture her, now in full evening dress, holding a gun and facing down a grizzly.

"This is my husband, Raymond," she said, looking up at the tall man beside her.

"So kind of you to come all this way," he said with a noticeable lisp that was endearing and somehow welcoming. I'd been expecting the owners of these properties to be snooty, but so far that wasn't the case at all. "We can't wait to see your performances— what a welcome change it will be." He then introduced Howie and the girls to a few of the trail guides who'd be wilderness companions for the guests over the next few days, leading hikes, taking the men shooting and educating anyone who wanted to know about the area. Raymond explained that the guides served as professors of the wilderness, friends of the great outdoors, and they would be with us at all social occasions, during dinner and after, so we could continue the conversation into the evening. They'd grown up in the area and knew the terrain, the weather and the hunting patterns inside and out and were therefore treated with high regard. Raymond and the guides showed us around the room, pointing out different hunting trophies.

"Archibald has been eagerly awaiting your arrival," Anne said in a hushed tone, gently keeping me back from the tour. I tried not to act surprised at the mention of his name, or that he'd discussed me with her, but I casually glanced around the room. "He's in the far corner by the piano. Don't be too tough on him, he can come off as a big shot because he's so respected on the business side of things, but deep down he's a real softy." She smiled and I had to bite my tongue. I was not about to engage in this conversation with our gracious host. "Not the kind of softy that'll be bouncing a baby on his knee, mind you, he doesn't slow down enough for that kind of life, as you probably know, and he tells me you two are cut from the same cloth."

"Well, I'm a show girl," I said a little roughly, though I knew my sharpness should be directed toward Archie and not Anne. "We don't tend to have those domesticated bones in our bodies."

"He tells me you're a city girl, but, boy, I hope you'll feel the privacy out here is worth every minute of that long journey. Manhattan can be exhausting, don't you think?"

"Sometimes," I said, knowing full well that her busy social life would be entirely different from mine. I thrived on the hectic city, the late nights, the secret speakeasies, the cramped and sweaty dance floors. She was speaking of society parties and philanthropic obligations and expectations.

"Even when I'm in Newport, you'd better believe the gown I wear to dinner, the food I serve and the guests I entertain will be in the paper the next day. I don't get a minute of peace. But out here it's secluded, it's protected, it's hard to reach, and the press can't get anywhere near me. I can wear what I want, when I want, and do whatever I please."

"Must be a relief." I tried to commiserate, but I was the opposite. I welcomed the press writing about me, flattering me, telling the world what I was doing and encouraging them to get in on the fun. "How long do you stay out here in the summer?" I asked, trying to keep things light.

"We arrive in July, then off to Newport at the end of August," she said.

"Must be a lot of work, though, to maintain such a huge property."

"Oh, we're very lucky to have exceptional staff who live here year-round, and they keep us wonderfully self-sufficient. We have a small farm and gardens, and we grow our own vegetables, so we're always ready for visitors. We've had scientists, writers, statesmen, actors, and even Ziegfeld girls," she added, winking at me.

"Are we your first?"

"You are not, my dear, but you are certainly the most lovely. I can see why Archibald is so smitten with you."

"You know . . . ," I began, I just couldn't stand there a minute longer and listen to her speak of him as if he were some poor injured bird.

"Oh, my dear, would you excuse me for just a moment? I have to greet a guest who just walked in. . . ."

I stood in the middle of the room alone for a moment and felt Archie's eyes on me. Glancing over, I couldn't help noticing that he looked particularly modern and dapper in a double-breasted dinner jacket with those wider satin lapels that the more fashionable men were wearing these days.

Despite everything, I hoped that he'd make his way over to me. If we were going to be here at the same camp for a few days, I at least wanted to get the awkwardness over with. But just when I thought he might, the fellow from the steamboat appeared out of nowhere.

"Oli," he said, smiling broadly. "Remember me from the boat? Andrew Stark." He lifted my hand to kiss it.

"How could I forget?"

"You left me all alone down there," he said. He was tight already, as if he'd been leaning into the gin martinis a little too hard all afternoon. "It wasn't kind." He stepped toward me. "You can't leave me all hot and bothered like that, you know, you'll get a man in trouble if you leave him in that state."

"You got into that state all by yourself." I stepped back, no longer wanting to be associated with him but also unsure of who he was and what had secured him an invitation to the Belmonts' camp.

"Maybe, but babe, you're the only one who can get me out of it, if you know what I mean."

"I'm not your babe—"

"Everything all right over here?" It was Archie. He stood between me and Mr. Stark.

"Fine," I said stiffly, rolling my eyes. Archie looked from me to Andrew.

"Why don't you get yourself some air." He patted the guy on his back rather hard and nudged him away from me toward the back door. "You smell like panther piss, you're lit up like a store window, and we haven't even sat down for dinner yet," he said in a whisper loud enough for me to hear. "If I see you bothering this young lady again, or showing disrespect in any way, I'm going to have no choice but to punch your lights out."

He turned to Archie with a look of surprise.

"That's right," Archie went on. "Don't make me show you what I mean, go on."

I couldn't help smiling. I hadn't expected such a direct delivery, and neither had that drunk, but it certainly did the trick, and we watched him slink out the back door.

"Thank you," I said.

"He can be a real brute."

"I meant for the flowers in my cabin."

Archie looked mildly surprised.

"What? You think I couldn't have handled that boozehound myself?" I said.

He laughed. "That boozehound is Raymond's business partner's son, and he's always in spectacular form." He looked at me seriously. "Can we get a breath of fresh air before dinner? There's something I need to tell you."

I glanced around; everyone was still mingling and conversing. "I'm quite comfortable here," I said. I didn't see why I should have to leave this magnificent room.

"Then can we sit instead?" he asked, gesturing toward two wooden framed armchairs near the fireplace. I shrugged and led the way. Archie sat down, looking uncomfortably at the guests around us.

"I'm afraid that I owe you an apology," he said. "You weren't entirely wrong in your assessment of me. In fact, your instincts were right."

"Obviously," I said.

"At the time of our meeting and in the weeks that followed there was indeed another woman." He glanced at me, looking concerned, as if I might once again make a scene, and he quickly continued, as if hoping he might tame the situation. "I've been involved with a woman in Cincinnati for almost half a year now, and in what seemed to occur as a result of a natural progression of time spent together, rather than any deep interest or desire, we became engaged to be married."

I glared at him, not giving him the satisfaction of a response—he hadn't shared anything that I didn't already know.

"But upon meeting you, I had such intense feelings for you, I knew that the engagement wasn't right. I had never felt that way about her. It was more a pairing of convenience—her family knows my family, she lives in the city where much of my work takes place, where my family resides."

I shook my head to let him know that he was heading down the wrong path here. I didn't want to know about her or how neatly she fit into his life back home. I wanted to know why he was telling me this. He picked up on my impatience and quickly moved on.

"Ever since I met you at the Pirate's Den I haven't been able to get you out of my mind. I asked around to find out where you might perform and I finally discovered you were in Ziegfeld's show. It wasn't by chance that I caught that ribbon, it was sheer determination. Even though I knew nothing about you, I was incredibly taken. It was like electricity when we danced, and I felt compelled to know you. I also knew in that instant I couldn't go through with the engagement, not if I was capable of having such feelings for you. It took some time for me to unravel things, and when we went to dinner that evening and kept the restaurant open into the early hours of the morning . . . I admit . . . I had not fully untangled myself of my obligation."

I stiffened and readied myself to stand and leave. I'd wasted hours at dinner with him, indulged him. To think that I'd envisioned myself with him. I'd refrained from asking him to come up to my apartment—despite how much I'd longed for him that evening. I'd followed his "gentlemanly" lead, doing the appropriate thing. But how long I'd lain in bed that night picturing us together, something so ridiculously premature that I'd never done before.

He took my hand gently, insisting that I hear him out.

"Please, Olive. Don't give up on me so soon. I should have told you, but I was worried you wouldn't give me the time of day. I did know then that I would end things with Louise no matter what."

Louise. The name made me cringe.

"You were right to notice, of course, that I wasn't back to the city as much as I would have liked in those early days after meeting you. I felt that I must first wrap things up in Cincinnati. I didn't want to be the kind of man who wooed you in New York before resolving things back home. That was a risky thing to do on my end. I worried about leaving you confused, but I felt compelled to do things the right way. I wanted to do the right thing, in the right order."

I shook my head. I was at a loss for words. And that was rare for me.

"Olive," he said urgently, taking both my hands and turning me to face him. "Please tell me I haven't missed my chance."

"Where do things stand now?" I asked dryly, unsure what to think, if I should trust him. I'd felt betrayed and fooled.

"I've called it off, the whole thing. No matter what you decide, meeting you made me realize I was making a mistake. Everyone back home is shocked at the abrupt break and seems to feel I've done something terribly wrong, and now I realize how unkind it has been of me to let things go as far as they did when I never felt true love for her. But I've made my decision and it's final."

"And you and me being here, Archie, in the middle of the forest at the exact same camp, at the exact same time. Is this just a coincidence or did you have something to do with it?"

He smiled sheepishly. "I might have put in a special request with the Belmonts." He looked back at me and again quickly continued. "Don't get me wrong, they were thrilled, absolutely over the moon about the idea of you. They've heard about your voice and your performances and they love the Ziegfeld shows, and I may have put in a few good words with your boss."

"What? Your good words cost me my role in the *Midnight Frolic*," I said. "I was the star of that show, and now they've replaced me during my absence."

He looked surprised. "But I specifically spoke to Ziegfeld and he assured me that you'd be right back where you left off after the summer tour. He promised, man to man."

He didn't seem to understand how his interference had unsettled me. Who was he to manipulate my life without my knowing? And yet the intensity of his feelings had been responsible.

"Now they know they can plop someone else in my role at any time, and the show will go on. I'm no longer indispensable."

I was angry with him and I wanted him to know it, but I was also strangely flattered, despite everything he was telling me, that he'd gone to so much trouble to ensure we could spend time together.

"I realize now, as I'm saying it, how this may seem. It's just that after we talked that night, about traveling and exploring the world, I felt certain you'd love it here. I wanted you to experience it, to feel the beauty of it, and I thought how wonderful it would be to show you this, to spend time with you here away from the busy city, to get lost on a hike, to row you out to the other side of the lake and take a picnic. I may have got ahead of myself, dreaming all this up without your permission, but it was a dream and I went for it."

I shook my head. "I don't know what to think. I wasn't expecting this, that's for certain."

"You don't owe me anything, Olive. If you don't want to see me while you're here, I will stay out of your way"—he looked up as if to gauge my reaction—"but if you will allow me, it would be my absolute honor to share it with you."

A bell rang and everyone began to move toward the main doors and head outside for dinner.

"Let's go out," I said. "I don't want to keep Anne waiting."

Outside in the open air, two long tables had been set for dinner, all spectacularly lit up with candles and even tiny lights that hung in the trees above. The cabins and the main lodge surrounding the space were all lit from within, and the whole scene looked like something from a storybook.

The seating arrangements were such that our group was seated at one end of the table, while the rest of the guests were seated at the other end. My seat was smack in the middle, opposite Anne and

Raymond, with Ruthie and my fellow performers on my right and the rest of the guests on my left. When Archie took the empty seat next to mine, I raised my eyebrow.

"I suppose you had a hand in this too?"

"Guilty as charged," he said, flashing a bashful smile.

I hadn't decided what to make of his news yet, so I was as gracious as I needed to be as a guest at the table, but I didn't indulge him—instead I paid particular attention to our hosts.

Over the main course of sweetbreads, mushrooms and green lima beans, I asked Anne who else had visited the camp, fascinated by this whole world, hidden away in the mountains, that I'd known nothing about until just a few weeks ago.

"Oh, we've had all kinds—actors, lieutenant colonels, writers—hundreds. I can't think of them all."

"Who was the most interesting?" Ruthie leaned in and asked.

"Oh, it has to be the wife of the imperial emperor of China."

"She traveled with twenty-five personal maids," Raymond added. "Can you believe that? I thought Anne required a lot of help!"

Anne laughed. "It's true, they just kept coming out of the carriages. I had to worry about having enough beds."

"While we had dinner," Raymond jumped in, "our staff had to rearrange the cabins to sleep six or seven maids where there'd usually be no more than two."

"Three of her girls were assigned simply to watch her bedsheets, even when she was out of the room. If a breeze so much as ruffled her sheets, they had to be washed and changed immediately," Anne continued. "We found her delightful, but the staff needed a few days' break after she left with her entourage."

I thought I'd experienced luxury—having my own apartment with Ruthie, receiving mink coats and jewelry backstage from admirers and perfect strangers—but all this extravagance was unlike anything I'd ever known, and here in the wilderness was the last place I'd expected to find it.

The next morning, I woke to a racket and a rotten champagne headache. Someone, somewhere in camp, was singing their lungs out. I put my head under my pillow to drown it out, but it didn't help, and then I realized that it wasn't just any old fool, it was a man's voice, and a beautiful one at that.

Why on earth would anyone be crooning so early? Surely I wasn't the only one who didn't appreciate being roused when the sun was barely up. I peeked into Ruthie's room—she was sleeping soundly and snoring like an old man, so I left her to it and checked the clock in the kitchenette: a quarter to six. Absurd! If I'd really put my mind to it, perhaps I could have gone back to sleep; I could sleep anywhere through just about any noise, usually. But I was annoyed and intrigued, my head was splitting, and I had to know who would do such a thing at this god-awful hour. And the fact was, the more I listened, the more I had to know who that voice belonged to.

I threw my fur coat over my silk pajamas and robe, pulled the woolen socks that my mother had knitted for me up my calves as high as they would go and stepped into my rubber galoshes. I followed the voice all the way to the lakeshore, where it became apparent that it was coming not from our camp but from the other side of the lake or farther down the shore. I walked along the water's edge a little, but there was no way I was getting any closer unless I took to water.

The boathouse was a green two-story structure with a sloped shingled roof directly downhill from my cabin. Canoes were stacked inside and mounted from wall racks. A small metal rowboat sat calmly in the water, tied with a simple looped rope next to the deck, its oars already fixed in place. I climbed in, wobbling as I set foot inside, then I eased the rope off the dock and quickly took a seat on the thin wooden bench, hoping to calm the rocking motion. After pushing myself away from the dock with my oar, I began to glide into the thick grey fog engulfing Osgood Pond. I couldn't see where I was going in the early morning haze, so I closed my eyes and followed the sound.

It might've been August, but at that time in the morning it was colder than Greenland itself out there. I looked down at my outfit and had a giggle, quite sure that when my mother had sat by the fireplace in our family home, tiny needles clicking away, she hadn't envisioned me wearing these socks on occasions such as this. The mink coat, a gift from some stage-door johnny during my first week on the job, hadn't been on such an adventure either and would probably be ruined if it got sopping wet. But if I flipped this boat over, I'd have bigger problems than replacing my fur in the summer, in our remote corner of the Adirondacks. I'd probably damn near freeze to death.

As I drove the oars through the water, I realized that steering was much harder than I'd imagined. I tried to turn into the direction of the voice—deep and emotive, becoming clearer and more powerful the closer I got—but the rowboat, which had looked so inviting and romantic sitting under the eave of the boathouse, almost calling for me to get in, suddenly felt too big and cumbersome for me to manage. I had a moment of panic. I could no longer see my way back to shore, nor could I see where I was going.

I kept on rowing, scared to look down into the deep black water, realizing how impulsive I had been and wishing I could be more like Ruthie—she might seem like a free spirit at times, but she had a good head on her shoulders. I focused on the voice—Italian and familiar—and wondered if I could have made a mistake. Maybe it wasn't someone singing after all, maybe it was someone playing a Victrola as loud as could be, because the closer I seemed to get, the more it sounded like the operatic tenor Alberto Ricci.

"Hello," I called out. I was close now and began to make out the shape of someone through the fog. "Hello, who's there?"

The singing stopped, and when I was about eight feet away, I could see him clearly—Alberto Ricci, sitting in a green canoe in his white long johns. I couldn't believe it was actually him. Quickly plunging my oars in the water and paddling backwards to slow my arrival, I narrowly avoided a collision.

"*Buongiorno,*" he said, smiling right at me as if he'd been expecting company.

"Hello," I said, attempting to sound stern. I had to keep my composure. "I must say that your singing, your beautiful singing, out here in the middle of the lake, is waking up the whole of our camp and probably half of the Adirondacks. May I suggest that you save your practice for later in the day?"

"*Che bella,*" he said. "It's very nice to make your acquaintance. What is your name?"

"Olive," I said. "Olive Shine, I'm staying at the Pines Camp. We're the entertainment for a few days, the *Ziegfeld Follies*."

"Olive, the Lady of the Lake," he said. "*Ciao, bella.* So lovely for you to join me. Alberto." He rolled his Rs and I couldn't help smiling. I was meeting Alberto Ricci in person in the middle of a lake!

"I know who you are. Actually, I saw you perform at the Fairmont Opera House when I was just a kid; my mother is a big fan. Your voice is stunning, absolutely magnificent. But the hour . . . it's so early."

"Come—" He reached out his hands as if I might just drop my oars and climb into his canoe with him. When I didn't cooperate, he simply pulled my rowboat closer with his oar until they were parallel and we were facing each other.

"Now I see you," he said.

"I'd rather you didn't. You've most definitely cut my beauty sleep short!"

"And what do you perform in Mr. Ziegfeld's spectacular? Do you dance on your toes?"

"Dance, yes, but singing is my specialty," I said, suddenly feeling meek next to this idol.

"My dear, what better place is there to perform our morning exercises—these are the perfect conditions for our vocal cords—the moisture in the air, away from all that dry filth in the city. Do you live in Manhattan?"

"Of course."

"I do not know how you do it. How can you live and breathe there? Wait until you hear yourself here, it is so powerful, amplified."

"I know it's amplified! It sounded like you were singing into my ear while I was trying to sleep."

"Don't worry, I have something that will help you wake—" He held up an Icy-Hot Thermos. "The housekeeper made me some of your terrible American Maxwell House. It's all yours." He handed it to me, and I unscrewed the lid and took a sip.

"That's not just Maxwell House," I said, feeling the warmth of brandy or whiskey or some liquor on the back on my throat.

"Of course not, I said it's terrible—I have to add something to make the flavor."

"May I ask what you are doing here?"

"I'm staying at Paul Smith's Hotel that way." He pointed his oar to the other end of the lake. "I don't like to wake my friends and neighbors, so I paddle south." He grinned. "And what a treat, because I meet you."

I couldn't help laughing. I had dreamed of someday meeting this man in person. If I still had money coming in from the *Frolic* and the *Follies*, I would've spent my entire paycheck from Ziegfeld on a ticket to see him perform. I'd splurge on a ticket in the orchestra section, just so I could see him up close, without having to watch the whole performance through the opera glasses. And here we were in the most unlikely of places.

"Would you care to accompany me?"

"Where to?" I asked.

"To sing, of course."

We started with some vowel warm-ups and then sang together until the fog had cleared, the sun was out and the birds were singing above us. We sang "Ave Maria" at the top of our lungs as if we were onstage before a full audience, not in the middle of a lake, on our way to getting drunk on hooched-up coffee in our pajamas. We sang as many songs as we could think of in English.

"*O brava*, Olive," he said. "With some proper instruction you could go far." He nodded, looking serious, and I was both delighted by the compliment from such a talented and accomplished professional and slightly disappointed—I'd thought that all my years of lessons had been enough.

"This is quite a way to start the day," I said, lying back on my fur coat, feeling the sun start to warm up the morning.

"It's the only way to start the day. *Il miglior modo!*" he said. "The best way."

"Let's do one more, then I'm afraid I have to get back to the camp," I said. "We have our first rehearsal and then a performance tonight."

"One more," he said. "I have breakfast with my host and then I plan a long siesta. 'O sole mio' for *l'ultima*."

"Oh, I don't know Italian very well," I said. "I don't know it at all."

"You know this," he insisted. "You must."

Of course, once he began, I recognized the song and was able to sing along with the chorus, making up and filling in when I didn't know what came next.

We both laughed when we were done, he at the ridiculousness of me making up words, I'm sure, and I because the whole meeting had been so unexpected, so dreamlike, and I never could have imagined such an encounter.

"Learn Italian, Olive," he said, turning his canoe to face north. "One or two songs to start, it will help you in your career."

I smiled, excited at the prospect.

"Meet you again *domani*?" he said.

"*Domani!*" I said with my hands and my best Italian accent.

"*Domani,*" he said, turning his canoe in the direction of his hotel as my little metal rowboat rocked in his wake.

We rehearsed in the dance hall down by the bowling alley on the south side of the property, and early that afternoon we practiced on the outdoor stage near where we'd had dinner the night before. Howie gave us stage directions for five of the classic *Follies* numbers—including most of the acts I'd performed during my parents' disastrous attendance—and while the stage was nowhere near as smooth and polished as the New Amsterdam's, and it was a fraction of the size, we were able to make it work.

Usually when the company went on the road, they went for four months over the summer to cities such as Chicago, Kansas City, St. Louis, Cleveland and Philadelphia. They took over two train cars: one for the performers and crew, one solely for the scenery and costumes. This, however, was a one-month deal and we couldn't bring scenery because there was no way to transport it once we were off the train. It made the whole thing feel less impressive than our usual productions, but we still managed to put on a decent show.

After the performance, we changed and mingled with the guests around the bonfire. Ziegfeld had been right: they were all grateful and complimentary for the entertainment. Archie was sitting with a group of people on the far side of the bonfire. We caught each other's eye and I saw him excuse himself from his group and walk over to me.

"You were spectacular as usual," he said.

"Thank you, we had to make do with what was available."

"Honestly, you could have been unaccompanied with no stage and no fancy costumes and you would have had us all on our knees."

I smiled.

"Join us. . . ." He motioned to his friends. I wanted to, but I didn't want to appear too eager to let him off the hook.

"I should stay," I said, looking back to my fellow performers. "We were in the middle of discussing the show."

"Ah." He nodded, though I sensed he knew I was making him work for his forgiveness. "Maybe tomorrow, then," he said.

"Maybe," I said coyly, and I had to force myself to turn and slowly walk away.

CHAPTER FOURTEEN

The next morning, Archie showed up at my cabin wearing his hiking clothes—plaid britches, a button-down shirt and lace-up boots.

"I know you leave in a few days, so I thought I'd try and persuade you to let me take you on a short hike."

I hadn't stopped thinking about what he'd told me before dinner two nights earlier, and I'd hoped he'd make another attempt to spend time with me. If he was telling the truth and the engagement was called off, then I didn't see any harm in getting to know him.

"What do you say?" He smiled.

"I say if you can wait ten minutes for me to put on my sporting togs, then I'll be right with you."

He smiled. "Capital," he said. "I'll meet you in the main lodge."

So, where are we going?" I asked Archie. He was walking next to me along a pathway leading away from the cabins, through part of the camp that I hadn't yet explored.

"We're going hiking."

"But where? Isn't there a destination or something, a place that we're trying to get to?"

"Not really." He laughed. "We'll hike through some conifer trees and a hardwood forest, according to the guide, and we'll pass by Black Pond."

"So, we're just walking for the sake of walking? There's no place to stop and have a refreshment?"

"Agnes, the housekeeper, packed us some sandwiches."

"Well, I'd do things a little differently around here if I were the owner of all this land. I'd have bar carts all along the trails," I said, half-joking. "I'd make it a lot friendlier to the average show girl."

"There's nothing average about you," he said.

"I'm just trying to know my onions about the purpose of hiking," I said. "I'm used to having a goal in mind, and then I do the things necessary to get there. It's how my brain works. I always have to know what I'm reaching for next."

"Hiking is about the journey," he said. "The trees you see along the way, the nature, the views, the fresh air."

"Did you know there's a tuberculosis-curing hospital near here in Saranac Village?" I asked. "Where people come for weeks at a time specifically for the fresh air."

"I didn't."

"It's true. Anne told me about it, they get cured purely from fresh air. There are cure chairs and cure porches, and apparently there's a whole industry up here dedicated to curing people. It sounds like my cup of tea—lounging and breathing air." I laughed.

We walked through the tall evergreens and I took a long, deep breath.

"Is it really over, Archie?" I asked. I had very little experience with relationships thus far, but what I had experienced had all been based on lies and distrust. I simply couldn't allow myself to fall for him again if I wasn't sure I could trust him.

"I promise you, Olive, it's completely over," he said, and I nodded, believing the sincerity in his eyes.

We walked on and something hung in the air between us. He seemed thoughtful and serious all of a sudden, and I wondered if I'd missed something.

"There is one other thing I feel I should tell you," he said quietly.

"Okay," I said. "It can't be any worse than what you already shared." I laughed, but he remained stoic.

We walked along in silence for a few moments; the trail was taking us uphill and our deep breathing was suddenly audible.

"I was married once," he said finally. We had reached the top of the pathway, and trees opened up to reveal a view of the pond, where reeds were swaying gently at the water's edge, making a lulling, hushing sound.

"Oh."

"My wife, Clara, fell ill when she was pregnant, less than a year into our marriage. She went into an early labor, and I lost them."

"Oh, Archie," I whispered, shocked by this terrible revelation.

I was suddenly jolted back, in a flash—the fear, the smelling salts, the nuns. I had to wrench myself from its hold to something, anything comforting to say. It was just so awful.

"They actually . . ." I didn't know how to ask.

"Yes, both of them, gone. It's difficult to speak of. It was a horrible time in my life," he said. "Nine years ago. She would have made a wonderful mother."

He kept looking out at the pond, as if talking to me about it directly would be too much for him.

"I've come to terms with the fact that I may never be a father, and I'd be okay with that, I suppose, but then there are the times that I can picture it so vividly, how it would be, where we would go, what we would do." He shrugged and seemed to come out of his daze a little. "I don't know."

I'd heard of it, of course, dying in childbirth, but I hadn't known anyone who'd actually experienced this loss, and the death of both his wife and child was so devastating. I pictured Archie, young and excitable, a new bride, a child on the way, a whole life ahead of him, and then suddenly it was all gone, he was left alone. What he had shared was so deeply personal, and I was surprised and yet grateful to him for entrusting me with his past. I reached out and touched his shoulder, and then I put an arm around him and squeezed.

"I don't talk about it too often," he said, turning to me, his soft, caring eyes, a sweet, generous smile. "It's just too sad," he added.

"I'm sorry, I j-just . . ." I stammered for words, confused at my swell of emotion. "I just feel for you so very much."

"Thank you. I wanted you to know I'd been married before. No more secrets," he said.

"No more secrets," I said, feeling a pang of regret. He'd been so honest with me, sharing a piece of his past that I wouldn't have known about if he hadn't brought it up. I should do the same, tell him my secret, but I couldn't, of course I couldn't. His was a tragedy that happened to him, something out of his control. Mine, well, that was my own damn fault.

"You're easy to talk to, Olive," he said, and I smiled. He was right, there was an ease between us. If only I could be truthful. "Come on . . ." Archie began walking again. "It's this way."

He walked slightly ahead through a narrow pathway with trees on either side, the sunlight blocked out by the canopy of leaves, except for a few small openings where the sun streamed down in beams. I followed closely behind, and then he reached his hand back, without looking, and grabbed mine, knowing exactly where I was. I looked down at my hand in his. It was such a simple gesture, but a rush of warmth came over me. We walked like that for a while, until the path broke into a fork.

"Left or right?" he asked.

"Which way did the guide say?"

"I don't know—he drew me a map, but I left it in the cabin, fig-ured we'd find our own way."

The way he said it made me smile.

To the left was a low wooden bridge crossing Black Pond, with reeds and lilies growing on either side of it. The sun was shining, and birds were dancing about. To the right, the pathway led deeper into the forest.

"What's that?" I asked, pointing to a structure high up in a tree down the wooded path to the right. "Let's take a peek." I tugged his hand before he had a chance to respond. "I think it's a tree house."

Growing up with three brothers, I'd always wanted to prove that I could do what they could. There was a field with cows down the

183

street from the house we grew up in. My brothers liked to go in there and try to get the cows riled up, even though the cows never seemed to care about having visitors. I stayed out of the field for the most part, avoiding the massive cowpats at all cost, but the trees surrounding the field were perfect for climbing. There was an old oak they favored, especially hospitable with its knotted, aged trunk and branches and its well-worn foot holes. When my brothers climbed trees, they always seemed so free, high up in the branches, their own private hideaway—a boys' club where no one could reach them, no one could hear what they talked about. It didn't seem to matter what was going on below them, they were immune to it, like birds cruising in the wind currents.

I started climbing so I could see what they saw, feel what they felt, but they made the ascent look easy. When they weren't around, I'd climb onto the fence and attempt to pull myself up, but I didn't have the arm strength they had, and even one or two branches up seemed terrifyingly high. My father would have locked me in my room for a week if he'd seen me up there.

When I was eight or nine, my brothers were all playing ball by the field with their friends and I casually walked over and started climbing. Knowing they hadn't noticed yet, I kept going, pumped with adrenaline, not looking down. Just one more branch, I told myself, then just one more. The branches were getting thinner and weaker the higher I got, and I finally had to stop. I looked up. I was near the top of the tree and could see clear across the field and beyond for what felt like miles. As the girl of the family, I'd been missing this. This freedom, this rush. I was on top of the world. Then I looked down and gasped. I was so high up. I clung to the tree branch I was perched on, frozen. The muscles in my feet cramped up, and I was paralyzed with fear.

"Erwin," I cried. "George!"

They couldn't hear me. They were caught up in a game of ball farther down the street, and though I could hear them laughing and calling out to one another, they couldn't hear me. Even my voice was stuck, as if my mind couldn't let me yell too loud, in case it threw me off balance. Eventually Junior, he must have been five or six at the time, grew bored with the ball game, his brothers and their older friends, and he wandered off closer to where I was. I called out to him and asked him to get help.

"Geez, sis, are you nuts or something?" Erwin said after Junior ran and got him. "What were you thinking?" He looked up at me, clearly irritated that I'd interrupted his game and gone someplace I obviously wasn't supposed to be. He climbed up and guided me in getting down, telling me where to put my feet and which branch to hold. "Don't go climbing places you can't get down from," he said as we worked our way slowly to the bottom.

"How was I supposed to know I couldn't get down?" I said, almost in tears.

"Just go back to your singing and dancing and dolls, and stop being such a pest," he said. "Bother your own friends, not us."

I ran toward the tree ahead of Archie as we got close.

"You're not seriously going up there?" he asked as I began to climb up a rope ladder hanging down from the tree.

"Hold on to the bottom of it, will you?"

Before he could protest, I was already making my way up to the top, where I reached over and grabbed one of the branches, hoisting myself up to the next and the next until I was on the platform. It was a massive tree, and that old oak back in St. Cloud probably paled in comparison, but I'd been to a lot of places I wasn't supposed to be since then. This height didn't faze me anymore.

"What a view," I said from the top. "Join me." I looked down at Archie, so handsome and fit in his hiking gear. He looked as comfortable in plaid britches and rolled-up sleeves as he did in a sharp tailored suit and fedora. I liked that about him, how he could seamlessly glide from one environment to the next.

"I don't know if it will hold my weight."

I pretended to jump up and down. "Feels sturdy enough to me."

"Good Lord, you're making me nervous." Archie began wrangling with the ladder, swinging all over the place with no one to hold it still. "I can't very well leave you up here alone when you're exhibiting such reckless behavior," he said, breathing deeply when he finally reached the top.

"Wise," I said, giving him a hand. "Very wise."

The tree house was tall enough for us to stand, and the platform encircled the entire trunk. On the far side there was a window cut out, providing a panoramic view of the water and beyond.

"It's beautiful up here," I said.

"It sure is," Archie said, standing behind me and placing his hands gently on my waist. I turned around and we were inches apart. "Olive," he began, as if he were about to ask me a question, those dark brown eyes, serious and intense, looking right at me. But before he could say more, I kissed him.

CHAPTER FIFTEEN

On our last day at the Pines, Archie planned an excursion to Paul Smith's Hotel, where it was rumored Alberto Ricci would be treating his fellow guests to a couple of songs. I had it on good authority from the man himself that this was in fact the case. Archie arranged for two Concord coaches, each drawn by four horses, to deliver the guests at the Pines to Paul Smith's in the late afternoon so we could enjoy refreshments outside on the hotel's lakefront prior to dinner. There was space for twenty guests in total, and Archie invited Ruthie and me to join him.

"What are you wearing?" Ruthie asked, pushing open the door to the bathroom in the cabin, where I was smoothing my hair with a comb and water, curving the ends so that they gently touched my jawline.

"Haven't decided yet," I said, dampening the comb again, attempting to tame an unruly fringe that wanted to flick left when it was supposed to lie straight across my brow. Ruthie stood behind me watching in the mirror, then she ran her fingers over the short red waves set in place to frame her face.

"You're so lucky," she said. "I could never do a razor-sharp bob like you."

"Why would you want to?" I turned and cupped her red hair. "Your hair is so pretty."

"But yours is so dramatic and startling."

I turned back to my reflection and admired my new style. "That's exactly what I'm going for."

I powdered my nose, put some rouge on my cheeks and lips and looked in my closet. This would be the last night that I'd see Archie for a while. The pale peach dropped waist was a favorite of mine—I usually wore it with white gloves and a long string of pearls; it was the ideal dress for the occasion but too subdued for my mood.

"Is this too much?" I asked, grabbing the dark navy dress heavy with beading. It was not the most comfortable dress for sitting and dining, but it felt amazing to dance in, layer upon layer of beaded tassels swishing and jumping with every step. Ruthie came out of the bathroom and smiled.

"It's a lot."

I held it up and looked in the mirror. The contrast of my pale skin against the dramatic dark beading and my almost black hair was just what I wanted. "It is a lot," I said. "It's perfect."

Ruthie decided on a turquoise hanky-hem dress that was definitely more appropriate for the afternoon-into-evening affair.

Carefully we climbed into the first coach.

"You really like this guy," Ruthie said in a whisper.

"Who?"

"Archie. I don't think I've ever seen you like this."

"Like what?"

She tapped my knee and laughed. "Excited, anxious, checking in the mirror five times before we left the cabin. You care about this one, that's all."

I rolled my eyes.

"It's a good thing, Olive, it's nice."

We spent the afternoon at the Casino—which was actually a boathouse, named not for all the gambling that apparently went on there but rather because it meant "little house" in Italian. The second floor was the men's billiards room, with a separate card room for women—the owner had originally thought it was unseemly for men and women to engage in such activities together, but we all threw those cautions to the wind and commingled anyway. We went on a boat ride as the sun was setting and then ate dinner at tables set up along the lakeshore. Alberto performed as we ate dessert, and he insisted that I join him for "Ave Maria," which earned us a standing ovation. I couldn't believe I was actually singing to an audience with Alberto Ricci.

Later that night, back at the Pines after everyone had said good night and gone back to their cabins, Archie and I stayed up, watching the last of the embers glowing in the firepit.

"You were magnificent today," Archie said, pulling me closer to him on the wooden bench. "Stunning in every way, and the way you and Alberto sang together, honestly, it was perfection."

"Oh, Archie, you're too kind. I think Alberto's voice can make anyone sound good."

"I hardly think so, Olive. On the contrary, I'm sure there are not many who could sing with him and sound halfway decent. You have a beautiful voice." He kissed me. "And a beautiful smile." He kissed me again. "And a beautiful neck." I let my head fall back. "And beautiful shoulders . . . Olive?" he asked softly.

"Yes," I said. "Yes." And he took me by the hand and we walked back to his cabin.

As soon as the door closed behind us, he slowly removed my dress, kissing me softly with each inch of skin he revealed. We moved toward the bedroom, and I urgently unbuttoned his shirt, desperate for us to touch.

"Archie," I said. "I should tell you . . ."

But he kissed me again.

"Archie . . ." He kissed my ear, my neck, my collarbone. "Archie, you drive me wild."

He picked me up and carried me the rest of the way.

Afterwards we lay in bed, his strong, muscular arms wrapped around me. I felt blissfully stunned. I'd never been with a man before, not like this. The one other time didn't count; it had been so different, so unwanted. This was how it was supposed to be—this incredible intimacy—this overwhelming rush of emotion.

The only singing I heard as I rushed out of the cabin in bare feet, my shawl wrapped hastily around my shoulders, was the sound of coots and warblers making themselves known well past dawn. Our *Follies* group would be packing up and moving on to the next camp after breakfast, and I'd promised to meet Alberto on the lake one more time beforehand. He was staying only a few more days, and then he'd be heading to Philadelphia for a show, then back to Italy.

Archie and I had both slept in, and when I woke, I had to peel myself away, not wanting to leave him sleeping soundly next to me, but eventually I tiptoed out of bed. I climbed into the first boat I saw and rowed out on the lake in hopes of catching Alberto at the tail end of his vocals, just to say goodbye.

"Yoo-hoo," I called out. The lake was smooth as glass, and there was barely any fog. I could make out the shape of his canoe from a long way off, but there was no sign of Alberto. *"Ciao, Alberto,"* I called out. Could he have gone for a swim? I wondered. But the water was calm all around, and the air was too cold at that time in the morning.

"Hello," I called again as I approached. He popped up from lying flat in the canoe with an arm over his eyes.

"I thought you do not make it," he said, rubbing his eyes.

"I thought you'd drowned," I said.

"I did. In last night's wine. My head is booming."

"Does that mean we're not warming up?"

"Absolutely not. But the air out here is helping *il mio mal di testa.*" He rubbed his temples.

"I know how you feel. I didn't go to sleep until three in the morning. Archie and I sat out by the campfire."

"Are you *innamorata*?"

"Well, it's a bit soon for that," I said, feeling myself blush but unable to keep from smiling at the thought of Archie's touch.

"I always know immediately if I'm in love."

"You make it sound like it's a regular occurrence." I laughed. "How many times have you been in love?"

"*Molte, molte.* Too many times. You?"

"*Molte,*" I said with my hands.

The truth was I'd never been in love before. I hadn't allowed myself the time or inclination—I'd had one goal, of becoming a star, for as long as I could remember.

And yet the thought of leaving the camp and not seeing Archie again for a while weighed heavily on me. I'd be traveling to the other camps for the rest of the tour and it was only mildly likely that Archie would be in Manhattan upon my return. I'd taken every opportunity I had to be around him during my time there. I walked by boccie ball games in the afternoon, I stayed around the campfire long after the other performers went to bed. I even found myself wanting to rush through rehearsals to see him again, and now, after last night, the thought of our lives continuing on without each other outside the confines of the camp felt all wrong.

"How do you know if it's really love?" I asked.

"You just know, Olive." He smiled. "But be careful. Men like that, wealthy, important, they don't like performers—singers, dancers, actresses."

"Oh no, Archie loves that I sing. In fact, our second meeting was during one of my shows. I landed in his arms. It was wild. . . ." I was about to tell him the whole story of flying off the stage and meeting him on the dance floor. But Alberto wagged his finger at me.

"Honestly, Alberto, he's not like that."

He shrugged and lay back in his canoe. "You should audition at the Metropolitan Opera House."

"I'm not good enough for that."

"Maybe, maybe not. Get good enough. I make the introduction next time I'm in New York. Always you keep aiming higher. Ziegfeld is good for now, but always you think, What's next for Olive?"

"If I could just keep on with what I'm doing I'd be happy, but sometimes I feel as though it could all slip away."

"It could," he said matter-of-factly. "It always could. That is why you must be careful."

I tried to brush it off. Be careful? What did that even mean?

"Be careful with your heart, be careful with your talent," he continued. "That is all."

We traveled throughout the Adirondacks for the next several weeks, each camp more impressive than the last. There were imported English clay tennis courts, croquet lawns, trails flush with wild raspberry bushes, late night swimming parties and retinues of servants that outnumbered the guests three to one. We met and mingled and performed, and Ruthie was right, it was quite a lovely way to spend a month in the middle of summer. But by the end of it, I was ready to return. I missed the city and I missed Archie. I couldn't wait another minute to be back in his arms.

CHAPTER SIXTEEN

We were ready in less than fifteen minutes after the lights went down. Ruthie and the girls knew that if they hurried, they could catch a ride with Archie and me in his Buick, which waited for me outside the stage door most nights. He didn't mind that the girls piled in and tagged along, as long as they got there quick—before the late night crowd began crawling out of the midtown theaters and restaurants and making their way to the clubs. Archie had a table reserved in the back of Grotto, 42, a fancy establishment where you had to be someone or know someone to get in, and he was ushered past the heavy black gates and through the brass-studded door in a snap. He liked to get settled before the crowds began filling in and the dancing began. Drinks were $1.25 a pop, but Archie took care of all of us, which the girls loved because it meant they didn't have to agree to date some dud just to have a little fun.

I liked that he took care of my gang. Most of us were making decent money as Ziegfeld girls, between $40 and $75 a week if you were really lucky, but by the time we paid for a place to live and bought the clothes, shoes, makeup and accessories necessary to live this kind of life, and go to these kinds of places, to be considered a "new woman," as the papers were calling us—modern, independent ladies who liked to earn our own money and make up our own minds—we had little money left to eat, and drink, and share in the reckless moral debauchery that we all got blamed for. So it was nice of him to treat everyone.

"What are you having, ladies?" he asked as the waiter headed over to our table.

"Brandy. I'm only drinking brandy from here on out," Ruthie said.

"Why's that?" I asked.

"Didn't you hear? One of the gals from the *Scandals* almost died from some bathtub gin at a speak downtown."

"That's not going to happen here," Archie assured us. "I'll get you whatever you want, but I promise you this place has the good stuff."

"That's what they all say," she said.

"They import wine from Europe and spirits from South America and Canada," Archie said.

"Brandy," she repeated. "No one can fake the smell and taste of cognac."

"I'll have a cherry on top," I said with a smile.

"Two parts champagne, one part gin, one part orange juice, a dash of grapefruit and a trickle of cherry brandy," Archie told the waiter, who wrote down the concoction. "My girl Olive here invented it," he said.

"No, I didn't, you did."

"Okay, fine," Ruthie said, "twist my arm. If it's got brandy in it, I'll have what she's having."

"A round for the table," he said, counting the ladies I'd brought with us for the evening, as well as his friends who'd joined our table. "Make it ten, and bring these ladies a menu—they've been performing all night."

Before long, some of the middle tables got pushed to the sides or taken out back to make way for a small dance floor in front of the jazz band. Once the girls had some food in their stomachs and some hooch in their veins, they were up and dancing. I hung back with Archie.

"I don't want you to leave town again tomorrow," I said. "I'm going to miss you terribly."

"Believe me, I don't want to leave, but I have to head back to Cincinnati if I want my company to keep running. Are you sure you can't come with me?"

"You know I can't. I've got shows every night this week. Who else would fly offstage if not me?"

"Yes, into another man's arms," he said with a schoolboy's sulk.

"I landed in a lady's arms tonight, and it was far more exhilarating than the sweaty palms of some apple-knocker from out of town. You can rest assured I've only got eyes for one big-timer, and that's you." I leaned in and gave him a kiss. He grabbed my chair and pulled it closer to him.

"Why don't you stay at my suite in the Plaza while I'm gone—keep the bed warm?"

"It'll cost a fortune to keep it while you're gone, and I can stay at my own place." The thought of waking up there, padding around in a plush robe and ordering breakfast in the room overlooking Central Park sounded dreamy.

"Olive, you must," he said. "Besides, you'll be doing me a favor—I've leased it for the whole year—I wouldn't want it to sit unused until I return."

I smiled. He seemed to mean it. "Well, if you insist."

"Just promise me you'll talk to Ziegfeld and ask for some time off. Next time I want to take you with me and introduce you to my friends and my family. My mother's going to adore you—she's a big fan of the arts."

"I'd love to meet her." The fact that he wanted me to meet his mother felt quite serious, but strangely it didn't terrify me as I might have expected. In fact, it made me feel closer to him, and though I couldn't quite picture what might lie ahead, something about the mystery of it all left me feeling excited. I was curious to meet the woman who raised such a thoughtful, generous and driven man. I'd seen how hard it had been for my mother to keep three boys on track, teaching them manners, instilling respect, helping them find their interests, which would hopefully lead to success, so even without meeting Archie's mother I admired what she'd accomplished.

"And after Cincinnati I want to take you to Paris."

I laughed. I didn't mean to, but the two cities hardly seemed to belong in the same sentence. Paris sounded so much more evocative.

Archie kept on. "It's a sin that you haven't yet been."

"Oh, Paris . . ." I put my hands on my heart. "It's calling me—just be careful, because I have a feeling I'm going to fit right in there and might never want to return."

"First stop, we have to go to the Folies Bergère—that was Ziegfeld's inspiration, you know. And then the Louvre."

"And the Eiffel Tower," I said.

Archie rolled his eyes. "Sure thing, but knowing you, you're going to have more fun ducking into the cafés and meeting some of the expats than you are playing a wide-eyed tourist."

Archie had made a point to be in Manhattan when I returned home from the Adirondacks and we'd spent every spare minute together. After just a few short weeks in the city, I was already having a hard time imagining my days without him. We'd fallen into a routine. He had business dinners while I performed, and he often brought his work associates to the *Frolic* after. He picked me up from my show each night, and we either headed down to the Village, stayed in Times Square or jetted up to Harlem. We both stayed in his suite at the Plaza, then in the morning he'd order room service and we'd try alternating techniques to cure our hangovers. Archie swore by a fernet and Coca-Cola and rubbing vinegar on his temples, while I could get by on a cold glass of tomato juice, plain toast and a nap, which didn't work out so well for me on rehearsal days. Those first few weeks back in Manhattan together were nonstop, each of us wanting to show the other our version of the city and to show each other off to our friends.

We went to the Cotton Club one night, to a boxing match in New Jersey the next, to dinner at a politician's town house the next. What I loved most about Archie was his ability to fit in wherever we went—he appreciated the opportunity to explore new and different places, and he was fascinated to meet people with all different lifestyles. He could hang his hat at an uptown club just as well as he could at a speakeasy in the Village. We were like chameleons, the two of us, not too fancy but perfectly at home getting all gussied up and mingling with anyone we might meet.

After the Grotto closed, we went to Tony's for a nightcap.

"Ruthie and I are dead set on heading up to Harlem," Pauline said, tugging on my arm. "Tell Archie and his friends they have to come."

"I want to, but we can't tonight."

"Come on, Olive, you've got some life left in you."

"Of course I have," I said. "But Archie leaves tomorrow, so I'm going to make sure he gets a good night's sleep."

We walked up to the Plaza arm in arm. "Mr. Carmichael, welcome back," the doorman said, holding open the glass door to the towering marble palace. I felt like a million bucks walking through those doors with Archie by my side. At the beginning of the summer, I could never have imagined being taken with someone so mature and businesslike and yet so fun and dashing. I wouldn't have thought it possible for me to take my eyes off the stage for more than a minute for a man, but the funny thing was I was having a grand time onstage and a grand time off. It was as if I were proving everyone wrong. I could have it all.

Archie led us over to the manager at the front desk. "I wanted to let you know I'll be heading back to Cincinnati tomorrow for a week or so, and Miss Shine will be staying as my guest in my suite."

"Of course, Mr. Carmichael, I will be sure to let the staff know."

"Thank you, I'm glad to know she will be well taken care of, and if there's anything she needs, anything at all, please make sure she is attended to."

"As you wish, sir."

CHAPTER SEVENTEEN

I sat in the plush grey velvet chair, looking out the window while I sipped my tea. The fall leaves were aflame in the treetops outside. I crossed my legs Indian style and massaged the arches of my feet, painful lately from wearing my dancing shoes for so many hours each day.

Archie had been gone two days but it felt like two weeks, and the Plaza was less magical somehow without someone to share it with. I took the elevator to the lobby and went to the telephone booth to try to reach him, but when I picked up the receiver, I felt a sudden urge to call home.

"Flatbush six-seven-two-seven," I said to the operator.

With the exception of a few letters that I'd sent home to my mother letting her know my whereabouts, I hadn't actually seen my parents or my brothers for over a year.

"Mama?" I said when she picked up.

"Olive," she said with a sigh. "Thank God. I've been worried about you."

"I've missed you, Mama." As soon as I said it, my eyes filled with tears, and the sudden rush of emotion surprised me. I'd been busy lately with the nightly performances, rehearsals, a few more commercial sittings and now spending time with Archie every spare minute I could get. I was the happiest I'd been in a very long time—ever, really—yet something about not sharing that with my mother made it all feel less real somehow. It was as if I couldn't really enjoy this new life I'd built for myself if I couldn't share it with my family, if I couldn't have their blessing. It was a thought that lurked around in the back of my head, brushed aside. But now, hearing her voice made me want her approval, and my father's, more than ever.

"Is everything okay?" my mother asked. "Where are you?"

"Everything's wonderful. I'm at the Plaza."

"The Plaza?" She sounded skeptical about this, and I could hear a thousand questions running through her mind.

"Oh Mama, I have to see you, to tell you everything. I know it's been a long time but can you come here? We could have tea."

"Of course, Olive. Tell me when and I'll be there."

The following afternoon I got to the Palm Court tearoom early. It was an impressive, airy space with live palm trees reaching up to the glass ceiling, enormous marble columns and mirrored doors. I wore a below-the-knee cream chiffon dress with a dropped waist, white lace gloves, cream cloche hat and the string of pearls that Archie had given me. I sat watching the entrance for her arrival and jumped up when I saw her.

"I'm so relieved to see you." She took my face in her hands when we were seated. "It's been far too long. Oh, Olive, your father's very . . ." She looked down, almost as if ashamed.

"It's okay, I know." I nodded. I wanted to ask her about him, if he'd eased up even just a little, if he might be open to a visit, but apparently the answer was no, not yet. "Isn't this place magnificent?" I looked up to the domed yellow-and-green skylight.

"It is, but what are you doing here?"

The waiter approached our table.

"We'll have anchovy canapés and the stuffed celery to start," I said. "Oh, and Mother, you must try the cassoulet of lobster. Would you like that?"

"Just tea," she said demurely. "Thank you."

"The new season just started. The *Midnight Frolic* is going really well," I said, but I saw my mother look down as I said it. The word "frolic," perhaps, was off-putting. "It's a late night revue, a way for audience members to see more of the show," I said, gauging to see if this satisfied her. "I'm the star of that show, Mother. I'm not in the *Follies* anymore, I'll tell you about that later. . . ." I trailed off when I realized she wasn't really listening, or interested, smoothing the tablecloth, looking around the room, slightly uneasy.

"What are you doing here, Olive?" she asked again.

I paused. I couldn't force her to care about the show. "I have a beau."

Almost immediately my mother's face started to light up. "Well, that's good news. Your father will be thrilled."

Her response made me tense. Why did it have to be this news that gave her the greatest thrill, not my well-being, not my success? I tried to settle myself and revive the excitement I had just felt in anticipation of telling her about Archie.

"I can't wait for you to meet him. He runs a gas company in Cincinnati, but this is his New York home." I spread my arms open as if to suggest he owned the place. "I have my apartment, of course, with Ruthie, as I told you in my letters," I quickly added, not wanting her to get the wrong impression. "But it's lovely to come here for lunch or tea now and again. They treat me very well here, even when Archie is away on business."

She looked around the room as if to see what all the fuss was about. I suddenly felt silly, as if I were showing off, as if I needed to impress her, as if I wanted her to go home and tell my father how well I was doing, that I had made it, without compromises. Was that what I was trying to do?

"How is the apartment, with the girls?" It seemed to pain her to ask—the thought of her only daughter living independently in the big city like a sinner.

"It's great," I said, sipping my tea. Ordinarily, my mother would have loved it here at the Palm Court, ornate and luxurious, but she seemed too uneasy to be impressed.

"Is he kind to you, Olive?"

"Oh Mama, the kindest."

"And does he know about . . ." She paused, and I tensed, wondering what she might bring up. "You know, your performing?"

"Of course he does! Ugh, Mother, you are starting to sound like Papa."

"I'm just asking because you know how men can be."

"He's not like other men. We met at the theater, he's cultured, he's seen the world. He collects art," I blurted out. "My performance was what drew him to me."

She nodded. "Don't get upset, darling, I'm just saying that sometimes what attracts a man to a woman is not always what he wants in a wife."

I rolled my eyes. She didn't understand and she wouldn't until she met him for herself. I was agitated all over again and I didn't want to be. I wanted her to be happy for me, to trust in my ability to choose a man who wanted me for who I really was. I knew she had reason to doubt my judgment, I'd made mistakes, but I wasn't the same girl anymore, I'd grown up.

Forgetting myself for a moment, I slipped an Egyptian cigarette out of my jeweled cigarette case, placed it in its ivory holder and held it out for a waiter to light. When I looked up, my mother was staring at me with her mouth open.

"Olive, what are you doing?"

I froze for a second. Never in a million years would I have anticipated lighting a cigarette in front of my mother, but it was too late to pretend that it hadn't happened, so I chose to go on. "Oh Mother," I said quietly. "We're modern women now. It's okay."

"It's not okay," she said in a hushed voice. "It's not ladylike, Olive, smoking is a man's habit."

"Times have changed," I said, wondering momentarily if I really believed it.

She closed her eyes and took a deep breath. As she did so, the waiter approached and I leaned into him, expecting a match to be lit and held out for me. I'd already pulled out the cigarette, I might as well smoke it. But I was mistaken.

"Miss Shine," he said firmly, "smoking is absolutely not permitted in the Palm Court."

"Excuse me?" I said, taken aback. "I happen to know for a fact that Mr. Carmichael is free to smoke when and where he wishes."

"Yes, in the Oak Room with other gentlemen only," he said.

It took me a minute to comprehend what had just happened and then compose myself. In a matter of seconds, I had not only disgusted my mother but been rebuked by a waiter in front of her.

"My good man," I said after a moment's pause, "last I heard this was a free country, and I don't intend to do anything to change that."

"Madam . . ." He began to look stricken. "I apologize for the inconvenience, but this is just not the kind of establishment that encourages such behavior from young women. I can have an ashtray taken up to Mr. Carmichael's suite if you'd prefer to continue your tea in your room."

My mother looked from the waiter to me, and I could see the pieces falling into place. I'd been staying here in his room, and she knew it. It felt horrible to let her down, but I wasn't about to let her see me treated like this, so I looked in my purse and found a book of matches. While the waiter stood glaring at me in horror, and my mother probably did the same, I lit a match and brought it to the tip of the cigarette.

"We're quite all right where we are, thank you," I said, trying to enjoy the moment of defiance, but as I brought the cigarette to my lips I saw my hand tremble ever so slightly. Finally, I looked over to my mother, and the disappointment on her face was crushing.

"We can't have them treat us like that, Mother," I said after the waiter stormed off. "It's wrong, we have the vote now, we must stand up for our basic freedoms."

The waiter appeared at our table again. "Right here, please," he said, and he instructed two younger waiters to place a Japanese screen around our table, shielding the other diners from our view. "The sight is offending our guests."

"Now, if you'd said the smell was bothering them, I might have put it out," I said. "But if they can't stand to see a young woman exercise her rights, then maybe they need an education in how the modern world works."

The waiter turned on his heel and left, and my mother began to collect her things. I reached out and put my hand on hers. "Where are you going, Mama? Don't let them bully us into leaving."

"It's not them," she said softly. "It's you." I saw her eyes fill with tears. "Your manners, your lack of etiquette, of decency—living here as an unwed woman with a man you've only just met—even your lovely hair . . ." She reached out and tucked a piece of my cropped hair behind my ear. "It's all gone."

She stood, pushed in her chair and gently placed her handbag on her arm. "Olive, you're forgetting who you are."

"You're wrong, Mama," I said, almost in a whisper. "For the first time in my life I know exactly who I want to be."

CHAPTER EIGHTEEN

We had barely begun the second act of the *Frolic* when the doors flew open and about twenty policemen burst onto the scene, followed by a handful of men in suits who barked instructions.

"Everyone freeze!" one of them yelled.

The orchestra stopped abruptly, and some girls dashed offstage to grab their clothes while the rest of us onstage froze. We'd heard of raids where men and women were arrested by federal agents—I'd seen them photographed in the paper, publicly shamed for dancing or mingling in an alcohol-serving establishment. The last thing I needed, after my disastrous meeting with my mother, was my picture in the paper in handcuffs, but I couldn't tear my eyes away from the vulgarity of it all. One minute there was music and dancing, appreciation and harmless enjoyment, many guests spending their hard-earned money on a late dinner, and the next people were running and cowering and scared. I was scared, too, terrified, actually, with no idea what would happen. What if we got hauled away? Where would we be taken, how long would we be kept there, who would I have to call to get released?

The irony of it was that Ziegfeld hadn't wanted to sell alcohol in the first place. He would have been quite happy to serve the best food alongside the most desirable dancers and call it a night. Many of his elite regulars, however, asked him to store and serve their private wine collection behind the bar—which technically didn't violate the rules. And the rest of the guests, well, they insisted that hooch and watching the show went hand in hand, and if they couldn't have both, they threatened to take their business elsewhere. So reluctantly Ziegfeld appeased them, getting his hands on bottles of champagne for a pretty price. At the first sight of agents, the rumor was that the barkeeps knew to pull a hidden lever that sent an entire row of champagne bottles into a crate in the wall of the bar.

"I'm not selling this!" Ziegfeld shouted at the agents, clearly distraught as they stormed in, not caring to differentiate between what he was selling and what he was storing and serving.

I'd never been in a raid before, but I always thought the goal was to arrest as many patrons as possible for purchasing liquor and fine the owners so much that they'd be forced to shut down or pay off the police. But this raid seemed different. They weren't making arrests. They weren't even harassing Ziegfeld. Instead they headed straight for the bar.

"There's nothing here!" we could hear Ziegfeld yelling at them. "These are private wine collections, collections that they already had in their homes. These are not for sale, I assure you!" But the agents didn't care, and it was strange to see the all-powerful Mr. Ziegfeld ignored. One agent picked up bottles of vintage red wine, pulled out the cork with his teeth and took a swig. Then they formed an assembly line of sorts, agents behind the bar picking up bottles, some worth as much as my rent, I'd guess, and throwing them over the bar to another agent, who threw them across the room to another, who dumped it all into a large open-topped barrel. Some bottles just clanked in, but others shattered. Wine and bourbon spilled out onto the carpet. Some agents missed—intentionally, it seemed—shattering glass and spilling hooch all over the beautiful space. It was dreadful. Patrons ran for the doors and the agents didn't try to stop them; they were intent on emptying out Ziegfeld's entire stock of alcohol.

When they left, we all gathered out on the red and sticky dance floor. I was so relieved that I hadn't been arrested but devastated at the sight of it all. Ziegfeld surveyed the damage.

"It's horrible, Mr. Ziegfeld," one of the girls called out, starting to sob. "It's awful what they've done to this place, they have no right."

He shook his head and took it all in. "This doesn't matter," he said. "This can all get cleaned up. This dance floor will be mopped, the linens will be washed, and the tables and chairs put back in their place. All evidence of this raid will be gone after the cleaning crew comes in and does its job, so don't worry about that. What matters is that our patrons come to us for an exclusive, luxurious good time. They trust that my staff will treat them with the utmost respect, they will eat the finest food, and they will be treated with dignity. My patrons don't deserve this. If we cannot operate without this kind of disrespectful intrusion, sending our moneyed clientele out into the streets like criminals, then I don't even know if we should go on." He shook his head, and some of the girls gasped. I tried to remain stoic, though inside I knew I was in hot water. I might not be in the *Follies* anymore, but with Howie's help I'd become one of the stars of the *Frolic*. I couldn't fathom him closing it down. I'd have nothing.

"It's been a bad night, Flo," Howie said, stepping in and taking him by the arm. "Let's not jump to any rash decisions tonight. We can beat this ridiculous Volstead Act, we can prove that those wine bottles belonged to patrons fair and square, and that they weren't being sold. They didn't see the champagne—it's all in the back as planned." I imagined Howie was also starting to worry and working hard to set Ziegfeld on the right track. "You make money with tickets and dinner. If you can't sell hooch, people will still come."

"Sure they will," one of the girls agreed.

"We almost got taken off to jail," Lara wailed. We turned and gave her a look—we were trying to keep our jobs here, not make things worse.

"No one's going to jail," Ziegfeld said. "I'm going to get all this cleaned up, and I'm going to take some time to think things through," he added at last. "Ladies," he said, turning to us and smiling, trying to act as if he weren't shaken from the experience, "take the next week off, get some rest, let's meet back here in a week, and I'll have a plan."

With that he left, leaving a group of nervous young women behind him, wondering if they'd get paid, wondering how they'd make their rent, worrying about their future.

He just got spooked," I told Archie when I met him at the Plaza that evening. We lay back on his bed after he'd just called down for oysters to be delivered. I didn't feel like going out after all that, not yet, anyway. "He's been raided before and the show has gone on. This shouldn't be any different," I said. But part of me was scared that the agents had gone too far this time, and he was getting tired of it.

"Can he still make a profit, though?" Archie asked, turning his head toward mine. "Without the alcohol sales? I'm not so sure he can. Between the costumes and the stage design, he seems to pay out a lot to make that place as luxurious and swanky as possible."

"I sure hope so," I said. "I don't know what I'd do without that show, it's everything to me."

"Everything?" Archie asked.

"Well, not everything," I said, reaching over and running my fingers through his hair. "But it makes me very happy to be on that stage, you know that."

"I sure do," he said. "But I think there are other things that could make you happy too."

"Oh, really?"

Archie leaned in and kissed me. His soft lips on mine, his smooth, clean-shaven cheeks, the hint of his cologne, it made me forget everything else for a moment. He wrapped his arms around my waist and pulled me toward him.

"You make me happy," I said.

He began to unbutton my blouse, but there was a knock at the door.

"The oysters," I said, giggling.

"Don't go anywhere," he said, straightening himself up and tucking in his shirt. "Stay right where you are."

I lay on the bed and listened as he opened the door. "Right here will be fine, thank you," Archie said. "Oh, and we'll be needing two glasses sent up."

"I see," the waiter said. "I'll send them right away."

When Archie returned with a silver cart, a tower of oysters and an ice bucket, I told him about the way the staff had treated me in the Palm Court with my mother.

"They suggested that I was some kind of prostitute, staying in your suite while you were away," I said. "Honestly, they were terribly rude, in front of my mother, too."

"That's terrible! We can't have your reputation tarnished like that. I thought since I was away on business they would understand you were simply my guest, but I think I've been too greedy, wanting to spend so much time with you. Maybe I should get you a suite of your own."

"No, I have my own apartment. I suppose I should stay there once in a while."

"But darling," he added as he opened his closet and took out a bottle of champagne from his stash and placed it on ice, "it's unheard of for a woman to smoke at the Plaza."

"How was I supposed to know? Where do you get that from, anyway?" I asked, nodding toward the bottle.

"From Europe via Canada via a guy named Eddie."

"Aren't you going to open it?"

"Not until it's cold."

"Just put some ice chips in mine, it will be fine."

He shook his head. "That would be a sin, to put ice chips in Moët and Chandon. Do you know how hard it is to get your hands on this?"

I grabbed it from his hands, popped the cork to the ceiling and took a sip. "It's not that difficult," I said with a grin.

Archie threw up his arms in defeat, collapsed onto the bed next to me and took a swig from the bottle.

"Anyway, why is it unheard of for a woman to smoke here?"

"It just is, it's the Plaza. I'm sorry I didn't warn you. And your poor mother."

"Well, that wasn't the only thing that disappointed my mother."

"Go on."

"The waiter let on that I'd been staying here, with you, and she was horrified."

"Oh, Olive. Would it help if you introduced me, to show them that I'm a respectable gentleman?" he asked, continuing to unbutton my blouse.

"Respectable?"

"As respectable as they come," he said, kissing my neck.

"The best thing we can do right now is lay low. I certainly don't want her to tell my father—he'll disown me for good if he knows I've been staying here with you as an unwed woman."

"Agreed. I haven't even met him yet, I certainly don't want him to have a bad opinion of me." He drank from the bottle. "I have an idea," he said suddenly. "Let's get away from all of this. Let's go upstate to the Adirondacks this week. I have some business to take care of up there, and nothing would make me happier than to have you join me. We can stay at the Pines again." He looked at me to gauge my interest. "Come on, it's beautiful at this time of year. With all that hoopla at the club tonight, I think getting out of the city and spending a few days in the country is probably exactly what you need."

"It sounds lovely, but I have to be back at the theater in a week, that sounds like a quick turnaround."

"We can leave tomorrow. I just have something I need to take care of in the morning, then we'll take my train car, no waiting around. I'll have it connected to the most direct trains and we'll get there in less than twenty-four hours. I'll make sure you enjoy the journey as much as the destination."

He wasn't kidding. We boarded the train early and were greeted by the same butler I'd met the first time I saw his railcar.

We sat on the two-seater facing the windows.

"I do love a good adventure," I said, smiling.

"And I love your spontaneity," Archie said. "I could tell from the minute you flew off that stage and landed in my arms that you had a wild streak in you." He ran his fingers across my wrist, and just one touch sent a shiver up my arm. I felt like a teenager around him.

"I've always been thrilled by the feeling of not knowing what comes next," I said. "I've craved that feeling of excitement since I was a child, but growing up my family didn't share that sentiment." I leaned back on the plush down-filled cushions. "They wanted to know what their immediate future held, they were a family of planners and organizers, with routines and schedules and set dinnertimes. I've always been the outsider in that regard. I'm telling you, even what we ate for dinner was planned out. On Mondays, we had baked ham with carrots and peas. Tuesdays, lamb chops and mashed potatoes. Wednesdays, my father met friends at the club, so we had leftover baked ham sandwiches and apple jelly. Thursday was broiled veal cutlets and fried tomatoes."

"That would drive me crazy," Archie said.

"It was the same thing week after week. If there was a change to be made, and that was a rare occurrence, my mother wrote it on the blackboard in the kitchen. Every day was so predictable."

I thought back to the conversation I'd had with my mother at the kitchen table before I moved out of their house in Flatbush, her hint at disdain for her domesticated life. I'd always been so resentful of those mundane dinners, I'd never considered for a moment that she might feel the same way.

"Maybe that's why you grew up to be such a daring thing," he said. "You rebelled against the routine."

"Probably."

Early that evening after lounging all day, watching out the window as the countryside flew past us, enjoying card games, Archie told me it was time to dress for dinner and presented me with a gift box wrapped in a large silver bow.

"May I?" he asked before he untied the bow, took off the lid and tilted the box toward me.

"Wow," I said, picking up an emerald-green dress with three tiers of fringe that swished gently with the motion of the train. The appliqué on the bodice was treelike, with gold and green leaves, and it felt reminiscent of the lush greenery we'd been passing through all afternoon. "It's stunning, thank you."

By seven P.M. I was freshened up and dressed for the evening ahead. Outside, day was turning into night and the sky was a rich shade of blue. The lounge had been transformed and was set up as an elegant private dining salon, with the sofa moved to the end of the room and a romantic table for two in the center. Archie stood by the window, handsome in a black tuxedo. He turned and looked at me.

"A vision," he said. "That's always my favorite part—seeing you walk into a room. You look beautiful."

"I feel beautiful, thank you," I said, giving a little twirl, letting the fringe of the dress sway from side to side.

Miniature hors d'oeuvres were brought out to us two at a time— stuffed mushrooms, salmon mousse and toasted bread, olives and even oysters.

Archie took my hand and walked me over to the gramophone. We danced to Bessie Smith's "Back-Water Blues," and I felt as though I could stay on that train with him forever. Suddenly the city and stage seemed so far away.

Once we sat down, the butler came out of the kitchen with a tray perched on his shoulder with two beautifully molded individual Jell-O salads—each one about six inches tall. "Look how they jiggle." I laughed, shimmying in unison with them.

"This is quite a spread for a train ride," I said. "How is all of this even possible?"

"Anything is possible if you want it badly enough—you know that."

He delivered the masterpieces to us, slices of tomato, cucumber, celery and green pepper, captured midrotation and suspended in clear yellow gelatin. It danced in front of me with the motion of the train, and it almost seemed a shame to cut into it.

"So, Olive, I've been thinking about the Pines Camp."

"Oh, me too—it's such a magical place. I never dreamed I'd like it so much when Ziegfeld first told me about it."

"What if I bought it for you as an engagement present?"

"What?" I laughed, but my stomach flipped with the thrill of his words. "What do you mean? We're not even engaged."

"Well, that's something I've been wanting to talk to you about." He stood from the table and came around to where I was sitting. Everything else seemed to happen in slow motion. He reached inside his jacket pocket and pulled out a small seafoam-green box with a white bow, then took a step back and was down on one knee in front of me. I couldn't believe what was happening.

"Archie," I said in a whisper, suddenly overcome with emotion. "What are you doing?"

"Olive May McCormick Shine," he said, taking my left hand in his and kissing it. "I love everything about you, and I don't want to spend another minute of my life without you by my side. Would you do me the great honor of being my wife?"

I put my hand over my mouth, stunned. I couldn't believe what was unfolding. I couldn't speak.

"Olive, my darling, will you marry me?"

"Yes." I stood and pulled him to his feet. "Yes, Archie, nothing would make me happier." I kissed him.

"Well, then let me place this on your finger before you change your mind," he said. He opened the box and took out a huge emerald-cut diamond ring with two baguette diamonds on either side.

"Oh my," I said, breathless, stunned all over again.

He slipped the ring onto my finger and kissed my hand. "This, my love, this is where it all begins."

CHAPTER NINETEEN

There was a dusting of snow on the ground when we reached the Pines Camp, even though it had been a crisp fall day back in Manhattan.

I'd been caught so off guard with the engagement, and the fact that I'd said yes, that I hadn't given much thought to what we'd be doing once we arrived.

"I'm surprised Anne's here at this time of year," I said.

"She's packing up some of her belongings, and we're going to sign the paperwork."

"You were already buying this place?"

Archie smiled. "I've been talking to them about it since the beginning of the summer, but I want it to be yours. I know how much you enjoy socializing and entertaining, and this is the perfect place to do that. We'll change anything you like to make it more accommodating."

This was starting to sound like a lot of fun. Ruthie had been right—any place this difficult to get to had a certain appeal, an exclusivity that made it seem even more mysterious and magical than it already was.

"It's nice to see you again, Olive," Anne said as we climbed down from the carriage. She was wrapped in a fur shawl, looking elegant as usual.

"We're so happy to be here." I was beaming. I knew it and yet I couldn't help myself, I was desperate to tell someone the news.

"Olive?" She looked inquisitively from Archie to me. "Archie? What is it? You're keeping something from me."

"We're engaged!" I jumped a little and held out my hand. It wasn't the way she would have announced it, I'm sure—she would have waited for us to be seated inside, luggage unpacked, sipping tea from bone china—but I wasn't her, and I was giddy with excitement.

"I am thrilled to hear this," she said. "Raymond! Come on out here, we have some fantastic news—and let's put some bubbly on ice!"

We spent the next few days touring the property and meeting the rest of the guides we'd somehow inherit with the camp. Jose showed us around and walked us down to the vegetable garden and the small farm that housed chickens, two dairy cows, a goat and some sheep. And the stables! Four beautiful horses were being fed when we passed by.

"What are we going to do with all of this, Archie?" I asked when Jose went into the stables. "It's lovely, but I don't know what to do with these animals."

He took my hand and led me into the chicken coop, where he opened a little door at the end of an enclosed shed. He reached in and took out two eggs.

"We're going to make omelets!" he said. "The staff live here year-round, they know what to do. They'll take care of the animals, just like they'll take care of the property, and in the dead of winter they'll fill the icehouse with blocks of ice from the lake so we're well stocked for summer. Believe me, Raymond and Anne have this place running like a well-oiled machine."

Being in the wilderness was freeing. The air was clean, the views of the lake and the forests beyond were magnificent. Jose rejoined us, and as we were about to head back up the hill to the main lodge, I saw one of the horses had stuck her head out of the stall and was watching us.

"Here, feed her these and she'll be your friend for life," Jose said, placing a few carrots in my hand. "This here is Lady. We think she might be going to foal early next summer."

She stretched her neck out and started nudging my hand impatiently. "All right, Lady, hold on." I opened my hand flat and let her take a carrot off my palm, her wet lips and nose making me laugh. She munched on it quickly and sniffed my hand for more, so I held another one out for her and smoothed down her long, muscular neck.

"Some people say if you blow in their nostrils it helps them bond with you," Jose said. "I think it's an old wives' tale myself, but some horse folk swear by it."

"I'll come back and visit you, Lady," I said, admiring her long eyelashes, her sharp eyes looking at me.

Later that night after dinner with the Belmonts in the main lodge, Archie and I collapsed into bed.

"How far did we walk today?" I asked.

"A long way."

I lay on my back, stretching my legs one at a time, pointing my toes. "What if we got married right here?" I asked.

"Here?" He propped himself up on an elbow and smiled. "I thought you'd want to do something ritzy in the city, at the Plaza or someplace."

I lay back. "My whole life is pretty ritzy. I have so much glamour onstage and our city life is so fun and extravagant. I love it, don't get me wrong, but this would be special, different and real."

"Our friends could join us here," Archie said.

"Can you imagine the fun—transporting everyone up here by train and boat?" I said. "It would be a party before the party even begins."

"It should be summer," Archie said.

"End of summer, or Ziegfeld will be furious if I'm not there for the midsummer shows."

Archie laughed. "Whenever you want, Olive. I will be the luck-iest man alive."

I snuggled into him. "And I will be the luckiest girl."

CHAPTER TWENTY

Back in the city, Ziegfeld called a meeting and told us the show must go on. He said he refused to be bullied by some crooked agents attempting to hold up an absurd and crooked law, so we all, very gratefully, got right back to work.

But one month later I was already asking for a few days off to attend the wedding of one of Archie's business partners in Cincinnati. Ziegfeld wasn't thrilled about my leaving right before opening the new holiday show, but I knew it was important to Archie for me to meet his mother and his business associates, and this was the ideal opportunity.

Archie had been in Ohio on business for a week already. He picked me up from Union Station in his hunter-green Rolls-Royce Phantom, and that baby could purr. The late November air was biting, so I quickly pulled the windows shut.

"Are you crazy driving around in this weather with the windows open?" I asked. "It's freezing out here, and I just fixed my hair and face."

"Everyone's going to love you no matter how you look," he said, leaning over to give me a kiss.

"Keep your eyes on the road, darling, precious cargo here. I have to get back in one piece, the Christmas show's starting in a week."

"Don't I know it."

"When will I meet your mother, Archie?" I was quite looking forward to finally meeting the woman who'd raised this fine man.

"She'll be at the wedding, so definitely today."

"Oh good, I'll be on my best behavior, then." I laughed. "I have to say, this is a beauty," I said, running my hand along the dashboard of the car. He had a thing for cars and kept them in a garage at his family home, which he promised to show me over the weekend.

"She's my newest addition and she's one of my favorites."

He draped his right arm over the back of the seat and around my shoulders.

"If you love cars so much, why do you have a driver in the city?"

"The fun really comes when you're driving like this, out on the open road, no one honking at you, no streetcars competing for space on the road."

I shrugged. "Makes sense, but seems a shame to keep them locked up here in Cincinnati."

"Are you pulling my leg? It gives me something to look forward to when I come home."

It was pretty and all, the greenery, the mansions with the huge lawns set back from the roads, but I couldn't imagine calling a place like this home, not a streetlight in sight, let alone a billboard.

"Don't squint your pretty eyes like that," he said, taking my hand on the white leather between us. "I grew up here, remember, it will always feel like home to me."

It had taken me eighteen hours to get there in Archie's railcar. I rode through Pennsylvania, Maryland, West Virginia, and, oh, I lost count of the others. After a while, though, no matter how luxurious, staying in one train car with no one but his butler, William, to converse with, I began to go a little crazy.

"I can't wait to get on the dance floor, Archie. My legs are falling asleep."

"Not long now, Olive," he said.

We arrived just before the ceremony began and slipped into a pew in the back. Flowers were everywhere, the groom standing at the front of the church anxiously awaiting his bride, the guests chattering, hats bobbing. And then the room silenced as the bridal processional began.

I'd attended a few weddings before, but I'd never been particularly interested in the details until now. Just the sound of the organ, everyone turning to watch the bride enter the room, arm in arm with her father, filled me with unexpected emotion as I began to imagine what our own wedding day would feel like. I longed for things with my father to be patched up by then. I hadn't seen him since I'd moved out of their house in Flatbush over a year ago and I couldn't picture a day so special without my family at my side.

Afterwards, Archie drove us to his friend's house for the reception.

"Here we are," he said, turning into a long brick driveway and through an ornate wrought-iron gate with two stone columns on either side. At the top of the driveway was a palatial home. A stone staircase led up to the white stone house. There were four columns in front, and between them were two cathedral windows flanking a shiny black front door. It was magnificent.

We were greeted and led into a crowded, stately room, and after just moments I heard a woman's voice call out over the others.

"Archibald!" A woman in a long rose-colored dress with long sleeves and a high neck strode toward us as if she owned the place. "I didn't see you at the church."

"We were in the back, Mother, we made a quick exit," he said.

"And you didn't think to drive me?"

"I assumed you'd have your driver. Was I wrong?"

She rolled her eyes. "That's not the point." I was starting to feel uncomfortable; she'd made no move to acknowledge me.

"Well, Mother, be that as it may, finally, allow me to introduce you to my fiancée, Miss Olive Shine. I'm so happy for you both to meet." He said it so proudly, and I loved seeing his face as he spoke.

"Welcome," she said, though the way she stood a few feet from me, her hands interlaced in front of her, seemed to suggest the opposite.

"So nice to finally meet you, Mrs. Carmichael," I said. "I've been so looking forward to it. I just arrived off the train, literally moments before the ceremony began."

"Lovely," she said as she turned and walked toward the reception area decked with white chairs, white flowers, white linens. "This way," she said. "I've seen to it that you're seated at my table."

Archie squeezed my hand as we followed behind her, and I wondered why he hadn't warned me about her before now.

"Tell me," she said to me once we were seated, "how was the train ride?"

"Very comfortable, thank you. But I'm glad to be here. I've never been to Cincinnati before and I've been so eager to meet Archie's family, especially you. You've done such a fine job with this gentleman." I smiled at Archie, but it was as if his mother didn't even hear me.

"A city girl," she said with what I thought seemed a hint of disdain.

"Well, now I am," I said, reaching into my purse for my cigarette case out of habit when things felt tense or awkward. But recalling the incident at the Plaza, I quickly changed my mind. Archie was such a kind, warm soul—all my friends commented on how easy he was to talk to, how they felt they'd known him for years when they'd only just met—so I hadn't expected his mother to come across so icy.

Archie came to my rescue and took me around the room, introducing me to some of his work associates and their wives. They were pleasant, some a little too interested in the fact that I was a show girl, but mostly, I gathered, it was because they'd never met one before. And then, as we were finally making our way toward the dance floor, Archie made an abrupt turn in the opposite direction and took me with him.

"Where are we going?" I asked.

"There's someone I'd rather not—"

And then a woman's voice called out. Younger than his mother's but shrill just the same. "Archibald, is that you?" Archie kept walking. "Archibald, I know it's you." He slowed his step and turned.

"Louise," he said.

Oh, it was *that* Louise.

She was attractive, I'd give her that. Blond, with high cheekbones and a disproportionately large mouth. Two slightly less attractive women stood at her sides.

"Archie, darling, no need to run away with your tail between your legs." She laughed. "This must be the—"

"Louise," Archie said quickly, "this is Olive Shine." And then he dropped his head slightly, as if he couldn't believe he had found himself in this situation.

"Nice to meet you," I said. I could think of plenty of other things to say, but I imagined this was hard for her—to see her former beau in her hometown with his new fiancée. Or maybe she didn't know that part. Just as I thought it, she took a good hard look at my ring and smirked.

"You don't let the grass grow under your feet, do you, Archibald?" She shared a look of disgust with her two friends.

I bristled, but Archie squeezed my hand, so I kept my powder dry and refrained from giving her an earful.

"Well, I wish you two the best of luck," she said with a snort and that oversized mouth, laughing almost, and it infuriated me. Then the three of them walked off.

"Archie . . ." I turned to him. "Why didn't you tell me she'd be here?"

"I didn't think she would be, honestly. I'm sorry."

"And your mother, she acted as if I were some acquaintance, not her future daughter-in-law."

"She just takes a little time to warm up, that's all."

But I wasn't about to be dismissed, and I wanted to get some dancing in before dinner was served—it wouldn't hurt if it also bought me a little time before having to face his mother again.

"You're feeling blue about all this, aren't you, Olive," Archie said. "I really wanted this to be special for you, meeting my family and friends. Sorry about Louise, she's just sore about how things ended. She's very traditional, you know, a real—"

"Forget it, Archie," I said, kissing him so he'd stop talking about that dreadful woman. "Put it out of your head. We're here to have a good time, and I know one way you can make it up to me." I tugged him toward the orchestra.

"You've got that wild look in your eye, Olive—I don't know if they'll appreciate the style of dancing you like, the way they do in Manhattan."

"Do you really care what everyone thinks?"

Archie shrugged. He did care, but I was convinced he cared more about me.

"Please, darling," I said, skipping toward the orchestra. "Let's have some fun."

Archie paused for a second and then relented. "Let's," he said, and led the way.

We danced the Charleston, and Archie let Cincinnati have it. A few couples danced around the perimeter, a one-two up, one-two up, but boy, did we put them to shame. Archie didn't hold back, arms were swinging, legs were kicking, he turned me and touched the floor, pulling out all the stops. I always loved a man who could dance. And me, well, let's just say I gave them a good show.

We returned to the table as the appetizers were served. By the

Nicola Harrison

time we sat down, I felt one hundred times better. It was as it always was—a good dance could get rid of any bad feelings, just shake them loose and send them off to God knew where—anywhere but in my head. It worked for Archie, too, I could just see it in him.

But his mother glared.

"I've been sitting on that train for twenty-four hours straight," I said cheerfully. "Had to let off some steam."

She muttered something and dug into her shrimp cocktail.

"Mother!" said Archie, who was sitting between us.

"It's all right, darling," I said. "I can fend for myself."

Archie looked stricken by her remark, or maybe it was mine, but I wanted to show him that I could defend myself without losing grace. "I completely understand that this new development in the way of women is a regional phenomenon, picking up speed on the East and West Coasts of the country first, but Mrs. Carmichael, I assure you it will be here in your hometown soon enough if it's not already, so it's best to prepare yourself." I speared a shrimp with a cocktail fork, dipped it in the sauce and took a bite. "I don't know what you just called me, a flapper, perhaps, but I assure you I don't take it as an insult. Us new girls are able, independent individuals seeking freedom of thought and expression, casting off the shackles of fear." I'd read those words in a newspaper article on the train just that day. Lecturer Helen Ferguson Buchanan had defended us in a speech at the First Universalist Church and I was all for it. "The rise of flapperism is nothing but the flood of feminism that has been kept down through the ages and is now rushing through broken barriers to its new level." Thank God for Helen Ferguson Buchanan!

234

Mrs. Carmichael kept her head down, staring at the damned shrimp. I tried to keep up my cheerful banter, but the tension at the table was stifling. I looked to Archie, and he gave me a look as if to say, "Stop while you're ahead." But the silence was killing me.

"And it's not just women, you know, Archie is really quite progressive. He can—"

"My Archibald is nothing like you," she finally erupted in a deep, low growl. "He was raised with respect for manners and decorum, and we hardly envisioned any son of ours spending time with a show girl."

"Just hold your horses, Mother," Archie said. "Olive here was also raised in a good family. Her father is—"

"I don't care who her father is," she spat.

"Well, then you should care who she is, because as you very well know we are engaged to be married. Olive is an exceptionally talented performer in the Ziegfeld shows, Mother," Archie said firmly.

"One of the most sought-after shows in New York City," I chimed in. "You should come for a visit sometime and see for yourself." I tried to lighten the mood a little, but Archie wasn't done.

"More than that, she's a brilliant opera singer and has been approached by the Metropolitan Opera House." Mrs. Carmichael raised an eyebrow and so did I—that was a white lie. I'd told him what Alberto had suggested, but I certainly hadn't acted on it. I wasn't about to correct him, though. "And Olive's right, women in New York these days have a lot more freedoms, Mother, you're just not used to that here. But you need to catch up and fast."

"Well . . ." She blinked a few times, retracting her chin into her neck more than I thought possible. I think she didn't expect to be scolded by her son. "If you're a singer," she directed to me, "then drinking is going to do nothing to help your vocal cords." She nodded toward my bourbon.

"Excuse me for disagreeing, Mrs. Carmichael," I said as demurely as possible, since I didn't want to embarrass the woman any further, "but on the contrary, I actually find that it relaxes me and allows me to expand my diaphragm more than usual."

The other two couples at our table looked wretched, and I felt for them. They'd come for a lovely wedding and were being held captive at this table by a family feud.

"Do you know what?" I said, leaning over and touching the shoulder of the gentleman next to me. "I didn't even get your names. We were so busy talking politics over here. I'm Olive."

I drank down the bourbon, and when the dinner plates were taken away, and Archie was chatting with some colleagues at a neighboring table about business, I set out to find a refresher. When I approached the bar, however, I saw Louise, and she saw me. She quickly turned her back.

"Hi there, Louise," I said. "Just looking for a cocktail, not a cat-fight." She turned back to me. "Look, I know these things can get messy, bumping into a former flame."

"Messy?" she hissed. "Is that what you want to call it? Archibald called off his engagement to me, which had been well-known and celebrated news in these parts. Our families go back years. And for what? A gold-digging actress he just met."

"Whoa there, soldier," I said, shocked by her insulting accusations. "I'll have you know that I make my own money, thank you very much, and I didn't know that Archie had a penny to his name when I first met him. You can rest assured that his money is not what I'm after."

She shook her head.

"As for you and your engagement, I don't know what to tell you about that, Louise. Maybe a friend to this family is just the last thing he wants or needs."

I stood there alone for a few moments while she and her girls walked away.

"Oh, don't worry about her, dear." A middle-aged woman sidled up next to me at the bar. "She can be a real pill, everyone around here knows that."

"Thanks . . ."

"Peggy," she said. "I'm a friend of the family."

"Olive," I said.

"Oh, we know who you are, darlin'." She laughed. "You've been the talk of the town. His mother can be tricky, too, but you'll get the hang of things, and when you bring a baby or two into this family all will be forgiven. Everyone's sort of waiting on pins and needles for it, especially after"—she lowered her voice to a whisper—"everything that happened."

I must have looked dumbfounded.

"Oh dear," she said. "You do know about Archie's first wife, don't you? Have I gone and said something I shouldn't have?"

"What? Yes, Archie told me, such a terrible tragedy. Just unimaginable to lose them both like that. But he's not really the family type anymore."

"Yes, well, he's let a bit too much time pass between then and now if you ask me, but I'm sure it's hard to fall in love again after something like that, and there was so much pressure for him to find someone and carry on the family name. And, well . . ." She looked in the direction of Louise. "That's what that was, pressure from his mother, but he just needed to find the right one, and now it looks like he has." She squeezed my arm. "You just don't waste any time with all that," she said, reaching over and patting my stomach, "and you'll be just fine."

I danced the heck out of that reception, and I drank all the bourbon they would serve me. At some point, Archie took me back to his family home and settled me in my room.

"I hope you'll give my mother a chance, Olive," he said as he put me to bed. "I'm sorry about the way she spoke to you, but sometimes she doesn't realize the effect she can have on others."

After my chat with that Peggy woman, Archie's mother seemed like the least of my problems. But I wanted to tell him that his mother should appreciate me, someone who's pulled herself up and worked hard to get there. She of all people should appreciate that, after seeing Archie create his own fortune and then provide for her, buy her an enormous house and pay for her luxurious lifestyle. Maybe now that she was firmly situated in high society, she didn't want to let anyone in who might rock the boat. But even in my drunken state I knew better than to bring that up. Mothers were generally sacred territory.

"She made me feel unwelcome," I said simply, my head spinning from the hooch. First, I had been rejected by my own family with a curse that I'd never meet a reputable man who'd want anything to do with me, and now, after meeting the man of my dreams who wanted to marry me, his family was rejecting me, too. It felt rotten, and so did my head.

So when Archie came in the next morning with a telegram from Ziegfeld saying that I was needed back in New York and had to catch the next train out of town, it couldn't have come at a better time.

Archie handed it to me.

"What can he be thinking?" he fumed while I pored over the message. "He can't just expect you to drop everything and go back to New York so soon. You're not needed back there until Wednesday."

"It says there's an emergency, one of the girls had to leave the *Follies* unexpectedly." We both knew what that meant.

"I haven't had a chance to show you around."

"I know, darling, but there'll be other times," I said, though I wasn't sure if that was entirely true, given the reception I'd received so far. "One of the girls has probably taken ill, or . . ." I didn't want to say it.

"Or she's with child, I know, Olive, but that's hardly your fault."

"Of course it's not my fault, but he relies on his top girls to keep things running smoothly, and he's asking me to replace her—in the *Follies*. I'll be back on top."

"Well, he's going to have to replace *you* at some point," Archie said, walking to the window.

His remark stopped me in my tracks. "Excuse me?"

"Maybe not right away," he went on, "but this year or next year, certainly sometime before we get married, he's going to have to find himself the next Olive Shine soon enough."

"Why would he have to do that?"

Archie looked at me, surprised. "Well, you're hardly going to carry on as a show girl once we're married."

"Why not?" I said, taken aback by his words.

He looked at me with genuine confusion. "Sweetheart, you didn't think your performing career would continue once we were man and wife, did you? I can't have you wearing barely anything, tantalizing every man out there with your beauty."

He meant it as a compliment, I could tell from the way he spoke, but I couldn't believe it. It was as if I were having the very same conversation I'd had with my father, but with Archie.

"I feel . . . I worry that there's been some misunderstanding," I said slowly, sensing that the life we were starting to build together was slipping through my fingers. "I never said I would stop performing. It's who I am, it's what makes me happy, it's my reason to live."

"Oh, Olive." He came toward me and took my hands. "I want you to be happy, I want to give you everything you've ever dreamed of. All that talk about traveling together, seeing the world, how can we do that if you're handcuffed to the theater night after night? I have to travel for work, you know that, and when we're man and wife I want you by my side. I'll go crazy if I have to leave you for weeks at a time. Isn't that what all this is about, love and companionship?"

He made it all sound so important, so lovely, and I wanted it, of course, I did—but I wanted my life, too—the life I'd built for myself. I looked out the window, at a loss for words.

"And Olive," he said, bringing me into his embrace, "what if we have a child, two children, heck, even three, a real family—close your eyes and imagine it, Olive."

"You said you didn't want that," I whispered.

"I didn't think I did, but now, with you, it's all I can think about."

I closed my eyes and saw nothing but blackness. It felt as if I were sinking, slipping out of his arms, the floor swallowing me whole. Tears welled up, and I kept my eyes shut so that they wouldn't escape.

"I want to give you the world, Olive," he said, "and I hope you want the same for me." But all I could hear in my head was, I can't, I can't, I can't.

CHAPTER TWENTY-ONE

I had never intended to deceive him. I'd thought there were pieces of my past that were best left untold—what good would it do to bring all that up now? It would send me to pieces, for one thing, and Archie would be horrified. Such things were best left unsaid, and yet now, as he was starting to get strange ideas in his head about a family, children, I didn't know what I was supposed to do. All of a sudden it seemed that deceiving him was exactly what I was doing.

I got back to New York in time to fill in for Jenna in the *Follies*, who'd been "taken ill." I learned her numbers and footwork fast, with more determination than I knew I had in me, especially after such a long and arduous train ride. I rehearsed every single day from sunup until sundown. So just as my future husband was telling me I should start thinking about giving it all up, Ziegfeld slotted me back into the *Follies*—temporarily, he reminded me, until Jenna returned, but we all knew that wasn't happening. It was thrilling to be in both shows again.

"I'm so relieved you're back in the *Follies*," Ruthie said when we'd opted for a night in back at the apartment rather than out at the clubs. "How does it feel?"

"Glorious," I said. "And exhausting, just the way I like it."

"You should listen to me more often. I told you you'd be back on top in no time."

"I know, I know," I said, sprawled on the white sofa, Ruthie lying on her usual spot on the rug. She reached up and grabbed my hand.

"Let me try it on again," she said, admiring my ring. "I think Lawrence is going to propose any day."

"Really?"

"I've been telling him all about your engagement, how romantic it was. I think it's got him thinking." She smiled. "He would make such a good husband and a wonderful father."

I sat up. "Do you want to have children?"

"Of course." She laughed. "I can't wait."

"But what about the shows?"

"What about them?"

"What will you do?"

"I'll be out the door so fast."

"You'll just quit?"

"Olive, can you imagine how nice it would be not to have to work so damn hard, not to have to watch our figures all the time? I'm going to learn how to cook and I'm going to play house all day long and, fingers crossed, it won't be too long before I'll have a baby. I've been planning for it since I was a little girl."

I looked at her, baffled. "I thought you loved show business."

"I do. But I'm going to love this so much more." She took off my ring and looked at it from all angles, then gave it back. "It sure is a beauty."

I slipped it back on my finger and felt a pang of envy shoot through me. How nice it must feel to have that kind of certainty and confidence in her womanhood. Outwardly I might come off as independent, appearing to demand respect, but inside I was questioning everything, inside I was starting to crumble.

Two long weeks later, Archie joined me once again in Manhattan. We celebrated our reunion with a night out and he was keen on introducing me to one of his friends in the art world.

"We should start thinking about our guest list," Archie said as we walked to the waiting car outside the Plaza, an icy December chill biting our faces.

"Yes," I said, although I was sharply aware that in the past two weeks I'd been avoiding the subject of the wedding, in my mind and in conversations with the girls.

"It doesn't feel right to start planning a wedding without my mother," I said, knowing full well that this wasn't the only thing bothering me.

"Well, I need to meet your family, Olive. I have to ask for your father's blessing, for heaven's sake. We're doing things terribly out of order. It will certainly make me feel better to have things out in the open, and I'm sure it will make you feel better, too."

"I know," I said. "Of course we'll tell them. Soon, maybe this weekend."

But I knew I'd delay it as long as possible. I knew they'd be happy, no doubt about it, and that was the problem. It would make things better all around. My parents would be thrilled to meet Archie, a handsome, wealthy, responsible businessman who was willing to take on their wild and unruly daughter. This was exactly what they'd hoped for, and now that I was making it a reality, my father would no longer have to worry for me. I'd give in and get off the stage and he'd be getting exactly what he wanted, and he'd probably tell me that.

Ever since Archie's announcement at his mother's house, that he'd like me to stop performing, travel, see the world, I'd grappled with it. I loved Archie, but I didn't like the idea of throwing in the towel on this life I'd so desperately wanted and worked hard for. And yet I understood what he meant: to be truly man and wife, we'd have to meld our lives together. How could we really do that if I was tied to the stage? I wondered. I knew deep down that I'd have to make changes for our life to work together, but I wasn't ready to admit to anyone that I'd let it go.

"Anyway," I said, changing the subject, "tell me something about your friends we're going to meet tonight. What do I need to know?"

"Gertrude is an art collector too, far more invested than me, and she's a sculptress also, though I haven't seen her work, so I don't know if she's any good."

"Is she going to abhor me too, because I'm a show girl?"

"Good Lord, no! Wait until you see her studio, she has a penchant for the young and unknown artists. She likes to seek them out and bring them to the surface. Her family's very well-known, so she has the means to bring these struggling artists to the light. It's really quite admirable."

We walked into what I thought was going to be a small dinner party on West Eighth Street and MacDougal and found instead a throbbing soiree in what looked like a combined art studio and gallery.

"Gertrude," Archie said after we removed our coats, "thank you so much for having us. This is Olive Shine, my fiancée."

"I've heard so much about you," she said, hugging me tightly. "A Ziegfeld girl in the flesh, and a beauty at that! Come on, you two. Archie, I've been so eager to show you the new work."

Dressed to the nines in a beads-and-lace dress, she pulled us through the crowd to a room to the left of the action. We walked through dancing and music and laughter, and I wondered if everyone was high from the strong fumes of oil paint and turpentine that filled the space.

Art of all kinds was everywhere—half-finished on easels, on the walls, stacked on the floor. But in the smaller room the paintings were dark and somber—gritty scenes of poverty and desperation in streets and speakeasies that I recognized.

"Hey, I've walked by that place!" I said, pointing to a dingy bar scene with barkeeps tending to patrons. "McSorley's. I heard the beer is terrible. Basically water."

"Ladies don't drink beer," Gertrude chided me. "And they wouldn't let a lady in even if you paid them."

"Speaking of," Archie said, "I'll be right back with refreshments, and it certainly won't be beer for you two," and he went off to find us some juice.

"It's a John Sloan piece," Gertrude went on. "Really captures the ambience, doesn't he? And I love his figures. I know what's going on in that barkeep's head by the slump in his shoulders."

It was a bit moody for my taste. I didn't know much about art, but I preferred things a little more vibrant.

"Is that a portrait of you?" I asked, pointing across the room to a huge painting of a woman lounging in a green-and-blue pant ensemble on a purple-draped velvet sofa. "It's fabulous."

"Isn't it just! It's a Robert Henri. My husband won't let me hang it at home because he doesn't want his friends to see his wife 'in pants'!" she said with a mock gasp. We both laughed. "Really! It's absurd. So I hung it here, in my haven."

Archie and I had a grand time mingling with all of Gertrude's guests. Archie was fascinated by her artist friends, some of them intent on showing the truth, as they called it: real life, people working, hardship instead of the "elite idealism" that they said other artists portrayed.

On our way back uptown at God knew what hour, I snuggled into Archie in the back seat of the car. I loved that he wanted to show me every corner of his varied world. It was one of substance: artists, creators, people not afraid to speak their minds. I couldn't believe I'd gotten so lucky to be with a man who was able to talk to me about the arts and didn't care if we were kicking the sawdust-covered floors at a downtown speakeasy or climbing into bed at the Plaza.

We made love that night on the soft white sheets, the smell of fresh winter air in his hair and the taste of gin on his lips. And when I was just about to drift off to sleep, he pulled me into him.

"I have an idea," he said, brushing the hair off my face, my eyes half-closed. "What if we move back to Cincinnati after we get married?"

I didn't bother opening my eyes, just half chuckled and pulled the sheets around me. "You're hilarious," I whispered.

"I'm serious. You saw all that beautiful art tonight, wait until I show you my collection. It's all in storage at my mother's house."

I pushed myself up on one elbow and stared at him. Surely he was joking.

"This Plaza arrangement is temporary," he said. "Once we're married you won't need your apartment and I won't need this. We'll need a proper place to call home. I'd like to have my art on display, especially since you are so creative yourself. It thrills me that we can enjoy it together."

"Bring it to Manhattan," I said.

"There aren't enough walls in New York City."

"Don't be absurd," I said.

"And besides, the city is no place to raise a family—"

"Archie," I quickly cut him off before he had a chance to finish that sentence, "we can live our lives any way we want. That's what I love about us, we're not your average couple, we're unconventional. We dance with the dancers and drink with the drinkers, remember?"

"That was Frank who said that, not me."

"Who cares? We march to the beat of our own drum, we don't have to follow those guidelines about marriage, and all that people think it entails. As long as we're happy and in love, we can make any arrangement work."

I kissed him, hoping it would seal my words, persuade him to believe me.

"I don't know, Olive," he said, sighing and lying back on his pillow. "I—"

"I'm tired," I said, suddenly feeling wide-awake. "Let's just talk about this in the morning." I turned onto my side and hoped to God that we'd never talk about this again.

One thing was clear: something in Archie had changed. When we'd met he'd said he didn't want to become a father, I was sure of it, not after what he'd been through with his first wife. I'd specifically taken hold of this information, storing it away, while recalling all too well what the doctor had told me, that my uterus had ruptured, that I couldn't bear more children. But now small tears were starting to appear in what I thought had been an impenetrable bond, an ideal courtship, two people who thought the love they had for each other was all that mattered, the only thing they needed. Maybe I had been wrong.

CHAPTER TWENTY-TWO

Six months later—summer 1929

Does everyone have a drink in their hand?" I asked loudly, making sure everyone in the group could hear. It was almost noon and I had dressed in a royal-blue-and-white polka-dotted, dropped waist dress. Who cares that we're at the camp out here in the middle of the woods? I thought. If I was hosting my family and friends, it was going to be fabulous.

"Mother?" I called over my shoulder, to be sure she could hear me. She was standing at the back with my father and Junior, while my friends were crowding around the barkeep, who'd set up shop by the firepit as I'd instructed, and George was getting friendly with the girls. "We have mimosas made with fresh-squeezed orange juice and French champagne—thank you, Canada. And for anyone who needs a cocktail while we're walking, you'll find bar stations set up along the way."

We were once again at full capacity, as we had been every week since summer started. Along with my family, who, as I'd anticipated, were far more cordial with me now that I was almost a married woman, there was Ruthie and Lawrence—Ruthie hadn't wasted any time, she'd married him in December and was now almost seven months pregnant—Emily and Lou, Willis and Anne-Marie, and Lillian, Gladys, Lara and Pauline. Archie would be joining us that weekend along with a few of his guests, and Alberto was there with his friends Chester and Michael, but they'd been here before and knew their way around just fine. We were already halfway through summer, and I'd made sure that each and every week had been a riotous good time. The wedding was only a month away, and there was still work to be done to get the camp ready, but I supervised that while entertaining our guests—intent on keeping myself busy at all times.

"I'm going to start the tour so that you'll know your way around this place and will feel perfectly at home during your stay." I did this whenever we had a fresh round of guests. I remembered Anne Belmont making us feel so welcome when we arrived, and I intended to carry on her spirit of warm hospitality, while making things a whole lot more fun.

"There's so much I'm eager to tell you about, so let's get started," I called out, raising my glass in the air. It was noon, but I'd been drinking mimosas for the past hour while getting ready that morning. "We're going to start at the boathouse, come along." We stood next to the first cabin and looked down at the boathouse, the perfectly still lake behind it mirroring the sky. "As you can see, the roof of the boathouse is under construction. It had a peaked roof, which was pretty, but I'm having it flattened—can you guess why? It's going to make an ideal deck for sunbathing, with a perfect view of the lake, don't you agree?" I looked across to Ruthie, but she was chatting with one of the girls. The deck and the stairs leading up to it would be ready just in time for the wedding weekend. "And there are plenty of rowboats and canoes available anytime you please, just come on down, and take one out for a spin."

I continued on, leading them down a trail that passed by the boathouse, and then took a left over a walking bridge we'd built that led to an adorable Japanese teahouse nestled on a tiny island with windowed doors on all four sides, providing the most beautiful panoramic view. It was one of my favorite places to take in some solitude—though, to be honest, that never really happened these days, I was too busy entertaining.

"Gentlemen, you can fish off this bridge, all fishing gear is at the boathouse."

I stumbled just a bit as we crossed back over the bridge. "Whoops," I said, my heel caught between the boards. I was laughing and grabbed the rail to steady myself. Maybe I should have had some toast before I started in on those mimosas, I thought. Emily's husband, Lou, stepped forward to help me, but I yanked my shoe free and waved him away. "I'm all right." We continued up the trail around the back of the main lodge and down to the bowling alley and billiards room.

"Anytime you want to bowl, simply let the staff know and someone will come down and pick up your pins for you. We have three, or maybe it's four lanes—so I highly suggest making a party of it, and there's almost always someone down there serving drinks, so don't be shy."

We went inside and I showed them the bowling alley. George picked up a perfectly smooth, carved ball, rolled it down the left lane and knocked down all the pins. We all cheered. Lillian and Lara gave him a kiss on each cheek at the same time and his face flushed. He was in heaven. The barkeep came around and topped up our glasses. I was feeling warm and happy, just the way I liked it.

I'd made many changes to the camp that summer. I felt that if people were going to come all this way from the city to spend a week here for relaxation, they shouldn't have to walk more than a hundred yards for a drink, so I set up bar carts throughout the grounds. We kept walking on the trail that led us to the highest point on the property and allowed us to look out onto all sixteen of the cabins, the lake, and the treetops.

"By next week, I'll be watching and waiting for bathtubs to be brought up this very river by tugboat, where they'll be delivered right onto the lakeshore down there and installed in every one of these cabins. You can't have a retreat into the Adirondacks without a fabulous bathtub to soak in, don't you agree?" I wasn't talking to anyone in particular, I was just performing my routine to this small audience.

I showed everyone where to go for meals, where to play tennis and boccie ball, and then directed them to some of the best hiking trails on the property. Ruthie looked rather exhausted after all the walking, so I took everyone toward the main lodge, where lunch was being served.

Reluctantly, in early June, I'd informed Ziegfeld that I'd be getting married at the end of the summer and after that would no longer be able to perform in the *Follies* or the *Frolic* or any show at all. I'd justified it to myself with the promise of seeing the world—Paris, Florence, London. I'd wrapped up the June show, spent almost all of July at the camp throwing one monthlong party and planned to return to the show for my grand finale toward the end of August, one week before my wedding. Everyone would be there for my final, farewell show. I tried not to think about it too much by maintaining a steady stream of visitors. As one group left, another arrived, so I never had a chance to dwell on this decision that I'd grappled with for months. The constant visitors and the constant party, as well as the hooch that I drank pretty much continually, helped to ensure I wasn't too saddened by it all.

Lunch was served, drinks kept flowing, and by four P.M. that afternoon I was knockered and needed a nice long siesta so I could rouse and get the party started again for dinner.

"Mother," I called out rather loudly when I got up to walk back to my cabin and saw her sitting on a carved wooden swing and looking out to the lake. "Are you having fun?"

I plonked down next to her and the swing shuddered in my clumsiness. She shook her head but didn't take her eyes off the lake.

"What is it?" I asked, wishing I'd gone directly back to my cabin, where my head would be hitting the pillow at this very moment.

"What are you doing, Olive?" she asked with a sorrow in her voice I wasn't expecting. I'd thought everyone was having a grand old time. "And what is all this?" She motioned to the cabins and the main lodge.

"I thought you'd love it here," I said.

"Why are you making all these changes, flattening the roof so you can sunbathe, shipping claw-foot bathtubs up the Hudson River, a bar at every corner? It's absurd, how much does that even cost you?"

"What difference does it make how much it costs? We're getting it ready for the wedding," I said. "That's what you wanted for me, isn't it, for me to get married so you wouldn't have to worry about me anymore?"

She shook her head. "You're drunk all the time."

"I am not drunk," I said, trying to sound as sober and as offended as possible.

"Is this what you gave that poor baby up for, this life of debauchery?" she said in a low whisper.

"Mother," I said, looking around to see if anyone was nearby, "don't speak of such a thing again."

My mother slowly peeled her eyes off the lake and glared at me.

"What choice did I have?" I asked. It was the question I'd been asking myself over and over ever since Archie had proposed. It was the question I'd been trying to quiet, to ignore with a constant flow of new guests to the camp and a constant flow of champagne. It wasn't until I fell for Archie that I could even fathom what it could mean to have a baby; but now it was too late, and worst of all, he didn't even know the truth. No one did, not even my mother.

"I don't know, Olive," my mother said, standing up from the swing. "Maybe I led you astray—it just seems as if it was all for nothing."

———

All the champagne I'd consumed seemed to have drained from my veins, and I felt horribly sober. I couldn't be alone with my thoughts in the cabin, but I didn't want to be around any of our guests either. I walked through the towering pines to the farm to find Jose or Eugene. I'd asked Eugene to organize a group hike the following day, and I thought I'd take my mind off things by checking on the itinerary. He wasn't there. No one was there, in fact.

There were eggs in the coop, but I wouldn't have anything to carry them in on my way to the kitchen. I'd hoped to see Lady in the stable, but she was out in the field with the other horses. She looked rounder, her stomach fuller and dropping.

"Can I help you with something?" Eugene asked, startling me as he rounded the horse stable with a bucket and a rake, sleeves rolled up, galoshes caked in mud.

"Oh, you gave me a start!"

"I apologize, ma'am. I was just refilling the horses' feed."

"I was only wondering how Lady's feeling."

"She's started walking about quite a bit now," he said. "Doesn't want to stand still, you see that?" He pointed out to the field, and sure enough she was pacing. "That could mean a couple of days or even less now," he said. "I think after today we'll have to separate her from the rest."

"Why?" I asked.

"If she foals with the other horses around, they might get too close. We had a mare foal a few years back and the male got up close and stepped on the little one's leg. We had to put her to sleep before the foal was even a few hours old, very sad day that was."

"Oh, Eugene," I said, suddenly overcome with sadness. "That's just terrible." A chill came over me and I looked around to see where I could sit for a minute.

"It was sad," he said, beginning to rake out the stable. "Sorry. . . ." He looked back at me, seeing the pain in my face. "Sorry, you see things like that happen all the time when you're with the animals this much, probably a bit startling to regular folk. Have I upset you?"

"No, no, I'm fine. I'm sure you see all kinds of things." I felt a sudden desperation to get back to the privacy of my cabin. "Let me know how it goes with Lady," I called out as I backed away. "I'd like to know when things start happening." I walked briskly back to the cabin, hoping I wouldn't see anyone.

I couldn't get through the door quickly enough. I shut it behind me, bolted it and then, wrenched by heavy sobs, crumpled to the floor. Everyone was here at the camp—my friends, my theater girls, Alberto, my parents, even my brothers. Archie would be here in just a few days, and our wedding plans were coming together. My grand finale would be a huge success and a final celebration of my time as a Ziegfeld girl, and yet everything felt so horribly, horribly sad. I loved Archie so very much, but I was leading him, unknowing, into a trap. Into a cruel, deceitful lie.

CHAPTER TWENTY-THREE

It was two weeks before the wedding. The sunbathing roof deck was complete, the cabins freshly painted, seven of the sixteen bathtubs had been shipped and pulled up the banks to the cabins by some thirty men, then installed. The rest would have to wait. A steamboat full of orchids would arrive from Manhattan a few days prior to the wedding, along with a shipment of hooch. The only thing left for me to do was go for a final fitting of my wedding gown in Manhattan and bring it back to the camp.

That and my final performance.

Archie had been at the camp with us for the past two weeks, rolling up his sleeves and working with the staff to ensure that everything would be perfect. While he'd originally planned to join me in Manhattan for my final send-off, he now needed to stay behind and await the special delivery by way of Canada to ensure that our wedding wouldn't be dry. I understood the precariousness of the situation; it would be a middle-of-the-night delivery and Archie felt he should be there in case of any mishaps. So I asked Alberto to accompany me to the city, and we'd be back before the guests arrived for the wedding.

We took Archie's railcar—it had been put to great use that summer, shuttling our friends back and forth. Alberto's friends Chester and Michael also rode back to town with us. We were all dog-tired from the week's activities. As soon as the first leg of the trip was complete, Chester said he planned to sleep the rest of the way. I probably could have benefited from the sleep, too, given all the wild parties I'd been throwing, but I was too eager for my performance. I'd have three days to rehearse and then, showtime.

Alberto and I sat at the table and chairs by the window. I tried to read a story in an old issue of *McClure's,* but I kept reading the same few lines over and over.

"Archie is a good man, Olive, very welcoming," Alberto said. "Nice of him to put up with all of our *canto forte.*"

"I know, he's very patient." I thought of all the late nights by the fire, Alberto, his friends, and me singing our lungs out. "Though he has to allow me to let it out somewhere, especially now that I'm giving up the stage."

Alberto shook his head. "You told me when we first met on the lake, that you would never give it up, you said he would never ask you to."

"I know." I nodded. "I didn't think he would." I looked out the window and sighed. "But things are different now. I didn't know back then that I would be in love with him the way I am now. I didn't know that I'd want this life, companionship. Until I met Archie, I honestly thought it wasn't for me. But now I can't imagine my life without him."

Just this week Archie had spent two full days pitching in with the workers, painting the guide boats, repairing loose boards on the deck and making sure all the chairs at the boathouse were in good shape for picnics. He told me he wanted everything to be perfect for me and all my guests.

"I don't want a lifetime of flings, Alberto. Now I know what's possible, and I don't want to lose him. Don't you want that kind of companionship, especially as we get older?"

Alberto looked thoughtful. I followed his gaze to the sleeper carriage, where Chester was resting. We'd never spoken of such things, but I knew there was more than a simple friendship between them.

"Sometimes you can't have everything that you want," he said.

I understood what he meant, but it wasn't my place to press him to tell me more.

"Will you have children, Olive?" His question got my attention, and I turned, silent, to face him. Alberto waited patiently for me to answer.

"No," I said in a whisper.

"Archie, he doesn't want a family?" Alberto seemed struck by this.

I shook my head. I couldn't speak of it; the thought of it all made me want to curl up in shame.

"Olive, if Archie wants the babies, then I understand. Of course there is no way to be Ziegfeld girl and have the babies. But if he doesn't, then why you have to stop—why? You can go on, Olive, you don't have to waste this talent."

"It's complicated, Alberto," I said. "It's just far more complicated than that."

"I don't understand, Olive. Why can't you have your love and also have your life, why you have to choose?"

"Because he doesn't want me dressing that way. I think it will be an embarrassment to his family if I am this show girl, entertaining other men when we are man and wife. Most of the girls leave the show when they marry."

"I understand, but you are not those other girls. I just worry that you will be unhappy. When I don't sing I am *infelice, miserabile*. I might as well go away and *morire* if I cannot sing."

I felt the same way. All summer I'd been putting on a show, hosting as many people as possible, inviting all my theater friends so that we could re-create the thrill of performing at the camp, so I could feel that camaraderie that I felt in the dressing room and backstage. I'd been drinking and drinking to make everything louder, more rambunctious, to make the everyday moments spectacular. I knew I should stop, but I wanted to shock people, I wanted people to talk, I wanted word to travel back to the city about what fun everyone was having, just as word had traveled about the shows when I was in Manhattan. But I knew it was all a farce, something I was doing to trick myself into believing that everything was going to be okay, that everything wasn't going to change.

"Just being a wife, Olive, it's not enough for you. I've seen it before, you won't be happy. Maybe you should have the babies, at least it will keep you occupied."

"Alberto," I snapped, "can we please stop talking about it?" But as soon as I said it, I regretted it. I'd offended him with my outburst.

"I'm sorry, I don't mean to be so brash, but can we change the subject?"

He nodded and went back to reading his paper.

"Well," he said after a few moments, "maybe it won't even matter. If this country's economy *va in bagno* the way my friend Roger tells me, then the theaters will be first to go."

"What are you talking about?"

"Here." He tapped the page he was reading.

A CRASH IS COMING AND IT MAY BE TERRIFIC, the headline read.

"I've met him," Alberto said. "Roger Babson, he's *molto intelligente.*"

"I've heard Archie and his friends speak of him recently—he's the statistician, right? They said he's full of baloney. Apparently he's been saying the same things for years and years."

"'Sooner or later a crash is coming, and it may be terrific,'" Alberto went on. "'Factories will shut down, men will be thrown out of work, the vicious circle will get in full swing and the result will be a serious business depression,'" he read out loud.

"Yes," I said, "that is quite depressing. Can we talk about something more uplifting?"

"'There may be a stampede for selling which will exceed anything that the Stock Exchange has ever witnessed,'" he continued reading. "'Wise are those investors who now get out of debt and reef their sails.'" Then he looked at me and raised his eyebrows.

"Alberto, please, you are boring the pants off me." I sighed.

"If he's right, we are in big trouble," he replied, showing me with his hands just how much trouble. I couldn't help smiling at his lovely

Italian way. "No one goes to the theater or the opera when men are losing their jobs, I can promise you that."

I leaned in and read the article over his shoulder. "President Hoover doesn't seem concerned. Look," I said, "he says the market is sound, and he's the president of the United States of America."

"After your wedding, I will go to Europe and I will stay some time. I fill my schedule with European tours for the next year or more. You should try the same. If you want, I arrange a meeting for you and my European booker next time he's in town."

"Alberto, I told you," I said. "This is my grand finale."

The words hung heavy in the air between us. I could see him out of the corner of my eye, and we both stared straight ahead, the gravity of my statement sinking in. After a while he turned his eyes back to his paper, and I looked out of the window, filled with a sense of dread.

CHAPTER TWENTY-FOUR

What a wonderful feeling it was to walk through those familiar heavy glass theater doors and into the dressing room. Relief swept over me when I saw my mirror and dressing table in the corner—someone had decorated it with flowers and even made a banner with my name on it. I'd been gone for two months already, but mercifully they didn't let me see if my corner had been assigned to one of the other girls. At least on the surface, it was as if I'd never left.

"She's baaack!" Gladys called out the moment she saw me, then Pauline, Lillian and Lara ran to me as if I were a long-lost friend.

"You silly girls," I said, loving the attention, wrapping my arms around them, "I just saw you at the camp."

"I know, but it's dull without you here with us," Lara said.

"And with Ruthie gone too," Pauline said, "it's just not the same around here."

"She's right. Ziegfeld just brought in twenty new ponies for the upcoming season," Lara whispered. "Half of them don't look much past sixteen!"

Gladys sauntered over and took my hand. "Will you all stop gossiping and give the poor girl some space?" And with everyone following alongside, she led me out the door to the rehearsal room, where we sat down to put our shoes on. "So, tell us everything. Have you been practicing for your wedding night?"

"Oh, Gladys!" I said. "You don't change."

I took my T-straps out of my bag.

"Hey, I almost forgot," I said. "I brought gifts." I had with me a box filled with little bottles of maple syrup. I'd written the name of each of the girls on tags tied with ribbon to each bottle. "Gladys, Lillian, Pauline," I said, taking out the first three. "These are from our sugar maples at the camp. Eugene tapped the trees last spring and we still have some left. You all have to come back up in early spring when the snow melts, we're going to have a sugaring-off party when the sap starts to run."

"My goodness, Olive," Gladys said. "You're turning into a darling little farmer."

"Well," I said, bristling slightly. "Makes for a fine maple bee's knees."

"What, no honey?"

"That's right—our barkeep makes them with maple syrup instead, lemon and plenty of gin."

"Now that's more like it."

———

Along with some of the old standards, Howie had updated the choreography of one of my favorite acts to make it fresh—a sassy number that felt very apropos. It featured me and all the girls going shopping, each girl pulling me in a different direction. The set was much improved, too, like a real department store. We danced from a makeup counter to a jewelry section, each girl wanting advice for different reasons. I was needed and wanted by each of them, but I had to keep pulling away, checking the time, and eventually I made my way up that famous Ziegfeld spiral staircase. At the top Eddie Cantor stood in silhouette, waiting. I kept running back down a few stairs, just one more thing to attend to, but eventually I reached the top. In the spotlight, I sang a final farewell number at the top of the staircase and then joined arms with Eddie and together we walked down the other side of the staircase. One final kiss to the audience and we exited stage left.

We ran through all the numbers over and over, and it felt so good to be moving, dancing, singing. It reminded me of those early days when I first joined the *Follies* and worked so damned hard every day to get caught up, to be as good as the other girls, to perfect that Ziegfeld walk. How quickly I'd made friends, how generously they'd welcomed me—me, the new girl from Minnesota.

Because I'd been away from it for two months, my body felt less malleable than before, and by the end of the day my muscles ached and my feet pounded. But I loved the physical reminders that I was back where I wanted to be, doing what my body craved.

My mind had been full lately, spinning and churning with thoughts of the wedding, thoughts of Archie, our future, my future, my final show and the aftermath, but for those few days of rehearsal

I tried to push all that out of my mind. Just enjoy this time with the girls, I told myself, relish this last performance, you'll face whatever comes next when it comes.

We went out for dinner on the first night, but after being out of practice, I was too dog-tired to rehearse all day and dance all night, so we piled into Pauline's place in Inwood—the same apartment I'd shared with Ruthie—and stayed up late chatting instead.

"You are so lucky, Olive," Lara said when we were sitting on the living room floor drinking hot cocoa that Pauline fixed for us. "Archie's not just rich, he's handsome, too, and he seems like he's really in love with you. How'd you find one with all three? Everyone I know settles for two, sometimes even one out of three."

"He's one heck of a guy," I said.

"And you don't have to do this anymore," Lara said.

"What's 'this'?" I said.

"Performing, making money, sitting on the floor with us girls."

"But I want to do this," I said, "I wish I could do it forever."

"No, you don't," Gladys chimed in. She had made it clear for some time now that she wanted to find the perfect johnny to take care of her.

"I do," I insisted. "It's all I've ever wanted to do."

"You say you do, but we're getting on, Olive, you're just about in your mid-twenties and I'm . . ." She paused. "Well, no one needs to know the exact details, but I want to leave show business on my own time, not get kicked out of here to make way for those young ponies coming in."

"Ruthie settled for one out of three," Pauline called out from the kitchen.

"That's not true," I said. "Lawrence is a good fellow."

"Sure it's true. Lawrence loves her a good deal, but he's not a looker, and he's not rich."

"Who cares if he's rich?" I said. "And he's a looker in Ruthie's eyes, and that's all that matters."

It felt good to be back with the girls, but talking about Archie made me miss him. What I didn't miss was hearing the desperation in these girls' voices, the idea that they all needed a man to rescue them, take care of them, provide for them. They were all so beautiful and talented, and Ziegfeld did have a way of drawing out each girl's individual talents, I'd give him that. I just didn't believe that we needed someone to save us. We'd all made it this far, many of us had made sacrifices to become Ziegfeld girls, and if I was going to leave it behind and marry Archie, it was because I was in love with him and I wanted to, not because I needed to.

The final performance was on Friday night, and it had barely seemed to begin before it was time to start climbing those stairs for the finale. Alberto and Chester were in the front row, Ruthie and Lawrence were a few rows back, and I recognized so many other faces. I felt beautiful in the costumes again. I wore a beaded white figure-hugging dress. It was weighty and glamorous, its beaded tassels tapping at my thighs as I took each step. At the top, I turned and looked down at it all, 1,702 seats, a full house, the look of expectation on every face in the audience. They'd given me so much, this sea of people, night after night, warming me with their applause, sending vibrations through my bones with their cheering. I'd been loved by all these friends and all these strangers. I sang my final lyrics with passion, and I couldn't have wished it to go any better, there wasn't a stronger note to leave on: the audience roared, they stood, they applauded. I breathed it all in, aware that it was all about to end. Did I really have to let this go? Did I really have to leave all this behind? I swept my right arm out to the audience, reaching from left to right to capture the thunderous percussion of applause, and then my left arm, sweeping across the theater from right to left. Both arms now outstretched to either side, I raised them up. I felt so victorious, my body absorbing it all one last time. I closed my eyes and the applause kept coming, and while I loved it, relished it, I pictured Archie's face, smiling, his hand reaching out and taking mine, and I felt a separate sense of peace. Opening my eyes again, I mouthed, "Thank you," then I linked my arm with Eddie's, descended the staircase and walked off the stage into the wings.

After the show, the girls took me out and we danced all over town. It was as if it were going to be my last night ever in the city—which of course wasn't the case—but despite that moment of calm onstage, something in me began to feel frantic, delirious, desperate. The final performance had come and gone, and now I had to think about my future. I loved everything about Archie, but every time I pictured walking down the aisle toward him, standing there smiling, his eyes shining, proud and handsome, I started to feel anxious and scared.

I danced with some gent at the Rand and almost let him kiss me, for God's sake. I was being reckless, and I wasn't even sure why. When it nearly happened, I quickly took myself off to the ladies' room and confronted myself in the mirror. *What are you doing? Get a grip on yourself.* But after returning, I was handed another drink and pulled onto the dance floor, and I let the music and the hooch lure me back into the night.

I don't remember going home. It must have been at some ungodly hour, I'm pretty sure the sun was already up. I vaguely recall one of the girls, or maybe two, hoisting me up the stairs. All I know is that I woke up on the living room floor in Pauline's apartment. Lara and two new girls, whose names I couldn't even recall, were strewn about me, one in an armchair, one on the floor, one on the sofa.

I woke before the others, and I should have gone back to sleep, but I couldn't. My mouth was as dry as sandpaper, and I needed to stop the pounding in my head. From the minute I awoke I had that uneasy feeling, unsettled. I tried to get comfortable, hoping it was just that we'd barely eaten dinner, too focused on having fun, but all I could think was that I had to get out of that apartment. I didn't want to talk to the girls about the final show, about what would happen next, about the wedding.

I fumbled around in the curtain-drawn darkness, even though it was surely past noon. I changed my clothes, splashed my face with water and tiptoed out the door and down the stairs. I'd promised to visit Ruthie before heading back to the camp, since she wouldn't be able to travel again for the wedding. The sunlight stung my eyes as I blindly hailed a taxicab.

Hello, darling," Ruthie said as I reached the landing of her fifth-floor walk-up somewhat out of breath. "You look terrible." She took me in her arms and gave me a good long hug. I had to reach over her firm, protruding belly and stick out my rear to hug her, and once I was there, I didn't want to let go. "Come on in," she said, taking my hand. "Can't have my new neighbors seeing you in this state."

"Oh, Ruthie, I feel terrible. I've got a wooden mouth and about twenty carpenters in my head."

"Well. You had a lot to celebrate. Sit down, I'll make you some tea."

I sat at the kitchen table and looked around. Her apartment was small and sparse but clean and on a quiet, tree-lined street. You could see the bright green leaves of the treetops right outside her kitchen window.

"It's lovely here, Ruthie," I said, taking it all in, then looking at her, noticing for the first time how much she'd changed. I'd seen her at the camp just a few weeks before, but it was as if I hadn't been paying attention then. From the back, her figure was still slim; it was just her belly that had grown. Her face was fuller, rounder, but it made her look younger and more innocent, cheerful.

"We haven't decorated yet, I'm still trying to get the hang of this whole being-a-wife business." She laughed. "Look, Lawrence bought me a waffle iron." She pointed to a metal contraption that took up almost her entire countertop. "I haven't a clue how to use it."

We both laughed, but it made my brain hurt, so I put my head in my hands and squeezed my eyes shut.

And then I stayed there.

I could hear Ruthie pouring the water into the teapot and the clunk as she took cups down from the cupboard. A ripple of emotion rose up from the pit of my stomach and began pressing at the backs of my eyes.

"Oh, honey," she said with a sigh. "What's the matter? You really didn't want to leave the show, did you. I could tell by the way you were carrying on at the camp." She sat down across from me and pulled my hands away from my face. "I know how much the theater means to you."

I tried to speak, but a big sob came out instead. "It's not about the show," I finally managed. "It's Archie."

"What about Archie?" she said, shocked. "I thought you were madly in love."

"I am, we are . . . that's the problem."

"I don't understand."

I looked up at her worried face and felt trepidation at saying it out loud for the first time, to anyone. But she was watching me expectantly.

"I've been lying to him all this time."

"What do you mean? About what?"

"I can't have children," I whispered.

The worry lines on her forehead softened and her expression changed from one of concern to one of pity, shock.

"I can't have children," I said it again, louder. "I didn't think I'd ever want to, and now I do but I can't, and I haven't told Archie, and he wants a family, and I'm going to trap him, and I'm never going to be able to give him what he wants. I love him so much, and yet I'm going to ruin his life, crush his dreams." Tears streamed from my eyes. "And I hate myself for it all," I cried, "for everything I've done! And when he finds out the truth, he's going to hate me too."

The words seemed to be spilling out of me, and I realized that I was losing control. I felt horrible and yet compelled to keep telling her the awful truth.

"Oh, Olive," she said. "But how do you know? How could you possibly know such a thing?"

"Because I gave my baby away," I said, sobbing loudly, realizing how dreadful it was to be saying this to Ruthie, only a month away from giving birth herself, how despicable I must seem. "I got pregnant by some man in California and I gave that poor baby away when she was just days old, and I had just turned twenty, and, oh, Ruthie, there was all this blood!"

"Olive!" She pulled me to her and held me tight, but I couldn't stop.

"They said something tore, my uterus, I think—and I'm pretty sure it was my punishment. God took one look at me doing this inexcusably cruel, selfish thing, and he punished me by damaging me, so I couldn't do it again to another innocent baby."

At last I fell quiet. Ruthie sat back, took a deep breath and, probably without even realizing, rubbed her belly with both hands. "Let's keep God out of this, shall we?" she said gently. "What's done is done. You weren't married, you would have been disowned, and you probably couldn't have taken care of a baby then, anyway."

"Of course I could, I just didn't want to. I wanted to perform, I wanted to live my life, I wanted the pregnancy to be over as soon as possible so I could move to New York and follow my dreams. And now I have this beautiful life all laid out ahead of me and I can't live it. It's all going to be a big lie, and"—the tears started filling my eyes again—"Archie has no idea about any of this."

"Why?"

"I don't know, I just couldn't bring myself to tell him, I was scared I'd lose him."

Ruthie stood up and poured me some tea, added several spoonfuls of sugar and some milk and set it down in front of me.

"I thought Archie didn't even want children," she said.

"That's what I thought when we first met."

"How old is he, anyway? Thirty-eight?"

I nodded.

"Well, he should have gotten started earlier."

"But he did. He had that awful tragedy with his first wife and their child," I said, "and he told me that ship had sailed for him. But after we were going together for some time he started to change his tune. He started saying he could imagine what it would be like to have a child with me, he said he felt happy and hopeful. And then he didn't stop talking about it, planning our future, and I just let him. And, honestly, I felt the same way he did. I never could have imagined having a child before I met him, but now"—the tears welled up in me again—"I think it would be the most beautiful thing in the world."

Finally talking about this with Ruthie, after two and a half years of keeping the secret pushed down deep inside, made all my regret and remorse rise up to the surface.

"I never thought I could give up the stage. I used to think it was the only time that people approved of me, that the only time they truly loved me was when I was performing, when they'd stand up and clap their hands together with such enthusiasm, and at the *Frolic* when they'd slam their mallets on the table, and I'd feel the vibrations.

That, Ruthie, that felt like love to me, that felt like the best kind of love there was. I thought it was the only kind of love I'd ever need."

Ruthie nodded slowly. "And then you met Archie."

"Yes," I said. "And then I felt what real love was—true and connected. Archie makes me feel like the most adored woman who ever lived. And last night, when I was singing that final number, and they were all clapping away, and I was taking it all in, I thought, This is nice, how very kind of them to appreciate me like this. And then I thought, I can't wait to tell Archie about it, I can't wait to be in his embrace again, to lie next to him in bed, to hold his hand."

Ruthie sighed. "You have to tell him, Olive."

"I can't."

"You have to be honest with him."

"If I tell him, I'll lose him, I know I will. He'll be repulsed by what I did, sending that sweet baby off into the world alone. Oh God, when she was so helpless." It was as if I were realizing the magnitude of it all for the very first time, and another wave of sobs rose up in me.

I took a deep breath and tried to regain my composure. "There are plenty of young, beautiful, capable women who would gladly marry him and bear his children," I said, trying to be realistic.

"Oh, stop that kind of talk. But Olive, I'm telling you, if you walk down that aisle and then he finds out afterwards that you kept this from him, then you will most definitely lose him. You might be married, but he won't trust you. He may not be able to forgive you, and then you'll be alone in a loveless, resentful marriage for the rest of your life. You both will. Tell him now, Olive. You have to, it's the only way."

I nodded. I knew she was right, I just didn't know if I could.

CHAPTER TWENTY-FIVE

When I returned to the camp a few days later, it was quiet. Plants had been delivered and set up around the property, giving the camp a tropical feel. An inviting aroma of baking came from the kitchen. I didn't see Archie, who must have been out with one of the guides. We'd had so many guests all summer that I'd almost forgotten what it was like to hear the birds, the gentle rustle of the breeze in the trees and the stillness. In less than a week the wedding guests would start to arrive, staying at the camp or at Paul Smith's Hotel. We'd get caught up in the hosting and the entertaining, and we'd have few moments to ourselves, and then the wedding would be upon us, and I'd be walking down the aisle. Archie would be standing under the trellis, the lake in the background, and he'd be smiling and . . . I shut my eyes. Stop it, just stop thinking, I told myself. I needed a distraction. Everything was too quiet, too still.

I changed out of my city clothes and put on my trousers and my galoshes and walked down to the farm. Eugene was there, and when he saw me approach his face broke into a huge smile.

"Is there news?" I asked.

"There is," he said. "She had a filly. Come and see."

I slowly approached the stable and peeked my head into the stall. Lady stood proudly next to her foal, who was skinny, all legs, her coat fluffy like a rabbit's. She had almost exactly the same markings as Lady—golden brown, three white feet and a white spot on her nose.

"Oh, Eugene, she's magnificent." I wanted to reach out and touch her.

Lady stepped forward, pushing the foal slightly behind her as if to protect her from me.

"It's okay, Lady, I'm just looking," I said.

"She's been tending to her, watching over her while she sleeps, the little one hasn't left her dam's side."

"When was she born?"

"Yesterday. Lady barely needed any help, she knew exactly what to do. The filly came out hoofs first, her nose resting on her legs, back up, just as she should. They bonded right away. Little one nursed quickly, and she stood herself up within thirty minutes of being born."

"A strong one," I said quietly. "I knew she would be."

"Once she stood, she was a bit too excited, wobbling around her dam for a good hour, getting used to her legs. She didn't want to get any rest, but Lady got her settled. You should be able to go in there soon and see them, but we're letting them alone for now."

Eugene seemed so proud of them both.

"Does she have a name?" I asked.

"We've been waiting for you, Miss Olive. We asked Mr. Carmichael, but he insisted that you should be the one to name her. He said you'd like that."

I felt my eyes go glassy. "That's sweet," I said. "But I wouldn't know what to name her. I don't have any experience with that kind of thing, I wouldn't know where to start."

"You don't have to have experience to name a horse." He laughed. "You just have to look at her and say whatever first comes to your mind when you see her."

I stared at her for a moment. "Grace," I said. "That's what I think of when I see her."

"Well, then, I think we have a name."

I nodded. "Thank you, Eugene, for taking such good care of them. You've done a fine job."

Back at the cabin, I downed a shot of whiskey, then lay back on the bed.

I tried to picture what would happen if I followed Ruthie's advice and was honest with Archie, what would happen to me if he heard the news and left me. I'd never been afraid of the future before. Unlike some of the girls who'd been terrified of getting too old or finding themselves on the street the minute they turned the dreaded three-oh, I had always believed, maybe naïvely, that everything would work out and I'd be just fine. I hadn't thrown myself at those stage-door johnnies; sure, I'd let them take me out, but I hadn't been desperate to get married, I hadn't been scared that I'd lose my beauty, my figure, my youthful ways. I'd somehow believed that I'd make it, but now I wasn't quite so sure.

I thought back to those first days in the *Follies* dressing rooms and hearing some of the girls talk about getting older, as if they were all going to catch scarlet fever and drop dead on their thirtieth birthdays. It had seemed so far away. One of the principals had turned and caught me eavesdropping. "Just you wait and see," she'd said. "You may be one of the youngest chicks in the coop now, but it creeps up on you fast. You'll be staring thirty in the eye before you know it."

I'd thought she was wrong. It had seemed like a lifetime from where I was then. If I weren't getting married and leaving the stage now, how much longer would Ziegfeld even keep me around? I wondered. When he had fresh, new, interesting-looking seventeen-, eighteen-, and nineteen-year-olds knocking down his door just as I had, would he still want me then?

When I pictured life without Archie, it was bleak and miserable. I'd be alone, heartbroken, regretful, and soon enough I'd be out of work. I'd be broke, an old maid. Childless. What would I be good for? A governess, perhaps—if a family would even take me, a former show girl. It would be a fitting punishment, to take care of someone else's children. But I couldn't do what I knew I should, I simply couldn't tell him.

I heard the front door open, and Archie walked into the bedroom in his fishing gear. He looked so handsome, his cheeks slightly pink from the sun, his hair tousled.

"Olive!" he exclaimed, surprised and smiling. "I'm so happy you're back, I missed you like mad." He strode over to the bed and hugged me, long and hard, but then he stopped himself. "I should change, I smell like a fisherman. Give me two minutes."

I walked to the living room and poured Archie a whiskey, refilled my glass while I was there, then walked out to the porch and sat on the wooden bench, feeling strangely still.

"Much better," Archie said a few moments later, coming up to me and taking me in his arms. "God, I missed you." He squeezed me, gave me a kiss and then took a deep inhale as if breathing me in. I handed him his drink and he sat down next to me. "So how was the grand finale?" he asked.

"Good." I nodded. "It was good."

"Good? That's it? Was it not well attended?"

"No, it was fine, a full house."

"Well, that's better than good, isn't it?"

"Yes," I said. "Better than good."

"And you got the dress? I see you have something hanging in the bedroom. I'm sure it's extravagant and very special, and I wouldn't want anything less." He smiled. He was so excited, it made me want to cry. "I won't peek, don't worry. But when did you get back? You should have had Agnes come and unpack your bags, they're still sitting by the door."

I nodded again. I swallowed hard. "The thing is, Archie, I loved it. I loved being on that stage again. I loved the applause, I need the applause."

"Olive . . ." His smile dropped slightly. "We talked about this, remember?" He tried to laugh a little, but it came out just like breath, a puff of air.

"I just don't think I can be happy without it." I remained stoic, hard, and yet I couldn't believe what I was hearing myself say. "I won't be happy if I don't perform, if I'm not a Ziegfeld girl, or if I'm not on the stage, singing, dancing, entertaining. And the thing is, I know you don't want a wife of yours to do that."

"Olive," he said, but I kept on, not letting him speak, not letting him talk me out of it.

"It would ruin your reputation and it would ruin the good name you built for your family, but I need to do this. I have to do it."

"What are you saying? Don't be silly." He smiled, but I didn't smile back. "We can talk about this, Olive. Don't say something you'll regret. Just think about what you're doing here, just think before you say another word. Please."

He took my hand, but I pulled it away.

"I don't think I would make a good wife. I don't cook, I can barely keep track of my things, let alone run a household."

"I don't care about any of that stuff, you know that. We'll make it work," Archie said.

I clenched my jaw. "I'm sorry, Archie." I felt light-headed. It was disorienting, as if I were hearing someone else say these words, not me, but I forced myself to go on, coldly. "I've made a terrible mistake. I can't marry you. I'm so very sorry."

Archie stared at me, stunned, as if I'd punched the air out of him. I didn't think he could speak, and yet strangely I could—these cold, callous words coming out of me. He sat down on the wooden chair next to the bench, staring out at the lake.

I watched him to see what he'd do next, to see what I'd do next, and then he stood up again.

"This is ridiculous, Olive. You can't do this to me," he said. He was angrier now. "You can't call this off just days before the wedding. It's all planned. Agnes has been preparing for days, the guides have worked nonstop all summer to get this place exactly the way you wanted it. You!"

I stood there doing nothing. Not even reacting.

"Some guests are already on their way," he said, and then the enormity of it all began to fall on him. "Our families, Olive! It will humiliate everyone involved. You can't do this. I won't allow it."

"I'm sorry," I said.

He paced and then looked at me, softer now. "You've got cold feet, darling," he said, as if this possibility had just occurred to him. "This happens to a lot of people, I've heard, days before the wedding."

"It's not cold feet. I know what it is."

"Well, then, what the hell is it?" he said, louder this time. "Something's happened, did something happen in Manhattan?"

"No," I said. "Nothing happened in Manhattan, I just—it was a mistake. This was a mistake."

He sat down again, then he dropped his head into his hands. "I don't understand," he said to himself. "I just don't understand."

I couldn't watch. I walked back into the bedroom, picked up my bags and carried them out to the main lodge.

"I need the rest of my things picked up from my cabin, and I need to go to the Blue Mountain House immediately," I said, my voice shaking, to whoever might hear. "Now!" I shouted.

People emerged from the hallway, other rooms, and began to scurry around. The carriage was brought up front, and my bags were packed in the back within moments. They must have wondered what on earth was going on, but from the look of me and the intensity in my voice, they seemed to know not to ask questions. My world began to spin, and I thought I might faint. In a matter of minutes,

I had entirely changed the course of my life and I was in the midst of walking out on the only man I'd ever loved. I had no idea what I was going to do next.

Archie walked out of the cabin when I was seated in the back of the carriage. He looked devastated, in shock.

"You're making a huge mistake, Olive," he called out. "If you do this it's over, there's no turning back." He walked up to the carriage window. "Don't do this, Olive, you're going to regret it."

"I know," I said in a whisper. Then I turned to face forward as the carriage began to pull away.

CHAPTER TWENTY-SIX

Before I boarded the train to head back to the city, I called my parents from Blue Mountain House. I felt sick with anxiety waiting to connect and was immediately relieved when Junior answered.

"It's Olive," I said, my voice already starting to break. "I have a message that I need you to pass on to the rest of the family."

"I'll get Pa on the line, he's in the living room."

"No, no," I said quickly, "just tell them, tell them to cancel their plans for the Adirondacks, the wedding is off."

"What?" he said louder than I wanted him to. "What do you mean the wedding's off?"

"What do you mean the wedding's off?" It was my mother now, she must have heard Junior and grabbed the receiver from his hand.

"It's over, Mother," I said, the tears running down my cheeks all over again. "There isn't going to be a wedding."

"No," she said firmly. "Not again, you're not doing this to us, Olive, you're not humiliating this family again. What did you do?"

"I . . . I . . ." I suddenly couldn't speak. What could I possibly say to make her understand? "We can't marry," was all I could manage.

"You have to fix this, you do whatever it takes to fix this. He is a good man, Olive. You go back to him and you make it right, do you hear me?"

"I'm sorry," I whimpered into the phone. "I'm very sorry," I said, and I hung up the phone. I took a few deep breaths and then, before I could talk myself out of it, I picked up the receiver again. This time I called the New Amsterdam and asked Ziegfeld's secretary, Mrs. Parham, to pass a message on to the girls. It was a painful and humiliating call to make, but at least this way I'd have to make only one call and the word would get out in time for them to cancel their travel plans.

On the train, I sat and stared straight ahead at the seat in front of me. My tears had finally run dry and my eyes burned. I was frozen. I couldn't move. All I could do was try to consider what might happen next. I seemed to be able to think only a few hours ahead; everything else seemed insurmountable. Ruthie and I had given up our apartment months ago, and I couldn't possibly face going back to my parents' house in Flatbush—not now, with my tail between my legs, a failure just as my parents had predicted. So I decided to go to the Saint Agnes Residence, one of the boardinghouses for women that I'd heard a few of the theater girls mention. There were other boardinghouses around town, all strict with curfews, simple and affordable, but Saint Agnes was the only address I could recall.

I took a taxi from the train station and arrived on the steps at 237 West Seventy-fourth Street just before four P.M. I should have known from the name that it was a Catholic house, but the sight of the elderly nun opening the door in her black-and-white habit sent me immediately back to Birdhouse Lodge, and I had a sudden urge to turn and run. I looked down at my trunk, which the taxi driver had left at my feet, and knew I didn't have any choices.

"I was hoping you'd have a room available," I said quietly.

"Come in, dear," she said. "I'm Sister Dorothy, come and sit in the parlor and we'll talk."

I did as she instructed and, once I was seated, she sat across from me.

"Now, dear, it's thirty-five dollars a month, you get your own room, shared bathrooms, three meals a day and maid service to change your sheets once a week. You can do your washing in the laundry room. This is a women's-only residence, no men whatsoever. Those who disobey the rules will be asked to leave."

I nodded.

"Do you have your three references for admission and a doctor's letter showing you're in good health?"

"No." I shook my head, a new dread creeping through me. "I didn't know I needed any of that."

"Oh, yes, dear, we can't let just anyone in off the street. We have to think about the health and safety of our residents. Would you like to come back tomorrow when you have your letters gathered?"

"No," I said, suddenly desperate. It was already late afternoon; where was I going to go if I couldn't stay here? Ruthie's house, I supposed, but she was so pregnant and her apartment so cramped, and I could hardly lug this trunk all over town. I was exhausted, physically and mentally. All I wanted to do was be shown to my room and allowed to sleep for a hundred days. I spoke before an idea had fully formed. "If I can get the reference letters, doctor's note and the money by this evening, could I stay here?"

"Well, yes, we have a room available, but it's already quite late."

"May I just leave the trunk here until I return? I promise I'll be back before eight o'clock."

Though it was the last place I wanted to go, I hailed a taxi and headed to the New Amsterdam Theatre. I couldn't bear facing the girls and Ziegfeld himself, all of them now knowing that the wedding had been called off just days before I was supposed to walk down the aisle, but I had no choice.

I took the elevator up to Ziegfeld's office and mercifully didn't see any of the girls on my way in.

"Miss Shine," Mrs. Parham said. "What a shock, I mean what a surprise. I was so sorry—"

"It's a bit of an emergency," I said, cutting her off before she could say any more. "Is he in?"

"Let me check, dear."

In my sad new circumstances, I was becoming everyone's "dear," and it stung.

A few moments later, Mr. Ziegfeld opened his office door and nodded for me to come in, but not before six young girls who looked as though they couldn't have been more than fifteen walked out, all rosy, flushed cheeks and giggles. Surely not, I thought. They'd have to be at least eighteen to be cast.

"Miss Shine," he said with those same puppy-dog eyes his secretary had given me. "I was saddened to hear your news," he said as he closed the door behind me.

"Yes, thank you." I nodded, looking down to the floor. I hadn't prepared myself to speak of what had happened. Just the thought of Archie brought tears to my eyes; I knew I would fall apart if I had to speak his name.

"But you see, your role has already been recast, Miss Shine," he said matter-of-factly.

"It's what?" I said, looking at him directly for the first time. I hadn't planned to speak to him about returning to the show either, not yet, anyway. I needed some time to get myself settled, set up a place to live and mentally prepare myself to face an audience and the girls again. But once all of that was straightened out, I had planned to come back.

"I'm sorry," he said. "I never could have predicted such a change of heart. I had to think of future shows, and we've just completed extensive auditions to cast the upcoming season," he said, returning to his desk chair and resting his elbows on the desk as if to let me know he had work to get on with. "Contracts have been signed."

"But I was your star in the *Frolic,* don't you want me back for that, at least?"

He shrugged. "We have a new star."

"Who?" I asked rather loudly, shocked that this could all transpire so quickly. But he didn't dignify my outburst with a response. His face remained expressionless. It took me back to that night in the car—when after refusing his advances, I'd stared at him, trying to get a glimpse of what would happen next. This time I knew there was nothing I could say or do to change his mind.

"Well, that is disappointing, but it's not the reason I came," I said, eager to mask my vulnerability. "I was hoping you could write me a letter of recommendation for the Saint Agnes Residence. I need it today so I can stay there tonight. I would also like to ask Howie for a letter if he's here, and I need a doctor's note, so I was hoping I could ask the stage doctor for a letter."

Ziegfeld looked exasperated. "It's already five o'clock."

"If I don't have these letters, I won't have a place to sleep tonight," I said. "And if you could possibly not mention that I was a performer, rather state that I worked at the theater, perhaps as an assistant or secretary, I would appreciate it." I looked to the ground, the humiliation in asking for this almost too much to take. I wondered how many times he'd seen his biggest stars fall from grace. I wondered if he even cared. To him I was just one of hundreds of women who would pass through this theater.

"I'll have Mrs. Parham take care of these letters for you, but it might take a while, you can wait outside her office."

"Thank you," I said, and as I turned to walk out of his office, I felt a wave of desperation come over me, a sudden realization that this might be the last time I'd set foot in the New Amsterdam. I abruptly turned back toward Ziegfeld, who was walking me out of his office, and found myself just inches from him. I placed my hand on his arm and let it run down to his hand, where I stopped and squeezed. "I appreciate your help," I said, looking up at him. He pulled his arm away, and I suddenly felt sick at what I'd done in a moment of hopelessness. I quickly turned again and hurried out the door, stunned that I could feel even lower than when I had walked in.

"Oh, and Miss Shine . . . ," he said.

"Yes." I felt wretched but forced myself to perk up slightly. Maybe he'd had a change of heart about the show.

"Best of luck to you."

Having sat in humiliation for what felt like hours while waiting on the letters, I returned, exhausted, to the residence and was at last allowed a room. I tried to stay in bed. A week would not have been long enough. But the nuns knocked on everyone's doors early for breakfast. They wanted doors open, they wanted to peek inside and be sure there were no visitors of the opposite sex, no funny business going on. Most of the women were secretaries and were up and off to work early. Lying in bed with the sheets over your head was not encouraged, so on the third day I dressed and went to the parlor room, where I wrote out a telegram, then walked to the post office to deliver it.

DEAR ALBERTO STOP
I WOULD LIKE TO SPEAK TO YOUR EUROPEAN
BOOKER STOP
I NEED TO FIND WORK AS SOON AS POSSIBLE AND
CAN TRAVEL STOP
I AM STAYING AT THE SAINT AGNES RESIDENCE IN
NEW YORK STOP
YOUR FRIEND STOP
OLIVE

The next day, a messenger boy delivered a telegram to the residence.

MIA CARA OLIVE STOP
MY BOOKER HAS YOUR NAME BUT SHOWS ARE
BOOKED A YEAR IN ADVANCE STOP
I WOULD LIKE HE MEET YOU IN THE SPRING IN NEW
YORK STOP

WE MEET TOGETHER STOP
PRENDITI CURA DI TE STOP
ALBERTO

After that, I had to force myself to get out of bed. I knew I needed to find work so I could pay my way, but my head felt so heavy, I wanted to close my eyes any chance I could get. All day, every day, I was pining for Archie and kept wondering what he was doing, if he was still at the camp, if he had gone back to Cincinnati, if he was in Manhattan. I briefly considered asking at the Plaza if he was in residence, but what was the point? They wouldn't reveal that information for one thing, and even if he was there, then what? I couldn't go back now. Nothing had changed. I'd still lied to him, backed him into a corner without his even knowing, and on top of that, I'd publicly humiliated him. I'd called off the wedding and then I'd left him with the dirty work of letting the guests know that it was over, that they should cancel their travel plans. I imagined there were some he couldn't reach, some already en route whom he had to face and possibly even host. Before all this I'd been riddled with guilt and anxiety, but this feeling that I'd hurt him, abandoned him without warning and then made him be the one to face the burden and humiliation of announcing it publicly, it was horrible. I'd forced him to despise me, and I'd sealed my fate.

I wanted it to go away, all of it, the way I felt, the light through the curtains, the noises of other people speaking. I couldn't stand any of it. I wanted to be numb. I wanted to sleep. I wanted to never wake up.

The worst of it was that I didn't really understand what I had done or why I had done it.

But those nuns kept knocking.

"Breakfast!" one of them bellowed as she knocked and then opened the door a few inches. "Breakfast," I heard her say again as she moved on to the next door. If I wasn't up and dressed and down for breakfast, she'd be back to throw the door wide open. "This is no place for lollygaggers," she'd said the previous day. So I got up, went down for breakfast—or coffee, since it was all I could stomach—and then walked around the block a few times until the secretaries had scurried off to work and I could return to my room, where they'd leave me alone for a while. I walked slowly, the collar of my mink turned up and pulled around my face. The coat was far too wintry for a crisp day in early September, but I didn't care. I wanted to hide.

A newsboy at the corner was waving a paper as I approached. "Stocks recoup as bulls again rule market!" he shouted, calling out the headline far too loudly. "Read all about it. Sensational gains!"

I thought back to the conversation with Alberto on the train when he'd read out Roger Babson's warning that an economic crash was coming, and he'd said that no one would go to the theater if that happened. Babson had obviously been wrong, and so had Alberto. Archie had said it was all horsefeathers and he was right. The thought of him made my stomach twist. It was hard to swallow; just thinking of him made my eyes tear up.

"Five hundred bottles of liquor seized on Bay State Veterans train!"

I looked at him and saw the look of desperation in his eyes. "Two cents, miss, read all about it. *The New York Times*, just two cents."

When he saw me feeling around in my pocket for change, he tried diligently to make the sale with whatever other news he could recall. "Typhoid outbreak under control," he said. "Water shortages loom."

I handed him two cents, and he gave me the paper and immediately began selling to other passersby, clearly not wanting to miss a second of selling time.

Back in my room, I sat on the bed and mindlessly turned the pages of the paper.

78-YEAR-OLD MICHIGAN GRANDMOTHER CHARGED WITH BOOT-LEGGING IS KILLED TRYING TO FLEE JAIL. Absurd, I thought, then went to the next one. And that's when I saw it, a small article on page thirty-one.

HE LIKES CINCINNATI, SHE LIKES MANHATTAN; CARMICHAEL AND SHINE PART WAYS

The wedding is off for businessman Archibald Carmichael and chorus girl Olive Shine after a blowup at his summer house, the Pines, in the Adirondacks.

Sister-in-law Edna Carmichael, who spent time with them at their camp this summer, said she had an opportunity to observe Miss Shine's "unusual way of doing things. Most of the guests she invited were broke," said Carmichael. "She had a penchant for high-class bohemians whom she fed and clothed, and she acted as if she already ruled the place. She spent money like an empress, drank excessively and used outrageous language even in the presence of guests." She added, "It's no surprise that my brother-in-law eventually saw that they were not suited."

Mr. Carmichael is said to be returning to his hometown of Cincinnati, where he will reside, and plans to reunite with former fiancée, Louise Moyer.

I stared at the small rectangle in horror. I read it over and over again, fixating on that last sentence. This was horrible. I couldn't believe how much hurt and insult could come from one tiny three-inch column. How could this happen so fast? How could he go back to someone he didn't even love? My heart was beating fast, and I could barely breathe. I crumpled the page into a ball and threw it across the room, then fell onto the bed, sobbing into my ink-stained hands, realizing for the first time the magnitude of what I'd done and how permanent it was.

There was a knock at my door. I put the pillow over my head. Another knock, louder now.

"Miss Shine?"

I checked the clock—it was two P.M. Another knock.

I threw the covers back and stomped to the door. "It's the middle of the afternoon, I've had breakfast, I don't want lunch," I shouted. "I don't have a job to go to. I'm not a secretary. What do you want me to do, go and sit on a park bench until the others come back? Can't you leave me alone?"

It was the young one this time, Sister Theresa, slight and mousy, wearing wire-rimmed glasses. She stood there looking shocked, and I felt terrible all over again. I hadn't expected it to be her. I'd seen her around the house, talking to the other residents, and she had seemed to be quite sweet. Not that I'd spoken to her, but she'd always seemed accommodating, cheerful. I'd even wondered if she envied those girls in their day dresses heading out into the city.

"You have a visitor in the parlor," she said quietly.

For a second my heart jumped. What if it was Archie? And then it sank. Why would it be? I took one look at myself in the mirror. I looked gaunt, my skin was grey, my hair looked as if it had been glued to my head. I had dark shadows under my eyes. I didn't care. I put on a cardigan and walked downstairs.

Ruthie was leaning back in an armchair. She looked uncomfortably large.

"Olive," she said sympathetically as soon as she caught sight of me. I could have kept on walking. I didn't want to see her. I didn't want to see anyone, but I forced myself to go in.

"Hi, Ruthie," I said.

"How are you?"

"As well as can be expected. Aren't you supposed to be having that baby soon?"

"Two more weeks, apparently," she said, looking drained. "Listen, Olive, I've come to apologize. I feel terrible, I haven't been able to sleep since I heard the news. I gave you bad advice and I feel awful, just awful about it." The tears welled up in her eyes.

"What are you talking about?"

She looked at me, distraught. "This is all my fault, I told you to tell him"—she cupped one hand around her mouth and whispered—"about the baby. And now you're here," she continued, "at a boardinghouse, alone. I'm so sorry, it's the pregnancy, it's making me not think straight."

I waved my hands. "Oh, God, Ruthie, stop, stop, stop." This was

all so exhausting—everything I did created problems I didn't antic-
ipate for people I loved. "None of this is your fault."

"Of course it is."

"I didn't tell him. I didn't tell him about the baby, and I didn't tell
him I can't have any more children."

"What?"

"I couldn't do it," I said. "I knew how his whole family back home
was desperate for him to become a father, to carry on the family
name. I knew that was what he wanted too, so there was no point.
He might have asked me to stay, but he would have regretted it later.
I would have ruined his life, crushed his hopes and dreams. If we'd
married, I would have been a constant disappointment to him, a
letdown, and I don't want to be that to anyone. I'd rather be alone
for the rest of my life than know that I was one big disappointment.
It's bad enough being that to my family."

Ruthie sat back and seemed to take it all in, to understand, but
then she shook her head. "But he wouldn't have to know, Olive.
Some people can't have children. And he could accept that if he had
you. He wouldn't need to know about the cause."

"But *I* would! *I* would know. And our life together would rest
on a lie. You're right, he might feel sorry for me if he didn't know
the truth, even sad for me, but I wouldn't deserve his sympathy. You
said yourself I had to tell him! That's the trap I'm in. Even if I did
tell him, he might *think* he could accept that, but he'd regret it, and
I can't knowingly cause him anything but happiness."

She knew me, and she was watching me, her eyes wide with regret, knowing I couldn't live like that.

"I think about that poor baby now," I went on. "All the time I think of her, where she is, who took her in, what she looks like. She'd be two. I just think, What was it all for? For me to end up sitting here, alone, back with the nuns?"

"Oh, Olive. What are you going to do now?"

"Ziegfeld doesn't want me, so go back to that agent Moses Sherman, I suppose, see if he can find me some work. But nothing's going to pay the way Ziegfeld did. I guess I should try to get used to living here because I don't know how I'm ever going to afford anything else."

Ruthie shook her head and sighed. "We were on top of the world, you and me, not too long ago."

"You still are," I said. "I'm the only one who's made a mess of things. You never wanted to stay in the show, you always dreamed of this."

She nodded and smiled. "We're going to look at buying a house in Westport after the baby's born—you know, have a little more space."

"You're going to make a real good mother, Ruthie," I said, feeling a pang of loss at the thought of her moving away, even if it was just outside the city, with a husband and baby and a house. Everything I never thought I wanted suddenly looked quite beautiful.

"I'm sure Moses will find a new show for you," she said. "Or you could talk to Texas."

"The nightclub hostess?"

"Yes, Texas Guinan, have you heard about her new place? Eadie went on to make a heck of a lot of money with her at the El Fey before it shut down. Your father isn't going to like it, so don't go inviting him to a late night show." She laughed halfheartedly. "But it'd get you back on your feet."

I nodded. "It's not a terrible idea, I suppose."

"You'll work it out somehow, Olive, you always do."

CHAPTER TWENTY-SEVEN

The following evening, I forced myself to get out of bed, put on a face and pay a visit to Texas at her spot, the 300 Club. I'd squandered almost every penny I'd made in the *Follies* and the *Frolic,* and I had only a handful of years left before I'd be too old for the show girl roles anyway. But while Ziegfeld's girls were getting younger and younger, and prettier, too, the nightclubs were a different story—they generally loved to have former *Follies* girls onstage. Texas welcomed me into the club as if I were a longtime friend.

"Come on in, my little," she said. Her voice was gruff, and she was known for having the rudest mouth in town, but somehow she seemed maternal.

She walked me through the club, where long rose-colored chandeliers hung from the ceiling. The walls were draped with green-and-gold tapestries, and the floor was carpeted with plush red velvet. We passed through the crowded room and back to her office and dressing room, which was also decadently set up. In the lights, I could see now that the years hadn't been all that kind to Texas—her hair was a brittle blond, her makeup heavy and her skin seasoned, presumably from all the late nights—but she was still striking in her own way. I didn't know if it was the way she spoke or the way she looked, but she commanded your attention, and it was no surprise she'd been so successful as the queen of the nightclubs.

"Thanks for meeting with me," I said. "I don't know if you recall, but I met you a few times with Archibald Carmichael, when your club was the El Fey."

"Oh, I recall. I don't forget a pretty face on the arm of a big butter-and-egg man."

"A what?"

"A rich fella—" She laughed a hacking laugh. "One of my patrons was handing out fifty-dollar bills to my girls as if they were nothin'. I asked him what business he was in, that he could throw around so much cash, and he said dairy produce, so I been calling 'em butter-and-egg men ever since."

I laughed, thinking that $50 could go a long way for me right about now.

"You were hot stuff in them Ziegfeld shows, people been talking about you for some time. So what'd you do? Smash some eggs? I'm guessin' if you're coming here to see me, things didn't work out with Ziegfeld."

"Yes. I, w-well . . . ," I stammered.

"I don't care about the particulars." She picked up a coffee mug and took a slurp. "Want a coffee?"

"Got anything stronger?"

"You're going to have to get some Fred to buy you that, darlin', unless you want to hand over thirty-five big ones for a bottle of 'champagne,'" she said, suggesting some concoction that they passed off as the real thing.

My God, that would've paid rent at the boardinghouse for a whole month. "Coffee's fine, thanks."

She stood up, went to the door and yelled out, "Leon, two hot coffees and two oranges." Almost immediately a boy not more than seventeen brought us exactly that, and Texas began peeling her orange and eating it right there.

"Go on, then, tell me, what brings you?"

"I left Ziegfeld's shows, I just had my finale and thought I was going to be done with all this, but my circumstances changed, and I'd like to be back onstage, making some money."

"You made a good name for yourself, better than I ever did on the stage. I was a show girl too, you know, then I went off to Hollywood and made some westerns. I was Hollywood's first cowgirl, you know, the whole world would have known it, too, if it hadn't been for that damn, good-for-nothin' war interfering with the release date."

"I've seen some of your films, you're very good."

"Better at this, though," she said. "I like getting people to do things, and getting them as inebriated as possible makes it easier for them to do things like part with their money." She laughed wholeheartedly and clasped her hands. "So, we all love a Ziegfeld girl and we'd love to have you. But I like a specialty act, what are your best tricks?"

"Singing is what I do best," I said. But I didn't feel like myself; my confidence was in the gutter, and for the first time since I could remember, I didn't even want to sing.

"Well, we sure would love that, but unlike the theater, which is civilized, we got hustlers and mobsters and writers and mayors coming through this joint. We got millionaires and senators all spending big for Moët. They don't want just a pretty girl singing a pretty song, they want a touch of scandal and skin, so make sure you show 'em what you've got, doll."

I nodded.

"But we ain't no bordello, either. You can go to Polly's for that, and hey, if you're hard up you certainly could—I don't ask questions, but there's none of that going on under my roof. That's not how I make money off my girlies, you got that?"

"Of course," I said. I couldn't believe I was even having this conversation. Only a few weeks ago I was set to become Mrs. Archibald Carmichael, yet here I was being warned not to become a lady of the night.

"Don't look so stirred up, doll face. I have to say it. Some girls come in here looking for the wrong type of business, I just have to set things straight. I might be a foulmouthed broad, but I ain't no madam."

"I understand."

"Come back in the morning, and we'll get you set up with a costume and music. You just think about what you want to sing—something cute, something sassy. It's going to be grand, girly, don't worry, we'll get you back on top in no time."

The 300 Club was one of the most expensive clubs in town, tinged with far more illicit activity than Ziegfeld's *Frolic*. Publicly, Texas announced that she had only setups for drinks and that if people brought their own flasks of hooch, that was their business—but that was a lie. The bottles were stored in the house next door and passed to the barkeep through a hole in the wall. Raids and arrests were frequent—and Texas herself had spent a night or two in the slammer. I'd seen her picture in the paper as she was let out, with a quotation that read, "I liked their cute little jail. . . . I don't know any other time when my jewels felt so safe."

If my family hadn't liked my performing on Broadway, then they sure as hell weren't going to like me in late night speakeasies. But what did it matter? I thought. I'd already disappointed everyone I cared about, so there was no point in stopping now. To make a big, flashy comeback, I decided on a voluminous pink feather cloak with little more than tassels, pearls and lace underneath. I'd be singing "I Want Someone to Make a Fuss over Me," and I'd make sure they did.

Club performing was different from appearing on Broadway. Texas called herself the hostess, but she was more like the ringmaster, and we, the scantily clad chorus girls, were the acts in her risqué circus. She was funny and brash and insulting to her patrons, and they loved her for it.

"Hello, suckers!" she said on my first night in the show, her raspy voice silencing the room as the music ended, and Naughty Maureen, the "titillating tap dancer," left the floor.

"Well? The girl can dance, didn't I tell ya the girl could dance? Give her a big hand, would ya?" she said, and the crowd did just that. "I just had a fella come up to me, not a regular," she said, taking a seat on a stool center stage. "And he says he's been overcharged. I said,

'Whaddaya mean you've been overcharged? Lemme see your check. Why, you poor sap. Sucker, you had two telephone calls and a bottle of champagne. Whaddaya expect? Don't be dumb.'"

Everyone laughed.

"Listen, suckers," she went on, "it's only money. Why take life so seriously? In a hundred years we'll all be gone. I don't need your money. Give me plenty of laughs and you can take all the rest." But that was all horsefeathers, too, because she was notorious for driving prices up and making a fortune from running her clubs.

I waited offstage, a few nips of whiskey in, ready for my entrance.

"Now, this next little girl is someone you all know and love," she said. "Give a big welcome back to the stage to this little one, former Ziegfeld Folly Miss Olive Shine."

I sauntered onstage wrapped in feathers and began to sing. It felt good. I didn't have to do any fancy footwork or think about the precision of the Ziegfeld walk. I started off slowly as I made my way to the grand piano, brushed past the pianist, a much older gentleman called Bones. I ran my hand along his shoulder, then climbed up a few steps at the rear of the piano and arranged myself sitting on top. Toward the end of the song, I threw off my feather cloak and bared almost all. The crowd cheered and it was nice to be back. But it didn't give me the thrill I'd expected. Instead, my mind went to the money. Please the audience and you'll increase your pay, I thought. Make them happy, they'll buy more booze, Texas will have more money in her pocket and she'll be more inclined to raise my pay. I'd never thought about money like this before. It hadn't mattered. As long as I could be on that stage, I would have done almost anything.

It was five in the morning when I left the club. The sun would be

up soon, and West Fifty-fourth Street was quiet except for the last
few patrons leaving the 300. I hailed a taxi to take me to the boardinghouse and was asleep by the time I arrived.

I fell into a new routine, sleeping all day and staying out at the club
all night, an arrangement that the nuns at Saint Agnes wouldn't have
liked one bit if I hadn't lied through my teeth, telling them I took
a job as a nurse's assistant working the night shift. I was grateful to
have money coming in. It made me feel slightly less desperate for the
future, but it definitely felt like work. For the first time, performing
felt like an obligation.

We changed up the numbers nightly, so that repeat customers
wouldn't have to watch the same acts night after night. I sang "Oh!
How I Hate to Get Up in the Morning," which Irving Berlin had
written when he was drafted in the army, and I think the audience
liked that I put my own spin on it. But the only time I didn't feel that
I was putting on a whole lot of worthless razzle-dazzle was when I
sang the rueful songs "What'll I Do?" and "When I Lost You," also
by Berlin but written when his wife died of typhoid fever, contracted
on their honeymoon in Havana. Somehow feeling the sadness and
regret in his lyrics made me feel less alone and more truthful.

CHAPTER TWENTY-EIGHT

It was Sister Theresa, I could tell from the sound of her quick, light step coming down the hall. "Olive, visitor in the parlor." We'd become friendly, she and I. She saved me a boiled egg and a piece of bread from breakfast most mornings, and I ate them at the kitchen table around lunchtime. Afterwards, I helped her prepare for that night's dinner by peeling potatoes or chopping onions. I didn't have anything else to do during the day, and by lunchtime I'd usually caught up on enough sleep to make it through the rest of the day and night. She'd asked me about my nursing duties and it felt wrong to lie to a nun, especially one who was being so kind and helpful, so I told her it was against hospital policies to discuss the ins and outs of it all, I had to respect the patients' privacy.

"Who's the visitor?" I called out after she'd knocked, but she was already making her way back downstairs. It could only be Ruthie again, but I was surprised Lawrence had let her leave the house when she was due to have that baby any day now. Maybe it was one of the other girls, Pauline, or maybe Gladys. I quickly dressed, smoothed my hair, then went downstairs.

"Mother!" I said, shocked, seeing her sitting tightly on the edge of the tufted cream-colored armchair. Her face was pale. She was dressed in a black day dress and matching coat, with a single string of pearls—formal for the daytime at a boardinghouse. I quickly glanced down at my jodhpurs and sweater, something I wore most days at the house when no one except the nuns would see me. They were comfortable and sporty and reminded me of my days at the camp. My mother also glanced at my attire, then shifted in her seat and pressed her lips together.

"Olive," she said. "Here you are."

"Here I am."

"We had to track you down. You know, it would have been nice to receive a letter telling us of your whereabouts."

"I know, I'm very sorry. I meant to, I was just trying to get settled after ..." I didn't want to talk to her about the canceled wedding, about Archie. My stomach clenched at the thought of him. I couldn't bear to be questioned about it all, not yet, and her visit had caught me so off guard.

"Yes," she said stiffly. "I can imagine it's"—she looked around—"quite an adjustment."

I took a deep breath, preparing myself to be bombarded with questions: What happened? Why did he leave you? What did you do? How are you going to make this right? But instead she simply sat there, her hands folded in her lap, her face pained. It was distressing to see her like that, looking as if she might burst into tears. I wondered if my circumstances were causing her all this pain. Despite her look of upset and disapproval, some small part of me felt cared for, that she had come to find me, to check on me. Maybe she didn't want me to be alone.

"Thank you for coming," I said, but she just looked at the floor. "Is everything okay, Mother?" I asked finally. And when I said it, the tears sprang from her eyes.

"Oh, Olive," she said quietly, quickly trying to wipe away her tears.

I was wrong, this wasn't about me, this must be something terrible. I hurried to her as sudden thoughts of every possible horrible thing that could happen flooded my brain: Junior, George, Erwin, my father.

"What is it?" I asked, taking her hand in mine.

"It's your aunt May. She died."

"No," I gasped. "That's impossible."

"We just found out yesterday morning."

I found it hard to catch my breath, a terrible ache in my heart. She'd helped me so much, given her kindness so freely. We had kept in touch too little since I'd left Rockville more than two years ago, with the exception of the occasional letter and her declined invitation to the wedding. At the time, I remembered wishing she could attend, wishing she could meet Archie. I knew she would have been happy at the thought of me getting married.

"But she was so young," I said, trying to comprehend it.

"I know. She had a heart condition that we knew of most of her life, so I suppose it was inevitable at some point. The doctor had warned her. But she'd seemed fine. Even though we knew about her condition, it seemed to come out of nowhere."

"I didn't know about it," I said hopelessly, as if it would make some kind of difference now.

We'd been through such a tremendous seven and a half months together, it was hard to fathom. But the truth was that since leaving my aunt in Rockville, my thoughts had been elsewhere, caught up in the excitement of my glamorous new life, pushing away the thoughts of my pregnancy, the baby, what had become of her, not allowing myself to think back to that time. I had no idea what Aunt May's days had been like after I left.

"I can't believe she's gone," my mother whispered.

"Mother, I'm so sorry." I felt terribly guilty to think that my mother had been forced to track me down, probably calling the New Amsterdam Theatre and getting the runaround before finding me here, all while she'd just learned of her only sister's death.

I should have gone to see them as soon as I returned to the city.

"Was anyone with her?" I asked. Aunt May had lived such an isolated life, the thought of her dying alone was unbearable.

"A neighbor found her." My mother put her head in her hands. After a few moments she took a deep breath and seemed to pull herself together. "Your father and I will take the train to Rockville tomorrow. We'll have a few days to take care of her affairs," she said. "The funeral is on Saturday."

"What about the boys?"

"George will stay with Junior, make sure he gets to school."

I nodded. It really should be me helping out.

"I thought you'd want to know."

"Of course," I said. "Thank you."

"I'm sorry for whatever happened between you and Archie. I

sensed from the way you were acting in the Adirondacks that there may be some trouble looming. Of course I have no idea what that might have been."

"It's my fault," I said. I knew she was waiting for more, but it was all I could manage. She deserved more of an explanation, she was my mother, after all, but I was devastated to hear the news about Aunt May. I simply couldn't begin to talk about Archie.

My mother stood up and put on her coat. "I'm sure it hasn't been easy for you."

That night I went to the club early. I couldn't sit around at the boardinghouse. I kept thinking about Aunt May, how I'd thought of her so fondly over the past two years but had never really let her know how grateful I was to her for helping me. We'd exchanged only a few letters, and I regretted that now. But there was more—her death seemed to seal another regret. I'd always wanted to know if she'd ever received word about the baby, if she knew whether she'd been adopted by a local family or one from another state. It would be impossible to demand such information from Birdhouse Lodge after I'd signed those papers, but I couldn't help wondering. I hadn't asked her, though. Instead, I'd sent the occasional bland letter about my shows, wishing her a Merry Christmas, telling her we'd love to pay for the train ride to the Adirondacks, saying I understood when she'd written that it was too far to travel.

Why hadn't I asked about the baby, my baby? Maybe I'd been too scared to revisit that time in my life. Giving her away had seemed the only choice I had back then, but was it really? Looking back,

I wondered if it had been decided too quickly, too hastily, without much regard for the permanence of it all.

Now, when I thought back on those months with Aunt May, despite the urgency of the situation, I realized they'd actually been quite enjoyable, hidden away, just the two of us talking, reading and gardening, nurturing the baby growing inside me. It was easier to think back on it now and appreciate it. Though I'd been purposefully pushing it out of my mind, there was so much I still wanted to say to her. She was the only other person who'd known me in that way, and I'd just assumed that she would always be there.

"Hey there, girly," Texas said, swinging the dressing room door wide open as she marched in. "The early bird gets the worm, except there's nothing but snakes out there, girly, and don't you forget it." She laughed. I tried to smile back at her. "Why the long face? Who died?" she said, laughing again.

"My aunt, actually. My mother just told me today."

"Oh, doll face, I'm sorry. I've got to work on my punch lines. Were you close?"

"Not always, but a few years ago I went through something ..." I looked up at her. Hell, it was Texas I was talking to, she must've been through just about everything. "I got pregnant and stayed with my aunt in Minnesota to wait it out, then I gave the baby up for adoption."

"Oh, honey pie, that's a tough one."

"I had to hide the whole thing from my family," I said, strangely relieved to tell someone. "My aunt took such good care of me, never batting an eye in judgment. I just wish I'd spoken to her again, I wish I'd thanked her better, let her know what it meant to me."

"She sounds like a good lassie. You going to her send-off?"

"I can't." I sighed. "It's this weekend, I've got this," I said, motioning around the club, "and I can't afford the train ride."

"How much is it?" she asked.

"Oh, I don't know. A train to St. Cloud, then another to Rockville, probably fifty dollars at least."

She pulled a roll of bills out of her bustier and started counting.

"Don't you worry about the show. The show will go on, it always does. You go and you pay your respects," she said, placing a wad of bills on the table in front of me. "And when I'm pushing up daisies, you do the same and show up for my funeral. I want everyone I ever knew to be there. Nobody wants to be forgotten."

I pulled up to Aunt May's house in a taxi a little after noon on Friday. It had taken me three trains and forty-seven hours to get there. When I walked through the gate and up the pathway to her home, it hit me—this had been her whole world, this little house.

I had one small travel bag that I slung over my shoulder before I knocked on the door. I could hear people inside, so I knocked again.

"Coming," came my mother's voice. She opened the door almost absently, as if she were expecting it to be a delivery of flowers or something. And then she swung back around and stared at me. I, too, stood frozen, staring—not just at my mother, who'd seemed so fragile just days earlier and now seemed flushed, youthful, but at the little girl she was holding on her hip.

The girl, no more than a toddler, looked at me curiously with wide green eyes, her wispy dark hair falling in all directions against her milky-white skin. She reached out a hand toward me, then pulled it back, quickly hiding her face in my mother's shoulder.

"Olive!" my mother said finally.

"Mother."

"We weren't expecting you. How did you get here?"

"Train. Three of them, actually. I wanted to attend the funeral but didn't know how to reach you."

"Yes, yes, of course, how nice." All that youthful color had suddenly drained from her cheeks.

"Who's this?" I asked, though as I said it, I felt my legs start to tremble under me.

"This?" She seemed stunned, as if I'd asked an absurd question. "This? This is Adeline . . ." She paused again. "Your cousin."

"Addie," the girl said, peeking back at me, smiling, reaching her hand out again to touch me.

"My cousin? Whose daughter?" I asked, but my mother ignored the question. I placed one hand on the door frame to steady myself and reached the other out to the girl. "Well, hello there, Addie," I said, giving her hand a gentle shake. "It's nice to meet you."

"Come in," my mother said. "Your father's going to be surprised. You come in and take a seat, rest for a minute, you've had such a long journey. I'd better go and let your father know you're here," she said, flustered—panicky, it seemed, at the thought of sharing this news. I couldn't take my eyes off the girl, and she didn't take her eyes off me, looking over my mother's shoulder as she was whisked out of the room.

Several minutes later, my mother reappeared with my father by her side, the little child no longer on her hip. They stood stiffly in front of me.

"Hello, Olive," my father said.

"Hello, Papa." I was so tired and wished I could hug him, but I could see it wasn't going to be that way. He was angry about my aborted wedding, just as I knew he would be.

"Good of you to come," he said, as if I were some random neighbor coming to pay my respects.

"Yes, it's so unexpected and sad," I said.

"It certainly is." There was a cold tension in the room. "Well, I'd better get back to the yard, it's a mess," he said, and he turned on his heel to go back out the way he came in. I looked at my mother questioningly.

"Papa," I said, "you have to forgive me—" But he was already leaving the room.

My mother and I stood in the room in silence as I watched the door he'd walked though.

"He has a hard time understanding your choices," my mother said. "Quite frankly, we all do sometimes. You tend to make decisions that have vast repercussions for your life and ours too. Some people can adapt to that kind of thing, and others can't. Your father, I would say, cannot."

I sat back down again; a swirling, unsettling feeling had come over me.

"Can I have something to drink?" I said.

"Of course." My mother left for the kitchen, but after a few moments I got up and joined her.

"It's so hot in here," I said. "Can I open the window?" I leaned over the kitchen sink and opened it a few inches, feeling immediately refreshed by a rush of cold air. Outside in the backyard, my father was hammering nails into a fence post, and the little girl, wrapped up now in a hat, scarf and coat, was playing with a woman I didn't recognize. The child's face was striking and remarkably familiar.

"Who did you say the little girl is?" I asked, not taking my eyes off her.

My mother clanked about, opening the tin, spooning the tea into the pot, getting the cups down from the cupboard. The kettle began to whistle, and she seemed to let it go on longer than necessary.

"Who is she, Mother?" I asked, more insistent now.

"Your cousin," she said in a low voice. Then she finally looked at me. "Your aunt adopted a little girl."

I felt my stomach drop, and a wave of chills coursed through my whole body. I went back to the kitchen window and leaned toward it. She was laughing now, playing hopscotch in front of the lady. Adeline. It was a beautiful name.

I looked back to my mother. "She's mine, isn't she."

"Keep your voice down," she scolded.

"She is. I could see it the minute you opened the door. How? How could she have my baby? How could she not tell me? I signed the papers. I left Birdhouse Lodge without her. Aunt May wasn't even there. I don't understand. Mother, please!"

My mother grabbed me by the wrist and took me back to the living room.

"I don't know how, and I don't know why, Olive!" she said in an urgent whisper. "I don't know why she would do such a thing. It was wrong of her. She lived like a hermit, and that is no way to raise a

child, and she knew we had made a specific plan. A specific plan!"
she said, hitting her fist into the open palm of her other hand. "I told
her back then that she shouldn't have done it. She said she couldn't
stand to let some stranger take a newborn baby away."

"Wait a second, you spoke to her about this? You knew?"

She closed her eyes and took a deep breath, exasperated by my
persistence. "Yes, Olive, I knew. She told me a few weeks after she
brought Adeline home."

"What?" I yelled this time. "You knew about her the whole time,
and you didn't tell me? How could you not tell me?"

My mother looked at me, furious. "First of all, lower your voice
or I'm going to have to ask you to leave. Your father doesn't know
about any of this, and I don't want him to find out. And secondly,
why would I tell you? You didn't want that baby—you made that
very clear."

"I was nineteen, Mother! I didn't know what I wanted. You made
that decision for me! I was scared. All this time I've been thinking
about her, wondering if she's okay, if she's loved, wondering where
she is. And you didn't think I ought to know?"

"I've seen what you've been up to, drinking, and dancing, and out
all night. I hardly think you've been losing any sleep over this poor
child. Anyway, there's no point raking all that up now, what's done
is done, and Aunt May is gone." She narrowed her eyes and glared
at me. Was she suggesting that this was my fault? Had the whole
plan to involve Aunt May in my pregnancy secret been too much
for her heart?

"We're going to bring the child to Brooklyn, and your father and
I will raise her. We'll tell everyone that May had adopted a child and,

following her untimely death, it makes sense that her only sister will bear that burden."

I sat on the arm of the chair, weak. I felt as if I'd been punched in the stomach, repeatedly. A thousand questions ran through my head. Why hadn't Aunt May told me, would I have tried to stop her? Was this her plan all along? Was she doing this to fulfill her own desires to become a mother? I had so many questions that would never be answered.

I slid into the chair and put my head back.

"Oh God, are you going to faint?" my mother asked, irritated. "If your father sees you, he's going to wonder what's going on."

"I'm in shock, Mother," I said. This onslaught of information left me weak. I felt my mother lift my limp arms and hoist me up.

"Come on, Olive," she said, her voice softening. "Let's get you upstairs."

"I'm okay," I said. "Just let me be." But she'd already pulled me up to standing and was walking me to the narrow staircase.

Holding on to the banister, I made my way upstairs, my mother following, and sat down on the edge of the small bed that I'd slept in when I was staying with Aunt May. When I looked around the room, I realized that it was Addie's room now. There were building blocks stacked in the corner, knitted dolls lined up on the window-sill. Squeals of laughter rose up from the backyard.

"I need to see her," I said.

"You need to get some rest and pull yourself together." My mother sighed, shaking her head, and left the room.

Addie was running, arms out in front of her, chasing the birds.

She seemed so happy. I couldn't believe she was mine. I opened the window so I could hear her better.

"Look, look," she was saying to the woman who was outside with her, urging her to look at the birds, too. "Birdies," she said, then more squeals as she chased after them again.

I picked up one of the knitted dolls. It was a cream-colored bear wearing a hat and gloves and dark green pants. Someone had knitted this for her, and I felt so incredibly thankful. She had been loved. Aunt May had given her a start in life. And whether she meant to or not, Aunt May had given me a gift, too, one beyond what I could have imagined. This was an absolute miracle.

Once I'd taken some time to collect my thoughts, I drank down the water my mother had left by the bed and went back downstairs. Outside, I sat on the ledge of a low wall in the backyard near Addie and the neighbor.

"What are you playing?" I asked.

"Birdies," she said, pointing at them as I'd seen her do from the window.

"Big birdies," I said. "They look like they might be crows."

She clapped her hands together.

"I'm Maria," the woman said, "I live next door. You must be Olive. I was a friend of your aunt's."

"It's nice to meet you." I remembered her now. I'd seen her a few times when I stayed with Aunt May, but I didn't think we'd ever spoken. I had been hiding myself back then, while Aunt May purposefully avoided people, saying it was too hard to meet new people after her husband died.

"I have two girls, they're seven and nine. They love playing with Addie. And we all adored May. She was such a kind, quiet lady."

I nodded. "She really was. I can't believe she's gone."

Maria shook her head. "Me neither, such a shock. My girls came over to visit Addie that day, and when no one answered we got worried and came in through the back door. We found her in her bed. Addie had been trying to wake her."

"Oh, Lord," I said. "How awful." I looked over to Addie, who was pulling a little wooden dog on a string. She was only two and she'd already been through so much. My heart ached for her.

"It's very kind of you to have the reception at your home," I said. Maria had insisted, since their house was bigger than Aunt May's, and in return my mother was attempting to cook enough pies to feed an army.

"Of course," she said. "It's the least we can do." She paused. "What will you do now?"

"What do you mean?" I asked. But from the way she was looking at me, I realized she knew about me and Addie.

"Your mother said they'd take her to New York."

I nodded.

"She really is the most darling little girl," she continued. "So happy all the time, so well behaved, so easy."

I nodded again. What else could I add? I had no idea if she was well behaved, if she liked to take a bath, if she was a picky eater, a good sleeper, if cats made her sneeze the way they did for me.

"I'm sorry," she said. "It's none of my business. We just care for her so much."

"It's all right," I said. "I honestly don't know what I'll do. But thank you for caring about Addie, for being a friend to Aunt May. It's what they needed, I'm sure."

"We could keep her," she said suddenly, almost nonchalantly, as if we were discussing who should keep the leftover pies. "With us. She's known the girls since she first came home."

I was stunned by her offer and studied her face, taking in all that she had said, unable to respond right away.

"Well, you don't have to say anything now. Just think about it and know that we would be more than happy to take her in."

That night Maria, her husband and their two girls joined us for dinner, but I barely said a word. In a matter of a few hours everything I thought I knew had turned out to be wrong, and I was trying to absorb it all. Addie sat in a wooden high chair at the end of the table, and Maria's two girls sat on either side of her, while the adults sat at the other end of the table. My mother and Maria mostly discussed preparations for the next day, that my mother would bring the pies over to Maria's house the next morning before we all left for church, how Maria's husband would set out drinks, and another neighbor would bring lemon cake. I didn't attempt to partake in the adult conversation—I so desperately wanted to be seated with the children.

I couldn't take my eyes off Addie, the way she picked up her buttered bread and ate it, her lips and cheeks getting greasy from the butter. The way she grasped her fork in her hand and ate her carrots. I wanted to hold her fleshy hand in mine and walk her around the backyard, just the two of us, to spend time with her away from everyone else, to hear her high-pitched voice respond to things that I said. And then, as if she knew we shared a secret, she looked up at me and smiled.

There must have been fifty or sixty people at the funeral the next day, paying their respects to my aunt. I was surprised. She had barely interacted with anyone when I'd lived with her—but these were friends, church patrons, store owners, other parents from the neighborhood. It seemed that having a child in her life had coaxed her to mingle with humanity again. Several people spoke at the funeral about what a kind and generous person she was, how she helped others, how she'd watched other neighbors' children alongside Addie when they'd needed to run an errand, how she'd brought food to one family for a week straight when their child fell ill. I had seen this kindness in her when she took me in, but I'd known then that to others she was just an odd lady, the woman at the end of the street who kept to herself. The May they spoke of at her funeral had flourished. She'd reclaimed her life with Addie in it. My mother saw it, too. She wept quietly in the pew. I reached out and took her hand.

"This was how she used to be before Henry died," she whispered. "She was back to being May again."

It was a moving tribute. I imagined my own eulogy. Whom had I cared for or loved unconditionally? How had I helped people? Who had relied on me? I thought of Archie, how I'd been so cruel and cowardly to not tell him the truth, how I'd convinced myself that hurting him and abandoning him with no explanation was better than being honest with him. And now he was gone. I regretted it all.

That night when everyone had left, I told my mother that she should put her feet up and I would read Addie her bedtime story and put her to bed. My mother looked at me uneasily.

"That's all right, Olive, you don't have to," she said.

"I want to. And besides, you both must be exhausted after today. Let me help."

"You've been on your feet all day, Doris, let her help out for once," my father said as he settled into the armchair in front of the fireplace. I had noticed throughout the day that any time I'd tried to spend with Addie had been interrupted by my mother. This time I didn't wait for her to discourage me.

"Are you ready for story time?" I asked Addie, who was sitting in the middle of the living room stacking three egg cartons on top of one another. She nodded, so I picked her up and carried her upstairs.

I helped her into her pajamas in Aunt May's room, where she'd been sleeping in a makeshift bed next to my parents since I'd been staying in her room. I unfastened her two miniature pigtails and brushed her hair, and when I did, she grabbed my face with her two small hands.

"Pretty hair," she said, pulling gently on mine.

"Thank you," I said. "We have the same color. Look!" I swished my head from side to side, letting my short bob fly away from me. She did the same, laughing. In that moment, everything—the theater, the singing, the dancing, the nights on the town—everything seemed so frivolous and unimportant. How could I have not known how this would feel, to be sitting here talking to my daughter, seeing myself in her and her in me?

I read her a story, then I tucked her into bed, and by the time I was finished she was already asleep. Reluctant to leave, I kissed her forehead, noticing the softness of her skin, her innocence. I tiptoed out of the room and turned off the light, but as soon as I stepped outside the door, she was sitting up, crying.

"What's the matter?" I rushed back to her.

But she only closed her eyes, opened her mouth and wailed.

"You were asleep, Addie. Please, don't cry," I whispered, knowing my mother would be upstairs momentarily.

"Mama!" she cried loudly. "I want Mama!"

"Oh, I know, sweetheart," I said, crouching on my knees and hugging her.

"Mama!" she screamed even louder, swatting me away. "I want Mama!"

She'd seemed so content all day, so compliant with me when I read her a story. How had this suddenly taken such a turn? I wondered. Was it the darkness?

As I'd expected, my mother appeared at the door, rushed past me and picked up Addie, who continued to cry. But within a few moments she became quieter. She'd stopped screaming "Mama!" and had her thumb in her mouth, still sobbing, more softly now. I backed out of the room quietly, feeling foolish for having thought I would know how to comfort her. I had no idea how to help.

I sat down in the dark on my bed. In the course of twenty-four hours, everything that I thought I knew about the adoption had turned out to be wrong. The story I'd been telling myself, the secret

I'd been keeping, it was all a lie. Here she was, my flesh and blood, sleeping in the room next to me, suddenly in need of a mother more than ever, but she didn't know who I was. And I didn't know how to be her mother. My life was a shambles—but whether she meant to or not, Aunt May seemed to be giving me a second chance.

Addie was quiet now. I heard my mother leaving her room. Before I could talk myself out of it, I walked down the stairs and into the living room.

"Mother, Father, I have something I need to say," I announced as soon as I entered the room. "Adeline is my daughter. All you need to do is look at her to know it's true. I became pregnant just before you moved to New York. I know it was a terrible thing to do, out of wedlock with someone I didn't even know, but it happened."

A look of horror came over my mother's face, but I looked away.

"I stayed with Aunt May during my pregnancy and gave her up for adoption through the church." No one said a word. My mother now had her head in her hands, and my father's mouth was agape. "It was a terrible thing to do, to make an innocent child pay for my mistakes, I can see that now, but it was the decision I made. I didn't know until a few days ago that Aunt May had adopted her, but now, deep down in my heart, I wonder if she knew or hoped that I would come back for her."

I waited briefly for someone to say something. No one did.

"Well," I continued, "I have decided I will take her back to New York with me when I leave tomorrow, and we'll be together."

"Don't be ridiculous, Olive," my mother said. "Look where you're living. I doubt they're going to let a single show girl bring up a bastard child in a Catholic boardinghouse."

I cringed at the use of such vulgar words to describe Addie, asleep now right above us.

"I'll work something out," I said. I thought of the club. How would I make this work? The money was decent, but I could make the money only if I was working five nights a week. How could I do that while caring for a two-year-old? I hadn't thought it through, but I was angry now.

"Hold on a second!" My father's voice boomed over both of ours as he stood. "Doris, you knew about this?"

"Yes, I knew. My sister told me. Now sit down, Ted."

My father sat back down again and stared at the fireplace. It was the first time I'd ever heard my mother speak to him that way, and I'd never seen him so obedient.

"What will you work out?" my mother continued. "With what money?"

"I'm performing again."

"Where?"

I paused and glanced at my father, but he was motionless, looking stunned, staring straight ahead. I didn't want to tell them, but I didn't want to lie anymore either. "The Three Hundred Club, it's a speakeasy, it pays well."

"Well, that's exactly my point. How are you going to raise a little girl if you're out all night at a club? What are you going to do? Bring the girl to your shows, keep her in a cot backstage?"

"If I have to, I will," I said, realizing how ridiculous that sounded.

"Don't be absurd. Admit it, Olive, you're not fit to be a mother. You were unfit then, and you're unfit now. You've made your choices, now you have to live with them." She rubbed her temples and took a deep breath.

"Mother, that's unfair," I said quietly, questioning myself, questioning her. Was she right?

"We are fed up with your impulsive ways. Honestly, we've had it up to here."

I didn't know what to say. This was how they thought of me, this was how they'd always thought of me. I pictured them sitting at the dinner table at night, discussing how disappointing I had turned out to be, how I simply sought pleasure, thrills and happiness, nothing more. Putting my own interests first, before everyone else.

"We'll raise the girl—she'll be your cousin, and that's all there is to it."

My father stood, still staring at the fire. "This is a disgrace," he said, turning to glare at my mother and then at me. "You're a disgrace to this family," he said quietly, and he walked out of the room.

That night I lay in bed devastated, sobbing, biting the sheets so no one would hear. My own child was miraculously back in my life, but I was too much of a failure to be a mother to her. They were right, there was no way I could give her a good life—a single woman working in a nightclub. She wouldn't have a fighting chance. What was I thinking? It was heartbreaking to lose her all over again. How I wished I could turn back the clocks and start over.

The next morning, I picked up the small knitted doll sitting on the windowsill and held it to my cheek. Then I left before the sun came up and caught the train back to New York City, alone.

CHAPTER TWENTY-NINE

My first night back at the club I put on a show. One of the perks of the 300 was that we could change course at a moment's notice. I could tell Bones, the pianist, what I wanted to sing, and he could improvise on just about anything.

"I don't know about you, Bones, but I'm feeling a little blue tonight," I said as I walked onstage and the applause subsided. He played a few notes, as if the piano itself were responding to me.

"I sure do hope that getting up here and singing a few songs with this beautiful crowd will help cheer me up." He played another melody and then paused for me to sing the first few lines of "It Had to Be You" before he joined in. From there I went on to sing a few belters, where I really let the patrons hear my pipes. In the *Follies* we rarely had the chance to sing with such abandon, everything was so choreographed and rehearsed, done with restraint. Looking back, I might have even called it tame. The *Midnight Frolic* was where I'd really come to life, the place where I was allowed to be myself. But even then there was a limitation: Ziegfeld's eyes were always on us. Here at the 300 Club, as long as patrons were buying drinks, Texas let me sing what I was in the mood for, and tonight I was in the mood for the blues. I ended with Bessie Smith's latest—"Nobody Knows You When You're Down and Out." I sang it slow and soulful, sitting on the stool, with just Bones accompanying me. I forgot the audience was even there. I was singing for myself.

I took a bow and told them I'd be back. I sidled up to the bar and let some stranger buy me a drink, then another and another. I hadn't had a drink since I'd moved into Saint Agnes, so it hit me hard and burned my throat as it went down. I performed another set, all slow, solemn blues this time, and then I ended up at the bar again, letting someone buy me another drink. I didn't know if it was the same guy or a different one. It didn't matter.

"I'm unfit," I told him. I could hear myself slurring, but I didn't care. "That's what they say, unfit to be anything, really. A daughter, a sister, a *mother*." I said it as if it were a bad word. "I'm unfit to be a mother," I said it again.

"I think you're the berries," the young guy next to me said cheerfully. "A beauty, and that voice of yours, you could be anything you want to be."

"I used to believe that," I said. He kept talking, but I wasn't listening. I was staring into my glass. They were right, of course. Who leaves a baby with strangers to find other strangers to look after her? She was days old. I should have known that my aunt would go back for her; she had a heart. I was a shell of a woman. Selfish, so focused on getting to New York and getting my chance on that big stage that I almost managed to force that whole part of my life out of my head. I charged on ahead with my days, not even trying to locate her. Not even having regrets, not really, not until I met Archie and everything changed.

Archie.

"I'll take another," I said to the barkeep. He wiped down the bar and leaned on it, toward me.

"You okay there, Olive?"

"Good." I gave him two thumbs-up. "Another round, please," I said.

"Maybe it's best you call it a night," he said in a low voice. "Texas won't like to see you hanging around too long like this."

"I've got some good stuff back at my place," the fella next to me offered enthusiastically. "Scotch from Scotland, smooth as a whistle."

"Well, off we go, then," I said, standing and almost knocking over my barstool.

At that moment I didn't care what anyone thought of me, I just wanted the hooch to bring on that numbing feeling. I was close, I could feel it, but I wasn't there yet.

"You should stay, head backstage for a bit," the barkeep said. I knew him by name, but I couldn't for the life of me think what it was.

"Thanks for the tip, Fred, or Billy or Jimmy, or Joe." I rolled my eyes. "Come on. . . ." I linked my arm through the arm of the gent next to me. "What's your name, anyway?" He told me, but I immediately let myself forget it. "Lead the way."

I woke up on top of the covers, fully dressed in my fringe dress, my sequin headband pushing my left eye shut. I could hear the openmouthed breathing of a man next to me, but I didn't look his way. Instead I groaned as I rolled over and put my feet on the floor. I still had on my T-straps. With no recollection of what transpired after we'd left the club and no interest in finding out, I tiptoed to the door and left without so much as a glance in his direction. What did it matter who he was or what went on? I had to get out of there.

On the street in the bright sunlight my eyes burned, and I realized, when people were staring at my attire, that I'd left my fake nursing outfit back at the club. I couldn't very well show up at the boarding-house dressed like this. I hailed a taxi and banged on the back door at the 300, praying that someone would be there. Eddie, the doorman, let me in. He looked as though he'd been fast asleep, and I wondered if maybe he slept there during the day.

"Thanks, Eddie, I left some things in the dressing room. Can I go back there and get them?"

He stood aside and let me pass. "Five minutes," he grunted.

I tried to keep my head down as I walked up the front stairs and into Saint Agnes. Sister Theresa was in the lobby dusting, humming cheerfully.

"Good morning, Olive," she said. "Long shift?"

I nodded.

"Goodness," Sister Theresa said. "You look terribly tired." She looked concerned, trying to get a better look at me. I'd hastily washed my face in the dressing room but was sure there were remnants of last night around my eyes.

"Better get some rest," she said. "Oh, and you received a tele-gram." She rushed to the office, came back and handed it to me.

"Thank you," I murmured.

The telegram was from Alberto.

OLIVE BELLA STOP

MEET ME AT DINTY MOORES 8 PM STOP

46TH AND BROADWAY STOP

He was sitting at a table in the back when I arrived that night. I liked the place because they didn't give two hoots about Prohibition laws, and the bourbon they served was a heck of a lot more appealing than the corned beef and baked potatoes they were known best for.

"Olive," he said, standing and kissing me on both cheeks.

"I'm so happy to see you, Alberto." I meant it, too, since I hadn't been expecting to see him again until the spring. But I would've been happier if I'd had a chance to recover from the previous evening. I'd tossed and turned all day, barely able to sleep it off, and my head was still pounding.

"I'm starving, *bella*, I ordered the food already, are you hungry?"

I shook my head and Alberto waved down the waiter. "A drink for the lady," he said, "and maybe something *piccolo*? Something small for the lady?"

"Just a bourbon, please, on the rocks." I handed the menu to the waiter. "What brings you back to New York so soon?"

"My friend Chester, do you remember?"

"Of course."

"He's coming to Italy to visit me and I come first to travel with him. He has never been outside of the New York. Anyway, sorry I meet you so late in the day."

"Don't worry about me. I don't have to be at the club until eleven," I said.

Alberto shook his head. "I heard this, you are at the Three Hundred Club now. I no like it. It's *molto* bad for you, for your career."

My career. What a joke.

"You are my biggest fan, Alberto." I tried to remain cheerful around him, since he didn't deserve my terrible mood. "But Ziegfeld didn't want me back, the Three Hundred Club was all I could get, and the pay is decent. All the shows are already cast. Maybe I'll have better luck next season, but right now I need to make some money. Things are different for me now."

"I know." He shook his head. "Did you see him, Archie, again?" he asked. "He was very in love, and you also last time when I see you, before the wedding. What happened?"

The wedding. Planning it seemed a lifetime ago. So much had changed since then, and the thought of explaining left me weak.

"It's a sad story, Alberto. Thank you for asking. But it's a long one and I might end up in tears." I managed a wobbly smile. "And I have to put on a show tonight," I added as brightly as I could. "I can't show up red faced and puffy!"

"Okay," he said sadly, patting my hand. *"Capisco."*

The waiter delivered a mound of corned beef, carrots and cabbage for Alberto and he dug in heartily. I smiled at the sight of him devouring it.

He was such a kind man. I suddenly had an overwhelming urge

to tell him about Addie, but when I looked into his expectant eyes, I knew I'd only start to cry. What would I tell him? That I was an unfit mother—spending last night with a man I couldn't remember now? While Addie, left motherless in my aunt's house, was going to be brought back to a completely strange house in Brooklyn, where she'd be raised by two people who would take on this "burden" only because it was the right thing to do. Two people who were actually her grandparents but would never acknowledge that fact. They'd found me a burden, hadn't they? And yet who was I to pass judgment? I hadn't made it easy for them. If I'd done the right thing two years earlier, Addie wouldn't be in this situation now. And I would never have met Archie—let alone left and humiliated him days before we were supposed to walk down the aisle.

I knocked back my bourbon, and the waiter brought another round.

"You don't want to eat, Olive? Share with me, please?"

I shook my head.

"I get to the point, Olive." He grinned excitedly, rubbing his hands together as if he were about to let me in on a big secret. "I have a holiday show starting middle of November. We will travel Europe, and after there is *buono* chance we go to Russia. Chester will accompany me. I want for you to come with me, Olive. We will perform a section of duets together. We will introduce Olive to Europe and Europe to Olive. *Che ne dici?*"

I stared at him, speechless, and when I met his eyes, I realized he was excited, anticipating my response, a little puzzled even when I didn't reply right away.

I should've been ecstatic, jumping up and down for joy. After the recent turn of events in my life, the offer should have been something I'd be thrilled by, and yet my legs felt like lead, my feet were stuck to the ground. I couldn't feel anything.

Alberto hurried on, thinking I hadn't understood. "All the travel, the hotels, the everything, it will be arranged for you, Olive. Your only concern is to get yourself on the ship to Southampton, five days of luxury travel, and don't forget to bring your beautiful voice."

"I don't understand. You said everything was booked up. That I'd meet your booker in the spring."

"It is booked. It was. But I think of an opportunity, for you, because I don't like to hear about you in these nightclubs, it is, how do you say"—he placed his hand toward the floor, looked into my eyes and spoke very seriously—"*sotto di te*. Low, too low. And there, Olive, the money is very good, better than you ever see here. Because you perform with me, and in Europe I have the big name already."

Touring Europe with Alberto Ricci was an opportunity I could have only dreamed about a few years earlier. It could put my career on a whole new path. If I was well received, I could be taken seriously, seen not just as an aging show girl but as someone who could really sing. It was an opportunity anyone would grasp with both hands and never let go, but other thoughts were drowning me, blocking the possibility from entering my head.

I was thinking of Addie, here in New York; she'd be living in the same city as me. I didn't know if my father would ever let me in the house again, but I'd be closer to her, and somehow I had to find a way to be part of her life.

And then there was Archie, who had never really left me despite his absence. I knew it was over, I knew he'd moved back to Cincinnati, and he was engaged again to the other woman. But leaving? Leaving felt impossible. Leaving felt final.

"Olive?" said Alberto. "You don't say something? This is *molto, molto bene*," he said, using his hands. "We sing like we sing on the lake. You say yes."

"Thank you so much, Alberto. What an incredible opportunity," I said, forcing a smile. "You are so kind, so generous. This is just the kindest thing anyone has ever done for me."

"You say yes?" he asked again.

"Yes," I said.

A chill took over my whole body, and I had the immediate thought to take back my acceptance of his offer. Regret and remorse were seeping into every inch of my being. Don't be a fool, I told myself, you need this money to survive. Do you really think they're going to let you be part of Addie's life after you've already made such a mess of things? I was beating myself down with questions, torment running through my veins as Alberto sat across from me. They'll disown you, I continued to tell myself. You're unfit. You're unfit to be a mother. Leaving is the best thing you can do for the child.

Alberto drank down the rest of his bourbon and finished off the last of his corned beef, looking pleased, satisfied.

"*Bene*," he said finally, wiping his mouth with his napkin and setting it on the table. "It's October. You come pronto. We have to rehearse. We have to do *molto, molto* work. The tour starts in one month. I leave tomorrow with Chester. We send you your ticket, but to where?"

"Probably best to send it to the club," I said, thinking the less explaining I had to do to the nuns the better.

"And you come pronto. *Capisci?*"

"*Capisco.*" I nodded slowly, trying to take it all in. "I can't wait."

CHAPTER THIRTY

We crammed into Ruthie's living room a week and a half later. I'd already taken a few nips from my flask on the way over, reluctant to show my face, knowing that Pauline, Lara, Gladys and Lillian would be there along with a few others from the *Follies*. I couldn't avoid them forever, I knew that, but I still wasn't ready to be bombarded by all their questions about Archie.

Ruthie's baby was lying quietly in the bassinet, and I tried to make a fuss over him, but it only seemed to make me feel worse. Ruthie picked him up, a natural already, leaning in and kissing his cheek.

"Do you want to hold him?" she asked. "He's a real snuggler."

"He seems so calm with you, I don't want to upset him," I said.

"Oh no, he's such a happy baby." She handed him to me, carefully transferring him into my arms, making sure I was supporting his head, and I sat down on the sofa. He felt so delicate—the warmth and weight of him were surprising. He wriggled slightly, getting comfortable in my arms, and I felt overwhelmed to feel the life in him, overcome with longing.

"Ruthie," I said after a few moments in an urgent whisper, "take him, please. I had a drink on the way over, I shouldn't—"

"All right," she said calmly, placing a hand on my shoulder and squeezing. "You're fine, Olive, he likes you." Then she slowly took him from me.

I wanted to curl up and disappear. I didn't trust myself even to hold a baby. But, truthfully, no one really seemed as eager to hold the baby as they were to crowd around Ruthie. At first, they were fascinated by her appearance—she was beaming as she laid him down again in the bassinet—and the way her waist had nearly returned to its former glory. They marveled at her delicate cheekbones. Next, they peppered her with questions about giving birth, as if she were the first woman to do such a thing. Hearing Ruthie speak of her delivery brought the drama of Addie's back in force, but while Ruthie's sounded celebratory, mine felt wrapped in shame.

I hurried off to the kitchen to regain my composure but didn't have a chance—it was my turn to be swarmed and interrogated.

"What the heck happened?" Pauline asked, following after me.

"What do you mean?" I asked, stalling, realizing too late that I should have prepared a response about the halted wedding, something to say to shut them all up. But I barely seemed able to put one foot in front of the other lately, much less think through what they might want to know and make up a story. Several girls were around us by now.

"With Archie," she said.

"I wasn't in love with him," I said coldly. "And he wasn't in love with me."

"Really?" Gladys said. "That's what you're going to tell us? Come on, something must have happened."

"Nothing happened."

"Nah, I don't believe it. It was that night after your grand finale. Something was up with you that night, your nerves were on edge, and you were getting up real close with a fella or two. What'd you do? Go home with one of 'em, and Archie found out?"

"No," I insisted. "I did not, Gladys, so stop meddling."

She put her hands up and backed off a little.

"But what are you going to do now?" Pauline asked. "I mean, are you coming back to the theater?"

"Ziegfeld doesn't want me." I saw looks of shock cross their faces. We all thought we were invincible until our time was up.

"How are you ever going to find yourself another fella now, without the allure of the *Follies*?" Pauline continued in a low whisper, too stunned to hide her horror.

A few girls were stepping away, sorry, I guessed, for having pestered me.

"Everyone knows about what happened with Archie," Pauline went on. She never did know when to stop. "But I suppose it will blow over eventually. Someone else will come along."

I shook my head. "Honestly, it's the last thing on my mind."

I glanced over to Lillian, and when she caught my eye, she looked away. I wanted to ask her if she'd heard anything from Evelyn from her hometown, but I could already tell from the look on her face that she knew something.

"Is it true, Lillian?" I didn't want to show my weakness. In fact, I'd told myself I wasn't going to ask, but I couldn't help myself, I had to know. "Is it true what the papers said?"

"What do you mean?"

"About Archie, that he's going back to his former fiancée?"

Everyone went quiet and looked from her to me. It was obvious that they'd already talked about it.

"Go on, Lill," Gladys said finally. "Tell her what you know."

"I don't know much, I only know what Evelyn told me," she said, shrugging. "She hasn't been home for a while, alls I know is that they're getting married. The wedding is back on. They're having a Christmas wedding or something like that. At his mother's house."

Her cheeks turned pink—she was embarrassed for me, and it felt as if I'd been punched in the stomach all over again. Though I'd read it in the papers with my very own eyes, I couldn't stand hearing from Lillian that it was true. I tried to take a deep breath, but it felt as though someone were wringing out my insides.

"He has every right to move on," I managed to say as I pushed through the circle they'd formed around me in the kitchen.

Ruthie stood rocking the baby in the bassinet; he was cooing and she was smiling down at him, but when I reached her, she looked up with concern.

"I have to get to work," I said.

"So soon?"

"Sorry, I . . ."

"It's okay," she said. "It's a tough crowd," she added, nodding toward the kitchen, where we could hear them whispering. "Come back again when it's just you and me, and we can talk."

I hurried out of there even though it was only five o'clock and I wasn't expected to show up at the club until eleven. The hours in front of me seemed terribly long. All I could think to do was find myself a stiff drink, dull the pain, forget what I'd heard. Maybe I should just head down to the Village; I could kill a few hours at Chumley's. I knew I shouldn't, but I didn't know what else to do to calm my mind. How could he marry that woman, how could he move on so quickly and simply forget about me?

It didn't feel as if I had a choice any longer: going to Europe might be the best thing, the only thing, left for me to do—Archie was getting married. Nobody wanted me here, not Ziegfeld, not my parents. Addie was too little to guess who I was, who I could be, and they weren't letting me change that.

And yet, while performing with a world-renowned opera singer could potentially open doors to an entirely new level of artistic achievement, while earning money doing what I had somehow believed I was born to do, it all felt so daunting. How could I leave Manhattan now, knowing that Addie was just a few miles away, my own daughter? She might not know me as her mother, but might there be something I could do, some way to change that awful reality, despite my parents? At the very least, I would be close to her. And I couldn't bear the thought of leaving for Europe without seeing Archie again. By the time I returned, he'd be married.

"Excuse me, miss," said a man, bumping into me as he hurried past.

I'd been standing at the street corner, paralyzed by indecision, only dimly aware of my surroundings. My mind raced. Being close, was that enough if I couldn't see Addie? With Archie gone? The cards were stacked against me here, now. I needed to think boldly, but not impetuously, think ahead for once in my life.

If I made money in Europe and was successful, then maybe I could return to New York able to afford a proper place to live. It might be my only chance to show that I was fit to take care of a child. An opera singer was not a chorus girl. I crossed the street, walking absently with the flow of people on the sidewalk, not knowing where I was going. I went down several more blocks, thinking one thing, then turning it on its head, feeling a glimmer of hope in one instant, feeling useless the next.

One thing I knew: I couldn't keep falling back on the hooch to quiet the constant questions in my head, to dull the pain of all these feelings. Instead of walking into a speakeasy, I headed in the direction of Saint Agnes. I was certainly no churchgoer, but I was desperate. Maybe just being in the presence of nuns would give me the grace I needed. Dinnertime was approaching, and it wouldn't kill me to make more of an effort with some of the girls there. A distraction, maybe, and at least they didn't know anything about me or my past.

I sat down at the dinner table, a little sheepish for not being more sociable until now, but the girls from my floor made a space for me.

"Come and sit with us, Olive," Betty said.

"Are you coming from work?" Helen asked.

"No, just back from visiting a friend. I had some time before my shift tonight, so I thought I'd come down for dinner."

I helped myself to a plate of boiled chicken and carrots set out in metal dishes on the side table. The last time, the only time, really, that I'd spoken to the other girls, Kay had been about to go on a date with a stockbroker, so I asked her how it went. She laid her head on the back of the chair and smiled, pretending to fan herself.

"Yes, tell us, how did it go?" Betty repeated, laughing. "She hasn't stopped talking about him since."

"He took me to the Hotel Lafayette for French food, it was grand! And I'm seeing him again Thursday!"

We laughed at the exaggerated way she swooned about him; she was obviously smitten. The girls at the other end of the table joined in, too. I'd seen them in the halls but didn't know their names. Once the laughter subsided, one of the girls, freckle faced with ginger hair, still seemed to be chuckling. I looked over to her and realized it might be something else.

"Do you need water?" someone asked. She put one hand to her throat and the other was holding on hard to the edge of the table. Her face was getting pinker and pinker and she didn't seem to be getting any air in or out.

"She's choking!" someone yelled. Sister Theresa and Sister Dorothy ran into the room. "Someone help her, she's choking!"

"Olive," Sister Dorothy shouted, "you know what to do."

I immediately stood up from my chair but then froze. I had no idea what to do.

"Olive!" she screamed this time. "*Do* something!"

"Do what?" I screamed back. The girl was collapsing forward now onto the table, her face turning a darker shade of red. "I don't know any first aid."

The nuns ran to her side. Sister Dorothy gave one mighty blow to her back and then another and another, but nothing seemed to be helping. Everyone was crowding around her now, watching helplessly. Sister Theresa pried her mouth open and swabbed around the back of her throat with her fingers. At last a piece of carrot dropped to the table, and the girl gasped for air.

"Thank the Lord," Sister Theresa cried out, falling back, making the sign of the cross. They got the girl back in her chair and sitting upright. Everyone was fussing over her, getting her water, rubbing her back, but Sister Dorothy had a steely glare for me.

"Olive, in the office in ten minutes," she said, and walked out of the room.

The girls were turning toward me, wondering, no doubt, why a nurse's assistant couldn't have done more. I hurried up to my room and packed my belongings back into my trunk—there was no point in prolonging this, and I rushed to get it done. I closed up the trunk with trembling fingers and went downstairs to Sister Dorothy's office.

"Take a seat, Olive." There were three older nuns sitting in the room, staring at me gravely, and Sister Theresa squeezed into a corner seat.

"It has come to our attention that you have not been entirely truthful with us."

"I'm very, very sorry," I said. I had said that so many times over the past few weeks, and I meant it. They had been nothing but kind.

"Obviously, you do not work as a nurse."

I shook my head, my eyes glued to the floor.

"And we have *just* learned,"—she paused to glare at Sister Theresa—"that not last Thursday but the Thursday morning prior, you returned to the house later than usual, after the sun was up, smelling not of hospital disinfectant, but of cheap perfume and alcohol. You do not even work *at* a hospital, do you, Olive."

"No," I said. I couldn't believe Sister Theresa had spilled on me, but when I looked her way, she was sobbing quietly into her hand- kerchief. They waited for me to speak again, and the silence was painful. "I'm a show girl."

One of them gasped. If I hadn't been in such dire circumstances, I might have laughed. God forbid a show girl was in the house.

"I work at the Three Hundred Club, singing mostly, a little danc- ing," I said. "I knew you wouldn't let me stay if I told you the truth."

"You're absolutely right, we wouldn't have. We do not condone that kind of lewd behavior among the girls who are in residence with us, and we certainly don't appreciate being lied to," Sister Dorothy said. "I'm afraid we are going to have to ask you to pack up your things and leave immediately."

I nodded. I knew they had no other choice than to send me on my way, but the thought of finding another residence, getting what- ever reference letters that would require, again, and having to settle into someplace new, at night, all felt overwhelming.

"Is there any other way? Could I make it up to you? Could I at least have a few days to make other arrangements?" I was set to perform at the club in just a few hours; I couldn't ruin things with Texas, too.

"Rules are rules, Olive. We've been accommodating you in good faith. We have to maintain the highest standards, or the rest of the girls will think they can break the rules too. We must ask you to collect your things and leave."

"All right," I said, nodding slowly.

"You may make one phone call. And then you must be on your way."

I held the receiver to my ear, waiting for the operator to connect me, still unsure of what I was about to say.

"Mother," I said when I heard her voice, "it's Olive."

Silence greeted me on the other end. I waited a moment, hoping she would speak, but she did not. I wished I could tell her everything, how wretched I felt, but she hadn't even said hello. I couldn't bring myself to tell her I'd been kicked out of Saint Agnes. How could I possibly drop any lower in her estimation?

"I was thinking, I was thinking, perhaps I could come home."

There was a sigh. "Why would you do that? We've already discussed this. We will take care of the child."

"But wait, I'm not saying that. I mean, I could come home, to help out with Addie." Somehow, as I said these words, they made sense to me. Hope sprang up inside me as the words tumbled out. "I would like to. Mother, I've been thinking seriously—"

"Oh, Olive. *Have* you? It's not a good idea," she said tightly. "Your father is very angry."

"Well, maybe it will help if I'm there. I could help smooth things over."

"You do the very opposite of smoothing things over, Olive." She was speaking quietly; my father must have been in the next room. "You make a mess of everything."

"I won't this time. I promise. It could be good for Addie, if I were there to help."

"No. It would be very confusing for the girl."

"I'll go along with your wishes, I'll be her cousin, if that's what you want me to be. I need to know her. Why won't you let me?"

"Because you can't be trusted—you proved that in Rockville. And we can't have your brothers finding out. That's the last thing we would need. We cannot have this family dragged through the dirt with you revealing your relationship to the child when it pleases you. It's not fair to the other members of this family."

"But, Mother—"

"It's not a good idea, Olive, it will only make things worse. I'm not doing this to punish you, I'm simply trying to do the right thing, and not have our family crumble apart because of it. And let me tell you, things are precarious at the moment, very precarious. Your father is having a very difficult time with the news you sprang on him. And he's furious with me for lying to him." She added in a whisper, "He's barely speaking to me."

I heard crying in the background.

"Is that her?" I asked, suddenly feeling desperate. "Wait, does she need something?"

"I have to go, Olive," she said, and the line went dead.

I showed up at the 300 with everything I owned packed in my trunk. Texas took one look at me and shook her head. She agreed to let me sleep in the dressing room for a few nights but said I'd have to make more permanent arrangements after that.

But I couldn't sleep. I tossed and turned all night, thinking of Addie. Her cry at the other end of the phone line stayed with me.

I'd heard about women who, after having a child, developed a new instinct when their child was hurt or needed them. They could be fast asleep, and the whimper of their child two bedrooms over would immediately wake them. I didn't know what it was I had developed since finding out the truth about Addie, but I couldn't stop thinking about her. I pictured her eating at the dinner table, chasing the birds, falling asleep as I read to her, but I kept playing those few brief memories over and over in my head. They were all I had, and I yearned for more.

In the morning, I dressed and walked east to Fifth Avenue and West Thirty-eighth Street. The last time I had set foot in Lord & Taylor felt like a lifetime ago, though it was really just before I met Archie. I remembered splurging on the red dress and a few weeks later waiting impatiently for him to call on me so that I could wow him in it. Archie. I bit my lip at the thought of him.

I took the escalator up to the children's floor and wandered among the dresses, touching the delicate embroidery on the collar of a crisp white frock. I picked up a pale grey wool coat that had a dramatic flare. I imagined Addie putting it on and spinning. A tiny pair of patent-leather Mary Janes caught my eye—I'd had a similar pair as a girl. How was it possible that these past two years had unfolded—my performances, my nights out on the town, my falling in love—all of it transpiring while Addie was living with Aunt May? I should have known, should have been with her, watching her grow.

"Good morning, madam," the salesgirl said, startling me. "Are you shopping for something in particular? For someone special?"

"No," I said, suddenly flustered. "Not in particular. But yes, for someone special."

She looked at me expectantly.

"For my, I'm looking for my—my daughter," I stammered.

She gave me an uncomfortable smile and nodded. She was sensing something, as if she knew I was a fraud.

"For my daughter," I tried again. "She's two."

"Right this way," she said, turning to walk to another area. "You're looking in the wrong section. Age two and up is over here."

I followed her and glanced back in embarrassment at the clothes I'd been admiring. The shoes and dresses did seem small. My God, I didn't even know how to buy clothes for a child.

"This is brand new." She held up a soft knitted cream sweater with lace-trimmed cuffs and collar. "And it goes beautifully with this pinafore." She showed me a black velvet ensemble.

"It's very pretty," I said. But would she like it? Did she like to wear sweaters and pinafores? Would she care about her clothes at this age? I had no idea what she liked. The only person who had truly known was Aunt May, and she was gone, and along with her, all the memories of Addie's first years.

"Do you sell toys?" I asked.

"Toys?"

"Yes, toys, you know—the things children play with?" She was starting to get on my nerves.

"One floor up," she said, folding the sweater and placing it back on the table and then walking away with a sigh.

Upstairs there were dolls and cars and balls and hoops. A toy train, a pull-along duck, a sheep, a bugle. A building set, wooden blocks, a Tinkertoy set and more dolls—small, medium and large—knitted, molded, with hair, without. I ran my hand along them, waiting for one to call out to me, then I stopped at a white-and-brown rocking horse. Its head was probably taller than Addie. It had real horsehair for its mane and tail, a leather bridle and a saddle, all on a sturdy wooden rocker. I imagined telling her someday about the mare and her foal at the Pines, how the little one had wobbled at first on those spindly little legs, but once she got used to the feel of them under her, she couldn't stop prancing around. She just needed time to get used to her own strength, to know what she was capable of. I smiled at the thought of it, the thought of all the things Addie had yet to learn.

The size and shape of the thing made it awkward to carry up Fifth Avenue, and I had to stop a few times and set the bulky horse down, shake out my arms and stretch my back. I'd spent every dollar I had in my purse and was left with only a few coins to spare, but it felt good to spend it, and I had a little more that I'd saved tucked away in my trunk. I received some stares as I walked back to the club and offers of help from a few gentlemen.

"I'm fine, thank you," I said, walking on, struggling, but wanting the struggle, needing it.

I carried the horse through the front door of the club, past the doorman and back into the dressing room. I set it down next to my trunk, ripped a ribbon off one of my old costumes and tied it in a bow around her neck, then I sat back on the dressing room chair and admired her.

CHAPTER THIRTY-ONE

October 30, 1929

Lordy, Lordy, would you take a look at this?" The dressing room door swung open, and Texas walked in with a cup of coffee in one hand, an overstuffed paper bag under her arm and a newspaper held out in front of her.

I quickly sat up, pulling the one small blanket I had around me. For the love of God, it felt early. I rubbed my eyes and looked at the clock on the wall: nine thirty. I'd been staying there for a week, and I hadn't expected to actually see Texas in the mornings, or anytime during the day, but she acted as though seeing me sleeping on the sofa in the back room of her club were perfectly normal.

"'Stocks collapse in 16,410,030-share day!'" she read off the front page of *The New York Times*. "Geez Louise. Listen to this: 'Stock prices virtually collapsed yesterday, swept downward with gigantic losses in the most disastrous trading day in the stock market's history,'" she read aloud. "'Billions of dollars in open-market values were wiped out as prices crumbled under the pressure of liquidation of securities which had to be sold at any price.'"

She sat down at the dressing table, took an orange out of the paper bag and started peeling it.

"'Groups of men, with here and there a woman, stood about inverted glass bowls all over the city yesterday watching spools of ticker tape unwind, and as the tenuous paper with its cryptic numerals grew longer at their feet, their fortunes shrunk,'" she continued to read. "'Others sat stolidly on tilted chairs in the customers' rooms of brokerage houses and watched a motion picture of waning wealth as the day's quotations moved silently across a screen.'"

She finished the orange and started on another one. "Holy smokes," she said. "This could be bad, real bad."

"Texas, wait," I said as I grabbed my cardigan from the floor and wrapped it around my shoulders. "Texas, slow down a minute. I heard the newspaper boys talking about this over the weekend, but what does all of it mean?"

"It means, doll face, that we're all in the soup now. All those butter-and-egg men who come walking through our doors each night and put money in our pockets, they just lost all their fortunes."

"All of them?" My mind immediately went to Archie and then to my father. Both of them invested heavily in the stock market, and my father . . . well, he'd be in the thick of it down at the exchange.

"I would think so, at least anyone who had their money in the market, which they all did," she said grimly.

"Oh my God," I said. The money my father had been saving his whole life. And Archie, he'd worked so hard, building his fortune from nothing. "Can it really just disappear like that?"

"Apparently so. That's why I keep all my money someplace where I can grab it and run." She slapped the paper down on the counter and started peeling yet another orange.

"But . . . if they're losing all their cabbage, the last thing these fellas are gonna want to do is go home," she said, mulling it over. "So it could play out in our favor, maybe we'll be busier than usual."

"Sure, maybe the regulars will need some cheering up," I offered.

She turned again to the paper, its stories of desperation luring her back.

"Get this: 'Wall Street was a street of vanished hopes, of curiously silent apprehension and of a sort of paralyzed hypnosis yesterday. Men and women crowded the brokerage offices, even those who have been long since wiped out, and followed the figures on the tape,'" she continued. "'Little groups gathered here and there to discuss the falling prices in hushed and awed tones. They were participating in the making of financial history. It was the consensus of bankers and brokers alike that no such scenes ever again will be witnessed by this generation.'"

I had to reach my father, to see if he'd been affected by any of this. I quickly got dressed and walked two blocks down to the pharmacy, where they had a phone booth inside.

"Number, please," the operator said.

"Flatbush six-seven-two-seven."

"Hold, please."

I didn't know what to expect. The last phone call with my mother had been so awful, and the news might make things worse. What if they refused to talk to me and didn't want me intruding on them?

After a moment my mother answered. Even her "Hello?" sounded distressed.

"Mother," I said, "I heard about the stock market! How are you, how's Papa holding up?"

"Oh, Olive. Not good, not good at all. He was gone all day and night yesterday. He's in a terrible way, we all are."

"What can I do to help?" I asked.

"We had our life savings in the market," she whispered, and then she began to cry.

There was a scraping noise in the background, as if chairs were being moved across the floor, then my father's voice.

"Who is it?"

"It's Olive," my mother said.

"Let me talk to her," he said. "Give me the phone." I heard some shuffling as he took the receiver. "Olive?"

"Hi, yes, Papa."

"It's over, Olive, we're through, finished. We lost everything. We're ruined."

"Surely not everything!"

"Just about. I don't know what we're going to do." He sounded as if he might begin to cry, too. I'd never seen or heard my father cry. He'd worked so hard his whole life. "What are we going to do, Olive?"

It was a shock to hear my father, such a proud man, address me this way, as if he were looking to me for something like reassurance. The thought that I might ever provide it was astonishing.

"Papa," I said, "I'm going to come home as soon as I can."

"All right," he said, breathing deeply, as if trying to calm himself down. "That'd be nice, Olive. It really would."

I took a deep breath, too. Hearing him say those words meant the world to me; it was everything I needed to hear, after all the turmoil we'd been through. I only wished he weren't in such a bad way.

"Come soon if you can," he said quietly, as though he didn't want my mother to hear what he was saying. "I'm going to be out of a job by the end of the week. We can't stay here. We'll have to move back to Minnesota."

I walked back to the club in a state of panic. Everyone seemed to be rushing, and the sounds of the street clanged in my ears. But one thought rang louder than everything else: I couldn't let Addie leave again. I reached into my handbag and took out a letter from Alberto, along with my ticket to Southampton. It had arrived just two days earlier. I was supposed to set sail for Europe in a week. How was this going to work? How was any of this going to work? I needed to make money in order to provide for her, and touring with Alberto was my very best chance at doing that, but that would mean being thousands of miles apart.

Apart from Addie.

I peered down at the ticket in my hands, as if to decipher its print, but the words meant nothing except for one additional, inescapable fact: it would take me away from Archie, too.

I shook my head to expel the thought—I could not think about him.

———

That night the club was empty except for a few belligerent men drinking their last pennies away, apparently too scared to go home. Rather than putting on a show, I sat on the stool and sang a few numbers in the background. No one seemed in the mood to be entertained; the folks who did show up just wanted a rough gin and a smooth bar to lay their heads.

The next morning, I got up after just two hours of rest to buy a paper for myself and see what else had unfolded. I'd never been the least bit interested in the financial pages before, but I stood on the corner of the street scouring the front page, trying to get a better understanding of what was going on.

EXCHANGE TO CLOSE FOR TWO DAYS OF REST

The volume of trading in the last week has been so enormous that the organizations of the Stock Exchange houses have reached a point of complete physical exhaustion.

A picture on the front page showed stockbrokers and their clerks sleeping on the floor after working until the early hours of Wednesday. I turned the page.

ROCKEFELLERS BUYING HEAVILY

The manner in which the country's leading men have rushed to the rescue of the market, not only with words but with huge buying orders, has emphasized the public's conviction that the country's business fundamentals are entirely sound.

Well, that seemed a bit more optimistic, I thought. But the next night, the club was even emptier than the night before.

"This ain't good." Texas took a seat next to me backstage. "I heard some of the Broadway shows aren't even opening up. Apparently, some of the big investors in them took a hit too. I guess the last thing they want is more money spilling out onto the street. They don't want to pay the bills for all those lights."

"It's as if everything's falling apart around us," I said.

I felt in my pocket for my ticket. I'd been carrying it around with me at all times, scared that I'd lose it if I let it out of my sight. "I've been invited to go to Europe with Alberto Ricci," I said suddenly, holding out my envelope as proof. "I wanted to tell you, Texas, but then everything happened. I'm supposed to set sail next week."

She raised her eyebrows. I didn't know why I hadn't revealed this information sooner—she'd been so kind to me. But this had seemed too permanent, too real and so far away.

"Really? Alberto Ricci?" She looked impressed and maybe a little skeptical. I was, after all, homeless, sleeping in the dressing room of the 300.

"Hard to believe, I know, but he's a friend of mine. I'm just not sure I can go."

Her expression changed, and she turned serious. "You take that ticket, and you get on that ship, and you don't look back, do you hear me? Things could get worse, girly. It could get better, all blow over, but it'll probably get worse, and when it does, I won't have anything for you, for you or the rest of the girls. This club will shut its doors the minute it stops turning a profit. I don't work for the fun of it. So you go, and you ride it out for as long as you can, because there'll be nothin' for you here, doll face. Nothin'. And I'm sorry to say so."

It was hard to believe all the things we were reading in the papers—so the next morning, I showed up at the New Amsterdam Theatre, hoping to catch the girls before rehearsal started. I had to find out what was happening with the Broadway shows, and if I really was going to be leaving, I wanted to say goodbye. The girls were sitting in groups in the rehearsal room. I saw Pauline and Lillian across the room, and they waved me over.

"What are you all doing?" I asked. "Why's no one rehearsing?"

"We just got news," Pauline said. "The theater's dark tonight—no one's seen Ziegfeld for days."

"Oh, no!" Ziegfeld had always seemed untouchable.

"They're saying all his money's gone," she said.

"Lillian," I began, turning to her. But by the time I'd said her name, she'd taken me by the hand and whisked me to the other side of the room.

"Olive, listen to me. I've heard some news. I wanted to tell you but didn't know where to find you. Apparently, Archie lost every-thing, and Louise left him. The wedding is off."

"What?" I was stunned. She walked out on him at his lowest—and after everything I'd already put him through. But the fact was, my heart was pounding, too. I could barely breathe.

"How do you know?"

"Evelyn spoke to her family back home, and they told her it was the talk of the town. Local businessman ruined. And then Pauline's new fella? He's a lawyer, and he said he saw him a few days ago at his office, he was taking care of his affairs, trying to manage some of his losses, or something—"

"He's here in the city?" I had to see him. "Where?"

"He *was* in the city. Pauline's guy said he left, says he didn't know where to, but he *did* say he was never going back to Cincinnati." She looked at me, waiting for a response to the news she was imparting. "Sorry, Olive, I asked as many questions as I could, alls he knew was that he said he had to get away, out of the city."

"The Pines," I said.

"The what?"

"I've got to go." I kissed Lillian on the cheek. "Thank you."

I headed straight for Grand Central and managed to catch the last train out. I skipped a night at the Blue Mountain House. I didn't need to sleep, I just needed to see him.

It was a good twenty degrees colder at the camp than in the city, and I had left abruptly, with nothing but the clothes I was wearing and my handbag. I wrapped my cardigan around myself and paid the driver, though he seemed uneasy about dropping me there alone. It looked empty and barren except for a guide's car parked near the pathway to the farm and a few porch candles already lit.

"You sure you're all right here by yourself, ma'am?" the driver asked. I wondered if I'd made a big mistake, Archie could've gone anywhere, but something told me to listen to my instincts. "I don't feel right leaving you here alone," he said. "But if I don't head back now, I won't get to the main road before dark."

"I'm fine," I said. "Thank you, I can take care of myself."

Unlike the red and golden fall leaves I'd seen on the train ride out of the city, the trees in the Adirondacks were already bare, with a light sprinkling of snow on their limbs. It was as magical as it always had been, but my God, what was I doing here, the place where I'd fallen in love, the place where I'd caused so much pain?

Light shone from the main lodge, and I started walking toward it but then stopped and turned toward the cabin where Archie and I used to stay. At first it had seemed vacant, but when I reached the front door, I could sense that someone was inside. Music played faintly, there was smoke from a freshly lit fire, and a light shone through the front windows from the back of the cabin.

I knocked on the door before I could talk myself out of it.

"Come on in." It was definitely Archie's voice—it made me catch my breath.

I placed my hand on the doorknob, and the door creaked open.

"I'm in the back, Eugene," he called.

I opened my mouth to speak, but nothing came out, so I walked to the back of the cabin, out to the porch, and saw that he was outside stoking the firepit. I followed through the door he'd left open and walked down the uneven brick pathway toward him. Then I stopped.

"Archie," I said softly when he turned around. His mouth dropped open, as if he were about to say something, but he didn't.

"I heard the news, about the stock market, about Louise. I had a hunch you'd be here. I had to see you before I leave. I have something to tell you."

"Olive," he said, shocked. I was probably the last person he wanted to see. "What are you doing here?"

"Please, let me tell you what I came here to say."

He stared at me blankly, then nodded slightly.

"I owe you an explanation," I went on. "What I did was a horrible, terrible, unforgivable thing." It was cold and I shuddered involuntarily. "Can we sit down?" I glanced inside.

He nodded and led the way to the living room. We sat in the two worn leather armchairs in front of the fireplace.

"I have a daughter, her name is Addie—Adeline. I was nineteen and foolish. I didn't know the father." I looked down, ashamed to be speaking these words to the man I so admired. "He took advantage of me while I was on tour in California." A wave of nausea came over me, but I forced myself to go on. "I gave her up for adoption. There was a complication during the birth and they told me I wouldn't be able to have any more children." I closed my eyes and took a deep breath. "I should have told you from the very beginning, I should have been honest with you, but I was terrified that I'd lose you. Then when you started talking about having a family of our own, I just couldn't do that to you. I didn't want you to be childless if you wanted to be a father, not after what you'd already been through. It was cowardly of me, I can see that now. I should have told you the truth. Instead I ran, because I didn't want to disappoint you. I couldn't bear it if you resented me for the rest of our lives. It was selfish and I was wrong to treat you that way, keeping you in the dark, not letting you make your own decisions, instead making them for you." I finally allowed myself to look up at him, and I saw his eyes were filled with tears.

"I'm sorry, Archie, I'm so very sorry." And when I said those words that I'd been wanting to say ever since I had last seen him here in this very cabin, the tears ran down my cheeks. I wiped them away quickly.

"Almost a month ago, my aunt May died. She had taken me in when my family moved to New York. My mother arranged it, but no one else knew. I stayed with my aunt during my pregnancy, and when I went to the funeral, I discovered a secret. After I had the baby and left, she had taken in my daughter, too, as her own."

His eyes widened.

"Oh Archie, I thought she was gone forever. I thought she'd been adopted by strangers, that I'd never see her again. I've thought about her every day for the last two years, but I tried to force myself not to. I was doing everything I could to tamp down my thoughts, and then I found out that my mother knew about Addie living with my aunt, and she kept it from me."

"My God," Archie said under his breath.

"She's two years old. My parents have taken her to Brooklyn and they insist on raising her now. They say I'm unfit to be a mother." The words made the tears come again, and the fact that they were planning to take her away, back to Minnesota, was unbearable. But I willed those thoughts away. "I've made so many mistakes. I've hurt so many people. But I need you to know, Archie, that I have always loved you and I always will. I'm so, so sorry."

"I always loved you too," he said. He held my gaze. I saw the love and kindness in his eyes that I'd always seen in him, and I fought a mounting desire to rush to him, to be held in his arms, but I couldn't assume I would be welcome.

"Where are you going?" he asked quietly.

"What do you mean?"

"You said you had to see me before you left, where are you going?"

I nodded, forgetting for a moment that I was supposed to be leaving in just a few days. "I'm going to Europe to tour with Alberto, I don't know for how long. The theaters and clubs are going dark in New York. I'm lucky to have this chance." I wanted to tell him that I didn't feel lucky, that I didn't want to go, and now that I was by his side I didn't want to leave.

"I'm going to save all the money I make, and I'm going to send it back to Addie. My father thinks he's not going to have a job. I don't know what else to do—I'm sleeping in the dressing room at the Three Hundred Club, I can't take her there."

Archie stood and walked to the buffet. He poured a bourbon and offered it to me. I shook my head; I wanted to keep my wits about me. He took his drink and walked outside and stood at the firepit for a good ten minutes. It felt like an eternity. I wanted to follow him outside, ask him if he could ever forgive me for lying, for hurting him. I wanted to ask what he thought of me now, but I forced myself to stay seated.

I had said what I came to say. I had been honest at last, but if he wanted me to leave now, I didn't know what I would do.

"Do you want to be a mother?" he asked, walking back inside.

"More than anything in the world."

"Then you must be her mother. No matter what. And you can't wait. She's your daughter. Olive, when I said I wanted a family ..." He shook his head and rubbed his forehead. "When I suggested that we have children of our own, it was because I was so damned in love

367

with you. I'd never felt love quite like that before. I wanted to share it, I wanted everyone to see it, I wanted it to grow. Being with you made me feel like I could do anything. I could imagine us having a family, but that didn't mean it was the only thing I wanted. I wanted you, and I wanted whatever came next in our life together."

How could I have underestimated his kindness, his capacity for love?

"You should have told me the truth," he said.

"I know." I looked up at him. He was right, of course, but there was something I wanted the truth about, too. "What happened with Louise?"

He shook his head. "I went back home to Cincinnati and, I don't know, I was so lost, so confused. The whole idea of her was thrust upon me all over again, especially by my mother. She didn't care about my grief, she just wanted to keep up appearances."

"Why did you agree to it?"

"I was ashamed, I was spinning. The things you said to me came out of nowhere. I was broken. I wouldn't have married her once I came to my senses, I would have told her, but she got there first as soon as she heard the news about the stock market."

"I'm sorry," I whispered.

"No, please, it was a relief. I should have had my head on straight. I was just so devastated about you, about us. But Olive, I have nothing now. I've lost a lot of money in the market, maybe all of it. I don't know what the future holds. I don't know if I'll get any of it back, or if I'll be able to rebuild what I built before. The fact is, my fortune is gone. I've been knocked sideways this past week, hell, this past year. I don't know what's up and what's down. But what I do know is that I love you, I never stopped loving you, and I know you'd make a damned good mother."

I stood up, overcome with emotion. He walked toward me, took my hands and held them in his. I felt weak at his touch, the familiarity, the comfort.

"We could be a family, Olive," he said. "If that's what you want."

My heart was beating so fast I could barely get my words out. "But I can't give you children of your own, Archie, you need to understand that."

"That doesn't matter. We'll go and get your daughter, and we'll be together. No one, certainly not your parents, can tell you otherwise."

Tears streamed down my face. I couldn't believe the words I was hearing. I threw myself into his arms.

"And I should never have asked you to give up performing. That was a mistake. You were born to perform, your voice is meant to sing. We'll go and get Addie, and we'll go to Europe as a family," he said. "We'll be together as we always should have been."

I looked up at him and I kissed him. Archie loved me, I knew that now. But more than that, he understood me in a way that no one ever had.

CHAPTER THIRTY-TWO

We didn't call, didn't send a telegram, we just packed up Archie's trunk and scrambled to get to Brooklyn as fast as we could. We took his private railcar—its final run, he predicted—then went directly to my parents' house in Flatbush. If we were to board the ship to Southampton, we were going to have to move fast.

We arrived around ten A.M. after traveling all night, and we must have been a sorry sight. I was wearing the same clothes I'd worn for the past three days, but that was the furthest thing from my mind.

Archie held my hand as we walked to the front door.

"Olive!" my brother Junior cried, and threw his arms around me.

"I've missed you," I said. I hadn't seen him since summer, over five months ago, and he seemed taller somehow. His eyes flashed to Archie.

"How are you?" Archie said, shaking his hand.

"It's swell to see you both." He looked genuinely happy. "They're in the back," he said with a slight roll of his eyes. "Pop's on the horn. He's having a tough time of things," he added in a whisper.

My mother was bent over the dining room table wearing a thin flannel robe, writing feverishly in a notebook, and I could hear my father on the telephone in the next room.

She looked up, shocked to see us standing together. "Archie," she said, rising to her feet, holding the table. "What an unexpected surprise."

My father's voice went quiet in the next room, then the phone clinked as he set it down. A moment later he stood at the door, looking thinner than usual and a little grey in the face.

"Hello, Papa," I said.

His eyes darted from me to Archie. "What's going on?"

"A lot, Mr. McCormick," Archie said politely, breaking the ice and sparing me the need to respond. "We'd like to have a chat. May we sit?" My father nodded and pulled up a chair for each of us. "Olive has told me everything," Archie continued. "About the past, the child, everything is out in the open now, and we've decided to reconcile."

My parents stared at us.

"We're going to marry the first chance we get," Archie went on. "And . . ." He looked to me.

"And Archie and I are going to raise Addie together, we'll be her parents."

They turned, looking at me as if I'd spoken in another language. But there was something desperate in their eyes, in their effort to keep up.

"I am her mother, after all."

My brother had taken a seat in the corner. "Um, should I go and get George?"

"Yes," my mother said. "No, no, stay where you are."

I waited for someone to protest, and I was ready to fight back, my heart was beating fast. No one said a word.

"We're leaving for Europe this afternoon, in fact our ship sails at four P.M.," Archie said gently. "Olive has an excellent opportunity to appear in concert with Alberto Ricci. He invited her and wants to introduce her to his audience there. It'll be grand."

He was singing my praises, and I loved him for it. But my head was about to burst, and my heart raced while I waited for them to respond to what I'd proposed. I looked around, but there was no sign of Addie. "And we'll be taking Addie with us," I repeated, in case they hadn't grasped what I was saying. When I spoke, my mouth went dry.

"You're going to sing with Alberto Ricci!" Junior whistled. I gave him a quick smile, then looked back to my parents, trying to gauge their next move. Still no one said anything.

"Where is Addie?" I asked.

"She's in her room," my mother said absently. "Your room."

"Why?" And then, without waiting for a response, "I'd like to see her."

My mother nodded blankly, so I set my handbag down on the side table, took off my cardigan and walked up the stairs.

The door was ajar and I could hear her singing as I walked across the hallway. I peeked inside. She was sitting up in a small cot with raised sides, playing with her dolls. She looked up at me.

"Hello, Addie," I said softly. She immediately stood and reached her arms up. "Would you like to come out of there?" I asked, picking

---

her up, sitting her on my hip. She felt slightly heavier than she had in Rockville. "I'm so happy to see you, sweetheart, do you remember me?"

She nodded.

"Oh good! Because I've been thinking about you so often, and I was very excited to see you again. There's someone I'd like to introduce you to, he's downstairs. Would you like to go downstairs and see the others?"

She nodded again. "Dolls," she said, pointing at them in her cot.

"Of course," I said, reaching for them. "They should come too."

As I walked down the stairs with Addie and her dolls in my arms, I could hear my father's voice—not shouting, but elevated, agitated—coming from the dining room. My mother was joining in, and Archie was part of the conversation.

"Everything is gone, we're ruined," my father said.

"We can't even stay here," my mother chimed in. "We're finally settled, and the house is decorated, the boys are happy, and we have to pack up and head back to Minnesota with our tail between our legs."

"With our tail between our legs, that's right—and it's all my fault, I suppose?" my father snapped.

"That's not what I'm saying."

"I'm going to be out of a job, Doris."

"I know, I know."

"You don't know the extent of it yet," Archie said. "The market's still moving, it could make an upward swing, we've got to let things play out."

"You don't believe that," my father retorted. "I know you don't."

I turned away from the dining room and walked toward the kitchen instead. Addie didn't need to hear this.

"I bet your dolls are hungry," I said. "Should we have a tea party?"

Her eyes widened and she grinned.

"I'll make us some tea and sandwiches, and why don't you decide where we should all sit," I said.

She sat the dolls and one bear carefully in chairs next to her at the kitchen table, propping them up and reaching across to switch which doll sat next to her more than once. As I set out teacups and small plates, she arranged them in front of her dolls.

"Maria and Sophie and Teddy," she named them all. "And Addie ..." She pointed to herself. "And"—she pointed to me and hesitated—"and you."

"Oh, I'm Olive," I said. "But you can call me whatever you like."

She nodded uncertainly. "Ol-live," she repeated, struggling a little with the "l" sound. Then she began again, pointing to each in turn, "Maria and Sophie and Teddy and Addie and ..." She sighed, then pointed to me and said, "You be the mommy." She seemed pleased with her idea, poured some imaginary tea into a cup and held it up to her doll's mouth.

"Oh," I said. She was only playing, of course, but it made me catch my breath. "I would love that," I said, trying not to react with too much enthusiasm.

Archie walked into the kitchen as I pretended to feed the dolls and Addie nibbled on a sandwich.

"Is there room for one more?" he asked, crouching down at the table.

"Yes," she said.

"You must be the little Addie that I've been hearing so much about," he said, and she nodded back proudly. "My name is Archie."

She watched him, her small feet swinging back and forth beneath the table, then she slid a teacup toward him.

"What a wonderful hostess," he said, picking it up and pretending to take a sip. "You are just the most beautiful little girl I've ever seen in my whole life. And wow"—he looked from me to Addie with such a look of love that it brought tears to my eyes—"you look just like each other."

She smiled bashfully, but I could tell she was enjoying his attention, the dolls, the party we were having.

"And these are some very lucky dolls to have such a nice lunch with you both."

"A *tea* party," she corrected him.

"A tea party, of course. Well, later this afternoon I'm hoping the three of us will get to go on a big boat, and I've heard that they have the most wonderful tea parties with dancing and music. Would you like that?"

She clapped her hands.

Archie stood up and squeezed my shoulder.

"Go outside?" Addie asked, jumping down from her seat at the table, taking Archie's hand and pulling him toward the back door.

"Sure thing." He laughed. "I've never seen the backyard." He looked back at me and smiled.

My mother was still scribbling in her notebook when I reentered the dining room. It was strange and unsettling to see her so distant.

"Is everything all right, Mother?" I asked, looking over her shoulder to see what she was writing. It was a list of items from the house.

"No, Olive, it's not—nothing is all right. Haven't you read the papers, don't you know what's going on?"

"Of course I have." I sat down next to her. "I know that you've suffered a great financial loss, you told me when we spoke on the phone, but . . ."

"But what?" She looked at me, exasperated.

"Well," I said hesitantly, "it's only money."

"It's our life, Olive, it's fallen apart overnight."

"I know that feeling," I said.

We sat there in silence for a while. She rubbed her temples.

"You were right about Adeline," my mother said abruptly. "The girl needs her mother. I thought I could do it, but it's not ideal, not like this. And I was wrong about you. You've been good with her. You're going to be fine."

Hearing her words, I was finally able to breathe. I felt my shoulders drop, relax a little. I hadn't been aware that I'd been so tense. I wished she could tell me that I'd be a capable mother, a good mother, but she couldn't know that any more than I could. I'd settle for fine.

"I haven't always made it easy for you, and I'm sorry for that," I said. I didn't agree with all the things she'd said and done, but looking at her now, tired, somewhat defeated, I believed she'd always done what she thought was best. "Truly, Mother, I'm sorry for all I've put you through."

She looked at me and nodded. She looked grateful, grateful perhaps that I was acknowledging this. "You've always had an urgency in you, a desire to do things your own way. You've always known what you wanted, and you've gone after it. I have to admit, I never understood that about you."

"I don't know that I've always understood it either," I said. "I know that I've made some bad decisions, but looking back on my life now, I don't know that I'd do it any other way. If I'd done things differently, I wouldn't have Addie, and I wouldn't have Archie."

She stood up, wrapped her old robe around her and patted my hand. "I wish only the best for the three of you," she said.

It was past noon. We still had to pack up Addie's things, get back to the city, collect my belongings from the club, buy Archie and Addie a ticket and board the liner before four P.M.

In the bedroom, as we collected the last of Addie's dolls, my mother surprised me. She bent down next to Addie and smoothed her hair away from her face, "You're going on an adventure, dear. Olive and Archie will take good care of you." She kissed her head and stood back up, pulled a hankie from her sleeve and blew her nose. "You'll have fun."

Addie seemed quite excited by all of it. I knew that at some point I owed her an explanation. I didn't know yet how much to tell her, or when she'd need to know, but right then all we had to do was get to the harbor.

We piled into a taxi, and my mother and brothers stood at the door to wave us off.

My father walked to the driver's window and tipped the man. "Drive safe," he said. "Wait for them while they collect their trunk, and for goodness sake, get them to that ship on time."

"Everything will work out, Papa," I said.

"Oh, don't you worry about us, we'll be all right." He leaned in through the window and squeezed my hand. "It takes courage to do what you're doing," he said into my ear. "I'm proud of you."

CHAPTER THIRTY-THREE

We rushed on board the RMS *Olympic* in the final hour after quickly changing our clothes in the back room of the 300 Club, stuffing the last of my belongings into my trunk and transporting it all, along with Addie's rocking horse, to the ship with only minutes to spare. Archie suspected that we'd have no problem finding extra tickets because some people had chosen not to travel, given the new financial situation unfolding.

It was an enormous ocean liner, 882 feet long according to the steward, who showed us to our suite, with almost three thousand people on board, including the passengers, officers and crew. I looked around, admiring every element of our new surroundings, the carved oak writing desk, the ornate marble fireplace, the wrought-iron beds and embroidered linens. I wanted to remember every detail of this moment as we prepared to set sail.

"Do hurry back up to the promenade deck as soon as you can," the steward said once our luggage had been delivered. "We depart at four P.M. sharp, and everyone always wants a chance to say goodbye. We won't be seeing land again for five and a half days."

When I first moved to New York, I had marveled at how elaborately people dressed for the theater, but I'd never seen such splendor as I saw that day. Some women on deck wore fanciful, wide-brimmed hats with ostrich plumes and bird-of-paradise feathers, silk-and-velvet-trimmed shawls and dresses with ruffles and lace and beading, topped with the most extravagant jewelry. It was quite a display of wealth, as if everyone were fleeing the woes of Manhattan and taking their most expensive jewels with them.

The horns sounded and a brass band began to play as we felt the ship—assisted by a fleet of tugboats—start to pull out of the harbor and toward the Atlantic.

"Let's find a spot at the railing," I said, taking Addie's hand and linking my other arm through Archie's.

I was wild with excitement for all that lay ahead. It was shocking to think it had been only two and a half years since I'd arrived in Manhattan and knocked on Ziegfeld's door, all but demanding to be cast in the *Follies*, thinking that was the only thing that could make me truly happy. And yet now here I was, with the two people I desperately loved, two people whom only days ago I thought I'd lost forever, and soon I'd be onstage rehearsing with one of the most talented and well-respected tenors of our time.

Passengers leaned over the railing, waving frantically to their families and loved ones who stood on the pier to see them off. We'd already said our goodbyes in Brooklyn, but Addie started waving madly anyway.

"Goodbye," I said, joining her. "Goodbye!"

I picked Addie up so she could see everything that we could see, and Archie wrapped his arms around us both.

"I can't believe we're really doing this," I said, looking up at him.

"You bet your bottom dollar we're doing it, Olive Shine," he said, squeezing me tighter.

Everything had happened so fast. We were starting a new life together, the three of us, setting off on an adventure that was both thrilling and uncertain. As I looked out to the island of Manhattan, its tall buildings catching the last of the late afternoon sun, I'd never felt more confident that this would be my greatest adventure yet.

HISTORICAL NOTE

While I thoroughly enjoyed researching the life of a Ziegfeld show girl and all the details that go into the rehearsals and performances, I did take some liberties with show dates. Florenz Ziegfeld Jr.'s renowned *Follies* revues, inspired by the Folies Bergère of Paris, ran on Broadway from 1907 to 1931, with a break when his shows *Betsy, Rio Rita* and *Rosalie* ran 1928–1929. The *Midnight Frolic* ran from 1915 to 1922 and again from 1928 to 1929. For the purposes of this story I kept the *Ziegfeld Follies* and the *Midnight Frolic* running all the way through to 1929. The majority of the songs that were performed were taken from the 1927 *Follies* and 1928 *Frolic*, though I added in a few numbers from earlier shows, such as the *The Follies Salad* from 1919, when they were a good fit for Olive. The Pines, the fictionalized Adirondacks retreat where Olive and Archie spend time, was loosely based on a real-life retreat called White Pine Camp, where I stayed twice during the research for this novel and which I found to be a wonderful source of inspiration. In 1926

White Pine Camp was also where President Calvin Coolidge spent his summer and set up his "Summer White House." I first learned about the Great Camps of the Adirondacks when I wrote an article for a luxury travel magazine about a fancy seventy-five-acre estate and hotel called The Point that was originally the creation of William Avery Rockefeller II and used as his family's summer compound. Today it's a five-star resort that promises guests a taste of times gone by while "roughing it" in extreme luxury. Through my research for this article I learned about several other Great Camps built by Guided Age magnates along the rugged lakeshores of Upstate New York. Many of these camps were built in a similar design and construction, which became known as Adirondack Style, characterized by the use of local timber, Adirondack granite and rocks from the rivers. Families such as the Vanderbilts, Astors, Guggenheims and Rockefellers commissioned the building of these vast estates as an escape from the city. In learning about these camps I knew I had to set part of my story there and that Olive would fall in love with the wilderness in the end.

I referred to many invaluable sources in the research of this book, in particular:

The Ziegfeld Touch: The Life and Times of Florenz Ziegfeld, Jr. by Richard and Paulette Ziegfeld

The Days We Danced: The Story of My Theatrical Family from Florenz Ziegfeld to Arthur Murray and Beyond by Doris Eaton Travis with Joseph and Charles Eaton, as told to J. R. Morris

Ziegfeld Girl: Image and Icon in Culture and Cinema by
Linda Mizejewski

*Ziegfeld and His Follies: A Biography of Broadway's
Greatest Producer* by Cynthia Brideson and Sara
Brideson

*The Village: 400 Years of Beats and Bohemians, Radicals
and Rogues* by John Strausbaugh

*Capital of the World: A Portrait of New York City in the
Roaring Twenties* by David Wallace

Great Camps of the Adirondacks by Harvey H. Kaiser

*White Pine Camp: The Saga of an Adirondack Great Camp
and Summer White House* by Howard Kirschenbaum

ACKNOWLEDGMENTS

Thank you to my editor, Leslie Gelbman, for believing in this book; your astute editing skills, support and guidance are invaluable. And a special thank-you to my agent, Stephanie Kip Rostan, for your expertise and for guiding me through the world of publishing.

I am grateful to the entire team at St. Martin's Press for bringing this book to life and sharing it far and wide, especially Erica Martirano, Marissa Sangiacomo, Dori Weintraub, Danielle Christopher, Donna Sinisgalli Noetzel, Sona Vogel, Gail Friedman, Elizabeth R. Curione and Lisa Bonvissuto. Thank you also the team at Levine Greenberg Rostan, particularly Courtney Paganelli, Melissa Rowland, Cristela Henriques and Miek Coccia. I understand now that publishing a book really does take a village.

I wrote most of *The Show Girl* at The Writers Room in New York City, which has provided me a peaceful and productive space to write for close to ten years, and I'm so thankful for my talented writing workshop novelists who continue to inspire me every Thursday night: Donna Brodie, Mario Gabriele, Barbara Gaines, Sam Garon-zik, Joanie Leinwoll, Meryl Branch-McTiernan, Barbara Miller, Steve Reynolds and Rob Wolf, and especially our fearless leader, Jennifer Belle.

To my author and book-loving friends, and my early readers: Jamie Brenner, Fiona Davis, Suzy Leopold, Lynda Loigman, Amy Poeppel and Susie Orman Schnall, who have kept me sane through the last year with our weekly Zoom calls. I am extremely grateful to you all for your friendship and advice.

A huge thank-you to my friend and early reader Elisa Moriconi for your incredible friendship and support, to Suzanna Filip, for letting me write in your beautiful home, to my mother-in-law and trusted early reader Ginny Ray, and especially my parents, Michael and Jayne Harrison, for their constant love and support, and their tolerance for reading numerous revisions.

Much love to my boys, Christopher and Greyson, for joining me on this wild writing adventure—the books tours, the research trips, the many, many books lining our walls. And, above all, my love and gratitude to my husband, Greg—I cannot imagine any of this being possible without you.